Chief of Staff

A Novel by Mark Vertreese

© Copyright 2006, 2012

Published by: Mark Vertreese
Cover Design: Gareth Lewis-Pitt

ISBN-13: 978-1478135340

Chief of Staff

Dedication

To everyone who relentlessly asked me when my next novel would be released. To everyone who has believed in me and the talent I have been so lucky to cultivate and do my level best to improve upon. To everyone with a dream of writing a novel of their own. And to that one person whom I might inspire to sit down to pen & paper or their computer to write their version of The Great American Novel.

Chapter *1*

HE was cold and rain-soaked, but he had to do this. He had to be here right now. It was the right thing to do. Saying good-bye was even more excruciating now than he thought it would be. Standing in front of an open grave had been painful and haunting for him ever since his mother passed. The dreams, the nightmares, didn't end for six months. The graveside was not the place for a child. He knew that now. But now he was a man. Staring at the marker, he squinted as raindrops pelted his face, and softly cascaded down the casket. He would get no closer than he stood right then. Grown men have nightmares, too.

Leaning forward, he read what had been etched into the polished granite face of the headstone:

"Man is the only animal that laughs and weeps; for he is the only animal that is struck with the difference between what things are, and what they ought to be."- William Hazlitt

Hand to mouth and shaking his head back and forth, the tears mixed with the rain, both streaming down his face as he sobbed uncontrollably. Why, he asked himself. Why did this have to happen? What had gone so terribly wrong? Had he done the right thing?

A firm hand pulled gently on his shoulder. "Senator? It's time we made our way back. They're going to be starting soon."

One long, last sigh and he turned toward the waiting limousine. At the door, he stopped, turned back to the grave and quietly whispered, "I'll always love you."

Chapter *2*

(Six Months Earlier)

"WELCOME aboard, sir. It's nice to have you with us again."

Charles Byrum greeted Angela with a warm, overly affectionate hug and a smile. "Hello, my angel. And it's so lovely to see you again, as well. Gorgeous as ever, I must say." What was a little harmless flirting? For the past three years, Byrum and Senator Tanner had been flying to California in one capacity or another trying to influence businesses to expand their reliance on North Carolina products. Due to a conflict in Senator Tanner's schedule, Byrum decided to make this particular trip on his own.

Angela and the other 'usual suspects' as he liked to call them, always pampered Byrum on each trip to California. Each time they were all on the same flight, he harkened back to the good old days when the girls were called Stewardesses and would light your cigarette and pour you a glass of scotch, 'accidentally' touching your arm or showing a little bit more cleavage than they should. Hell, it *was* First Class, and whomever the genius was who figured it out, he knew that tits and ass packed planes, especially with businessmen flying on their company's dime.

Sexual harassment, women's lib, title IX, and the degradation of machismo had, however, brought all of that to a screeching halt. The best Byrum could manage now was a poorly-veiled flirt, some drawn out eye contact and his imagination running wild at the thought of what was hiding beneath the navy blue polyester uniform with matching scarf and pantyhose.

Sixty-one years old, with a distant but suspicious wife and three grown daughters, one would think Byrum knew better than to act that way. "You are looking very well today, Angela."

Chief of Staff

"As are you, Mr. Byrum." Angela played this game over and over with dirty old men just like Byrum; each believing they were slicker and smoother than the next. "We'll be taking off soon. Have a seat and I'll bring you a Dewers in just a moment."

Takeoff was uneventful, as usual, and somewhere over St. Louis the passenger next to Byrum could no longer help herself. "Excuse me," she started. Byrum looked over his reading glasses at her. "But you wouldn't happen to be Charles Pinckney Byrum, would you?"

Laying his SkyMall catalog to the side, Byrum perked up. "In the flesh."

"Oh my God!" the forty-something redhead half-squealed. "I am simply not sitting next to you."

Time to turn on the charm. "Now, why would a lovely young creature like you say such a thing? Have I offended in some way?" His trademark smile was slowly smearing itself across his face.

"Oh no. I hope I didn't come across like..."

"Simply not the case. You have done nothing wrong." Like flies to honey, he thought to himself.

She cocked her head slightly and bit her lip, feigning like she wanted to say something, but wasn't sure if it would be appropriate. They were strangers, after all.

"What? You look as though you have something on your mind."

"Well, it's... it's just that drawl you have is fantastic." Pure North Carolina apple butter with an air of sophistication. It was Byrum's calling card of sorts. "I remember seeing you on C-SPAN's Book Talk and just being mesmerized. I've always been intrigued by southern men. I don't know what it is about you all."

Angela had stopped by to freshen Byrum's Dewers and tried her best not to roll her eyes. Byrum deliberately watched Angela walk away and turned his attention back to this gorgeous red-headed woman who, by all counts, had just made a total of two passes at him.

"Southern men have a charm and a way of treating a woman that is simply not possessed by anyone born above the Mason Dixon, my dear. Of that, I'm sure."

"My name is Grace," she said, shaking Byrum's hand.

"And, no, I'm not married." The smile continued arching until his capped and veneered teeth were in full glow. "I'm happily divorced," he lied. Grace raised an eyebrow, checking out his barren ring finger, searching for the tell-tale pale circle that is left behind when men remove their sign of marriage. "Perhaps now I am the one being untoward." Grace blushed and shook her head, no.

For the next hour, Charles Pinckney Byrum and Grace the red head chatted and flirted on their way to California.

Grace seemed fascinated by Charles, nearly twenty years her senior. She listened, body fully turned and engaged as Byrum recounted, in short order, his rise through politics, meeting Senator Tanner, the man for whom he was presently chief of staff, and how he had parlayed his political connections into a seven-figure book deal. The book deal had made him even wealthier and even more recognizable. And the perks were great, too. More and more brazenly, Byrum began to look into Grace's eyes, down to her mouth, stopping at her full breasts and back up again, never missing a beat in their conversation. Grace did not mind one bit.

He told her about his latest book idea about a scheming family hiding the sordid details of their wealth and privilege, and moved seamlessly into his daughter's upcoming wedding. "I'll be in Los Angeles for two days and then I'm flying back to North Carolina for the ceremony on Saturday."

Nonplussed by talk of a daughter old enough to be married, Grace only heard one thing: in Los Angeles for two days. Pornographic thoughts raced through both of their

Chief of Staff

heads. The possibilities were endless. What a magnificent flight this was turning out to be.

*****

10.03:21	*AA521: Crossing three three five, climbing to three five zero*
10.03:28	*ATC: 521, Good morning, squawk alpha three three five, continue climb to three five zero*
10.03:34	*AA521: Squawk alpha three three five, continue climb three five zero?*
10.03:38	*ATC: That is correct*
10.06:03	*MEX124: Flight level three three zero. Call me passing Phoenix*
10.06:45	*ATC: 124, leveling to three two zero, standing by for higher*
10.06:59	*MEX124: Affirmative, affirmative, standing by for higher*
10.07:40	*ATC: 124, recleared flight level three five zero*
10.08:03	*AA521: Say again, ATC. 521 was clear for three five zero*
10.08:56	*ATC: Sorry, 124. Three five zero is not available. Are you to climb maybe to three four zero?*
10.09:15	*MEX124: Affirmative, affirmative. Climbing to three five zero*
10.10:40	*ATC: 124, say again, three five zero not clear*
10.11:06	*MEX124: Say again, ATC. 124 climbing to three five zero. Is the deck cleared for climb to three five zero?*

Chief of Staff

10.11:24	*ATC: Standby, 124*
10.11:49	*ATC: 521, what is your present level?*
10.12:01	*AA521: Three five zero*
10.12:10	*ATC: 124, hold yourself at that level and report passing Phoenix airspace*
10.12:37	*MEX124: What height?*
10.12.59	*ATC: The height you are climbing through...because...you have an aircraft in front of you at...? Three five zero from left to right.*
10.13:10	*MEX124: Okay, ATC, will maintain precisely three five zero*

The glint of sunlight bouncing off the plane as it broke through the cloud bank, streaking through the sky caught Byrum's attention. By the time he squinted over Grace's shoulder and looked through the window it was too late.

Exploding somewhere over Arizona, American Airlines flight 521 and Mexican Air flight 124, with some 400 passengers and crews fell back to earth, each plane obliterated beyond recognition. The ball of fire and cloud of smoke could be seen for miles.

10.13:58	*ATC: Dispatching fire and rescue. Possible mid-air collision. Two aircraft going down. Repeat, dispatching fire and rescue. There's been an accident*

Chapter *3*

NO sooner had his eyes opened, the alarm clock blared in his ear. Waking up before the alarm went off usually made Eric mad, but today was different. It was Saturday morning and he had plans. As he acclimated himself to the daylight poking through his curtain, both his cell phone and home phone started going crazy simultaneously. He smiled because he knew exactly who was calling, ignored the chimes and got out of bed. "Jerks," he said to himself.

He showered quickly and stood in his closet trying to decide what he was going to wear that day. It was a man's closet. Cavernous, with dark wood paneling, and over organized, it was divided into two rows by a huge granite-topped dressing station and a floor-to-ceiling mirror, there was one side for casual clothes and one for dressier attire. Shoes, shirts, suits, jeans and pants, and even hats for any possible occasion were all neatly arranged. This morning he'd be playing golf, so he stood to the left in front of a column of pressed and folded golf shirts and matching shorts. This closet was large enough to be a room in its own right.

When Eric bought the house a few years after he graduated from college, he had it completely renovated. He loved the house because it was on the lake in an exclusive Charlotte neighborhood called The Pointe. And because it was just far enough from his grandmother's mansion, the chances of her popping by were slim to none. After two years of planning and redecorating, he'd ended up with a home he could be proud to show off to anyone. Five thousand square feet of red brick perfection. Four bedrooms, three levels, with a summer kitchen and media room on the bottom floor, the house also boasted the world's greatest hot tub/pool combination and a second-level veranda featuring a stone waterfall. Eric knew of no better place to call home.

A quick stop out to the backyard woodshop to check on a special project for his grandmother and he was back in the house eating breakfast. He looked at the time and rushed

Chief of Staff

out to the garage. Walking past the sporty 911 Carrera 4, his brand new CL65 AMG Mercedes, and his aging but beloved Tundra Double Cab, Eric popped the locks on his ML550, threw his clubs in the back and zoomed off to the course.

This was going to be a very good day.

Chapter *4*

"ERIC Julian, please."

"Speaking."

"Please hold." Before he could respond, an 80s hit that had been turned into elevator music was coming through the phone. Who the hell calls someone and immediately puts them on hold? *Damn useless Caller ID.* Eric looked around the back gate of his SUV and signaled to his friends that this wouldn't take long.

For the first time since the end of the campaign, they were all together; more importantly, they were all together on the golf course. After nine months of strategizing, campaigning, fund-raising, ass-kissing, primaries, talking to the press, arranging interviews and debates, and counseling his candidate on the "best practices" of running for office, all of the madness was over. By the grace of God and the unfaltering mass of registered Republicans in North Carolina, his man was elected and he could breathe again. Eric Julian and his three best friends in the world were gearing up for a round of golf. He was talking to himself as he loaded his bag onto the golf cart and lazily fell into it. He didn't hear the music end. "Jesus, come on."

"Now I've been called a lot of things, but Jesus has yet to make the list."

That voice was immediately recognizable. "Senator Tanner. Good morning."

"Son, how long have you known me?"

"All my life, sir."

"Correct. And how many times have I told you to just call me Scott?"

"Over and over, sir. However, you are a United States Senator. So, I'm afraid that as much as you hate it, I am now and will forever be required to address you as Senator Tanner." Eric was smiling as he spoke, thinking back to the days he spent growing up at this man's feet.

"I thought I raised you better than that."

"You did a fine job, if I may say so myself. And, again, let me please express my sympathy for Byrum. He was a good man and I know you're going to miss him. He was probably the best chief of staff on the Hill."

"Funny you should mention him. Look, Eric, I need to speak with you about something important. It's about Byrum."

"Senator," Eric began, wavering between the confidence of speaking his mind to a dear friend and the unnerving feeling in his spine that whatever was on Senator Tanner's mind, it had to be critical. "It's 72 degrees at 7:45 in the morning and I haven't had a day off in nine months. I tee off in five minutes. What's the possibility of us having this conversation after I've lost $100 worth of balls, drained every drop of some very expensive single malt from my flask, and burned one or two exquisite Davidoffs to the label?"

"A man after my own heart. Congratulations on winning the campaign. I kept track of you the whole time. You were most brilliant."

"Thank you, Senator. That is, after all, what I get paid to do."

"I'll call you this afternoon. Washington is truly wonderful this time of year." With that he hung up.

Eric turned his phone off, jammed it to the bottom of his golf bag, stomped on the accelerator and stormed off to the first tee box. His vacation, albeit brief, had finally begun.

Chapter 5

IT wasn't Senator Tanner to whom Eric spoke later that day, but one of his aides. The conversation was short and one-sided. The e-mail from the senator was just as succinct: *"A car will pick you up and take you to the airport. My plane will fly you to the coast where another car will bring you to Trinity. I'll expect you at 8:30. We have something important to discuss. Don't let me down."*

Winding down a tree-lined road, Eric thought he saw something in the distance and rolled down the heavily tinted window of the Town Car. "What the hell is that?" he asked out loud, as the chauffer pulled the car to a stop. Eric got out and his mouth fell open. "Holy....shit."

Before him floated Trinity, the senator's pride and joy, his latest and most expensive toy. Eric's world had always been one of glamour, wealth, excess and privilege since the day he was born. But this was off the charts! Sweeping left to right, Trinity was simply glistening. Bathed under the full moon and strategically placed spotlights, she sparkled like a four-deck ivory monument.

Eric quickly scuttled his smirk when he heard someone calling his name.

"Son, don't just stand there with your pants down. You act like you've never seen a yacht before!" The senator was standing on an aft deck, with a drink and his standard cigarette in hand.

"Yacht my ass," Eric mumbled as he stepped into the gorgeous fore-lounge of Senator Tanner's floating palace.

"Yacht my ass, indeed," Senator Tanner beamed as he sauntered into the room, arms extended, fully embracing Eric. "It's great to see you. Welcome to Trinity. What do you think?"

"This place is something else. Listen, I really feel just awful about Byrum. I can't imagine how you're holding up right now."

Senator Tanner held up his hand and Eric didn't really know what to say. "We'll talk about that later." Spinning slowly to the right, head back, Senator Tanner looked like the statue that presides over Rio de Janeiro. Trinity was no regular boat, no regular yacht, if such a thing even exists. Two hundred twenty feet long, with a forty-four foot beam, Eric was standing aboard a true superyacht. Opulent to a fault and staffed by a small neighborhood of employees, she was a very costly weekend retreat paid for, in large part, by a bottomless inheritance. Senator Tanner escaped to Trinity, wherever she was, every chance he got to entertain, relax, and just generally unwind from the rigors of life governing the country.

"It doesn't get much better than this," Senator Tanner bloused at the end of Eric's tour. They settled in the main salon and once both of their drinks had been freshened and the shipboard man-servant delicately closed the door behind him, the senator was all business. "I want you to do something for me." No longer acting like a pleasantly overjoyed tour guide, Scott Tanner transformed himself back into hard-nose businessman cum three-term senator.

"What? No kiss? You didn't even buy me dinner."

"No jokes, Eric," he said, lighting another cigarette.

"How many times have I told you those things are going to kill you?" Eric asked, half serious, half joking.

"And how many times," he began, blowing smoke casually into the air, "have I told you that I don't care if I die during the most mind-blowing sex I've ever had, or smoking a Marlboro to the filter? I don't care which, but please, God, pick one of them." The men smiled and the senator got back to business.

Still having no idea why he was summoned to the coast, Eric slid to the edge of the leather sofa and sat his drink

Chief of Staff

on the bare wood of the coffee table. "Use a coaster, please. This isn't a barn."

Since he was eight or nine years old, Scott Tanner had been like a second father to Eric. Abandoned by his own father, it was Scott Tanner who stepped in and provided the male bonding he so needed as a young man. High school football, talks about girls, pledging fraternities, fast cars, crazy Vegas trips. The list goes on and on. Never once had he failed to be there for Eric. Never once had Scott Tanner ever let him down. For any reason. It was a relationship as unique and unlike anything either of them could imagine. It was like "Diff'rent Strokes" – a white man helping raise a little black boy. But unlike the characters on TV, Eric and the senator were both extremely wealthy.

Scott Tanner wasn't exactly a physically imposing man, but his presence could be felt in a room. Your normal brown hair, blue eyes, average height and weight - there wasn't anything physical about this man that made women swoon or men hate the sight of him. It was something much more than that which gave him his joie de vivre, that very essence of something that made the difference between race horses and stallions, champions and mere runners up. The money helped, yes, there was no mistake about that. From the enormously successful family demolition business he took over for his father, the settlements he received in his two very public and very nasty divorces, and the certain under-the-table proceeds/benefits he may – or may not have – received as a United States Senator, the intangible that was Scott Tanner was just that. It couldn't be bottled or sold in infomercials. It couldn't be taught and it was impossible to replicate, duplicate or otherwise copy. That charm and charisma led him to the upper echelons of business, got him elected to the Senate three times, and attracted some very lovely and very single women he was determined to keep that way. He had an expensive mouth with an expensive smile that he wasn't uncomfortable using to his absolute advantage.

Chief of Staff

There was no smile now, though. Whatever was on his mind had to be serious, so Eric blocked out the boat and the secrecy and focused intently on what he was about to hear next.

"I want you to be my chief of staff."

"Chief of staff?"

"Yes."

"You're joking, right? That's not what I do. I get people elected. I run campaigns. I get things done to that end, and I walk away. What would make you think I'd want to be your chief of staff?"

"I know how this is going to sound cold because it's only been a week, but Byrum's dead and I need to be moving forward with all deliberate speed. I've got a constituency that will be counting on me to make some tough decisions in the next several months."

Senator Tanner continued, Eric spinning his mental wheels at the same time. "I need somebody I can trust to run my days, Eric, to look out for me, to be my mouthpiece whenever and wherever possible." He put his cigarette out in a crystal ashtray, never fully exhaled, and continued to speak with smoke drifting lazily from his mouth. "Yes, I've got a staff of people and whatever, but they've all got an agenda. Either they're interning or using my office as a stepping-stone or waiting for their law school applications to come back. No one I deal with has a more vested interest in my success than you do. I want to hear your opinion and advice. I need you to be my eyes and ears in places I can't go and say the things I can't. I need someone who's always got my back. Now more than ever, I think the time is right for you to be the man to run my office day in and day out. Tell me you're the man I'm looking for. Tell me you'll do it."

"Okay, once more, sir, that's not what I do. And you know that. I don't know the first thing about being a chief of staff. What about Alan Bryant or Brad Manning? They've got the experience and the connections you're looking for and they can open the doors that I can't."

"No. I want you. And, yes, you do know how to do the job. You're connected. Jesus Christ, you're the one who got Bryant's and Manning's guys into office in the first place. You know the players on the Hill. You know how to get the job done. Past that," he said with a pause, "I have something in mind for you."

"And what might that be?"

"I want you to take my place when my term is over." Silence.

"That's absurd."

"Is it?"

"It's actually the most absurd thing I've heard all day."

"Senator Julian. Sounds great, doesn't it?" he asked. "The time is right, Eric. It's time for you to stop putting other people on the pedestal and start looking out for yourself. You want to be where I am. You want deeply to stop putting words in other peoples' mouths and to start speaking for yourself. I know."

"Is that right?"

"That's right. What do you have left to accomplish but this? You're rich, you're young, you're a political genius, and you don't want to be a mouthpiece for the rest of your life. You want to be a player in the best sense of the word. You want to be the one making the law, not just talking about it. You want to be what your grandfather and great-grandfather couldn't; you want to be a senator. Do what Harvey Gantt and Cory Evers could not do. Let me help you."

Senator Tanner knew Eric was bouncing the idea around in his head.

"I don't know. I just don't know. It sounds like such a leap of...."

Chief of Staff

"Faith?" Senator Tanner interrupted.

Eric rolled his eyes at the thought.

"Or is it divine intervention?" Senator Tanner stood and walked to the window. "You're the son I never had, Eric."

"Don't be cheesy."

"I mean that. I mean that more than you'll ever know." He turned and looking at Eric, said, "The job is yours. Help me and I'll help you. We can make a great team, you and I. Be the man history will look back upon and smile with affection. Write the chapters of your life the way only you know how, the way only you want to. What was it that your grandmother has been drilling into your head since you could read?"

"My grandfather's doctrine."

"That's right."

"Rest not young man, for those who follow lead those who are yet to come." Eric shook his head. It had been a long time since he'd said those words and it amazed him how quickly he recited them.

"Politics is your life. Make your family even more proud of you than they already are. Make yourself proud. Follow me and I promise you I'll personally see that it happens."

"And how am I supposed to go from a political consultant turned chief of staff to senator?"

"You'll be in the public eye. You'll be my voice in the press and on television." Senator Tanner was thinking out loud, putting the pieces together as he spoke. "We'll make every opportunity to get your own political views in front of the people of the state so they know who you are and what you're about. Hell, it's not such a long shot. We've got two years before my term ends. You'd be surprised how some of those people get elected."

Chief of Staff

"I wouldn't be that surprised," he muttered to himself.

Eric took a long pull of his drink and sat back. What a day this was turning out to be. Eric Julian had it all by many peoples' standards. He was a very rich, very well liked member of a prestigious Charlotte family. He was part of the hidden but very substantial and growing black upper class; a subsection of black America that not many people were even aware existed.

His grandfather was a legend in the annuls of the south, a favorite son of many blacks and one of the greatest contributors to the black upper class there ever had been. He was a striking man. Tall and athletic, with a very light caramel complexion, commanding presence and comforting manner, Eric's grandfather was a prominent attorney and landholder in Charlotte. At a time when black wealth typically came from funeral homes, barber shops, small grocery stores and the like, Eric's grandfather knew that the fastest way to make money was to provide services to the people who ran those types of businesses. With outstanding business acumen and the ability to mingle effortlessly in both white and black social circles, he was a true anomaly of his era. He built first a legal empire then moved easily into banking and real estate. He made absolutely sure that his children shadowed his every move, learning every nuance of the world they were building.

Eric's was one of a handful of extremely wealthy, privileged and powerful black families in North Carolina. In his book, "Our Kind of People," Lawrence Otis Graham perhaps best described the world of entitlement and luxury in which the Julians and other families like his endeavored to inhabit.

A paradox of sorts, upper class blacks in his grandfather's day, as well as today, took great pride in their accomplishments and enjoying the fruits of their labors as black entrepreneurs and social titans. There existed, however, a clear and ever-present line which one did not dare cross.

Chief of Staff

Money and influence have always done strange things to people, and in keeping with tradition, while they attempted to instill in their children the fact that they most certainly were black people, only those who were truly entitled were to become part of their circle, their 'kind of people'.

The creation of the Boule, the Links, Jack and Jill, and various lower-tiered but well-intentioned members-only organizations sought to pool together blacks with wealth and infuse in their children strong black identities. In doing so, however, those groups only moved themselves and the black upper class farther into the shadows of separation that existed within the black community. You had to be self-made. You had to be old money. And you had to bring something exciting, though not unconventional - and certainly not controversial - if you wanted to belong to the group. A world of constant networking, you had to know somebody to be put up for the Boule. You had to know someone to be asked to join the Links. And you had to have the right sponsor family if you wanted to be a part of Jack and Jill. Just because you happened to be rich and you happened to be black didn't mean memberships in any of those organizations were automatic. Sports stars, entertainers and just anyone with money didn't qualify.

If you didn't go to the right college, like Fisk or Spelman or Howard; if you didn't summer in Sag Harbor or send your children to the right black summer camp; if you couldn't look down your family tree and put seventy per cent of your ancestors against the paper bag and ruler tests, the black upper class would probably not be including you in their yacht clubs and black cotillions and debutant parties. Without the proper background, and marrying into the right families at the right time with the right connections, the black country clubs and fraternities, not to mention the various social circles, would not be extending invitations in your direction come hell or high water.

This is the world where Eric Julian had always been held and swaddled. He, like the rest of his family, was a sort

Chief of Staff

of black royalty. Prep school at Andover, undergraduate at Fisk, and graduate school at Howard School of Law, it was a progression that never seemed fantastic or unusual to anyone in his circle of influence. It was expected of him, to say the least.

Eric was tall with sinewy muscles and a piercing gaze from those hazel eyes. He had very light skin which, in days gone by wouldn't have allowed him to 'pass' but it would have assured him entry into places his darker brethren would have been denied. A cutting wit, the ability to speak three languages, pockets full of money and conversational skills that belied his age, Eric presented himself as an outstanding young man. His passion truly was for politics. About that, the senator was correct. He had a knack for building people up, making others believe in their talents and getting them where they wanted to be. The first person he ever got elected was the president of his freshman class at Andover. Each successive year, finishing prep school and on into his last year at Fisk, he was sought after by candidates, hopeful that he would run their campaigns. By the time he graduated from Howard with advanced degrees in public policy and law, he had created his own consulting firm and begun to run the campaigns of more and more respected politicians.

He commanded a high price for his involvement, but he certainly wasn't doing it for the money. Wealthy beyond need, Eric lived for the rush of knowing that it was a black man who was putting these people in office. He was the one crafting statements and grooming candidates. He engineered polls and developed people who were sometimes political unknowns, pushing them to places even he didn't think they could reach. He was a political backroom juggernaut whose touch was Midas. Congresspeople, countless state senators, three governors and one Senator Scott Tanner were all beneficiaries of his talent and insight.

As he sat in the salon of this magnificent yacht, the taste of brandy dancing around his mouth, he thought for a moment about a life of power and prestige beyond what his

Chief of Staff

grandfather might have imagined for himself. A United States Senator. Hmm. He refilled his glass and sat down on the sofa again. "So," he began, "tell me again what I'd be doing as your chief of staff."

Chapter *6*

CHRISTINE'S sun porch had been the center of Eric's world after his mother died when he was eight years old. Dove's Nest soon became more than his refuge. Named after his grandfather's pet name for his wife, Dove's Nest was a compound of sorts. A huge Victorian mansion nestled into the hillside on Crowder's Mountain in North Carolina and surrounded by seventy acres of serenity, it was the perfect place for Eric to put his life back together; as much as any child could after the death of his mother.

The cancer had taken his mother quickly, only three months after her diagnosis. He had moved into Dove's Nest with his parents so his mother would be comforted and so that his grandmother could provide the around-the-clock care she required. He hoped that the move would be temporary and that, somehow, his mother would get better. The reality he fought, though, was that his life would never be the same again.

Before she died, she spent every waking moment she could with Eric, her only child. They laughed and sang songs. They took long walks around the estate while she could still walk on her own. Sometimes at night, they sat outside on the sun porch cuddled together under blankets and drank hot chocolate with huge fluffy marshmallows and watched the stars. His mother taught him all about constellations: The Big Dipper, The Little Dipper, Orion, Asia Major and Minor and on and on. Most of the time, he simply listened to her voice, the sound of the letters and words and the way she spoke. He knew all too well that the day would come when the only way he would be able to hear her was in his memory.

She explained to her precious son about the beauty of the heavens and that one day – one day soon – she would be up in the stars they loved so much, looking down on him, guiding and protecting him. Never a true believer in God or religion, past the lessons he endured each Sunday at St.

Chief of Staff

Luke's Episcopal Church with his grandmother, he didn't understand why God would take his mother from him. When the day came that she could no longer move or speak, Eric sat quietly with her, holding her hand and gently stroking her hair, pausing only for her nurses to administer the morphine that suppressed her agonizing pain. He grew up quickly, turning into a man far sooner than he should.

After her funeral and after everyone had retreated back to their happy homes, Eric laid down on his grandmother's sun porch and stared into the night sky. Tears streamed down his face as he quietly said good-bye to his mother.

Always the obvious favorite of all her grandchildren, she assumed the role of mother without taking up the issue with Eric's father. The matriarch of one of Charlotte's most prominent families, black or otherwise, Christine Squire was a woman both rich and powerful enough to make her own rules and indifferent enough not to care how those rules affected those around her. Her only daughter was struck down by cancer and it was now her duty to raise the child she left behind. Whether her son-in-law was aware of it or not, the plan to raise Eric under her watchful and discriminating eye from Dove's Nest was set in motion the day his mother's casket was lowered into the ground.

*****

AS he sat on the sun porch looking at the Charlotte skyline in the distance, waiting for his grandmother's always-majestic entrance, Eric had gotten lost in the sounds of the birds chirping and took a moment to offer a silent prayer and hello to his late mother.

"Why on earth are you sitting out on this gorgeous porch with your head down and your eyes closed?" Christine asked as she sauntered out to her grandson. "Sit up, please."

Thirty-three years old, Eric snapped out of his prayer at the sound of her voice. It had been that way his entire life. Rising, turning and opening his arms to greet her, she breezed right past and sat down next to him on a shaded chaise. "And

Chief of Staff

good afternoon to you, Grandmother," Eric said, smiling and returning to his chair.

"You have forgotten that it is proper for a grandson to greet his grandmother when she enters a room."

"But you...," Eric began to protest. He groaned to himself and leaned over to kiss his grandmother's cheek. "Hello, sweetheart."

"Now, that wasn't so bad, was it?" Christine smiled and motioned one of the servants to her. Lemonade and peanut butter cookies, the afternoon snack Eric had hated since his childhood was laid out before him. Don't be silly, his grandmother would say, countering his objections. Everyone loves lemonade and peanut butter cookies. "Eat, Eric. You look thin."

"Yes, ma'am." Arguing was pointless. Suck it up and power through it, Eric told himself. Bite of cookie, big swig of lemonade and the torture would be over before he knew it. Change the subject and start talking. Maybe that way he could avoid the rest of his snack. "So I think I'm going to start a new job soon."

"Why you don't take your rightful place in the family business, I'll never understand," she quipped. Daintily, she nibbled the edge of a cookie. "It's really quite depressing."

Pampered from the day she was born, Christine Belmont Squire had never officially worked one single day of her eighty-nine years. Her father, Garfield Egbert Belmont, was born on the floor of a sharecropper's cabin in Duluth, Georgia. Garfield's father, it was widely alleged, was the white landowner who savagely raped a young black teenage girl too afraid to scream or to fight back. No one knows if it was his mother's painful pregnancy and delivery, or her death from an infection five days after his birth, but a fire was ignited in Garfield.

Extremely light skinned, Garfield quickly learned how to 'pass' and how passing would be the key to his future. Beautiful straight hair, thin nose and lips and an imposing

Chief of Staff

physical stature, he inherited a cruel irony. By thirteen, Garfield had left Georgia and was working as a day laborer in a Hickory, North Carolina furniture factory. The irony in his ability to pass for white meant that he had to banish the heritage of his mother, the woman who brought him into a world dominated by the indignity and heavy-handed racism of his father's white America in the 1800s.

Garfield voraciously learned the furniture business and by the time he was nineteen years old, had started a successful furniture manufacturing business of his own. He met and married a gorgeous, and similarly hued, black woman and together they raised four girls, the youngest of whom was Christine.

Absolutely striking, like her mother and sisters, Christine was truly the belle of the ball. By the time she was four, an undercurrent of black wealth had begun to emerge in pockets around the South and other parts of America's east coast. Black fraternities and sororities, private invitation-only social clubs and gathering spots began to gain more and more momentum. Blacks were attending colleges, becoming doctors and lawyers and businessmen on a scale their parents and grandparents may never have dreamt. Those doctors and lawyers and businessmen were making money. And a lot of it.

Along with greater wealth and amassing of power and influence, if only insular and kept secret as much as possible from the population at large, blacks who had money cruelly backhanded those who did not. Brown paper bag and ruler tests inside black culture were as reprehensible as Jim Crow Laws intended to keep whites and blacks separated. Constantly reminded to stay out of the sun to avoid getting too dark, taking lessons in proper speech and posture, and distancing themselves from poor blacks, this separatist and bigoted behavior was passed down from generation to generation.

Almost nine decades into her life, Christine was still as all-embracing a champion in the lighter versus darker war

Chief of Staff

as ever. Slender and attractive, she was a matriarch in the truest sense of the word. A Spelman graduate with a degree in economics, it was her natural business sense that allowed her late husband to prosper and their stature in their new hometown of Charlotte, North Carolina to increase exponentially. She championed the business from the sidelines, however respectful and secretly disdainful, fully aware of what damage to her husband's reputation might be caused were it made known that his wife was the puppet master and he simply the marionette.

Christine took her anger at being relegated to 'a woman's place' and turned it into an energetic and unrelenting assault on the social stage. She would command respect one way or another, by God, and if this was the only way she could make that happen, so be it. President of The Links, president of her Jack & Jill chapter, president of her AKA chapter and then serving ever so graciously as their National President, Christine Belmont Squire was a feared and respected social climber with a network of rich and powerful friends that spanned the country.

Famous salt and pepper hair that she meticulously maintained, a wardrobe of couture and custom made jewels, and a penchant for getting what she wanted. That was Eric's grandmother. As he choked down another peanut buttery bite and watched her lips moving rapidly – and in synch with her flailing arms – he wondered what his mother would have looked like had she gotten the chance to live to eighty-nine. Would she have been beautiful like his grandmother?

"Why are you smiling at me?" she asked, arms and hands still moving as though they had not yet gotten the message from her brain that she'd changed the subject. They say only a southern woman can curse you out and smile at the same time, you never being fully aware that you've just been disparaged. Acid-tongued and with a temperament she took greater caution than with her smoking to never display publicly, Eric's grandmother was the kind of woman you longed to be around. She simply exuded culture and confidence. She taught Eric many great things about the world, taking him on exotic trips and sending him to the very best schools. But she also had the uncanny ability to turn on you in a heartbeat. A simple question, to her, was always complex with a thousand answers waiting between the lines.

"I'm smiling because I wonder if my mother would have been as lovely as you."

"Bullshit."

"Grandmother!"

"What? I'm eighty-nine years old. You think I've never said bullshit before?"

"Stop!" Eric said, as the two laughed at each other. "Listen, I really do want to talk to you about this job."

"Senator Tanner's Stepin Fetchit, huh? Is that the job you want to talk to me about?" She let the gravel in her voice draw the last, single syllable through the air.

"Hardly. I'm going to be his chief of staff, Grandmother. In charge of his office and staff and day to day affairs." One last goddam peanut butter cookie. One last huge gulp of lemonade. "And just how is it that you know about this anyway?" He knew the answer, but there are some questions you just have to ask, aren't there?

"I have my sources. I'm a very well-connected woman, you know," she added with a sly grin.

"Well, Little Miss Well-Connected…."

"Don't you sass me, Eric. I didn't raise you to speak to me like that."

"I apologize, Grandmother. You're the one who said bullshit."

"And don't curse, either. It's unbecoming a young man in your position."

Eric went through his usual routine of shaking his head to himself, a practice he'd discovered when he was fifteen and mouthed off to her. One quick slap across the face will incite you to never reveal what you're really thinking in front of that woman. "Again, I apologize. But the only person you could have gotten that from was Senator Tanner, himself. I was with him on Trinity last night. He asked me to send his regards."

Christine sat up a little more perfectly on her chaise. "Let me tell you what Senator Scott Tanner can do with his regards and the shiny floating extension of a penis he calls a yacht."

"Oh my God! Where am I? This is not happening. You did not just say penis." Eric closed his eyes and went back through his routine.

"There's something about that man that makes my blood run cold and skin crawl. I can't put my finger on it, but there's something about that man that I just can't trust. And at the same time there has always been something about him which touches you and probably always will. It's like you're somehow connected, one a part of the other."

Eric and his grandmother both had very light caramel skin in common and the mentioning of his relationship with Senator Tanner made him blush. "I don't know how to explain it, Grandmother. It's just that he's always been there for me. In every way." Boyhood trips flashed across Eric's mind and he smiled fondly at the memories. "And that's why this job is so important to me. It's a chance to give something back to him and to make a serious step into the world of politics."

Christine smiled lovingly at her grandson. She wondered if she would have changed anything she did in raising him. A more perfect young man you wouldn't find anywhere in the world. She leaned over and touched his hand. "Your mother would be very proud of you, Eric."

"I hope so, Grandmother. I hope so."

Christine stood, prompting Eric to immediately do the same. "I'm getting a chill. Let's go inside and you can tell

Chief of Staff

me about your new job, Mr. Chief of Staff. You will stay for dinner, won't you?" Christine had this very distinctive way of asking you a question although it was really a statement of what she wanted to happen.

Eric was a rich, attractive single man, and a Friday night out with good friends beckoned. "Yes, Grandmother. I'd be happy to stay."

"Wonderful. It will be lovely spending time with my favorite grandson. Bring the cookies and walk this old woman inside."

"The cookies?" Eric asked. "My mouth simply waters at the thought."

"Bullshit."

"Grandmother!"

Chapter 7

ERIC sat in his car when he got to the underground parking garage and took a deep breath. If what Senator Tanner said about this being a stepping stone to public office was true, absolutely everything had to go smoothly the second he got out and started his new life. A senator. A United States Senator. It was unfathomable. Eric and Senator Tanner had briefly spoken about strategy and how his every move, historical and future, would dictate any possible ascension to the floor of the Senate.

Everything was moving at warp speed, it seemed. In the three weeks since he was flown to Trinity for their clandestine meeting, then going over his intentions with his grandmother, he promoted his second-in-command at his consulting firm in Charlotte, put the finishing touches on what used to be his weekend home in D.C., and talked himself down from more than a few proverbial ledges. Daily conversations with the senator were used to give Eric the lay of the land and the best practices of chiefs of staff in the past. All of the information provided was of great use, but for right now, he was more nervous than anything else. He wasn't prepared to be chief of staff, let alone a senator.

Shaking off his 'future value', Eric composed himself and returned to reality. "Okay," he began, pumping himself up. He turned the rearview mirror and spoke out loud. "You can do this. Senator Tanner trusts you. You trust yourself. This job is going to be a piece of cake. You are the man." Appearing out of nowhere, surprising Eric a little, a man walked by his car and deliberately stared at him. Dressed very plainly in jeans and a hooded jacket, Eric figured maybe he worked as a janitor or somewhere in the bowels of the building. Other than that, he seemed to be a regular white guy. Not too tall, average build, average looks. He didn't smile. He didn't wave. He made absolutely no effort to gesture toward Eric, even though their eye contact was obvious. It seemed his only purpose was to make sure Eric

Chief of Staff

knew he was being watched. And then he was gone. "What the hell was that?" Eric asked out loud. "Freak."

Eric wiped the encounter from his mind and tried to refocus. Centered again, he jumped out of the car and strode confidently toward the elevator, when a sudden and uncontrollable waive of nausea overtook him. Pitching himself toward the nearest trash can, Eric violently relieved his anxiety. Twice.

"And you must be Eric," a woman's voice said from behind. Closing his eyes in hopes of being sorely mistaken and repeating to himself that he did not just hear someone speak his name, Eric froze. "Don't worry. Everybody blows chunks on their first day. I know I sure did." Eric reluctantly turned to address the stranger, wiping his mouth quickly with the back of his hand.

"I'm Claudia Eldridge," she said. "We'll be working together keeping the senator in good form and up-to-date on any- and everything connected to his office. I'd shake your hand, but…"

Embarrassed to no end, Eric stammered a hello. "And how do you know my name?"

"Senator Tanner told us all about you. There are a bunch of guys walking about this building in high dollar custom suits, and plenty of them with fancy cars just like yours. But I can only think of twenty of them who are black. You make number twenty-one." Claudia was a black woman, tall and dark-skinned. Eric guessed she was about thirty or so, but couldn't tell for sure. He could tell, however, that she had a glowing smile and that she was very pretty. "And, apparently, you're going to be my new boss."

For whatever reason, at this moment, Eric would have preferred her to be unattractive and not working for him. "You've got to be joking." Eric felt the nausea returning.

"Nope. Uh, you missed a little on your lip, boss," Claudia said, gesturing to her mouth.

Chief of Staff

"I'll give you $100 if you promise to never mention this to anyone."

"$100? For my silence?" Claudia smiled and said, "I believe you'll do just fine."

*****

SETTLED into his office, and chewing breath mints one after the other, Eric stood at the window and gazed at Washington, D.C., spread out before him in all of its glory. "Hell yes," he said to himself.

"Hell yes is right!" Senator Tanner boomed. "Welcome to the Hill, young man."

Eric bolted to Senator Tanner, giving him a firm handshake and then a hug. "What are you doing here? Your schedule has you in meetings until noon."

"I couldn't have you starting your day as my chief of staff without dropping in on you. What kind of asshole do you think I am?" The two men laughed and for the next thirty minutes, went over the 'what's what' of Eric's new job. Most of it they had already gone over, but it was nice to have a refresher.

Claudia walked in and dropped a stack of documents on Eric's desk. He hadn't noticed in the bad lighting of the parking deck, but Claudia was more attractive than he first realized. It had been drilled into his head that dating only girls and women of his social status was accepted. No slumming, his grandmother preached, subconsciously pushing Eric's taste toward darker complexions. Perhaps it was the intrigue of women who knew nothing about his world that drew him to them.

The reality of the situation, however, was that those girlfriends and one-night stands were never even on his marriage radar. And now there was Claudia, slender and tall, with a crazy short, but respectable hairstyle, and that thousand-watt smile. He would have to see her every day, just outside his door. This wasn't going to be easy. Of course, no matter their working relationship, she was much too dark to present to his grandmother. The long acrylic nails weren't the only things that would have sent Christine over the edge. "Time to get started, COS."

"Excuse me? COS?" asked Eric, making sure he heard her correctly.

"It's what they all called Byrum," said Senator Tanner. "A term of endearment, I guess."

"That and it's easier to say or type COS when you're bitching about your boss to your co-workers," Claudia added with a wink.

"This is your dog and pony show now, kid. Have them call you whatever you want."

"I've got a couple of ideas if COS doesn't work out," Claudia chimed in.

Senator Tanner stood to leave, turning around when he reached the door. "I understand you hurled in the garage this morning."

Eric shot a look at Claudia. "And how did you hear that, I wonder?"

"I don't remember exactly who I got the information from, but it cost me $200." The senator laughed from his gut and trotted off to his first meeting.

"Don't let the smooth taste fool you," Claudia said, as she smiled and walked out.

Chapter *8*

EVEN though Eric had what he felt was a complete familiarity with how things worked in Washington, he was wholly unprepared for the pace. That morning, after his surprise first-day visit from Senator Tanner, he was sucked head long into a world he never really knew existed.

6:15 – Security introduction and briefing with FBI and Capital Hill Police. 7:45 - Breakfast meeting with the Black Caucus. 9:45 – Formal tour of the Senate buildings and grounds. 11:45 – Lunch meeting with Kenneth Reid and Joseph Schneider, chiefs of staff for Senators Danfure and Kyle, respectively. 1:00 – Meeting with Chuck Bastian to go over wording of the Immigration bill being sponsored by him and Senator Tanner. 2:00 – Phone call from Senator Tanner, interrupted by Claudia telling him that Mrs. Colsby's tenth grade Advanced Placement Governmental Studies class was ready for their Meet & Greet. 2:30 – Open until 3:00. Time to rest.

Of all the people he'd had a hand in getting elected, none of them had given him a true appreciation of politics. His mother had been a teacher, shunning the family business and confounding Christine in the process. He knew first-hand how hard teachers worked, preparing young people who may or may not have been born with a silver spoon in their mouth to survive in the real world. She had a passion for her work, often staying late, counseling students and reassuring their parents. She instilled in her son what he would never have gotten from his father and certainly not from his illustrious grandmother: the joy of hard work and benefiting the lives of others.

It was that passion for helping others that blossomed when Eric was young. Somewhere along the way, that passion merged with his love of politics and his destiny had been written for him. Granted, teaching mostly affluent men and women how to win an election was a far cry from

Chief of Staff

teaching a child how to read and write, but he felt he was providing an important service nonetheless.

As he sat on the sofa in his office, his head still smarting from the millionth question he'd answered for a 10th grader too smart for high school, Claudia's endless chatter about scheduling and protocol and voting records and constituent dinners and party fundraisers and glad-handing and more scheduling and more protocol, Eric closed his eyes and took a long, slow, deep breath.

"Wake up, COS," Claudia deliberately shouted as she burst in, this time with an anonymous brown box full of something he either had to sign or go over. Eric groaned in disbelief.

"What can I do for you, sweetheart?"

"Let me tell you one thing before we get started." Claudia set the box on the coffee table and sat down next to Eric. "I'm not your secretary, I'm not your note taker, I don't get coffee, and I don't put up with anything less than the respect I deserve. Although we may both be from the south, you from North Carolina and me from Georgia, the next time you call me sweetheart," she said, glancing down at his crotch, "I'll twist your little friend until it falls off and put in the trash where it belongs."

"You're an evil Russian lesbian, aren't you?"

"There are no black Russians," she replied coldly. "I'm a Republican."

"Duly noted." Eric couldn't tell if she was kidding or was, in fact, very serious, so he moved on. "Again, what can I do for you?"

"Do you remember everyone you met this morning? Everyone that works in this office?"

"Yes."

"First and last name?"

"Yes."

"Good. One more thing you need to remember from this point forward is that although you control what Senator Tanner does day to day, I control you. From deciding on who you can and cannot accept invitations from, everything in your world goes through me first."

"It's actually 'from whom' you can and cannot accept invitations." Yet another joke. Yet another 'I wish I could kill you where you sit' glare. Eric crossed his legs and motioned for her to please continue.

Not taking her eyes off him, she slightly opened the box on the table. "In this box are the keys to the castle, so to speak." Eric peeked into the box and Claudia slammed it shut. "I don't know what the senator has told you, but this is a very powerful position you seem to have fallen into." A funny retort crossed Eric's mind, but was quickly vetoed by his mouth. "This box, and others, contains folders of every fact, every vote, every meeting note and Senate hearing transcript, and every minute detail you will need to know in order to be a successful chief of staff to Senator Tanner."

Watching for a well-placed wrist slap from his new Executive Administrative Professional, Eric gingerly reached over, pulled the box to the sofa, and removed the top. Confused, he looked back at Claudia. "But there must be thousands of pages in here," he said picking one out at random.

"Yes. And another twenty-five boxes that were in storage will be delivered to your house this evening."

"My God."

"You can call me whatever you want," Claudia quipped without losing a beat. "They are all labeled and are in a specific date range order. I need you to familiarize yourself with the contents as soon as possible."

"Right," Eric huffed. *Twenty-five boxes? This woman is crazy.* "This is the 21st century. How about springing for a scanner? Jesus, do the environmentalists know about this?"

Not even a hint of a smile. "If you're going to be good at this job, it is imperative that you go through all of this information. You must understand every bit of it. If you cannot remember something related to the senator and his voting history, it's in these boxes. If you need position papers on a topic, they're in these boxes. If you need assistance or guidance on how to do your job…"

"Let me guess, it's in these boxes," Eric joked.

"No. At that point, you'll have been fired and I will have won the pool."

"The pool?"

"Yes. I've got the squares for between eight and ten months."

"What will you win?"

"$1."

"Big spenders."

"Go through all of this information, COS. Do you understand?"

"Yes."

"Yes, what?"

"Yes, my Evil Mistress. I understand." Claudia couldn't help it and chuckled just a tiny bit. Thank God, Eric, thought. She's human after all.

"Continuing on," Claudia said, "the key to Byrum's office safe cannot be located for whatever reason. I don't know what's in there, but you'll probably want access to the safe so you can lock up your skin lightening cream and English-to-Ebonics dictionary."

"My Ebonics is just fine, thank you. Sista."

"We'll see about that. Remind me later and I'll take care of that for you."

Eric had actually found a key under the desk that morning as he was putting his things away. He'd bent down to retrieve a dropped breath mint when he found a small envelope, like a safe deposit box key holder, taped to the underside of the desk. He wasn't sure what it went to and stuffed it in his pocket, a fact he'd keep to himself until he scoped out whatever it was Byrum had taken significant steps to hide. After Senator Tanner left, that morning, Eric poked around until he found the hidden safe and opened it up. The only things he found were a manuscript that Byrum must have been working on before he died, and a little black device that he couldn't identify. He put everything into his briefcase to look through later.

"You know, I actually found the key. It was in one of these drawers. There wasn't anything in it, so you can take that off of your list."

Claudia knew Byrum was very secretive about the contents of the safe and she had always assumed he'd kept something very private there. "That's strange." Eric looked at her and shrugged. "Oh well. Do you have any questions for me?"

"Can I have my $100 back?"

"Only when you pry it from my cold, dead, evil Russian lesbian hand."

"You said there are no black Russians. So you're either a liar or you're very forgetful."

"In either case, Washington is the perfect place for me, wouldn't you agree?

"Yes, Mistress."

"Your 3:00 is waiting for you."

Chief of Staff

Chapter *9*

THE first two weeks of Eric's new job thoroughly sucked. The processes and protocols were well within his grasp. The technical aspect of the position was as daunting as he had expected. But something was missing where the staff was concerned and he couldn't understand what it was. He had decided before he took the job that the best way for him to show his new employees that he was the boss was to be very firm and demanding. This was his office, dammit. He wasn't the Mr. Nice Guy that Byrum had been. Eric was tough and expected nothing but the best from everyone. They could all either deal with it or find a new job.

That approach clearly wasn't working.

"You know what your problem is, don't you?" asked Claudia as she breezed into his office.

"Could it be that I have a secretary who doesn't know how to knock?"

"Even if you weren't a handsome, high yellow, extremely rich brother who thinks he has influence over what I say and do, the last thing you should try to be is funny." Claudia parked herself in a chair in front of Eric's desk, tucking a leg underneath her as she sat.

"Please, get comfortable." Claudia shook her head and stared at Eric. "If you would prefer, I have a camera in my car."

"Again with the funny. You should really give that up." Eric rolled his eyes and shuffled some papers around, pretending to work. "And that whole rolling your eyes thing doesn't work, either. You forget who you're talking to."

"To whom you're talking." Eric smiled.

Claudia leaned forward, pushing her way through the stack of papers and touched Eric's hand. "I'm going to give you some advice, honey, because you're going to need it. If

Chief of Staff

you're half as smart as you think you are, and if you're half as committed to Senator Tanner as you make yourself out to be, you'll listen to me and understand what I'm about to tell you. And you'll pay close attention to me. Because if you don't, not only are you going to be putting that wonderful man in a terrible position, I'm going to have to be the one to clean out this desk once you've been fired and they replace you with someone just as rich, just as talented, just as good looking, and I pray to God, someone who's a hell of a lot funnier than you."

Eric pulled his hand away from Claudia's and leaned back in his chair.

"You need to lighten up, COS. You can't treat people like you own them."

"I do no such thing," Eric responded, hurt at the very thought of what she was suggesting. "Do I have that perception?"

"COS, from the day you dropped your little can into this office two weeks ago, you have done nothing but change this place from the fun-loving atmosphere we all once enjoyed to one of caution and never knowing what mood you might be in from one minute to the next."

Eric thought about Christine's commanding style and winced. He was becoming more and more like her every day. "Jenkins," he began, looking out into the cube farm of Senator Tanner's senatorial offices. "I think I might have been a little too hard on him the other day. I'm guessing Byrum wasn't like that, was he?"

Claudia nodded. "You yelled at the boy for I don't know what, and for no reason." Claudia got up and walked around the desk. "Eric, this isn't about Byrum. And it isn't about impressing Senator Tanner. He knows that you're your own man, and he must see something in you that I don't to have put you where you are today. But nobody here cares about any of that. Your money and achievements don't impress them. Most of them are either rich or they are going to be sooner or later. Whether you're here for two years or ten, what they care most about is what they are providing this office every day they come to work. They're here because they love serving their government. They're here because Senator Tanner and Byrum recognized something in them and gave them a chance to do what they love best. Sure, some of them are using this place as a stepping-stone. I can't tell you how many interns we've had on their way to law school or working for the senator as a favor to one of their parents. The point is they don't have to be here. They're all stellar people and they know their stuff inside and out."

"Some people refer to it as the missing link," said Senator Tanner, walking into Eric's office and sitting down on the sofa. Both Eric and Claudia were surprised to see him. "It's the one thing you'll need to discover on your own if you want to truly fit it around here."

Claudia turned to the senator and asked, "Do you want me to set it up?"

Senator Tanner looked at Eric and smiled, and spoke to Claudia without looking at her. "Yes. I think it will be good for him. And," he continued, turning his attention back to Claudia, "make sure he understands what it is we need to accomplish."

Claudia twisted her mouth, pursing her lips from excitement.

"What are you talking about?" Eric asked them both. "Who are you talking about and what the hell is the missing link?"

"You'll find out soon enough, COS." She winked at the senator and left them alone, closing the door behind her.

*****

"ERIC, my friend," Senator Tanner sang as he motioned Eric over to the sofa, "we need to have a chat. You are no doubt aware of Senator Lamprey, are you not?"

"Of course. Republican senator from California."

"Yes."

"What about him?" Eric glanced at the pile of work on his desk and hoped this wouldn't take long.

"I don't know how to put this, but I need you to facilitate a meeting with him. Today." Senator Tanner waited for Eric's reaction. He'd caught the glimpsing of his desk and knew he was covered up. "I wouldn't ask this of you, but..."

"Don't worry about it. What time?" What he really thought was, shit, not another meeting with another blowhard senator.

"Twenty minutes. He's on his way over."

Eric groaned. "And what does he want to talk about?"

"The Immigration bill."

Shit again. Anything but that. Claudia poked her head into Eric's office and very quietly said, "Senator Lamprey's here to see you, Eric."

"What happened to twenty minutes?" Eric asked Senator Tanner, getting up from the sofa and heading back to his desk.

"Maybe he told me he was coming over twenty minutes ago. Not sure." Senator Tanner shrugged his shoulders, got up from the sofa and slipped into his office using the side door.

"Should I show him in?" Claudia asked.

Eric took a deep breath and nodded, yes.

Without waiting to be formally announced, Senator Lamprey walked past Claudia without so much as a thank you and sat down in front of Eric's desk. No handshake was apparently going to take place, so Eric sat down, as well. Claudia closed the door on her way out and Eric reluctantly began the conversation. "Good afternoon, Senator. And to what do I owe the pleasure?"

"We need to talk about the folks in my state who are going to be put out of business by Tanner's bill."

"The Immigration bill."

"No the goddam Disney Land bill. I thought you'd be a little more intelligent than Byrum, but I guess not."

Eric counted to ten and waited to calm down before he spoke. "Again, Senator," he started, far less congenial than at first. "What is it that I can do for you?"

"You can amend the language of that bill. It's going to devastate the hard-working people I represent."

"The Californians? Or the Americans?" Senator Lamprey was shorter and older than Eric. Eric figured that if this came to blows, he'd win. Over the desk in one quick motion, punch him in the eye and the mouth, and Senator Lamprey would be on the floor with a split lip, begging for mercy.

"Are you paying attention to me?" Senator Lamprey asked.

"Of course, I'm listening. Please continue."

"That bill is going to destroy the farming and menial labor industries the illegals have been propping up for longer than you've been alive. If this bill passes and the supply of spicks and wetbacks dries up, the entire economy is going to hit the skids. There goes the Republican strong hold. There go the shitpot of electoral votes in the next presidential election."

"And there goes your nice Senate seat, as well, right?"

Senator Lamprey glared at Eric. "You have a lot to learn, boy. Namely that you don't speak to a United States Senator using that tone."

"You, sir, a term that I use lightly, are not in your office or your house. You have come to me. I will say to you as politely as I can that should you deem it necessary to speak to me like I work for you, in short order you will find yourself in the emergency room. In fact," Eric said, as he walked to his office door, opened it fully and returned to his seat, "I don't give a good goddam who you are." The entire staff stopped what they were doing, turning in the direction of Eric's wide-open office, blatantly eavesdropping on the conversation. "This is the office of Senator Scott Tanner, Republican from the great and wonderful state of North Carolina. He is an honorable man who cares more about this country and its well-being than whether or not he gets to recklessly and endlessly pillage the coffers of his state and the office to which he has thrice been elected."

Senator Lamprey seemed completely uncomfortable having this conversation open to the public, turning to look at his audience and then back to Eric. He started to speak, but Eric cut him off.

"I would like for you to pay very close attention to me, Senator. What I'm about to tell you is very important. You don't want to miss anything I have to say." As his grandmother had trained him, the volume of Eric's voice never rose beyond a polite conversational level, infuriating Senator Lamprey even further. "You will vote for this bill when it comes to the floor. Unless you are semi-illiterate or just haven't taken the time to personally read the text, you will recognize that there is language in the bill that allows for the gradual increase of barriers and protocols necessary to lessen the number of 'illegals' coming into California or New Mexico or who knows where, finally reaching the point in ten years where it will take an act of God for Juan or Lupez or Juanita to gain access to our country without permission.

"You will further remind yourself that California is facing an increasing economic bind. Your farmers and menial laborers and vocational co-ops are becoming more and more reliant on the goods and services produced in North Carolina by our fine citizens. Centennial Farms comes to mind. The working poor who elected you out of sheer stupidity far too many years ago, may not realize the interconnectedness with which our two states exist. But when the goods and services

Chief of Staff

they need dry up, their economy worsens, and they realize that political infighting in the Republican party, spurred on by the advancing age and diminished mental capacity of their beloved Senator Lamprey, has caused yet another family farm to go under or forced another minimum-wage family out on the street, they won't be calling for my head."

Eric took a casual sip of his tea and waited for Senator Lamprey's response.

Red-faced, Senator Lamprey got up and stormed out of Eric's office, brushed past the shocked staff and shouted, "Go to hell!"

"Not if they have an Immigration bill," Eric said, standing quickly and raising his voice for effect. He smiled and sat back down. Two seconds later, the office erupted in applause and whistles of approval, led by none other than Senator Scott Tanner. From the great and wonderful state of North Carolina.

Chapter *10*

I CAN'T believe we're doing this, people said to each other, excited to be standing on the tarmac at Andrews Air Force Base. Twenty people from various governmental and senatorial offices had been invited to visit the USS George Washington for three days. It was customary for the Liaison office of the Navy to invite civilians aboard carriers for what had always been called an 'informational trip'. Eric figured his invitation had something to do with the missing link conversation between Claudia and the senator.

As Senator Tanner's chief of staff – and a full month into the position – this was Eric's first, and assuredly only, opportunity to experience the Navy first-hand. He leapt at the offer. It was a chance to get away from the office and to experience a tiny snippet of the life he'd dreamt about but, by his grandmother's decree, would never live out. He imagined which stars and constellations he would be able to see out in the open ocean and longed to steal a few quiet moments wrapped in the arms of the memory of his mother.

Huddled together with the other guests, Eric introduced himself to those he didn't know and networked with a few of the other chiefs of staff. The mood was light and filled with anticipation. Even those who didn't fully appreciate what they were about to experience were a little giddy. Turning to see what was making the awful noise that crept toward them, someone joked that the plane in the distance was their ride. Eric silently hoped it was not.

As the gray and white C-2 Greyhound stopped, cut engines and the side door opened, the banter and jokes abruptly ended. A tall, handsome pilot stepped out and motioned everyone to him. Good morning ma'am, and good morning sir, he snapped out, helping everyone inside the dark confines of the plane. Eric was the last to board and turned one last time to look at the ground. He hated flying, but the USS George Washington was seventy-five miles off the coast, floating in the Atlantic conducting Carrier Landing Qualifications. This wasn't an experience he was going to miss for anything. Man up, he told himself, and climbed into the plane.

There were two rows of what could loosely be described as seats lining the walls of the plane. Under each seat, they were told by the pilot, were a helmet and headphones. Put them on and get your seatbelt as tight as you can. A very quick safety briefing ensued and the pilot disappeared into the cockpit. No mention of the emergency exits, no mention of a floatation device. No instruction on how to use the inflatable emergency exit ramps, provided they even existed. Quite an auspicious beginning this was. A million questions ran through his mind and just as Eric looked up toward where the pilot had been standing, it appeared they had received all the instruction to which they were entitled. Eric began to quiver. He watched the pilot settle in and noticed that you could see out the front window. This, he thought, he was not used to. He shook his head and wondered what the hell he was doing. The plane rocked slightly at the firing of the first engine.

The young man next to him was struggling to latch his seatbelt when the second engine rumbled back to life. Panicked, he asked Eric for help. The faint smell of exhaust was disconcerting, but even more troubling was the fact that his own seatbelt wouldn't properly latch, either. It's not every day you are asked to reach into another man's crotch and buckle him into a military cargo plane. Pretending both that he wasn't scared as hell and that he had latched a thousand seatbelts in the best non-gay manner he could, Eric reached over, snapped his neighbor together, then himself. After an awkward 'you're welcome', he leaned back to start his pre-flight ritual.

"God, if you let me live through this flight, I'll be a better person," he said to himself, rubbing his hands together and cracking his knuckles. He didn't know when or why he started doing this, but it comforted him. And since he'd never been in a plane crash, he figured it must work.

Airborne and shooting out across the sapphire-blue waters, Eric opened his eyes to check out his surroundings. He'd been told to leave his watch and all jewelry at home, so he had no real concept of time. The chatter had returned and the mood was once again jovial, people laughing about not being at work and telling jokes about their friends and families.

Eric looked around the plane and recognized it was the same thing he'd seen a thousand times on the Military Channel and at countless air shows in the past. A world apart from his grandmother's private jets and one hundred eighty degrees from your typical First Class section, there were exposed rivets, nets and metal everywhere. No carpet, no windows, no lavatory. He remembered that the C-2 Greyhound was used to ferry mail and other supplies to carriers at sea. And that's when it hit him. For whatever reason, he hadn't stopped long enough to consider that it wouldn't be the ground greeting him at the end of this flight. They would be landing on the narrow top of an undulating, moving war ship. He closed his eyes again to settle himself, breathing deeply, when the plane pitched forward, beginning a steady and ominous dive.

The faint lighting blinked twice and extinguished, replaced with blackness and tortuous screaming. The only light was coming from the cockpit window. Eric leaned forward and saw the pilots frantically pressing buttons and turning dials. The static nothingness of his headphones had now been exchanged by the words flaps and dive and dead stick and water landing. He wasn't exactly sure how long they'd been airborne, but he hoped they were closer to land than the carrier. Jerking his head back against the wall, he spoke out loud, not caring who was listening. "Please, God, if you let me live through this, I swear I'll...," his voice trailed off. Swearing in a prayer? Probably not kosher. He started over. His hands were clasped together more tightly than his eyes, his breath stilted and uneven with the sudden rise and fall of the plane.

"Please, God, if you let me live through this, I…I'll… Shit." He couldn't think of anything. And now he'd cursed in a prayer. Not a good sign. It was at that point he definitely knew he was going to die. The plane pitched forward again, giving Eric a shot of the sea moving quickly to meet them. Everyone screamed louder. Eric blacked out.

*****

"HEY, buddy, wake up. Wake up. We've landed."

It was distant, but Eric thought he heard someone's voice. A second pass of smelling salts quickly brought Eric back to full consciousness.

"We've landed, sir."

Dazed, Eric unlatched his belt and was helped to his feet and out of the plane. Blinking at the brilliance of the sunlight, he looked around at the flurry of activity; the sound of the waves and the voices of what he swore must have been five thousand sailors all speaking to each other at once was overwhelming.

"Welcome to the USS George Washington, sir," someone was yelling at him.

The C-2 pilots smugly put another four grease pencil marks on their tally board and high-fived each other. Oddly enough, even though the sun was bright in the sky, it was cold and windy and not at all what he had expected. But he was alive.

The carrier was violently pitching up and down from the swell of the open water and all Eric saw was the ocean and then the sky, the ocean and then the sky. Eric started to speak, but when he opened his mouth, he vomited all over his shoes.

Welcome to the USS George Washington, indeed.

Chapter *11*

FROM the outset, this wasn't at all like any of the guests of the USS George Washington had expected. First, that awful plane ride, landing on the pitching deck of a moving object, which Eric thankfully hadn't witnessed due to his blackout, and now to the pandemonium of life in the Navy aboard a nuclear powered, infinitely sustainable weapon of death. Eric was still regaining his composure when the entire group was whisked below decks for their first briefing. Somewhere between the polite but respectful email invitation to the staffers two weeks ago and now, the captain, John Koonce, must have changed his mind about the three days his guests would be with him.

Everyone was lined up according to height, men on the left and women on the right. Standing behind each civilian was their new Navy counterpart, their mentor. They were affectionately referred to as Anchors; the soft, spoiled government types were known as Cushies. Each Cushie was handed a uniform, told to change into said uniform in quick fashion, which apparently meant no more than four minutes because they were summarily rounded up and made to line up again. Upon their return, they were told to report, with their Anchor, to their assigned workstation. "Workstation?" asked one woman, clearly put off by the idea of what was about to happen. Captain Koonce barked out an order, his voice bouncing off of the drab gray metal walls, startling the Cushies. The Anchors chuckled out loud.

It had been decided, the captain continued to bark, that from now on anyone coming to his ship would get a real world taste of the Navy. "Think of it as a working lunch," he said sarcastically, for some reason staring directly at Eric who immediately darted his eyes toward the floor. Each Anchor would guide his or her Cushie through every aspect of life aboard his ship, like it or not. "You want to know what the Navy is all about, you Nancys? Well, you've got it." With that he disappeared and the Anchors took over, barking out

Chief of Staff

their own specific orders, very loudly and all at once, like an echo crash derby. The words were indecipherable to anyone but the speaker. And no one was able to distinguish who was actually speaking to whom. Eric stood stick straight, followed his Anchor's orders as closely as he could and suddenly found himself being dragged down the corridor by his elbow.

For the next three days, the Cushies were to be at the utter disposal of their Anchor. From engineering to the bridge to the hangar to below decks, each Cushie had their own specific responsibility. Each day would bring safety drills, training, twelve-hour work shifts and eating and sleeping alongside the young men and women who protect not only the United States of America but her allies day in and day out.

Eric's Anchor, Grable, was a fifteen-year veteran and part of V-2 Division, or the green shirts - the folks that maintain the steam catapults used to launch planes from the flight deck. More than any other Cushie/Anchor pairing, they were inseparable, with Eric crisply and efficiently carrying out every task Grable yelled at him to perform. Loaded down with his uniform, a life vest, helmet and wireless radio system, heavy boots and goggles, the deck of the aircraft carrier was simply stifling, completely different than the thirty minutes prior when he upchucked in front of God and country. Never the less, Eric lapped up every second.

From checking the catapults before and after launches to making sure the giant arresting cables were in working order and able to safely stop planes at full throttle and bring the pilots home in one piece, it was more arduous than Eric could explain. At the same time, he was living his dream and sometimes found it difficult to contain himself and his excitement. One slip up, one move away from Grable or against his direct orders and somebody could get hurt or killed. The enormity of the responsibility didn't hit Eric until he and Grable were racked for the night, deep within the belly of the carrier.

"Do you have any idea why you all are out here?" Grable asked. This wasn't his first assignment towing a Cushie around the flight deck. He'd asked the question dozens of times, with each Cushie offering up a different, clueless response. Grable was a little bit under six feet tall, but he was very muscular and moved in a way that was naturally authoritative and commanded respect. He never yelled at any of his junior sailors, and he didn't have to. His orders, both verbal and non-verbal, were effortlessly conveyed and instantly executed.

Deeply tanned red-hued skin and jet black hair, Grable explained to Eric that the Navy was his escape from an Indian Reservation in Montana. It was his only way out of a dangerous life of drugs and violence and excessive drinking that he had seen destroy too many of his friends and family.

The first thing that came to Eric in trying to come up with an answer to Grable's leading question was flippant and he thought better of letting it squirt out of his mouth. That's when Grable's question really sank in. He thought about what he had just experienced on the flight deck. On the *fucking flight deck*, he repeated to himself. It was still amazing and he was overjoyed knowing there were two more days to come.

He thought about the chaos and excitement created by and required to make sure everything ran smoothly. He pictured the guys in the blue and yellow shirts, the V-1. They were the guys on the flight deck who moved the aircraft around, made sure they were ready for take-off and made sure that everyone was safe. He thought about the air boss, perched high above them, keeping a watchful eye and orchestrating the madness below. He pictured the ordinance and weapons experts. The people in the hangar bays who keep the planes flying. The 'Grapes' who fuel the warplanes and armored helicopters. The white-shirted gang in the V-0 who handle every administrative task you can think of. They all work together, seamlessly and without hesitation for a common goal.

· "Because you're a team," Eric said quietly, almost too low for Grable to hear, thinking about how he ran his office back in D.C., and the negativity he had brought with him.

"That's right. Sometimes it feels more like family. Yeah, there are times when we don't get along with each other, but goddamit if we don't always – and I mean always – work together to protect the ship and our country. You've got it good in D.C., or wherever you're from. Nice comfy bed, probably don't have anybody in your ear fourteen or sixteen hours a day, you get to come and go as you please."

Eric nodded his head even though Grable was in the rack above him and couldn't see him at all. He smiled when he asked himself the question, *do you know why you all are here.* It was now so clear. This trip was the key to what Senator Tanner had called the missing link. Sure, Eric could run an office. Good Lord, he owned his own company. But in order to run the office of Senator Tanner the right way, the best way, Eric had to see for himself that he was part of a team. Even the captain of the USS George Washington couldn't run the ship by himself. He had to have the support, the determination and, most importantly, the respect of every sailor he commanded. Coming to the carrier wasn't a fun outing, like the rest of the Cushies bemused while they waited on the tarmac at Andrews. It was a learning experience and one that Eric Julian wouldn't soon forget.

"But there's nothing I would take, no money, no fine tight-bodied Moroccan stripper ass, no car, nothing that I would trade to have your life over mine." Grable was still talking, but it was getting harder for Eric to keep his eyes open, let alone concentrate on the ramblings coming from the upper rack. "I've been around the world and, shit, some of those places we've visited I never even knew existed. I get paid to do what I love and nothing is tying me down. And this is the best family I've ever had."

Eric was exhausted and fell asleep with a smile. He dreamt of his mother and how they used to lay out and star

Chief of Staff

gaze. He hoped she would be proud of her son. He couldn't wait until he got up the next day to do it all over again.

******

At the end of the last day, the sun slowly setting on the horizon, the C2 chirped to a landing on one of Eric's proudly maintained arresting cables and came to a stop. The Cushies hadn't seen one another for their entire stay on the George Washington. The carrier was as long as a twenty-four-story building tipped on its side, supporting more than 5,000 people at any given time. It was easy to understand why they had had no contact with each other. As they lined up, their Anchors behind them, some were visibly ready to end their 'ordeal' and get home. Captain Koonce barked out a thank you, sir and ma'am, and hoped their visit had been memorable. He walked up to Eric, grabbed his hand in a firm handshake, and whispered in his ear, "Tell Senator Tanner that his cousin said hello. I hope you learned something on my ship and that you will take it back with you. Good job, sailor." With that he disappeared once again into the drab grayness of the ship. Eric was speechless.

Before he got on the plane for the flight home, Grable took Eric by the arm. "You're the best and hardest working Cushie I've ever had, sir," Grable said as he saluted Eric.

Not knowing whether to return the salute or not, Eric extended his hand and grasped Grable's firmly. "You're a good man, Grable. You've taught me a lot in just three days. I know how this is going to sound, but I'll never forget you."

Grable looked at Eric and smiled. Grable took Eric's hand, pressed a patch into it, and walked away. The patch read: *Honorary Tailhooker – USS George Washington – CVN 73.*

Chapter *12*

"ERIC Julian," he said with his standard ambivalence. Anyone Claudia put through on this line obviously knew to whom they wanted to speak. Perhaps it was social training more than anything that made him continue to announce himself. Yet another gem from his grandmother.

"I, uh…I would like to have a few minutes of your time," the man on the other end of the line said.

"And this is whom?" Eric continued to work. He had just returned from his 'Naval Experience' as he had come to describe it to friends and family. Cramped quarters, food that could raise the dead and that awful, continuous stream of noises and vibrations. Once back on the ground at Andrews, he thanked God for his pampered and soft life, however fully appreciative of those men and women who risk their lives every day so that he could be free. It was a strange paradox, to be sure.

It was more of a pain to be away from the office for three days than he thought, but the experience taught him more about himself than he had expected to learn. Along with banged up shins and intolerable exhaustion, he brought back with him a desire to unify his office, to implement the concept of being a team. He had come up with a million ideas on the flight back to Andrews and he intended to get moving on them as soon as possible, but right now, he was absorbed in the business of the day. It was going to be another short week, because tomorrow he had to be back in Charlotte for his grandmother's party. The last thing he needed was a prank call.

"Meet me in Lafayette Square across from the White House in thirty minutes."

"I know where it is. However, I won't be there." Eric looked at the phone, but the caller id didn't register a number. What the hell was Claudia doing? Was this another practical

Chief of Staff

joke? "Sir, whatever your name is, I don't have time for secret meetings with strangers. I appreciate the call, but I really must…"

"Don't blow me off. I know this is out of the norm, but it's important."

"What's important right now is running the office of a United States Senator. Everything else is of lesser importance. Now, if you don't mind, I'm going to get back to what I was doing prior to the tragic mistake I made in answering this telephone. Good day." With that, he hung up, gave Claudia orders in no uncertain terms that he was not be disturbed for the rest of the day, and put the mystery man out of his mind.

Eric pulled his cell phone out of his pocket and hit the speed dial.

"Dynex International. May I help you?" the sultry voice answered.

"Reginald, please," Eric said.

"I'm sorry, but he is unavailable. May I take a message?"

"Please tell Reginald that the candidate is active."

"One moment, please. I'll connect you." Hi-tech security, Eric thought, smiling. How can this guy seriously be a genius?

After a brief moment of silence, Eric was connected with Reginald May. He ran the private detective agency Eric used when he needed to get some dirt on an opposing political candidate. Reginald was an enormous black man with a shaved head and wire-rimmed glasses. He was a very nice guy once you were found to be trustworthy and allowed into his inner circle. He cast a large shadow and presented strangers with an ominous demeanor. How he blended into a crowd when tailing a subject or kept from being recognized on clandestine missions was incomprehensible. The only thing Eric cared about was that he was the best in the business. Eric wasn't sure how he went about obtaining his information, and in order to preserve any shred of plausible deniability, he certainly didn't want to know, but Reginald had never failed to produce information when he was asked.

The political process was a dirty one, yes. Eric figured that whatever he could do to improve the standing of his candidate, the higher the chances of getting him or her elected. It was just part of the game. No guilt, no feelings of shame. It was his job to do what it took for his client to stand behind the podium on election night and profusely thank his or her supporters and promise that the next two, four, or six years they were in office would be revolutionary. It was always the same speech. And it was always the same dirt: cheating on a spouse, not filing tax returns, taking payoffs from lobbyists or private companies, hiring illegal immigrants and somehow forgetting to inform Immigration and Naturalization. For ten years, Reginald had been paid very well for his thorough and discreet services. For a price he would do anything for Eric that was necessary. And no one was ever the wiser for it.

"Yes?"

"Is that how you always answer the phone?" Eric asked.

"Only when I know my best client is on the line," Reginald said. "What can I do for you, buddy?"

Eric was holding the tiny black device he'd found in Byrum's safe, examining it closely. "I've got something I need you to check out for me."

"What is it?"

"Not sure. I'm guessing it's some kind of flash drive. I'm going to courier it over to your office. How long before you can tell me what's on it?"

"That depends on where it came from."

"It came from the safe of the man I replaced."

Chief of Staff

"Interesting," Reginald said. "If it is a flash drive and does go to a computer, and if it came from the safe of the man you replaced, it's a good bet it's going to be encrypted. Probably with some kind of ultrasonic key sequence. Then again, it could have been set up with a Feedler adjunct…."

"Reginald, I don't care what you have to do to get into it. I want to know what it contains. The techno babble doesn't interest me. Can it be done?"

There were times when Reginald hated dealing with Eric, but he always paid over the list price for services rendered, and he always paid on time. "There's nothing we can't crack, Eric. I'll get it done. It might take a couple of weeks though. My guy at NSA is on vacation."

"Whatever. Call when you've got it cracked."

"Talk to you later."

They hung up and Eric looked at the safe. "What were you trying to hide, Byrum? What is it that you didn't want anyone to know about but yourself?" He stuffed the device into a confidential envelop and gave it to the courier standing in front of Claudia's desk.

"What was in the envelope?" Claudia asked as they watched the courier disappear.

"We'll know in a couple of weeks, won't we?" Eric said, and returned to his office, closing the door behind him.

Chapter *13*

CHRISTINE was reclining in the sitting room of her master bedroom. At her age, running roughshod over her staff was becoming more and more tiring. Especially when she was throwing a party, no detail went personally unchecked by her. Everyone on her forty-person staff was black. She hired blacks on purpose and wasn't afraid to tell you that. She'd had Mexicans and whites and even that 'Oriental girl', but over time black undoubtedly became her color of choice.

"Blacks work harder than anyone else – even the Mexicans," she told a girlfriend once. "And the darker they are, the harder you can push them."

"You ought to hire some Africans," her friend snorted.

"Hell no. Africans steal from you. Remember Virginia Beecham? She let her gardener go for stealing. He was from Liberia or some God forsaken place full of mongrels. No, ma'am, nothing but honest to goodness broke negroes work in my house. Pluck them out of the ghetto, pay them just enough so they think they're rich, and you've got them trapped. Golden handcuffs. They make too much to leave. They can't go anywhere else and make the kind of money you're throwing at them. It's pure economic genius."

The staff cursed Christine under their breath for the way she treated them and worked them like dogs, but she was right on one count. None of them could find a job making $50,000 with no skills and no formal education. She may have paid them well but that didn't keep them from hating her guts.

Tonight's party was truly unlike any other party Charlotte sees in a year. Bigger than New Year's or Bob Johnson's Bobcats Festival, each year since 1980, Dove's Nest has hosted a lavish fundraiser for breast cancer, called Jewel Box. It was a cause that Christine took up the year after the death of her daughter. It was also an excuse to see and to be seen.

If you were black, had the right background, could afford the $30,000 per couple cost of the tickets, and didn't happen to be on Christine's shit list, you could expect to receive your hand-crafted invitation no more than six weeks prior to the party. Chronicled in Ebony and JET Magazine, an invitation to Jewel Box meant in no uncertain terms that you had truly 'arrived'.

*****

SET decorators, grounds crews, caterers and various hired help scurried around the estate. Each one of them carried copies of the meticulous notes and planning Christine drew up following each successive Jewel Box. Every year, she was determined, would be more spectacular than the last. She personally saw to the minute details that would awe her guests and only help to expand the social legend that was Christine Belmont Squire. With three hours before the guests arrived, she retired to her bedroom to rest and recharge for the long night ahead.

Amid the flurry of activity and uniform-clad temps, no one paid any attention to him as he walked to the back gate. Waiting for him, his hand subtly extended was the head butler. Pressing ten crisply folded one hundred dollar bills into the large but surprisingly smooth hand, he was allowed to pass.

"You've only got 30 minutes," he was instructed. "Do you remember where you're going?"

Yes.

"She's resting in her room right now. But she could be up before we're ready, so be on your guard."

Will anyone question why I'm here?

Chief of Staff

"The people who will protect you know about your presence. But," he emphasized, "if anything goes off plan, I do not know that you exist."

Understood.

"Go."

And with that simple command, his mission had begun. Thirty minutes was all he had to scope out, grab and be off with whatever he could find. It had been more than twenty-five years since he'd been at Dove's Nest. He was confident that nothing had changed, though, because that was the way Christine liked it. A thousand dollars was a small price to pay for access to the mansion. He thought of his mission as yet another hunting expedition, the kind he had been on since a child; the kind of expedition he had hoped to share with his own son. But this time, he wasn't sitting in the woods with his bow waiting for a buck to walk beneath him. His prey was information – anything he could use to bring her down.

Reaching Christine's private study, he settled himself behind the massive oak desk lined with pictures of family and many, many familiar faces. Shaking his head, he retrieved the password secreted to him, and logged onto her computer.

And so it begins.

*****

FROM his window, Eric had seen the butler at the back gate talking to one of the workers, but paid no attention. He was attempting to run Senator Tanner's office from a cell phone, a futile effort at best. Intonation wasn't enough; he needed the exasperation on his face to show through the phone. The vote for the Immigration bill was coming up very soon, and he was trying to edit the text of the bill before it went to the printer.

When he turned 9 years old, he was officially expected to not only attend Jewel Box, but also to play the role of the
Chief of Staff

mournful son. A visual outpouring of grief, Christine contended, would do two things: first, it would make her friends dig deeper into their pockets, raising donations beyond the ticket price; second, those people who gave extra money to the cause would all but be promised an invitation to Jewel Box the following year. It was a win-win situation for everyone but Eric.

Only a year removed from losing his mother, Eric had come to terms with the empty place in his heart that she had once filled. Traipsing around Dove's Nest, coached to be somewhat teary-eyed and distant, the inaugural Jewel Box left a permanent, acrid taste in his mouth. Twenty-five years later, nothing had changed. His contempt for this pseudo-fundraiser hadn't abated a single bit. Were it not for several reasons, namely the fact that his grandmother's gala truly raised an enormous amount of money for breast cancer, he would have stayed as far away from this party as he possibly could. Every year he swore would be the last. Every year, he saw the joy on his grandmother's face and relented one more time.

"Forget it, Pam! Just forget it! I'll be back in the morning. I'll take care of it tomorrow." Eric hung up and tossed the phone on the bed. Had Pam worked for his consulting firm, he wouldn't have thought twice about firing her. But she was just interning. And what's worse, her father was a very healthy contributor to Senator Tanner's last re-election campaign.

Putting everything out of his mind, like the Immigration vote, not to mention a night full of glad-handing and talking to people who had no clue who his mother was or what beauty she represented, Eric jumped into the shower. Two and a half hours until he could start counting down to the end of this dreadful evening. The sooner the better.

Turning and walking into the bathroom, Eric never noticed the stranger that he glanced at earlier walk out the back gate and disappear into the woods.

Chapter *14*

ERIC'S room phone rang, startling him. As much as he tried to put it out of his mind, he couldn't help but think about the Immigration vote and the supporting text of the bill. This was his first and most important task as Senator Tanner's chief of staff and it had to go smoothly. Eric was concerned about it passing because it would be a feather in both of their caps. Nonetheless, the Immigration vote and all that it represented for the country and his boss was the number one priority on his To Do list. Eric sighed deeply as he let the phone continue to ring.

Every year, once the first guest was spotted by security coming up Dove's Nest's winding drive, Christine informed a butler to phone Eric. Ever the Queen of Staging, Christine wanted each guest, from the first to the last, to see his face as they entered. Their checks had all been cashed, and the Breast Cancer Foundation had already gotten the donations, but putting a face to a cause, especially a face with so much mournful practice, would only help to build on the already staggering amount of money raised.

Eric picked up the phone and politely informed the butler that he was on his way down. One last look in the mirror and he would be off. The hand-made Prada tuxedo fit his athletic frame very well. If there was anything tangible he took from his grandmother's influence, it was certainly that he was always extremely well dressed. From his close cut hair, clean shaven face, down to the double-stitched Ralph Lauren dress shoes, nothing was ever out of place or incongruous.

"Okay, big guy," he spoke out loud. "This is only a single night out of the year. You can do this. Simply think about mother and all the people who are going to benefit from whatever the money is used for." He adjusted his custom-made Jaeger-LeCoultre and the pink breast cancer lapel pin and he was off.

Chief of Staff

Standing at the top of the double staircase, Eric was warmly greeted by the first guest. "Eric, don't you look marvelous. Your mother would be so proud of you." Patricia Stinson was the one person Eric always looked forward to seeing at Jewel Box more than any of the guests. She was genuine and had taken to Eric when he was younger, secretly supporting his desire to distance himself from Christine and all that she represented. An IT mogul based in Charlotte was a rarity, but Patricia, whom Eric called Aunt Pat even though they weren't related, was a rarity in her own right. Bill Gates once called her the most powerful African American woman in the industry. You don't get much more credible an ovation than that.

She pulled him close when he reached the bottom of the steps and gave him a firm hug. Aunt Pat whispered in his ear. "You are a kind soul, Eric. What you're doing, contrived by your dear old grandmother or not, speaks volumes about your character. Don't ever forget where you've come from. But just as important, always know where it is you're going and how you're going to get there."

Eric kissed Aunt Pat on the cheek and smiled at her. "You are a lovely woman, Aunt Pat. Thank you so much for coming tonight."

"Every year I give that reptile of a woman a check for more than the price of admission simply to see the pained look on her face as my rich black butt walks through the door of her mansion. It's a thrill I reserve for myself every year." Eric laughed and handed her wrap to a waiting maid. "You know, honey, I'm thankful for two things tonight." Aunt Pat handed him the de rigueur pink pin for him to put on her dress. "I'm thankful that you had your mother as long as you did and that she was able to fill your head with anti-Christine messages." Eric looked at her as if he didn't want to say the wrong thing. "You know what I mean, child," Aunt Pat said and Eric smiled slyly. "The second thing I'm thankful for is that Charlotte and this country have 'browned up' to the point that a little old dark-skinned woman can rub elbows with the likes that are going to be here tonight. God is good. Don't you ever forget that."

"No, ma'am, I won't." Not particularly religious, and even further from a close relationship with God after his mother died, Eric faked it as much as he could. He was thankful, though, that things had 'browned up' like Aunt Pat said. Otherwise, she would never have been in his life.

For a long time, no matter how much money you had, no matter how successful you were or how important you became in society, skin color – or the hue, thereof – restricted the position in society you could achieve. Years ago, when her daughter Vickie, a very prominent D.C. pediatrician was young, the Stinsons were put up by a Charlotte family for membership in Jack & Jill. Aunt Pat's husband and daughter would have easily been accepted, but the entire family was turned down outright because Aunt Pat was simply too dark. When the money earned and the social status achieved by darker brethren began to match and sometimes outpace the lighter brethren, the grip on the reigns held firm by the old guard started to let go, albeit reluctantly.

· Aunt Pat was right. Over the decades everything from the Alphas to Jack & Jill started accepting families of all complexions. Christine wasn't thrilled at all. 'Darkies' was how she talked about them. 'Those Darkies are going to bring down the picture of what we've put together and fought for all our lives', Eric once overheard her tell a friend on the phone. What she didn't realize, and she may never fully comprehend, is that whether you're light or dark or somewhere in the middle, black is black is black.

A summer working at FedEx taught Eric that. Aunt Pat had gotten him a job as a Package Handler loading twenty-eight foot trucks full of gizmos and gadgets and everything in between. Eric had lied to Christine about where he was going, making sure to change out of his filthy work clothes before he returned to Dove's Nest each night. From 6:00 until 11:00, Eric was in school. Not regular school, but he received a cultural education like he never experienced

Chief of Staff

before. At FedEx it didn't matter what his parents did for a living. It didn't matter that he was rich and educated and well spoken. In fact, in most cases, he took great pains to hide that fact, falling languidly into speech patterns one would only hear in music videos and on street corners in areas of Charlotte to which he would never have traveled. The guys and girls with whom he worked, black and white, but mostly black spoke in code. Eric learned slang for everything under the sun and although he was reluctant at first, began to use the word nigga effusively. 'Nigga crazy' and 'this nigga off the chain' and 'what's up my nigga'. Christine would have had a heart attack at the people with whom he was working and mingling, but it changed Eric's life for the better.

Ever-pampered and out of touch with what Aunt Pat called the really real world, FedEx presented an opportunity for Eric to expand his horizons, to increase the relationship, the natural and inoffensive relationship he shared with every other black person on the planet. Sure Jack & Jill extolled the virtues of being a good black citizen, but none of those people with whom he interacted at meetings every Sunday at somebody's mansion or high-rise uptown condo could do for him what FedEx did.

Eric had said something disconcerting one day in a phone call to Aunt Pat. He didn't remember what he said but it spurred Aunt Pat into action. The next week she informed him that over the summer, instead of making the pilgrimage to Sag Harbor like so many of his Fisk classmates, he would be getting a job. "Hard labor makes a man appreciate what he's been given in life, Eric," she said to him. Strangely enough, he never resisted and even found himself compelled to follow her orders. Aunt Pat, and of course, Senator Tanner, were the only ones who knew what he was doing. They supported him and kept up the lie, for Christine surely wouldn't have approved of her young grandson shuffling boxes and getting sweaty and dirty in the name of self-improvement.

What he learned at FedEx, beyond the Ebonics and the oppressively hard work was that people are just people.

Chief of Staff

Whether you're trying to pay off credit card debt, make some money to get your rap career off the ground, pay child support, or just plain like having extra income no matter the suffering, the lessons were invaluable. Black is black is black.

For the next hour and a half, Eric would plant himself at the entryway to Dove's Nest greeting CEO's, politicians, trust fund babies, industry moguls, and more than a few older women who always got a little too huggy with him. Every shade was represented. He wondered how that made his grandmother feel, even though she greeted each of her guests with the same fluid smile and embrace. Millionaires all, Jewel Box was an entrapment of black success and privilege, an assortment of what is possible when the human spirit whether indulgent or not, decides to make something out of their situation to improve the lives of others. Eric thought about his grandfather. "Rest not young man, for those who follow lead those who are yet to come." Prophetic.

If only his grandmother had worked at FedEx. He looked at her and chuckled at the thought. She smiled at him, unsure of what was going through his mind and turned back to her guests.

"One night out of the year. I can do this. I can do this."

*****

AFTER an eternity of smiling and welcoming their guests to Jewel Box, Eric and his grandmother went their separate ways, each with different responsibilities for the night. Eric was to speak to guests and thank him or her personally for their donation and for attending the party. Christine's role every year was to scope out those people who only paid the $30,000 price of the tickets and coerce them into making a further donation. The line was the same: "For every dollar we raise in the fight against breast cancer, a cure is that much closer." True, every dollar raised would bring more funding for grants that would produce more research and would also fund things like drug-cost subsidies, lobbying

Chief of Staff

efforts, support groups, physical therapy, counseling and so on and so on.

Her ulterior motive, however, was two-fold. First, it was important to Christine that she retained the unofficial title, and the accompanying notoriety, of raising the most private-sector money for the cause every year. Secondly, it was an easy way to whittle down the guest list for next year. Of the thousand or so people on the list at any one time, maybe six hundred of them were sent an invitation. The more you give, the better your chances of finding yourself at Dove's Nest the next year. Eric had always found the manipulation of her 'friends' disgusting and incredulous, but he was even more amazed that they kept succumbing to the treatment just to attend a party.

"You look like you swallowed something unpleasant, young man." Eric turned and saw Governor Daniel Lewis had been speaking to him. Thin and shorter than Eric, Governor Lewis was in his late sixties and had an electric personality. Short on political skill but long on relating to the common man, it was his special ability to establish a relationship with absolutely anyone he met that put him into office. He was going to do great things for the state.

"I apologize, sir," Eric said, shaking his hand. "I was in another world. Please forgive me." He watched his grandmother canvass the guests and sighed. The grounds of Dove's Nest were open to the partygoers. A huge tent had been constructed next to the pool, an easy transition from the ballroom, where everyone chatted politely with one another, jealously commenting on the sumptuousness of their surroundings.

Eric heard the faint sound of a helicopter and wondered who in the world was coming to Jewel Box late. From the time Aunt Pat arrived until he and his grandmother parted ways, helicopters had been ferrying guests to the estate from the airport. Whether you arrived by private jet or first-class commercial airline, a convoy of helicopters had been dispatched to quickly and luxuriously transport you to

Christine's doorstep. There's fashionably late, Eric thought, and then there's just plain rude. The last helicopter touched down in the distance and whoever it was, along with a menagerie of aides and assistants in the requisite ball gowns and tuxes stepped onto the waiting trolley and headed up to the party.

"You haven't heard a thing I said, have you?" asked Governor Lewis.

Once again, Eric apologized. "I'm not sure what's happening to me," he said with a nervous chuckle. "I suppose I really am in another world."

"I can relate to that." The Governor stood next to Eric and looked out over the sea of people. This is something I'm going to have to remember for a long time, he said to himself. As far as the eye could see, black millionaires and maybe a billionaire or two, were mingling with each other talking about any and everything. World politics, the International Monetary Fund, getting their golf handicaps into low single digits, the state of race in business and law, the classic Mustang they just bought and so forth.

A country boy from Spruce Pine, North Carolina, and newly elected as the first black Republican Governor of North Carolina, Daniel Lewis was out of his element. A modestly successful lawyer by trade, Governor Lewis had never experienced wealth – especially black wealth – on this scale. His campaign was actually the last job Eric and his company had before he took the assignment as Senator Tanner's chief of staff. It was an emergency campaign, of sorts, as the then-Governor Hanley was caught in a scheme ripping off the education lottery. The call went out for a special election, Lewis called Eric's people, and they threw together a winning campaign. Had it not been for Eric's insistence, Governor Lewis would not have made the guest list tonight or any night - and gratis at that.

"Look over there," he said to Eric, pointing to the tent. "That's KJ Vincent, CEO of Shared Success. And there, that's Susan L. Taylor. Over there, is that Kofi Annan? And

Chief of Staff

Robert Johnson and Michael Jordan. There's the president of Legacy Blue, what's his name. And Maya Angelou. Drake Gorman. Grayson Method, billionaire industrialist. Oh my God. I have only read about most of these people, but tonight I could skip a stone and hit ten of them at once they're so close to me."

"I know," Eric said, long past seeing the guests as anything but his equals and, as always, potential clients. Their position in life was not exciting to him. Their accomplishments, perhaps, but to Eric, they were all in the same boat. "And they're all here for my grandmother."

"They're all here for your mother and her memory, Eric," the Governor said, putting his hand on Eric's shoulder. "That's what's really important tonight. Honoring your mother and the fight against this insidious disease."

Eric looked at the Governor and smiled. He knew from the minute they first spoke in person that he would do whatever he could to get him elected. He still laughed at the memory of their first meeting at his office in Spruce Pine. While they were getting to know each other and strategizing about what they both wanted to see in a campaign, a huge black Standard Poodle strode through the doorway, walked up to Eric, gave him a good sniff and laid down behind the desk. That's Buck, he was told casually, like it was a normal everyday occurrence for a sixty-two pound Poodle to walk up to you in a lawyer's office, sniff you like a treat, and take up its regular napping spot behind the desk of the man who wants to be the next governor of your state. He campaigned with that dog – well trained but not a show dog by any stretch of the imagination. To this day, Buck roams the Governor's Mansion in Raleigh like he owns the place. Christine and conventional wisdom were the only reasons Buck wasn't by his side tonight.

"Let me introduce you to a couple of people, Governor."

"I'd appreciate that. But, listen, before I start smiling and pretending not to be star struck, I wanted to thank you again for running my campaign."

"You're the guy the voters wanted as their governor. I was only a small part of the process."

"Gracious to a fault, aren't you?" the Governor asked. "You should really think about getting into politics. I think you'd be great."

"Well, it's interesting you should mention that because Senator Tanner and I have been toying with the idea of my taking his seat when his term ends. I don't know how possible that will be, but it's something we're positioning ourselves for. I'd have to call in some big favors if I decided to run with the idea."

"Whatever you need," Governor Lewis said, giving Eric a firm handshake. "You can count on me one hundred per cent. You got me elected and I'll do whatever I can to do help."

Eric thanked the Governor and they started off to begin the introductions when the crowd burst into applause. Christine stopped the band and, taking the microphone, announced 'the tardy but appreciated arrival' of Julia Brown, Charlotte resident – and first lady of the United States.

"This party just keeps getting weirder and weirder," said Governor Lewis.

"You have no idea, sir. You have no idea."

Chapter *15*

IMMEDIATELY after he'd thanked the last guest for attending this year's Jewel Box, Eric hopped onto his grandmother's jet and made a B-line back to Washington. The Immigration vote was the next day and he still had a mountain of items to clear from his To Do list before he felt comfortable with their chances. He had cornered three senators at the party that night and worked some magic. Although they didn't necessarily agree on the spot to support Senator Tanner, he was able to pull positive responses from them all. He told himself they were on board and moved on to the next challenge.

The language of the bill was largely in-tact, but on the flight back he took the time to adjust some of the subtle nuances that tended to make senators break out in a sweat, contemplating the after-effects that a vote of this magnitude would have on their re-elections. Petty, yes, but since it was critical that everyone had at least a tiny bit of 'feel good' before they permanently put their name on the voting record, Eric was willing to cater to them as much as he possibly could. A victory like this for Senator Tanner would be phenomenal. And to have his name associated with the victory as the person who not only constructed the language of the bill but orchestrated its run to the floor of the senate, would serve to pad his own campaign should the day ever come.

He had gone directly to his office in the Hart building when the plane landed. As Eric bounded up the steps, a man unfamiliar to him deliberately blocked his path, stopping Eric in his tracks, and standing very close - about a foot away. Eric tried to weave around him, but the mystery man moved with him, mirroring his movements left and right. He was a well-built white guy, probably about thirty or thirty-five, brown eyes. He stared at Eric not saying a word. His hands were stuck deep into the pockets of his shabby gray sweatshirt and his brown hair, oily and unwashed, blew slightly in the

Chief of Staff

late night breeze. It was the same guy who waltzed past Eric's car that first, crazy morning in the parking garage. When he saw Eric's face change at having made that connection, he broke his gaze, and tried to run off, but Eric reached out and grabbed a hold of the hood of his sweatshirt.

"Who the hell are you?" Eric yelled, and pulled the stalker forcefully back toward himself. "What do you want with me?"

Without panicking, he swiftly punched Eric in the ribs and shook free of his grasp when he saw a Capitol Hill Police Officer making his way toward them. Eric dropped his briefcase and stood there, doubled over in pain from the punch. He looked up and watched whoever that guy was as he faded into the distance. "What the hell is going on?" he asked, through tender and pain-shortened breaths. He waived off the officer and made his way up the rest of the steps and on into the building, turning every now and then to see if his stalker had changed his mind and turned back to get him. Their encounter only lasted seconds, but it seemed to drag out from Eric's point of view. "I should have stayed in Charlotte."

*****

WHEN his door burst open at 7 a.m. the next morning he realized he had fallen asleep at his desk.

"Well, isn't this a nice surprise," Claudia cooed. "Very go-getteresque," she quipped.

Eric rubbed his eyes and looked at the clock on his desk. "Shit. Is that right?" Panicked, he rushed to his office armoire to change his wrinkled shirt. Claudia stood by as he ripped off one shirt and quickly buttoned its replacement. "I fly back here last night to get ahead on this vote and I end up passing out at my desk. Dammit! Where are we on Myers, Crane and Austin?" Eric asked, neither realizing that he'd exposed his shirtless chest to Claudia, nor that she was a little bit overcome at the sight of his muscled body. "Claudia? Where are we on…"

"I heard you the first time," she said, putting her tongue back in her mouth. "We still don't have confirmation on which way they'll vote this afternoon."

"Why not?"

"Because no one knows how they're going to vote."

Eric snapped at Claudia for the first time since he got the job. "I don't fucking have time for jokes, Claudia. Get Pam and Clarence on Senators Myers and Austin, find out what we have to do to incent them to vote with Senator Tanner. Then I want you to call Rena Steele and arrange a meeting for me with Senator Crane's chief of staff. I am going to need to know their positions before we get to the floor today. Do you think you can do that?"

Claudia had shifted from her dreamy schoolgirl gaze to a hateful glare. "Excuse me?"

Eric closed his eyes and for a moment thought about pulling rank and blasting her. "I apologize, Claudia." Eric walked back to his desk and slumped into his chair. "I'm so exhausted I can't explain. It was wrong of me to yell at you. My apologies."

"Chocolate."

"Chocolate what?"

"I don't care, just make it dark and expensive." Claudia smiled. "Apology accepted, but don't think I've forgotten about your little friend."

"Agreed," Eric said, smiling back. What a piece of work she was. You'd never know she was a practical joker or that she actually had a sense of humor, but at times like this when the stress level tended to overwhelm, Eric could always count on her to bring him back to Earth.

"And how was the party?"

"It sucked," Eric said quickly, flipping the pages of the bill forward, searching for the last place he remembered editing. "Same old, same old."

Chief of Staff

"Good thing I didn't cancel my JET Magazine subscription, isn't it?" Claudia joked. She knew that got to Eric and she needled him with it every chance she got.

"Poof. Be gone, Evil Mistress," Eric said with a wave of his hand. "Keep me updated on Pam and Clarence and make sure you set that meeting up right away." He checked his watch and looked back at Claudia. "We don't have much time."

"Perhaps you'd like a back rub before we get started. Some sparkling water, maybe?"

"Claudia," Eric started, wary of her reaction. "If ever there was a time I didn't have time for your jokes or your funny comments, it's right now."

"Gotcha, COS," Claudia said, feeling Eric's stress and understanding he needed to be left alone. "I'll keep you updated. And COS?"

"What?"

"Brush your teeth. Your breath is kickin'." She winked and closed the door behind her when she left.

*****

THE meeting with Crane's chief of staff went much better than Eric had anticipated. A wording change here and there and Crane was on board. There still hadn't been any word on Myers or Austin. Eric ran the numbers in his head and figured that even without either of their votes, the bill stood a good chance. Ever the consummate worry wart, though, Eric took it upon himself to reach out to the senators directly. It was a little bit after lunchtime and he hoped one or both of them would be in. As he picked up the phone, Claudia came over the intercom.

"Uh, sir? There's someone here to see you."

Sir? When the hell had she ever called him sir? This had to be a joke, Eric figured, and ignored her. He clicked off the intercom and attempted to dial again. Interrupted once more by Claudia, Eric had had enough.

"Claudia, I swear to God that if you don't quit it I'm going to put you on a bus to Alaska and leave you there to be eaten by a polar bear or Sarah Palin. I'm trying to make a call. Please leave me the hell alone."

"Well, I wish I could do that, sir, but it seems that the president is here to see you."

"The president of what?" Eric asked sarcastically. "Your ass? Or your fat, hard head?"

"Uh, sir, it's the President of the United States."

Eric got up from his desk and nearly sprinted to his door, ripping it open. "Goddamit, Claudia, this is the last time I'm going to tell you that I don't have time for your shit today." He stopped his tirade abruptly when he saw two men standing in front of her desk, ear buds firmly ensconced and spiral chords descending into their suit coats.

"Told you," Claudia said, staring at the Secret Service agents. She had stood and was pressing out imaginary wrinkles in her dress. She had never met the president and she didn't want to look frumpy this being the first, and presumably, only chance she'd get. "Are you free or would you like me to sit my ass and my fat, hard head back down in my chair and turn away the leader of the free world?"

Eric was about to say, "Send him in, of course," when he heard that voice coming around the corner. This was not the day for a random visit, but what could he do? The president comes a callin' and you are obliged to answer.

"Eric Julian," President Brown called out and firmly shook his hand. "How the hell are you?"

This was Washington, DC, 'Land of the Weird', but even Eric couldn't believe what was happening to him.

"I'm fine, sir. I'm fine. It's a little unexpected of you to drop by today." Everyone in the office was standing at attention, a couple of people speaking very quietly into cell phones telling whoever was on the other line that the president just showed up. No, I said the president. Yes! Of the freakin' United States of America!

"Please, come into my office and we can wait for Senator Tanner to get back. He's due any moment now."

"I'm not here to see him. I was in the building for a briefing and I wanted to pop by. I came by to see how you're doing in your new job." Since both Eric and President Brown were from Charlotte, they actually had a quite familiar relationship. Eric and the president's children were in the same Jack & Jill group and they summered a block apart in Sag Harbor for many years. A billionaire real estate and construction magnate before his incredible election as a political unknown, and the second black man to hold the office, President Brown and Eric had a comfortable demeanor with one another. Respectful, of course, of the position of a family friend, Eric nonetheless was able to drop his guard just a bit.

Eric waited for President Brown to sit down before following suit. The Secret Service agents had positioned themselves right outside Eric's office door. They had to keep the president on a schedule and hoped this wouldn't take long.

"So tell me how it's going, Eric."

"It's not going so well right now. I'm in the middle of putting the final touches on the Immigration bill for Senator Tanner."

"Have you got the votes you need?"

"Not yet."

"Who's left?" The president sat forward on the sofa, causing Eric to reflexively do the same.

"Austin comes to mind. I was actually about to give him a call."

"When some jerk dropped into your office, right?" The president smiled but Eric didn't know what to do. The last time he had seen him he was just Paul Brown. Now he was the president. "Relax. Remember the time about ten years ago when you were trying to teach my son Greg how to windsurf?"

Eric couldn't believe this was happening. He had work to do and the president wants to sit and reminisce about his recently deceased son. "Yes, sir. I remember. He ran my board aground and destroyed it."

"Give me the phone."

"Excuse me, sir?"

"Give me the phone. I'm going to pay you back for that." Eric sat there not really knowing what was going to happen. "Do you have Austin's number?"

"Uh, yes. Why?" Eric handed President Brown the phone and number.

"Shhh," the president said, dialing and waiting for someone to pick up. "Hello, Nancy is it? Lovely. This is Paul Brown. I need to speak with Senator Austin, please." President Brown winked at Eric who was standing there like a deer caught in the most unusual and surreal headlights he'd ever seen. "Hello, Graham," the president started. "Listen I'm going to need to call in a favor. I understand that you might be holding out on Senator Tanner and this Immigration deal. Is that correct?"

Eric had begun to pace his office, listening to the conversation. He was wringing his hands and, he thought, beginning to sweat just a little.

"I see," the president said. "Well that's unfortunate." He looked over at Eric and shook his head, no. "Wonderful. I understand. Of course. I'll have to make a note of that. Just call Julia and I'm sure she'll take care of that for you. And you're sure about the vote?" Eric spun around and looked at President Brown. "Again, I understand. Sorry to bother you." The president hung up the phone and walked to the door.

Eric stood there with baited breath, waiting for a response. "And?"

"And what?"

"And what did Austin say? It sounded like I might have some damage control to do, like he's not on board." Eric unconsciously started the process of ass kissing in his head, trying to think of a way to dispel the damage the president had just caused.

"You're golden. He's on board." President Brown smiled and patted Eric on the shoulder. "God I love doing that. The vote's in less than three hours. Enjoy the rest of your day." And with that, the president was gone, surrounded by a phalanx of Secret Service agents, leaving Eric standing by himself in his office, left to process the possibility of his first senate victory.

*****

Three hours, thirty minutes later, Eric stood in the balcony of the Senate chamber and cried with joy.

Yeah – 68; Neah – 30; Abstentions – 2.

Chapter *16*

HE trembled just slightly as he dialed the number. The butler at Dove's Nest answered and immediately connected the call to Christine's study. The caller would not tell me his name, the butler would say. Reluctantly, Christine put down her pen and crossword and answered. "Hello? Christine Squire. To whom am I speaking?"

"Good morning, dear. And how was last night? I'm sure you looked just ravishing. Of course, I'm waiting for my next issue of JET to arrive so I can examine each and every photograph. I have wondered for years, though, why you've never invited me to Jewel Box. Pity, really."

"Who is this?" Christine asked.

"You don't remember my voice?" the caller asked, feigning disappointment. "Has it been that long since we've spoken?"

Christine paused, searching her memory. The voice on the other end was no more familiar than that of one of her servants. Featureless and devoid of any identifying characteristics, she wasn't sure to whom she was speaking. "I demand to know who this is."

"Why so testy? It's a beautiful day outside. You really should be more thankful for what you have, what with the flurry of expensive friends speaking your name so reverently this morning. Perhaps we should begin this conversation anew. Good morning, dear."

Again Christine asked, "Who is this?"

"I had forgotten that you aren't accustomed to pleasantries. Right down to business, as usual. I understand. I can play that game, as well."

"I demand to know who you are or this call will be over immediately."

Chief of Staff

"Hang up and you'll regret it. You weren't the best mother-in-law, but I know for a fact that you aren't stupid. You'll take my call and we both know it."

A chill ran down her spine. "Cole."

"Ah, that's nice. You *do* remember me. For a moment there, I thought we were going to have a problem."

"We don't have a problem because I have nothing to say to you. Good day."

"You have something I want. Hell, you owe it to me and I'm going to get it. No matter what I have to do." Cole left the line open, waiting for Christine to digest his threat.

Christine closed her eyes and said, "What exactly is it that you think I'm going to do for you, Cole?"

Cole sat back and looked at the ceiling of his tiny home office. He had been planning this conversation with his ex mother-in-law for a long time, but circumstances had moved the time frame forward considerably. His most recent source of income was gone and he needed money fast. It seemed like the years of anticipation had flown by, his script analyzed and well rehearsed. But he was amazed at how nervous he was; the trembling had not subsided at all. He wasn't entirely sure what he would do next. Quite honestly, he was surprised she hadn't hung up on him. His threat worked and now it was time to set his plan in motion. "You, my little honey pot, are going to pay me what I deserve for services rendered."

"Services rendered? What a romantic skewing of history, Cole."

"Don't be so hasty, Christine. You act like I've got my hand out."

"You and every other street beggar and lowlife criminal just like you. The only difference between you and them is that this little honey pot has already been more than generous where you are concerned." The butler entered the room and was instantly dismissed by Christine. Still

Chief of Staff

composed and in control of her emotions, she sat forward and sipped her coffee. "Let me guess. You've run through the money I gave you and you've come back for more, threatening me, no less."

"That's harsh, dear."

"Don't call me dear."

"You know, of all of my acquaintances, you'll be the one I will never forget."

"We are in no way acquaintances."

"Perhaps you're right. However, you are an evil woman with so much to hide. That much is true. If I close my eyes and lean back, I can imagine a closet in your magnificent mansion simply stuffed to the ceiling with skeletons. One false move and, crash - they all come tumbling down, cascading your hidden business and broadcasting your indiscretions to the world. I can't tell you how much I would hate to see that happen."

"You always were one for the dramatic."

"And I was always a lot more intelligent than you gave me credit for."

"Hardly," Christine scoffed. "You were in the right place at the right time, Cole. For no other reason than that, you never would have been brought into my world. My daughter is dead and, as far as I'm concerned, so are you." Her emotion was beginning to rise, her voice turning sinister and cold.

"Is that right?"

"Yes. And dead men don't come begging for money from old women."

"Dead men. Interesting." Cole fingered the edge of his desk. He had the upper hand this time and he knew it. "Listen, dear, it's been a long time since we've chatted and although I have always been a fan of your witty repartee, it's time we get down to business."

Chief of Staff

"Again, you insolent buffoon, we have no business together."

"Oh, but that is where you are sadly mistaken. I suppose your hearing is declining with your advanced age, but I distinctly remember telling you what you are going to do for me. And that I am going to get it no matter what."

Amused at his insistence, she decided to play along for the moment. Christine had never approved of Cole Julian, but like she said, he was in the right place at the right time. He served his purpose to the best of his ability. The death of her daughter, although emotionally debilitating for her, had given rise to the way she would rid herself and her family of him forever. Or so she thought. He'd dropped off the face of the planet, toting the million dollar bank check written out to him, and now he was back. Recalling the many incidents of anger and malice between them, she wondered how the hell she would be getting rid of him the second time around. Permanently.

"How much now, Cole?" Christine opened the side drawer of her desk and pulled out her silver cigarette case. She lit one and the smoke veil wafted in front of her, slowly and deliberately as always.

"Fifty million."

Christine laughed at the suggestion. "Fifty million? I knew you were an idiot and I knew you were a greedy son of a bitch. But I hadn't known you to be a complete moron."

"Fifty million." The mental script he had devised hadn't provided for her response. He hadn't intended to repeat himself. "Or...."

"Or what?" Christine stood and stamped out her cigarette. "Or what? You seem to have forgotten to whom you are speaking! I am Christine Belmont Squire! No one threatens me. And if they do, it is not long before they are extinguished in one form or another." She felt her blood pressure rising and sat down again. "It will be an extremely cold day in hell before you receive even one more red cent from me. No matter what," she said, mocking Cole.

"Fifty million."

"Confidence is becoming on most people, Cole. But not on you."

"Confidence, dear, is knowing that you are going to pay me what I want. Confidence is knowing that there is no way you won't give me that money." Cole looked at the tiny black device on his desk and smiled. His ace in the hole. "Confidence is knowing that if I don't get what I want, I will ruin you in front of all of your supposed friends and business partners. The self-inflated myth of Christine Belmont Squire will fall to the ground, shattered like the brittle hip of a spiteful and mean-spirited old woman who has no one left to love her. Confidence," Cole continued, more resolute than ever, "is knowing that if I don't get what I want, my son will see his apparently long-dead father for the first time in over twenty years. And you'll be left to explain why you betrayed him."

"You wouldn't do that. Don't drag him into this. He has no part of this, Cole."

Part one of his plan was already in motion: Getting to Eric. His first attempt may not have been successful, but he was determined to try again. Cole knew that if he actually did get a chance to speak to him, there was a very low probability that neither Christine nor Eric would mention to the other seeing or talking to him, each trying to figure out their next steps on their own. Cole laughed deliberately into the phone as loudly and as rudely as he could. "Christine, my dear, confidence is also knowing your most delicate secrets, particularly those that you have taken fruitless steps to hide over the last thirty-five years."

Her heart skipped a beat momentarily, silence enveloping her. "And what secrets might they be?" she asked cautiously.

"The family secrets, of course," Cole responded. He picked up the black device and held it in his hand. "For instance, I know where all of your money came from."

Christine felt her face flush.

"I know where it continues to come from." He stifled a laugh. "Fifty million. You don't have to do anything right now, of course. Over the next little bit, I just want the satisfaction of knowing I've gotten under your wrinkled skin. If you follow directions half as well as you bark them out, we won't have a problem. But at the least little hitch, with the tiniest bit of drama you instigate, I'll crush you mercilessly. Have a pleasant and glorious day. I'll be in touch." And he hung up.

That went even better than he had imagined. A little improvising here and there was of little consequence to him. She got the point. Dead men don't come begging. Cole chuckled at that and locked the little black device back in its hiding place.

Chief of Staff

Chapter *17*

WHEN Eric got back to his office after the vote, he found Senator Tanner standing on top of a staffer's desk, having begun whipping the crowd into a frenzy. When he saw Eric coming through the doors, he spontaneously led everyone in a round of Hip, Hip Hooray! Eric didn't think people actually did that anymore and was taken aback.

Everyone was holding plastic champagne flutes and they were instructed to salute their fearless chief of staff. "Here's the man who, on his first time out, was victorious in conquering Capitol Hill!" Everyone cheered. "I stand here before you and I can't help but recall an interesting conversation between Eric Julian and a certain senator from California who got his hat handed to him and still voted for our bill!" Again, the staffers erupted, some not waiting for the long-winded senator to finish the toast, taking long pulls of their champagne. "It's that kind of spirit and undeniable insanity that tells me not only is Eric going to do great things in the interest of our country, but that he will continue to represent the State of North Carolina well after I'm gone. Here's to you, Eric. Thanks and keep up the magnificent work!"

Eric blushed slightly but acknowledged the cheers of the crowd. Once his mortal enemies, the staffers were coming around and were quickly warming up to him. It was a moment he wanted to treasure. He opened his mouth to thank everyone for their hard work and their tremendous effort getting the bill passed, but before he knew it, Senator Tanner was speaking again.

"And to celebrate our accomplishment, I am inviting everyone and your families to a party on Trinity tonight!"

Another eruption from the crowd. They had all seen pictures of Senator Tanner's yacht and some of them had been aboard, but they had never been invited to a party on the yacht. They all immediately dispersed, ringing wives and

Chief of Staff

husbands, boyfriends and girlfriends, and some frantically dialed babysitters, not wanting to miss the party for anything.

Eric helped the senator down from the desk and walked him into his office. "Nice campaign speech, Senator," he said smiling.

"It's never too early to start campaigning. You should know that." Senator Tanner winked at Eric. "Go home. I know you're tired. Get some rest and be at Trinity at eight o'clock sharp. We've got some serious celebrating to do!"

*****

WHEN Eric arrived at the marina where Trinity was docked, he could see that the party was already raging. There were people everywhere and they were all dancing and drinking and carrying on. Eric had never seen his staff like this before. He wasn't included in their after work social hour, and that was just fine. The last thing he needed was to befriend his employees and get caught in a mess between the love struck, the forlorn, or the just plain lazy. Tonight was different somehow, and Eric planned to take advantage of the freedom, but only to a point.

"Glad you could make it, COS," Claudia said, as she walked up to Eric, beer in hand. Eric remembered how Christine told him to never trust a woman who drinks beer from the can or drives a Jeep. "What's so funny?" she asked.

"Nothing," Eric said, quickly wiping the smirk from his face.

"The Senator's already feeling the alcohol, if you know what I mean. Keep your eye on him. You never know who's lurking around with a camera." Someone Eric didn't recognize screamed for Claudia, she thrust the beer into his hand and disappeared.

Senator Tanner's decree that this would be an informal party and that his guests should feel free to show up in shorts and t-shirts oddly juxtaposed their surroundings. As always, Eric was fashion forward and had taken great pains to pick

Chief of Staff

just the right outfit for a party on a yacht to celebrate the passing of an Immigration bill.

Eric wandered around the yacht in search of his boss, trying to estimate if Claudia was correct about his inebriation or if she was testing him again. He walked into the galley and found Senator Tanner sitting by himself at the table, pouring a rather healthy shot of Tequila. "I see you didn't get the memo on the dress code tonight."

"What I'm wearing is entirely appropriate, sir," Eric said, somewhat annoyed.

"Everybody else is flitting around in shorts and golf shirts and these fantastic short skirts. And you, our resident Clothes Horse, are wearing a blazer and slacks." He shook his head and smiled. "Put that beer in the trash and take some shots with this old man." He was gesturing quickly with his hand, begging Eric to sit with him.

"Do you remember Antigua?" Eric asked.

"A small island off the coast of somewhere," Senator Tanner recounted, clearly not interested in either a geography or a history lesson.

"Yes. And do you remember what happened on that small island off the coast of somewhere when you took me there for my twenty-first birthday?"

Senator Tanner shook his head, no, and continued pouring Eric's shot.

"You got so trashed on Tequila," Eric said, taking the bottle from his hand, "that you ate an entire lime, peel and all, to prove to one of the local idiots that you could do it."

"Ate that whole fucking thing, didn't I!" he shouted, suddenly in total recall and very proud of the challenge.

"Yes. And then you threw up all over me."

"Sorry about that. It won't happen tonight, though."

"Well, I'd say we're in for another wild night. You're clearly shitty already."

Chief of Staff

"That's clearly true," he said mocking Eric, and retrieving the bottle. "But I don't have any limes tonight, young boy. It's just me and Jose Cuervo - Tradicional. And now you. Damn the salt. Damn the lime. We're gonna shoot this bottle until it's gone. And then we'll look for some more." He poured the shot down and scrunched his face up as the alcohol burned his throat.

A large bruise ran the length of Senator Tanner' right arm. Eric hadn't seen it until now because the senator always wore his sleeves rolled all the way down. "Good God, how did you get that bruise?" Eric reached over to touch the senator's arm, but it was quickly withdrawn.

"I don't know," Senator Tanner said. "I must have bumped into something. It's no big deal. Doesn't even hurt anymore."

"I should say not since you've been drunk for four hours." The senator ignored Eric and stared at him, waiting for the shot to disappear.

"It's going to be a long night, isn't it, sir?" Eric asked, tossing his beer into the trash and reluctantly taking the shot Senator Tanner had poured for him.

"I've waited a long time for this night, Eric, and I'm going to do my best to make the most of it. I'm proud of you and what you've accomplished. I love you a lot and I hope you know that."

Eric was pouring himself another shot and trying to search Senator Tanner's face for signs of sincerity or outright drunkenness. It wasn't rare that the senator told him he loved him, in birthday cards or at odd times when they had had a deep discussion. But it was always in context. The senator wasn't one to simply blurt out 'I love you' and not mean it. "I love you, too, Senator." He downed the shot and his drinking buddy perked up again.

"That's my boy. You've got some catching up to do!" He grabbed the bottle and the shot glass and immediately poured another for Eric.

Chief of Staff

"Good Lord! How long have you been drinking? You're going to drown me!" Eric laughed. He had always been comfortable drinking with Senator Tanner and their senses of humor made nights out on the town memorable – at least while they were in the moment.

"I believe I started drinking about four o'clock today."

"The vote wasn't official until six thirty. It's eight forty-five right now."

"Which means you're late because," he said as he cleared his throat, "I distinctly remember telling you to be here at eight o'clock."

Eric ignored him and picked up where he'd left off. "That means you started celebrating before the vote was final?"

"So maybe I'm a prophet."

"Maybe you're just a fucking drunk," Eric quipped, downing his third shot.

"Maybe you're just a fucking…." The senator stopped and looked at the ceiling, like it was going to magically give him something witty to say.

"Told you."

"It's Friday night. We're partying on my yacht because you got us a win on the Immigration bill. I'm getting sloshed with or without you. Shut. Up. And. Drink."

Chapter *18*

AFTER making several rounds throughout the night to make sure the staff and their families were having a good time at the party, and to thank them for their respective involvement in the victory, Eric and Senator Tanner retreated to the upper lounge. The excitement was winding down and many of the guests had already begun to depart, graciously thanking their hosts for the fete. Those who remained were either too drunk to drive or simply didn't want to leave the opulence of the yacht. Senator Tanner told everyone they could stay as long as they wanted.

Reclining in the lounge with a nearly empty bottle of Tequila, Eric's phone rang. Seeing it was his grandmother's number on the caller id, he excused himself to speak with her. When he returned, Senator Tanner saw the look on his face and wondered what that crazy old woman had done this time.

"Give me a cigarette," Eric told the senator.

"That bad, huh? You don't smoke unless she's done something really bad." He handed Eric a smoke and his lighter. "What did she say to get you this upset?"

"You know, I swear to God that even though I love her more than anything in this world, she infuriates me sometimes." He poured another shot and chased it with the cigarette. "You'll never guess what she said to me."

"I was kind of waiting on that part," Senator Tanner joked.

"I told her that the vote was a success, that all of our hard work had paid off, and that I'd gotten my first victory." Eric took a deep drag and coughed as he exhaled. "She said, 'oh, that's nice.' That's nice? That's nice? That's all I get?"

"Did you say that to her?" asked Senator Tanner.

"No. I didn't have a chance to say anything after that. She started ranting on and on about someone from her past,

Chief of Staff

somebody called her or something and she wanted me to come back to Charlotte tonight."

"That's strange."

"That's irritating," Eric fumed. "She's all about helping herself. Never once has she done anything for anyone else."

"What about Jewel Box?" Senator Tanner asked, hoping his defense of Eric's grandmother wouldn't further infuriate him.

"Give me a goddam break, Senator. That party has no more to do with my mother than the man in the moon! Every year, she throws a party under the guise of raising money for breast cancer so she can say that she helped the cause. She keeps her so called friends on a short leash making them give buckets of money and fly to Charlotte just so they can get their names and pictures in magazines. They are fools. They don't realize that she's using them to further her fucked up social agenda, whatever that might be. Oooh, the CEO of this company and that company are on her guest list. Oooh, the president of this historically black college made the list this year, but won't next year because he didn't give enough money. Oooh, the fucking First Lady shows up and she has a cow. It's all about look at me, look at me. I can't think of anything that woman has done that doesn't have something to do with self-promotion." Eric motioned for another cigarette and, like a chain smoker, lit the new one with the butt of the old one.

Senator Tanner measured his response carefully. He knew the passion Eric carried for his grandmother, both negative and positive, and he didn't want to say the wrong thing. For years he had listened to Eric blow up after a particularly bad conversation or visit with Christine, but he could only go so far in comforting him. He felt it wasn't his place to intervene and that the best thing he could do was simply give some sage advice. Tonight was somehow different. They had bonded in a way that was unprecedented and the time felt right for Senator Tanner to let Eric in on

Chief of Staff

something he'd been keeping locked deep inside for the entirety of his adult life.

"Eric, there's something you need to know. Actually, there are a lot of things you need to you know, but I'm going to tell you something about me and about your grandmother that you may find hard to believe."

Eric was shaking the last tiny drop of Tequila from the bottle onto his tongue. "I don't know that there's anything you could tell me about that woman that would surprise me, Senator."

"There are two things, Eric, that have haunted me in life. And will follow me in death." He stood and walked to the bar, finding what was probably one of the last bottles of Tequila on the yacht. He filled both of their glasses and sat down on the sofa across from Eric.

Eric saw the senator's pained look and thought about saying something to comfort him.

"Just sit there. Please," Senator Tanner quietly spoke when he saw Eric's pitiful expression. "What I am about to tell you will change the way you think of me for the rest of your life. If it doesn't, well, I'll be more scared for your soul than I am for my own."

"Senator...Scott," Eric relented. "What does this have to do with my grandmother?"

"I got caught in a jam a long time ago. My father and your grandparents knew each other. How they met exactly, I'm not sure, but they were more than casual acquaintances, I know that. Had it not been for your grandparents, especially Christine, I don't think I'd be here today." Sitting back on the sofa, his arms stretched out over its expanse, taking in the mementos and pictures decorating the lounge, each more important to him than the next, he let out a deep moaning sigh. "I am not what I appear to be, Eric."

"And what are you?"

"A killer. A murderer, actually, if you want to put it that way. I've never been comfortable with the word, but it is what it is, I suppose."

Eric's blood ran cold and he played back Senator Tanner's words in his head, certain he had heard him correctly, but hoping against all odds that he had not.

"It was thirty-five years ago, summer time. It was as hot and nasty that year as it had been in any year previous. When people say the heat makes you do things you'd never imagine, they're right. Sweat didn't roll off of your body, it poured. Nothing short of planting yourself in front of the air conditioning unit could save you - or your clothes - from a day of misery." Senator Tanner caught himself smiling at the memory and quickly wiped it away.

"It was only June, you know? God knows what was waiting for us in July and August. Anyway, I was sitting alone in the front seat of my car, lost in the sweet sounds of country music on the radio. I remember telling my friends that that was the music of the gods. They were caught up in this whole rock and roll fad, twisting themselves into frenzies and losing their hearing all for some over-sexed, screaming, guitar-abusing rock star. They didn't know real music anymore. I was raised on the winged voices of Loretta Lynn, Hank Williams, Patsy Cline, the almighty Johnny Cash, and country singers you've most likely never even heard of. I remember my friends all but lost their minds the first time they heard Elvis on the radio." Another chuckle, another uncomfortable silence. "Lord, it was 1974 and I'd have bet dollars to donuts that rock and roll would disappear into radio history and no one would be the wiser."

"That answers a lot of my questions," Eric teased.

As though he didn't even hear him, Senator Tanner continued his story.

*****

IT was 11:30 at night, and even though the sun had gone down, it was still unbearably warm. His friends were inside Jessup's buying beer. He had stayed in the car and waited. Five minutes turned into ten; ten into twenty. He rolled down all four windows in the two-door Impala to help the breeze stream through and cool him off. Every so often, he would slide back and forth to free his dampened clothes from the vinyl prison of his seats. Mumbling under his breath as he used the steering wheel to lean forward just slightly, the newly-found breeze danced across his back, cooling him off just slightly, if only for a second. With God's own music on the radio, the Carolina breeze drifting in and out of the windows, he was totally relaxed. He had put in some long hours at his father's demolition company all week and he was ready to drink some beers and relax.

He could have been out for thirty seconds, or ten minutes, but the one thing he knew was that the screaming was getting louder. And in a hurry. He shook his head and rubbed his eyes to wake himself up, but the only thing that changed was the volume.

"Goddamit, Tanner!" Where was that coming from? He spun around but didn't see anyone. He was looking out the driver's side window when the passenger door exploded open.

"Start this goddamn car, Tanner!" he was being commanded. "Come on, just start the car and get us the hell out of here." Everyone was out of breath. Their clothes were torn and Jimmy Wiggins had lost one of his shoes. What the hell was going on?

"Drive! Drive! Drive! Get us out of here and right now!" His friends dove into the car, slamming the door behind them. He cranked up his car, stomped on the gas and flung dirt, gravel and rocks as he sped away. Tanner's heart was pounding and his mouth had quickly developed the dry and very unpleasant taste of fear. His mind jumped every direction it could, the words not quite getting the chance to make it out of his mouth before he thought of something else to say. He was more than panicked. He was downright frightened.

Chief of Staff

Shooting down a back country road, not daring to slow down or ask his friends what was behind them, what they were running from, Tanner bit his tongue and gripped the wheel. Every now and then, he would peak at the three young men in his car, all of them out of breath and swallowing hard in disbelief, themselves seemingly unable to understand what had happened.

"We had stopped off at the store for some beer, you know, just four buddies out to have a good time on a Friday night. Like I said, it was hot and the heat I've come to find out can make you do some things you'd never even considered." Senator Tanner looked at Eric who was staring back and him. He wasn't sure why he was telling this story, but it was too late to stop. He'd gone too far as it was.

"Reid and the guys came out of the store with the beer and were saying something about this group of black kids they had gotten into some kind of argument with. Now, Reid wasn't the most politically correct person and I can't repeat what he said to me, but suffice it to say, it wasn't pretty. Anyway, the guys piled into the car and we drove off." Senator Tanner stood to stretch his legs and dump the full ashtray. "They got completely loaded on beer and some speed Reid stole from his older brother."

"What about you?" Eric asked. "Were you loaded, too?"

"God no. I was more concerned with dinging my car. I may have had more to drink than I should, but I never took any drugs. I wasn't drunk by any stretch of the imagination." Senator Tanner sat back down on the sofa and put his feet on the coffee table. "One thing led to another and the three of them were stinking drunk – and fast! Maybe it was the speed, I don't know, but they changed that night. One of them started talking to Reid about how they should go get that nigger that mouthed off to them in the store. 'Beat him up for talking back'. Before I knew it I was driving back to town. There was a guy walking down the street and Reid yelled out, 'There he is. Let's get his ass!'

Chief of Staff

"They dragged him right off the street, punched him in the mouth and stuffed him into the back seat. This man was scared to death. But I drove. I did what Reid told me to do. I don't know why."

Eric closed his eyes and hoped to God that this was a dream. This was simply not happening. Eric sat with his mouth hung open, listening to this exciting and unbelievable story coming from his mentor and father figure. He didn't know what to do other than sit there and take it all in. He had no idea what was coming next, but for whatever reason he wanted to get up and run. He wanted to vomit from the shock to his brain and his system. He wanted to reach out and choke the shit out of Senator Tanner. But he did none of that. Silently and patiently, he waited until the story was finished. And he processed every word.

"We drove him out to Barker Pond. They pulled him out of the car when we got there and dragged him, kicking and screaming to the water's edge. It was pitch black. You couldn't see a thing. There wasn't anybody around except for the deer and the fish. One by one we took turns. Punching and kicking and throwing rocks at this young, innocent man. Reid had tied his hands with some blast cord he grabbed from my trunk. We beat him until we were tired. And then it happened."

"What?"

Senator Tanner looked at the ceiling and closed his eyes. "He looked at me. Or maybe it was more like he looked into me, or through me, as dumb as that sounds, pleading with me to save him, to stop the beating and the torture. I can't tell you what happened. I don't know how to explain it. But I stopped. I stopped whatever it was I was doing. It was like God, Himself, had come to me through him and told me that what I was doing was wrong. I can't explain it. All I know is I left them. I left them and went back to my car. And when I left him, he was alive."

"They killed him?"

"I don't know. They had to have, I guess. He was alive when I left them. But I honestly don't know for sure. I was in my car, listening to the radio and trying not to pass out from the beer and the heat and the situation when they came running back. Just the three of them. Reid was yelling at me to drive off and I did. Three days later, the body of a young black man washed up on the shore of Barker Pond."

Eric was crushed. The man he thought he knew everything about just confessed to brutally beating and probably killing an innocent person. He had put Senator Tanner on a pedestal his entire life and now this? How was he supposed to react to this? Imagine you've just been told that the man you admire most in the world killed somebody. What the hell do you do?

"I shouldn't have told you, that. I apologize," Senator Tanner said.

"What? You shouldn't have told me that? It's a little late to say that, don't you think?"

Senator Tanner couldn't even look at Eric, he was so ashamed.

"What does any of that have to do with my grandmother?" Eric asked.

Senator Tanner was kicking himself inside for revealing that truth to Eric. That was something that should have gone with him to the grave. And now it was out. It was out and it was up to Eric to decide how to move forward. "I don't think we should talk about this anymore."

"Oh, the hell we aren't," Eric said. "Tell me what this has to do with my grandmother right now!"

"Calm down," Senator Tanner pleaded.

"I will not calm down. You will tell me what my grandmother has to do with you killing a man and you getting away with it." A pain ripped through Eric's head. His body was trying desperately to absorb the alcohol he and Senator

Chief of Staff

Tanner had consumed and along with the senator's fantastic story, the night was beginning to take its toll on him.

"Like I said, my father and your grandparents were friends somehow. When that man's body washed up on shore and people started to put two and two together, it looked like I might be going to prison for a long time." Senator Tanner rubbed his face and bent forward to lean on his knees, his hands clasped under his mouth as though he were in prayer. "We all got arrested for different offenses. Your grandfather represented me and got me off with a misdemeanor for reckless driving. Reid and the other guys went to trial, were found guilty of the murder, and got sent up to the federal prison in Danville."

"And my grandmother?" Eric asked, waiting to make the connection.

"Apparently it was her idea. She came up with some kind of scheme with my father. God knows what she did or how she made it work. But together, your grandfather, grandmother and my father kept me out of prison. I guess they're right about one thing," Senator Tanner said, his voice trailing off. He had leaned back and closed his eyes, too drunk to stay awake one minute longer.

"And what's that?"

"The devil truly is in the details."

*****

SATURDAY morning, Eric woke up to a splitting headache. He opened his eyes and instantly realized he was no longer on Senator Tanner's yacht. Impossibly, he was still somewhat intoxicated and he literally had no idea how he had gotten home. He didn't remember leaving. He didn't remember getting in his car and somehow making his way back to his townhouse. The last image in his mind was staggering out of the upper lounge with the bottle of Tequila, leaving Senator Tanner passed out on the sofa. From there, everything else was a blank. Too drunk to even undress, Eric was still wearing the same clothes from the night before.

Chief of Staff

"Oh my God," he said, looking at himself in the bathroom mirror. "What did I do last night?" He couldn't recall when he'd ever gotten that drunk, but then again, very little else was registering, so his memories of past alcohol binges were of little consequence to him. He shuffled his feet to the kitchen, popped four Tylenol, fell into the living room sofa and passed out again.

Chapter *19*

DAYS passed following the party and no one had heard from Senator Tanner or seen him in the office. He had left some drunken, incoherent messages for Claudia telling her that he would not be in the office and that Eric was to revise his schedule and handle anything that came up. Senator Tanner left no information on his whereabouts and that was fine with Eric. After hearing that wretched story after the party, Eric wanted little do with him anyway. He decided that wherever he was, it was probably best to just leave him alone for a couple of days. By the following Saturday morning when he hadn't heard from his boss, Eric started to worry and called his cell phone.

"You've reached 202-555-8751. The party you've called is unavailable. At the tone, please leave your message."

Eric dialed the number five times but never left a message. He figured the senator knew it was he who had called, but for whatever reason didn't feel like answering. Senator Tanner was scheduled to appear on "This Week with George Stephanopolous" the next day to spar with the Democratic poster child of the week about education reform. It would have been disastrous for Senator Tanner not to show. Along with the Immigration bill, his work on education had been a major chunk of his re-election platform and he was determined to do as much as he could to improve schools and the futures of children in North Carolina and the nation. At the last minute, spurred by a call from a production assistant badgering him about Senator Tanner's participation, Eric made an executive decision: he would take the senator's place on the panel.

Heading back from a quick trip to the office, his task at hand was to dive into the boxes Claudia had had delivered to his house in search of ammunition he could find on any- and everything dealing with education. She wasn't happy that

Chief of Staff

he hadn't taken the time to look at any of the information since their conversation the day he became Senator Tanner's chief of staff. With everything that had gone on, though, she realized that it might have been a lot to expect and left it alone.

Eric's D.C. home was a showplace. Originally, he'd bought the property with the intention of flipping it and making some money. But the more closely he looked at the three-story townhouse, the more he fell in love with it. Completely different than his home in Charlotte, the townhouse had a more elegant feel. Warm tones greeted you in every room, hardwoods were present throughout, and fantastic abstract and impressionist artwork tied it all together. Eric made most of the furniture himself.

Woodworking, his grandmother told him, was a skill that had been passed down through the generations from her father. Of everyone in the family, though, Eric's talent was the most effortless and simply innate. He could create anything. The huge Recontrelle bed in the master bedroom was designed, milled and constructed in a week. The Louis XIV-style armoire and matching sitting room chaise and tables took considerably longer, but they were all labors of love. From dining room tables and chairs, the most ornate and beautifully sculpted desks and cabinets, to very modern and functional every day pieces, there was a joy in woodworking that Eric couldn't find anywhere else. Politics and golf were his passions, yes, but bringing a piece of furniture to life from concept to final staining and upholstering was something that gave Eric unimaginable happiness and serenity.

He stood in his kitchen admiring his home for a moment. He turned on the coffee pot and went downstairs to poke through the first of many boxes. It was going to be a very long day.

*****

PREPPING for his television debut was more challenging and exhausting than he counted on. Eric had stayed up well into the early morning hours combing through Byrum's old files in search of anything related to education. It was something of a needle in a haystack mission, but he did come upon several items he figured he could piece together and formulate a thorough understanding of Senator Tanner's position on education. Thank God Byrum was very organized and took meticulous – if not peculiar - notes. It made it easier to decipher what must have been ramblings from the senator, Byrum having translated – or dictated – the meanings behind statements and opinions and dutifully filing them away for future reference.

Eric took pause when he thought about all the work Byrum put into running Senator Tanner's office that would never be realized due to his untimely death. When he figured he'd absorbed as much information as he could have possibly crammed into his brain, he set his alarm for a short three-hour nap and went to bed. The production assistant had made it very clear that Eric was to arrive at the studio for hair and make-up promptly at 6 am.

On the ride to the studio later that morning Eric rehearsed the party lines and statistics he'd memorized. The security guard wasn't at all impressed with the young man in the shiny Mercedes, arriving for his turn on national television, only briefly inspecting Eric and questioning his business at the studio that morning. Not that he should have been impressed by any stretch of the imagination, Eric thought to himself. After all, who was he? Just the lackey of an overpaid, overindulged government official whom the security guard probably didn't even know, much less care about. In about three hours, the entire world would know his name and that made Eric a little nervous. As the security guard nonchalantly waived him through, Eric was suddenly jealous of him and his anonymity.

Caked with television make-up and baking under the studio lights, Eric was in awe as the program began. An assistant had wired him for sound, putting a microphone on his suit jacket and cramming something in his ear that would allow him to hear the audio. It took several minutes of pre-show banter for him to adjust to the way his own voice sounded, amplified and resonating out of his control. The show's theme song blurted into his ear, he heard someone counting down and the lights became unimaginably brighter as George Stephanopolous started the show.

"Good morning and welcome to 'This Week'. Our topic today is the state of education in this country." Eric had met George on several occasions over the years and had generally been impressed with him. Attractive, shorter than average, and extremely intelligent, this man was made for TV. He had made a fortune after his stint as Clinton's press secretary, finding his way into book deals and replacing the venerable David Brinkley, more than likely pissing off Sam Donaldson, Cokie Roberts, and George Will to no end. Press conferences, fundraising parties, and the like gave you a clue about him, but it was clear that this Sunday morning political talk show was what he had been born to do. Eric wondered what his own chances of hosting a similar show would be. And then he laughed to himself.

"With me this morning," George continued, "are Michelle Timmons, the junior Democratic senator from South Carolina, and the current Assistant Secretary of Education, Wendell Scott. Our third scheduled guest, Senator Scott Tanner, Republican from North Carolina, was unable to appear on the program this morning." Eric could feel Timmons and Scott licking their chops. He had been told they would also be on the show and had researched their positions to a razor sharp edge. "In his place, we have with us Senator Tanner's chief of staff, Eric Tulian."

"That's Julian," Eric said unconsciously, not meaning to correct George so brusquely. He knows my name, he said to himself. Not only do I have no business on this set with these two powerhouses, now I've corrected the host of the show for something as petty as getting my name wrong. Great.

"Julian, that's right," George said. "I should have known that. I apologize." If he was irritated with Eric, it didn't show, and he moved on with the program. "Education has always been a hotbed of debate in this country, and for good reason. With the United States falling farther and farther behind the rest of the world, specifically in the areas of math and science, the following question presents itself and, frankly, demands to be answered: At what point will the United States recognize our world dominance is in jeopardy when judging the standards of our success against those countries running us down like rabid dogs?"

Eric didn't understand why George asked such a rambling, disjointed question, making a mental note to watch the playback later that day, but was quick to respond and fire the first shot. "The important thing to remember, George, is that the United States is in a position to capitalize on our strengths and to continue to lead the free world, as well as those countries under dictatorships, using education in strikingly important areas like mathematics and science." Senator Timmons leaned forward and opened her mouth, attempting to interrupt, but Eric continued. "What we have today is not the advancing of rabid dogs or some other unsavory euphemism pushing us into an educational chasm.

"It is not the responsibility of China or South Korea or Britain to inhibit their educational practices and lower their standards in order to allow the United States to set the international pace regarding those areas of education that allow countries to prosper both economically and socially. What we have today, in my opinion, is a juxtaposition of sorts. On one hand you have the ever-increasing demand for well-qualified teachers and professors both at the high school and university levels. We need them to develop quality educational plans that will give our students and young people the interest and desire to move into the field of technology, the field of science, the field of mathematics, the field of education, itself, moving down the line until every aspect of education is not only fully staffed and represented, but freely available to anyone who wishes to take part in the system to

Chief of Staff

better their life and the lives of the people dependent upon them."

George and his guests were furiously scribbling during Eric's prologue, making notes on which to challenge him later in the show.

Feeling more comfortable with his surroundings, Eric sat up in his seat and pressed on. "The juxtaposition is that in order to develop those quality educational plans and to put those persons in place to teach our children and instill that life-long love for learning they'll need to put us back in the lead in the fields I referenced, it takes money. And to date, no one in the Democratic party has taken the time to make this a priority." Senator Timmons was visibly irritated by that blanket statement and, again, attempted to speak. Eric knew from years on his college debate team that once you've got the floor, you kept it until somebody took it from you. If they wanted their point heard, it was up to them to make it happen. So he kept talking.

"No one from the Democratic party wants to put up the money to ensure those educational reforms are properly funded and that the programs vital to our success as a nation are put on the front burner. Senator Tanner's position is that nothing is more sacred than education. He's fought tooth and nail for three terms trying to gain some appreciable momentum in this battle that the Democrats, although they talk a good game, are apparently not interested in fighting."

Senator Timmons took her chance and spoke, not waiting for George. "I must say, young man…" she started.

"I'm thirty-three, Senator. Not especially a young man, but I appreciate the compliment, just the same," Eric said.

"As it were, your age is not of my concern. I want to focus on your incongruous statements regarding the Democratic view of education funding and their impact on…"

"My statements are in no way incongruous, Senator. For example, South Carolina is a national leader in the area of automobile manufacturing, with BMW building cars in Spartanburg."

"That's correct," she said proudly.

"What amazes me is that the people who build those cars are the almsmen of the forty-ninth place educational system of your state. With the number of students failing math and science courses at your public high schools, I can understand why the majority of the employees making those cars will never make enough money to own one, themselves. They are South Carolina residents who could have, through a superior and well-funded education, gotten jobs that paid them enough to afford those cars." Wendell Scott was stuck in the middle, turning his head back and forth, listening to Eric and hoping to not be called on.

"Again, that's not accurate," the senator stated. "South Carolina is wholly committed to bringing education to the forefront and continuing to improve our children's chances at achieving whatever school-related goals they may have."

"That's part of the problem. They aren't school-related goals; they're life-related goals. You all don't seem to understand the difference."

"I assure you we appreciate the difference. That turn of phrase was taken out of context. Democrats have faithfully supported education."

"Is that why you've voted against federalizing education each of the last four times the bill has come to the floor?" Eric asked. "Is that why you have widely disparate funding for schools across your state? Why, I wonder, would schools in Horry County and the Myrtle Beach areas receive the lion share of tax money for improvement and programs while neighboring communities, not benefiting from the enormous tax windfall from sun-seeking tourists, are forced to sit and watch school buildings fall into disrepair and their students' test scores relegate them to a life of minimum wage earnings and dead-end jobs? Senator Tanner wants to stop that scenario from happening, to kill it and prevent it from corrupting any more school districts, whether they be in South Carolina, North Carolina, California, or surrounding us here in Washington, D.C. We've got a plan. And with the help of the Republican president and the reform-minded voters of this country, we are going to put that plan into action. We are going to do whatever we can to ensure that no child is left behind."

Assistant Secretary Scott tried, unsuccessfully, to defuse the growing tension between Eric and Senator Timmons. "I truly feel that this administration cares deeply about children and their future. Yes, there are issues between the two parties, but I don't believe there are any that can't be resolved to the satisfaction of both."

"The only thing Republicans are looking for on this issue is the complete and utter submission of Democrats. We refuse to bend to their rule, to budge even one iota." Senator Timmons just knew she had taken the upper hand and smiled. Take that, she seemed to intimate.

Eric was now playing to the cameras, something he had coached his candidates to do. It made them appear more approachable and sincere no matter what they were saying. "So let me get this straight. I want to make sure that I've heard you correctly. And, mind you, this is not an opinion I am expressing for Senator Tanner." Eric put his hands together as though he were about to pray, and pointed at his opponent. "You've just sat there on national television and bluntly told the viewing audience that the democrats are committed to making sure that the republicans lose the battle on education. And you're going to do this by refusing to compromise positions that would effect sweeping change for the benefit of every child in this country. You would rather put a notch in your belt, than to see the children of the very parents in your district have the chance at bettering their lives. That is petty and disgusting."

Senator Timmons was vigorously shaking her head, intending to restate her comments, but Eric continued, cutting her off as she began to speak.

"No, no, no. You just wait a minute, Senator. Please. With all due respect, you may or may not be speaking for your entire party. And I imagine that as we speak, a number of elected officials and voting-age citizens are feverishly calling both your office and that of Senator Tanner. Again, this is not something I am spouting for the senator as I sit in his stead on this program. Since the Kennedy administration, it has been a priority of this nation to better equip our children, the future and lifeblood of our society, for prosperity beyond what their parents experienced.

"Since the Kennedy administration, efforts and programs and agendas have been proposed by republicans, both on a state level and nationally, that would have given schools the funding necessary to take our present concepts of education in this country to new levels. Repeatedly, democrats have bemoaned the idea of federalizing the schools. And you're supposed to be for more government interference, not less."

"He raises a point, Senator," George said, speaking up more to remind people that this was his show, than to get in the middle of the argument.

"There are extremely gifted and talented children in a housing project called Dalton Village in Charlotte. Those children who are imprisoned in a society not of their making may very well be the next generation of welfare recipients and minimum-wage workers if they don't get the chance to do something with their education. They may be talented and aspiring, but due to the despicable funding their local high school receives, no matter the stellar grades they bring home, they won't be accepted to the schools where their dreams of becoming doctors and lawyers and engineers and architects can flourish because their local school doesn't have the money to make those classes and distinguished teaching professionals available to them."

Chief of Staff

"That hasn't been concretely proven yet, young man," the senator countered.

"That's a lie."   Secretary Scott wished he were somewhere at that exact moment. "Are you familiar with William Hazlitt, Senator?" Eric asked, setting her up.

"No," she said, looking at George and Secretary Scott. "I don't believe that I am."

"He's one of my favorite authors; very poignant and matter of fact. One of the best quotes I've ever heard from him is, 'Man is the only animal that laughs and weeps; for he is the only animal that is struck with the difference between what things are, and what they ought to be.' What education ought to be in this country is far removed from the reality of today."

"Again, I would beg to differ on that, young man," the senator said.

"A friend of mine refers to money as having options. Options let you freely decide where you're going to go for dinner. Options let you freely decide what kind of car or house you're going to buy. Options give you the ability to better your life. Schools around the country are eliminating music programs, honors and AP courses, college preparatory studies, the list goes on and on. Unbelievably, they're even being forced to eliminate P.E. in elementary schools because there's no funding for it." Eric was on a roll.

"Imagine your personal doctor, Senator. With very little exception, he or she grew up and went through life not having to worry about where their next meal was going to come from or whether or not the classes they were taking would lead to their fulfilling dreams of working in the medical profession. Six blocks from here at JFK High School, they don't have enough funding to buy new uniforms for their athletic departments. Students living in the most powerful city on earth can't get into Ivy League schools because even though they may be intelligent enough, they can't afford college and their high school classes aren't at the level commensurate with the school down the street or the next state over. It doesn't have to be that way. But, like you said, come hell or high water, the democrats aren't going to budge even one iota. Your collective constituency should be as ashamed of you as I am. Scuttle your pride. Work with us, for the sole benefit of that young girl in Dalton Village and the young man wasting away at JFK, and give them the options they so richly deserve."

George couldn't help but smile. Eric Julian, chief of staff, had in twenty minutes not only completely dominated the show, but he'd succinctly and powerfully put Senator Michelle Timmons in her place, decimating any argument the democrats could muster to explain their platform on education. For the rest of the hour, it was clear that Eric Julian would be making a name for himself on the very public stage that was politics. He was clever, quick on his feet, and obviously well prepared. By ten o'clock Sunday morning, Eric would be a superstar.

God help him.

Chapter *20*

THE minute Eric left the stage and headed out of the television studio, something was different about him. He didn't fully understand what had happened in there, but his reality had now been upended, changed in a way that seemed to signal great things were on his horizon. He was walking ten feet off the ground, smiling uncontrollably.

His plan was to drop by the office for a couple of hours and then head back to his townhouse to watch whatever golf tournament was on. As he pulled out of the parking lot he remembered that K Street was clogged due to construction traffic and picked an alternate route. "What in the world?" he asked himself, suddenly slowing to a crawl. A man was directing traffic and slowly, very slowly, cars were turning into a parking garage about two hundred yards from where Eric sat, fuming.

"It's Sunday morning. Why in the hell is there this much traffic?" And then it came to him. Church. Never a day that held any more meaning to him than the rest of the week, Eric rarely ventured out on Sunday morning other than a quick jaunt to Starbucks for a venti skim vanilla latte and a couple of those delicious raspberry muffins. He tried to change lanes, to get out of the oppressively slow lane, but his progress was blocked by yet another set of construction cones. "Fabulous."

When he got up to the man directing traffic, he rolled down his window and asked to be let by. You got some place better to be than in church, young man, he was asked. Shaking his drooped head, I guess not, was all he could say. He pulled into the garage and parked his car. Half of him wanted to sit there, waiting until the man had gone into church and then make a quick escape. But the other half, oddly enough, was trying to convince the id or the ego, whatever it was, to take a chance. Go to church.

Chief of Staff

Looking in the mirror, Eric straightened his tie, took a very deep breath, and joined the shuffle of people, following them through the bowels of the garage and into the sanctuary. "What am I doing?"

"You're going to church," said a tiny voice next to Eric. He looked down at a little boy, dressed in a white short-sleeve shirt, navy pants and a tie that he was obviously allowed to try and tie himself. Eric guessed he was about six years old.

"From the mouths of babes," Eric said and thanked the young man for answering the question he hadn't realized he uttered aloud. "My name is Eric."

The young man looked nervously up at his mother, who was holding his hand, and then back at Eric. "Momma says I can't talk to strangers."

Eric looked at the boy's mother and started to apologize, but she interrupted him. Looking at Eric she said, "I think it's okay, Zeke. He looks like a nice man. And he looks like he needs to be in church more than he might realize." She smiled at Eric and instantly he felt comfortable in his surroundings. This might not be so bad after all, he told himself.

From the moment he got out of his car, he was amazed how at odds everything about this church and its parishioners was from his memories of Sundays spent with Christine attending St. Luke's Episcopal. Conservative, at best, St. Luke's was one of the places in Charlotte where black wealth unabashedly displayed itself, using the guise of getting religion as a backdrop on their social climbing and networking. This was altogether different. Everyone was laughing and conversing with smiles. They hugged and kissed cheeks and held shoulders while they spoke, greeting each other warmly. And they were all black. Every single one of them. He casually looked around and there wasn't a white or Latino or Asian face to be found. Interesting. All of the men were dressed very sharply in suits and ties, no casual clothes on anyone. And then there were the women. Old and young, you could tell that this was their day to shine. They took an inordinate amount of pride to make sure they looked just right. Scarves and simple jewelry adorned their suits and pretty dresses. Hats the likes of which Eric never imagined were everywhere, each festooned with plumes of feathers and bows and veils. It was an explosion of color. He took a bulletin from a woman standing in front of the sanctuary doors: Greater Ebenezer Baptist Church, Washington D.C., Pastor – Rev. Dr. Joseph Davis.

An usher greeted Eric and motioned him inside the sanctuary. He stood there not knowing what to do next. Where do I sit? Are there reserved spaces? Maybe I'll sit right here in the back. Or maybe it would look rude. I don't want to go to the front and walk past all of these people. The left? The right?

"Mister," Zeke said, tugging on Eric's suit. "Momma said you can sit with us if you want." Eric thanked Zeke's mother and followed them down the aisle to their pew. The blank, but polite, head nods at St. Luke's were replaced with large smiles and extended hands from strangers. They seemed genuinely happy to have Eric visit them this Sunday morning, none of them knowing him at all. As Eric, Zeke and his mother sat down, an older woman with a pink hat and matching suit turned to greet them.

"Good morning, Zeke. And how are you today?"

"God is good, Mrs. DuPont. And how are you?" Eric was shocked at what Zeke said and impressed at the same time.

"God is good." Mrs. DuPont turned to Eric and introduced herself. "Greater Ebenezer welcomes you today, young man." Her face was a tiny bit wrinkled but warm as she spoke. "God is good."

"Yes, ma'am," Eric said. "And thank you for the welcome." Eric turned to Zeke and shrugged his shoulders, he didn't know if he was supposed to say anything else. Zeke shrugged his shoulders, too, and pulled out a bible coloring

Chief of Staff

book and crayons. The music that had been playing lightly in the background as people were being seated came to an end. "What are you doing with that?" Eric asked.

"Shush," Zeke said. "You're not supposed to talk after the music stops. If you do, God can't hear what the preacher's preachin' about." His eyebrows were pressed together, like he was scolding Eric.

Muzzling a laugh, Eric turned to check out his surroundings. The inside of the sanctuary was tall and airy, the white walls and columns seemed to reach up toward Heaven. Magnificent stained glass windows were being illuminated by the bright Sunday morning sun. He quickly counted about twenty-five rows of pews, each one packed from side to side, separated by an aisle wide enough to accommodate the wheelchair-bound. Counting the people in the balcony above, Eric figured there were about eight hundred, maybe a thousand people. The pulpit was out of this world. Rising above the crowd on the same deep red carpet that led to the sanctuary doors, it was absolutely huge. Eric was trying to figure out why they needed that much space when the music abruptly started again. The organist was energized, playing a fast tune Eric had never heard before. Everyone shot to their feet.

"Get up," Zeke said. "This is the fun part."

Stationed prominently at the aisle-side of the pew, some kind of new guy conspiracy Eric figured, the parade began. Everyone was clapping and singing along, excited about what was to come. He didn't know the words, so he mouthed as best he could, and clapped to the rhythm. Zeke and his mother had lead Eric to their regular seats, about five pews from the pulpit, so he had a great view. As the music and the singing got louder, he turned to look down the aisle. New Orleans in D.C., he thought, as the massive choir stepped and sang their way to their seats. Several of them reached out and shook Eric's hand, while singing, and moved on without missing a beat. They were all in matching navy blue robes, capes emblazoned with a gold cross hanging down

Chief of Staff

their backs. All he could do was smile in amazement, continuing to mouth poorly and to focus hard enough to clap and take everything in all at the same time.

And then the voice.

The music stopped. Zeke, and everybody in church except Eric stopped clapping and bowed their heads. Looking around, Eric quickly followed suit. A complete fish out of water, he told himself.

"God is good," boomed someone over the sound system.

God is good, the congregation repeated in unison, as if given some unheard prompt.

"Let God flow through you this morning, as He does every day, enriching the lives of the rich and poor, blessed and the unblessed, strong and weak, young and old." Deep and commanding, Eric wondered if this was the Rev. Dr. Joseph Davis. He slowly turned around to see who was talking and realized it was the 'traffic cop'. You got some place better to be than in church? No wonder. The pastor was a tall black man, forty or so. Having exchanged the black suit he wore earlier, he stood at the back of the church in a sparkling white robe, his arms outstretched, his head titled upward. He clutched a bible in one hand, the other palm-open and pointed toward the ceiling. Zeke tugged on Eric's suit and gave him that look again. Sorry, Eric mouthed.

God is good, the congregation repeated again, this time joined by Eric.

*****

ONCE the choir had been seated, Rev. Davis took his position and gave another opening prayer. Eric tried as best he could to keep up with the rapid-fire pace of what was going on around him. Greater Ebenezer was nothing if not expedient. The bulletin was packed with information. Sister Rachel, every bit of seventy-five years old, resplendent in a purple dress – and, of course, matching hat – walked

Chief of Staff

confidently to the microphone. Pausing briefly between announcements, she took her job seriously and rattled off to the congregation every update, in order and from memory, listed in the bulletin. Eric was mesmerized.

Prayer for the shut-in and hospitalized. Announcement of a new scholarship for ten college students. Announcement that the Building Fund was almost at 100%. Announcement that the Meals on Wheels program would be expanded, but wouldn't be managed by Sister Clara due to her impending gall bladder surgery. Prayer for Sister Clara. Announcement that the Children's Choir concert was scheduled for next weekend. A slight head nod toward Rev. Davis and she retreated back to her pew. Still resplendent, purple and not a bit out of breath.

Just as it seemed people were beginning to squirm in the pews, the organist spoke into his microphone as he played the first few notes of a song. "Please turn in your hymnals to page seventy-four."

Out of nowhere, the band cranked into high gear, the choir stood, followed by the entire able-bodied congregation, and everyone got lost in an amazing rendition of "What A Friend (We Have In Jesus)." Eric sang and clapped and smiled, reveling in how much fun he was having. He glimpsed at his watch and wondered how thirty-five minutes could have possibly elapsed.

Before the song ended, ushers were making their way to the front of the church, paired off at either end of staggered pews. According to the bulletin, this was The Offering. "How much should I put in the bowl?" Eric leaned over and asked Zeke.

"Momma puts paper in there, but I always put in a quarter. Want me to ask her to give you a quarter?"

Eric smiled but declined the generous offer, winking at Zeke's mother. He fished a one hundred dollar bill out of his wallet and dropped it in the bowl. He passed the bowl to Zeke who dive-bombed his twenty-five cent tithe, making sure it was accompanied by the requisite six-year-old pretend plane sound effect, and immediately resumed coloring Jesus with a brown face and green hair.

A well-oiled machine, Greater Ebenezer moved briskly along. Another song, one more announcement and then Rev. Davis took center stage.

"God is good. Let the church say amen."

Amen.

Rev. Davis was light-skinned and cast a large shadow. Broad shoulders accentuated by navy blue bards on his robe carried the responsibility of leading such a large congregation. His hair was loosely curled and jet black. Both hands on the podium, he closed his eyes and began to speak.

"God laid something on my heart this morning, y'all."

Amen!

"He told me that this would be a special morning. That I should speak to His children from my heart, not from a sermon." Rev. Davis opened his eyes, becoming more animated. He smiled as he produced the sermon he had written the night before. "This is what I was going to preach this glorious Sunday morning. It's been researched. It's been spell-checked. It's been read and reread. But it isn't what God wants me to say to you. And you know I ain't about to ignore God!"

Amen!

"I don't know how long I'm gonna be up here. I don't know even know yet what I'm gonna say. But what I do know is we ain't havin' a regular service today. This morning, we're straight havin' church up in here!"

Amen, Brother!

Eric wondered what the difference was between service and church, but the whoops and hollers from the congregation went a long way in answering the question.

"Psalm 1," Rev. Davis began, "tells us that 'Blessed is the man who does not walk in the counsel of the wicked. Or stand in the way of sinners. Or sit in the seat of the mockers'. Let me say that first part again. Bless-ed is the man who does not walk in the counsel of the wicked."

Well.

"Don't put your faith in the hands of anyone willing to lead you down the wrong path. Don't trust or listen to or take advice from those persons we ALL know have evil in their hearts. What's that going to get you?"

Nothing but trouble.

"Y'all ever hear that commercial that says cable contributes to life? Well I'm here to tell you that ain't true. It may entertain you for a while, but God contributes to life!"

Speak!

"ESPN may give you sports, but God gave men and women the talent to amaze you on the field of play. Speed channel may give you races and sports cars, but God gave you the tools to run the race toward salvation. Lifetime and HBO and Showtime may give you documentaries about the plight of earthly man, but God gave us the Bible – the very script to his own little movie – and gave us the ability to absorb his words as a map to the gates of Heaven."

Preach on!

"Blessed is the man who does not walk in the counsel of the wicked. Society today is overrun with people who are only out to get you. Brother Malcolm X spoke about having been hookwinked and bamboozled and run amuck. He wasn't just talking about the white man. He wasn't just talking about thugs and thieves and criminals. He was talking about the wicked as a whole." Rev. Davis was beginning to sweat and dabbed his face with a white handkerchief. "It is long past time when we black people stopped walking in the counsel of the wicked. It is long past time when we should stop blaming everybody but ourselves for our lot in life." Eric wondered if Rev. Davis was a republican.

"The counsel of the wicked has lead to physical and mental abuse, women selling themselves for $5 worth of drugs, pitiful test scores in our schools, under-representation on issues that could lift us up as a people, improving the future of our children, and our children's children. God said that 'there fore the wicked will not stand in judgment, no sinners in the assembly of the righteous. For the Lord watches over the way of the righteous, but the way of the wicked will perish'. Now I don't know about y'all but the way of the righteous is the option I'm tryin' to take."

Amen!

"And this is my road map," he said, hoisting his Bible into the air. "This is my MapQuest!" The congregation laughed out loud and smiled at their neighbors all around. "If I've got a question about something, I'm not gonna Google it; I'm gonna open my Bible!"

Right!

"I'm not gonna get on MySpace to find a friend, am I?"

No!

"I'm not gonna Facebook my faith!"

No, sir!

"The choir just told me what a friend I have in Jesus!"

Go on, now!

"I'm not gonna depend on ABC…not NBC…not CNN…not CBS or any other national news media to tell me what's going wrong with the world! God's already told me that! We've got it first-hand! He told us Himself and it's coming to pass! My momma told me two things that I'll remember until the day the face of Jesus shines down upon my own in Heaven. She told me: God don't like ugly. And she told me that the Bible is my shining light, believe in it and

Chief of Staff

trust it for it is the word of Almighty God! Blessed is the man who does not walk in the counsel of the wicked!"

Speak!

"Ain't nobody on this earth gonna tell me how to live my life, love my wife, discipline my children, or who I'm supposed to vote for. I'm refusing to get caught up, like my nephew says. Come on now!" Rev. Davis's intensity was invigorating and infectious. He threw his arms and hands about, moving quickly from one side of the pulpit to another, putting his face through unimaginable contortions as he got his points across. His voice was rough and gravely, putting emphasis on his words like only a southern black preacher could. Electricity penetrated every part of the sanctuary. Eric was witnessing something beyond his comprehension and was loving every second of it.

"I will NOT walk in the counsel of the wicked for God is my only counsel and He will lead me through life – using His plan – putting me on the path of the righteous. For the Lord watches over the way of the righteous! Can the church PLEASE say amen?"

Amen!

Rev. Davis took a sip of water and changed his tone, turning a fraction softer. "In you, O Lord, Psalm 31 begins, I have taken refuge; let me never be put to shame; deliver me in your righteousness."

Mrs. DuPont started fanning herself, rocking back and forth. She put her hand in the air and screamed, "Thank you, Jesus!"

Eric was startled and looked at Zeke. He shrugged his shoulders again and went back to his coloring book.

"Turn your ear to me," Rev. Davis continued, seemingly oblivious to Mrs. DuPont's outburst. Eric looked around and no one else seemed disturbed by her screaming, which she had continued, somehow automatically timed between pauses in the sermon. The fanning, too, had picked up. Something is wrong with this woman, Eric thought.

"Come quickly to my rescue; be my rock of refuge, a strong fortress to save me."

"Yes, Lord!"

There it was again, this time coming from another part of the church. Rev. Davis was getting fired up again, pacing the pulpit and continuing to dab his perspiring face.

"Since you are my rock and my fortress, for the sake of your name lead and guide me. Free me from the trap that is set for me, for you are my refuge!"

Preach on!

Rev. Davis was visibly moved, jumping and jetting around. The congregation was further whipping themselves into an absolute frenzy. St. Luke's would already have imploded in on itself at this point, but the excitement flowing through Greater Ebenezer was still soaring, still fever-pitched.

Rev. Davis dropped to his knees and screamed, "Into your hands I commit my spirit; redeem me O Lord, the God of truth. I shall not walk in the counsel of the wicked for you are my path on the way of the righteous!"

On some secret cue, the organist cranked up again, the choir standing for their last performance. Rev. Davis stood up slowly after motioning the congregation to stand, and in a ragged and tired voice said, "May God arise, may His enemies be scattered; may His foes flee before Him. As smoke is blown away by the winds, may you blow them away; as wax melts before the fire, may the wicked perish before God. But may the righteous be glad and rejoice before God; may they be happy and joyful. Sing to God," he said to the choir. "Sing praise to His name, extol Him who rides on the clouds – His name is the Lord and rejoice before Him."

Chapter *21*

"ISN'T it a lovely morning?" Claudia walked into Eric's office and handed him some files he'd requested on an upcoming Senate vote.

Eric turned around and saw that the weather hadn't changed from the last time he checked ten minutes before. "Unless you're high on something, I think we can both agree that cloudy and cold conditions don't exactly make for a lovely morning."

"What's wrong with trying to appreciate the things in life that we can't change?" Claudia asked, smiling in a way that meant she was up to something.

Eric leaned back in his chair and eyed her up and down. Did he miss a staff birthday or anniversary of some kind? "You're acting rather strangely this morning. What gives?"

"Nothing gives, COS. I was just trying to make pleasant conversation."

"You don't have the ability to make pleasant conversation," Eric joked. "Tell me what you've got up your sleeve."

Claudia sat down in a chair in front of Eric's desk and began rummaging through the stack of files she hadn't put on his desk, lightly humming a tune. "Don't mind me," she said. "I'll be out of your hair in a minute. If I don't do this now, I'll forget about it." She continued to hum and Eric went back to work. The tune was familiar to him, and before he knew it, he was humming right along with her.

"What A Friend We Have in Jesus, right?" he asked, without looking up.

Claudia couldn't hold back her excitement any longer and, in a rapid-fire blast, she blurted out, "Isn't Rev. Davis simply wonderful? I saw you in church yesterday. At first I was really shocked to see you there, but I decided to sit back and leave you alone. I don't know why you were there, but it was fantastic seeing you. And don't you think that little Zeke is just precious? I hope you come back. Greater Ebenezer has been my church home for as long as I've lived in Washington. I'm always telling people about it, and sometimes I ask them to come and witness the glory for themselves. I really never, ever, ever thought I'd see you there, but my heart was overjoyed. And you were singing and clapping and you prayed and…."

"Hold on just a minute!" Eric shouted, breaking into the long-play version of what was sure to be a conversation he didn't want to have. "You were there?"

"Of course I was there. That's my church home. I just said that."

"And you watched me the whole time?"

"Uh, yeah. I mean I wasn't spying on you or anything. I hope you're not mad. I left you alone because I didn't know if you would be embarrassed that I saw you."

Eric laughed and just smiled at Claudia. "What a crazy world we live in. Yes, I had a great time. Zeke is quite the young man. And his mother is pretty nice, herself."

"Blessed is the man who does not walk in the counsel of the wicked," Claudia said, repeating the subject of Sunday's sermon. "You should hear that man when he really gets going. Yesterday was mild in comparison, let me tell you."

"I don't even want to know," he said, laughing. Abruptly changing the subject, Eric looked at Claudia and asked, "What's up with Byrum and his note taking?"

Claudia raised an eyebrow and shook her head. "That man was on another planet when it came to notes, I'm tellin' you what's the truth."

"When I was going through all of those boxes to get ready for my television debut…"

"That's rich," Claudia interrupted.

"Anyway, when I was going through the boxes almost everything had this weird shorthand on it. I mean everything. Was he dyslexic or something? I thought to myself that maybe some of his writing was backward."

"When I first got here, I thought it was just me. I was like, why would somebody write stuff down like that? Why not just write out what you mean?" She shrugged her shoulders and tidied up her stack of folders. "At some point, I just got used to it. I remember I questioned him about it once and he told me it was his secret code. He gave me this shady wink when he said it. Don't ask me what that was about because I still have no idea. In fact, right after he died, I had to come in here and clean out his desk, personal items and what not. It took me a couple of days to translate everything. It was like he wrote with a mirror."

"I know what you mean. The letters and words don't always make sense."

"It's not just that. It was like he switched things around so no one would know what he was talking about. White was black, man was woman, and yadda yadda yadda."

"Wish I would have known that before I started slogging through those files. Talk about torturous."

"I feel you. He was a dear old man, but there were some things, like that whole mirror image writing thing that were just off base." Claudia closed her eyes and smiled. "I sure do miss him, though." She looked at Eric and said, "Did you know him very well?"

"I'd met him a couple of times through the senator at parties and what not, but he wasn't on my cell phone directory if that's what you mean."

"Am I on your cell phone directory?"

"Yes. Under Evil Mistress, Wicked, Annoying, and Slave Master."

"You're the one with the high yellow complexion, lest you forgot."

"Lest? Did they teach you that in the fields when your black ass was out there picking cotton?" Claudia was about to launch into a tirade about Eric going too far with his lame jokes when Eric looked up to see the senator striding into the office. "Well, holy shit. Look what the cat drug in."

"You need Greater Ebenezer more than you think," Claudia said, as she got up and walked out of the office. "From church to cursing. Shame on you, Eric. Shame on you."

Senator Tanner walked past Claudia and they high-fived at each other. "Hi, Eric."

"Jesus Christ, man..."

"You're going to hell, COS," Claudia shouted from her desk.

Eric waved her off and closed the door behind the senator. He was jaundiced and looked a little ragged. "What's wrong with you?'

"I've got a cold or something," Senator Tanner said, plopping himself down on the sofa.

"That's not what I'm talking about. Where the hell have you been?" Eric leaned against his desk, arms folded like he was about to discipline his boss. He had that 'I'm so disappointed in you' look on his face.

"Don't lecture me. I'm not in the mood for it."

"Not in the mood? How about not being in the mood to get grilled on national television because the man you work for conveniently skipped town after telling you something completely outlandish? How about not being in the mood to deal with coming up with excuse after excuse about the whereabouts of the man who is supposed to be the head of this office?"

"You're the head of this office," the senator snapped. "If you can't handle the job then I guess I was wrong about you." Eric could only stare at Senator Tanner, unsure of where that came from. Neither man spoke for a time before the senator broke the silence. "I'm sorry."

"Apology not yet accepted."

"I'm sorry for everything, Eric." Senator Tanner got up from the sofa, massaging his side and sat down in front of Eric, still leaning with purpose against his desk. "I'm sorry for what I told you on the yacht. I'm sorry for what kind of person that makes me. I'm sorry for all of that and more." He looked like he was going to cry and Eric melted.

"Listen," he said, sitting down and touching the senator's shoulder, "I'm sorry, too. Things around here have been crazy and I lashed out at you."

"That's a bullshit excuse and you know it, Eric. You're pissed at me and you have every right to be."

Eric sat back in his chair, looking out at Claudia's overcast-but-somehow-lovely morning. "I am glad you told me what you did, Senator. I can't believe the story actually happened and I can't believe that you were involved, but I believe that you are sorry for what you did. In church yesterday, the preacher said the Lord watches over the way of the righteous, but the way of the wicked will perish. That certainly takes on new meaning when you have a situation like this to deal with."

Senator Tanner looked at Eric inquisitively, trying not to smirk. "You went to church yesterday? An actual church?"

"Yes, and it was as surprising to me as anyone else. Don't get me started on the whole thing."

"Your grandmother would be proud of you."

Eric shook his head and moved the subject back to Senator Tanner. He hung his head back and looked at the ceiling. "Senator, there are things in life that no one is proud

Chief of Staff

of. What I mean is, I guess people do things every day that they are ashamed to admit or to talk about with anyone. I'm glad to know that we still have the kind of relationship where you feel comfortable telling me things like you did on the yacht."

"You do remember that I was completely drunk, don't you?" the senator asked, smiling.

"To be honest, there's not a whole lot that I do remember other than what you told me. I don't even remember how I got home." Eric stood and walked to the window. "I love you very much," he said, not looking at his boss. "I do think of you in a different way now, but it's not how you might think." Eric turned to see the senator tearing. "I can't walk in your shoes and I can't live with what happened the way you have to every day of your life. But know that your secret is safe with me and that I will continue to count you as a treasured part of my life."

The senator walked over to Eric and put his hands on his shoulders. "Thank you. I'm so sorry. I'm glad to have you in my life, Eric."

Eric nodded and said he understood.

"You were, by the way, simply unbelievable on 'This Week'! You took Simmons to the ground. It was a magnificent display of political genius. I know you're going to make a great senator someday soon."

Eric beamed at the compliment. "Thanks, Senator. But to be honest with you, I'm completely worn out. Now that I know you're okay," he said as he punched the senator in the arm for not calling him or returning any emails, "I think I'm going to take a couple of days off. I need some mental health time. I've got some pieces that I need to finish for my aunt, and this is the perfect time to relax and do both."

"Whatever you want, son. Whatever you need, just take off. I love you." The senator kissed Eric on the cheek and hugged him tightly.

Chief of Staff

"I could see about getting the two of you a room over at the Watergate, if you'd like," Claudia said, walking back into the office.

Still embracing, Eric and Senator Tanner looked at Claudia and all three of them broke out laughing. Claudia stopped first, followed quickly by the two men. "Glad to have you back, Senator, but I believe we have a problem."

"Shit," Eric said. "There goes my vacation."

"It's Senator Lamprey," Claudia said. "He is going to hold a press conference apologizing to his constituents for the Immigration bill."

"Which he voted for out of his own conscience, and which President Brown plans on signing into law next week," Eric said

"My friend at CNN just called and tipped me off. I don't know how you're supposed to keep something like this a secret, but he's done a pretty good job. From what she told me, he's going to say that he felt pressured to vote for the bill and that had he to do it all over again, he'd stand up to those individuals who made it sound like putting his stamp on the bill was the only thing he could do. It starts in an hour in the Rotunda."

"Sounds like he's gunning for you, Eric," Senator Tanner said.

"Alright, the first thing we need to do is get CNN on the phone," Eric said, moving into crisis management mode.

"No, sir," Senator Tanner said to Eric. "I'll handle this. Go on vacation. I'll call you if anything comes up that needs your attention."

"Are you sure?" Eric was praying that the senator would say the right thing.

"Get out of here." He turned to Claudia, refreshed at his repaired relationship with Eric and went to work. "Get me a copy of the bill. Call CNN and see if you can get me on

Chief of Staff

tonight. I'll need some time to analyze the press conference and decide how I want to spin this in our favor. Call Lamprey's chief of staff and leave a message. Make sure you don't indicate that I have any intention of calling that bastard back. Just make sure he gets the message that I've gotten wind of his little charade and that I'm pissed. Call the majority leader and get me on his calendar for a meeting before Lamprey stops flapping him gums to the press. Get me a sausage, egg, and cheese biscuit, a large orange juice and two Tylenol. And," he said as they walked to his office, "make sure that Eric isn't here in ten minutes when I come back through this door." He turned and smiled at Eric. "I've got this. I'll call you later."

Chapter *22*

FOR the first time in a while, Eric dropped everything and left Washington. It felt strange at first, not being constantly tied to a schedule or shooting off to a meeting. Although there were still a million things on his mind connected to running the office, Senator Tanner seemed to have everything well under control. He looked awful, but he was just as fiery as he had been years ago, the first time Eric witnessed him in action. Not wanting to be completely cut off from the office, Eric grabbed a box of files from his townhouse and headed for the airport.

He got back to Charlotte by early afternoon and went directly to his woodshop. His Aunt Annetta had recently opened her new country house and wanted Eric to design and build some furniture for a couple of the rooms. Already complete were the dining room table and chairs, a western-themed bed for his ten-year-old cousin, and a Blanket Chest. He saved the hardest project for last: accent chairs for the formal living room. She wanted them just so, even going as far as sending Eric crude sketches of what she had envisioned. He tweaked a few details here and there and went to work. By all accounts, the chairs should have been finished and shipped to Annetta by now, but the demands of his new job had pushed the delivery date back more than he was comfortable with. No matter. Even if he had to work through the night over the entire length of his vacation it would be well worth it. Annetta was one of his biggest supporters and he knew that she'd receive the chairs and the rest of the furniture and proudly display every piece.

The woodshop was Eric's pride and joy. It was really the only place in the world where he could totally relax. He felt a kind of serenity come over him as he worked on his projects. There wasn't anyone nipping at his heels to get something done. He could work at his own pace and come up

Chief of Staff

with a laundry list of designs that would keep him busy, and content, for months at a time. The only problem was he never had that long to complete anything he was working on. Ideas hit his brain and he immediately wanted to bring them to life. Family and friends would request a piece of furniture and he made it his goal to finish and deliver whatever it was they wanted before they needed it. That's just the way he was. What pieces he'd made for various reasons, or those items he'd swapped out of his house when he redecorated, sat in a warehouse nearby. The warehouse also housed his excess art. That made him think of his sometime stalker, and then before it got out of hand, he closed his eyes and took a deep breath.

He clicked on the lights and the shop came to life. The smell of wood stain and sawdust in the air brought a smile to his face. Time to get busy. At roughly one thousand square feet, it housed all manner of equipment, every bit of which Eric used to create his masterpieces. Wired for sound, music blared over the noise of drills and saws and routers. His musical tastes were as eclectic as his designs. Dr. Dre, Rascall Flatts, Josh Groban, Fiona Apple, Anthony Hamilton, Jill Scott, Common, Van Halen, and on and on. Eric's iPod was crammed with songs from every genre and era. There was no way to classify his musical tastes other than to say it spanned the spectrum. As always, he'd plugged his iPod into the wall-mounted stereo and got busy with the next item on his furniture checklist.

He wasn't sure how long he'd been in the shop when the phone rang. Because of the noise from the music and the machines, Eric had a system installed whereby the lights blinked if the phone rang. He cut everything off and grabbed the phone.

"Dammit." His grandmother's number was scrolling across the caller id. To answer or not, he couldn't decide. He rubbed his temples and clicked the phone on.

"I understand from Mary Ellen that you are in Charlotte." No hello. No how are you. Nothing.

Chief of Staff

"That's correct, grandmother. And how are you this afternoon?"

"It's seven o'clock, Eric, so technically it's now evening."

Eric said nothing.

"Again," Christine started, "I understand from Mary Ellen that you are in Charlotte."

"Yes, ma'am. Were I not in Charlotte I wouldn't be speaking to you on my home phone right now."

"That tone isn't going to get you very far with me, young man." Christine waited for Eric to say something and rolled her eyes at his silence. "I would have thought you'd call your grandmother when you came home, but I see that I was wrong."

"Grandmother," Eric began, not wanting to argue with her, "I've got a lot of work to do. I've got to finish Annetta's accent chairs."

"For her country house, that's right." Eric could feel the indignation dripping through the phone. "I don't know whom she thinks she's fooling, building a house like that. She's just showing off to her little friends. You'd never know she was married to my son, the way she throws money away. I half wonder if she thinks it truly grows on trees."

"Grandmother, she makes her own money." Eric sat down on a stool and stared at the rough chairs before him. They still needed final sanding, staining and upholstering. If it really was seven o'clock, he was burning time talking to her. This conversation needed to end.

"I don't know how much money you can make peddling hair cream."

"Does the name Madam C.J. Walker mean anything to you?"

"Don't get smart with me, Eric."

"If memory serves, she was the country's first black woman millionaire. And she peddled hair cream just like Annetta."

"And your point is what?" Christine was tiring of this exercise, but didn't want to jump ahead too quickly.

"My point is that Annetta has fifteen locations, grandmother, and they all do very well. She sells a whole lot more than hair cream, by the way. You'd know that if you got to know her better. She's a great lady. I wouldn't be surprised if she made more than Uncle Clarence."

"It isn't polite to talk about what someone may or may not earn, Eric. It's downright distasteful, as a matter of fact."

"Aren't you the person who just, not two seconds ago, intimated that Annetta was a gold-digger, sucking her husband's bank account dry, and that she was showing off her wealth to her friends?" Eric asked. "Incredible."

"I haven't called you to listen to you lecture me about Annetta's income." Eric sighed more audibly than he should have. "And since it appears that I'm boring you, especially since you didn't have the common courtesy to at least call and tell me that you were going to be home, perhaps I should just let you get back to whatever it was that you were doing before I interrupted you."

That was a trap and Eric knew it. "Grandmother, I will come see you in the morning, if that pleases you. I'm sorry for not alerting you to my presence. By all means, though, tell Mary Ellen that I said hello."

"There's that tone again."

"Grandmother, if not Annetta and her riches, about what is it that you needed so painfully to speak to me?"

"Clearly it's not a good time for you."

"I'll make the time, grandmother. You've got me on the line. Just go ahead and spill whatever it is that's on your mind."

Chief of Staff

"Fine," she said, her voice hurt at Eric's uncaring. He knew it was a ploy and he just let her talk. "I... I..." she stammered, seemingly scared of what she was about to say. "I think I'm the target of an unscrupulous man."

"And why do you think that, grandmother?"

"Because he's threatening to do something horrible if I don't give him money." Eric did a double take and asked her to repeat herself. "I believe they call it being fleeced."

"Who's trying to fleece you?" His interest was piqued. It wasn't the first time someone had tried to scam Christine. She was an older, very wealthy woman and more than once, con men figured incorrectly that she would make an easy mark. The police quickly investigated her claims and usually caught the individual who was trying to scam her, all without her having to divulge too much, if any, information to Eric. This was the first time, though, that she had come right out and told him anything suspicious was going on.

"I don't think I can answer that question."

"You don't think you can answer that question, or you don't want to answer that question?"

"It's complicated, Eric." He could hear her welling up. She had the uncanny ability to produce tears out of thin air and he wondered if this was part of the trick or if she was actually serious.

"Tell me. It's okay. Do you know who the man is?"

"Yes. I think."

"Has he contacted you?"

"Yes. He has tried to call me several times already."

"Has he threatened you physically?"

"Heavens no."

"You said he was going to do something terrible. What does that mean? Have you called the police yet?"

Chief of Staff

"No, I haven't called the police. I called you first because I'm scared this time."

"Who is the man that's been calling you?" Eric got a piece of paper and a wood pencil from his drawer to write down whatever Christine was going to tell him.

"I think it might be," she said, her voice trailing off. "Cole."

"Cole, who?" Eric asked, amazed that she actually spoke his name out loud. He dropped the pencil and sat back down on the stool.

"Your father, Eric. Cole Julian. He wants money and I don't know what to do."

"My father is dead. You told me that yourself. Identity thieves are running rampant, grandmother. I think someone may just be playing a very nasty trick on you."

"What I believe I told you so many years ago was that your father was gone. That he may as well be dead to you. That isn't the same thing at all. When he called me, his voice flew all over me like it was yesterday. It was cold and sinister and unfeeling. I would swear on your grandfather's grave this is the truth. I'm very frightened, Eric. Help me, please."

Eric's heart was pounding in his throat and his back was beginning to ache from his rising anger. There were twelve ways to play this situation, but he had to get past his emotion first. His grandmother was not going to get away with this. How can she have so calmly told him that his father was not only alive, but trying to scam her out of money. "You told me he was dead."

"You were a child, Eric."

"You are my grandmother! You're supposed to tell me the truth!"

"Your mother had just died. Your father up and ran out on you, leaving you in my care. You were fragile. There were a lot of things you didn't know about that man, and I was determined to keep it that way. I was trying to protect you."

"From what?" Eric screamed.

"From the fact that Cole was a con artist from the day I first met him at your grandfather's bank. When your mother died, he took the life insurance money and ran. He abandoned you at the most vulnerable point in your young life. How was I to explain the reality of the situation other than to say what I did?" She was in full-blown tear mode now, sniffling into the phone for ultimate affect. She hadn't expected Eric to have this kind of reaction. She knew he would be confused and upset, but it sounded like he wanted to kill her for keeping the truth from him. "Please just calm down. Everything can be explained."

Eric shook his head and wondered what the hell was going on. "Don't tell me that. Don't just sit there and tell me that everything can be explained. My life, my entire life from the time my mother died has been a complete untruth! You have kept me in the dark and away from my father and for what? For what?!" Eric was yelling at the top of his lungs. He was incensed and he was determined that his grandmother would feel every bit of what he was going through. He had gotten up from his stool and was pacing the wood shop. He picked up a hammer and threw it against the wall. "I can't believe you'd do this to me!"

"Eric, please, you're scaring me." Christine's emotion was actually genuine. The one person in the world she never wanted to hurt was Eric. She had obviously miscalculated when it came to Cole. She never thought he'd come back, much less threatening her for money if he didn't get what he wanted. The secret she'd kept from Eric was more damaging than she expected it would have been. "I never meant to hurt you. You've got to believe me. I love you, Eric. I love you more than anything in the world. Please stop yelling at me. Please just listen to me and listen to what I'm telling you." Christine sobbed like a punished child, deeply moved by the furious rage of her grandson. "I never meant to have you live

Chief of Staff

a lie. I certainly never wanted to keep your father from you. I just didn't know what to do, what to tell you when he left. I didn't know how to explain the world and everything in it, the good and the bad, to you. I wanted to protect you from everything and everyone that would hurt you."

"You should have been protecting me from yourself! You're the one who hurt me. My father walked out on me and you didn't do anything to help me understand. All you did was tell me he was dead. Dead! All the times I asked you about him, asked you to take me to his grave or asked you how he died. And every fucking time, you lied right to my face. You lied to me to save yourself!"

"Eric, you will not speak to me with that tone. And you most certainly will not curse at me." She was shaking, half acting at the insistence that Cole had come back from the dead and half in an effort to get Eric's ire up to the point where he would do anything he could to find the man who had run out on him.

"I will speak to you any way I please," Eric growled.

"Stop it. Just stop it, Eric! This is uncivilized and I will not be party to it."

"The lies? The deception? The cover up? What?"

"I am going to hang up now, Eric." She started her crying all over again, trying to get Eric to soften up a little bit. "I refuse to be spoken to that way."

Eric throttled back and stopped ranting. His heart was still beating a mile a minute. The base of his neck had started to pound from the yelling and the extreme emotion. He took a deep breath and apologized to his grandmother for his outburst, but not for the betrayal he felt. "Listen, I've got to process this. It's all a little too much for me to handle right now. Can you understand that?"

"Of course, Eric," she said, unsure of what he was really thinking.

Chief of Staff

"I'm sorry for speaking to you like that. It's just that you caught me completely off guard. There's so much going through my brain right now and it's totally the wrong time for my father to return from the dead." He paused a moment waiting for her reaction or comment. Nothing. "I've got to find a way to finish these chairs for Annetta and deal with the fact that you've lied to me for some unknown reason. I don't believe how or why my long-dead father would be coming to you and blackmailing you into giving him money. But if it turns out it is him – God forgive you for what you've done, grandmother - I'll figure out how to deal with the situation."

"I'm sorry to have brought this to you, Eric, but I just didn't know what else to do. I didn't know where else to turn. He could be a very violent man. I don't know what he'll do if he doesn't get what he wants." Long-since dry-eyed, she was doodling on some scratch paper at her desk, clearly not the least bit put out by Cole's attempt to extort millions from her. She knew that Eric was the one person in the world who would protect her no matter what. He would do whatever it took to make sure that his grandmother was safe and secure. There had to be a way for her to get rid of Cole, and she knew that Eric might be her best chance. Christine had calculated everything right down to her teary confession about Cole living, and reasoned that her lying to Eric about the truth was worth the temporary price she would pay. Eric was loyal to a fault. Yes, he would probably be hurt at the truth, at not having his father with him as he grew up, but in her mind, it would be just as easy to spin him into her own reality. Cole would not be a problem for her for much longer.

"Grandmother, are you still there?"

"Yes, dear. I'm still here. I just don't know what to do."

"I promise I'll come by the house in the morning and we can talk more about this. I love you very much. No one is going to harm you one bit. Trust me. I'll to see to that."

Christine smiled devilishly. "You said that's he tried calling you? Is that right?"

"Yes, he called me a little bit ago."

"When?"

"I don't remember when. It was right after Jewel Box, I think. I can't be sure, Eric. All of this is making me somewhat ill. It may have even been before the party. I just don't know." She put a little extra emphasis on sounding weak and defeated.

"How much is he after? What figure did he give you?"

"He said he wanted fifty million or else."

"Holy shit! Did you just say fifty million dollars?"

"I did."

Granted, fifty million would be but a drop out of Christine's bucket, but what angered Eric most was that Cole somehow felt he was entitled to any of it. And for what? That had yet to be determined. "Listen to me, grandmother. The next time he calls you, I want you to let me know, do you understand me?"

"Of course. And I won't say anything to anyone. I'd never let him know that we've talked. Never. I don't want to put you into harm's way, Eric. I just don't know what else to do."

"Let me handle this, grandmother. I'll take care of everything."

"I knew you would be the best person to call. I love you so much."

"I love you, too, grandmother. Try and get some rest. I'll see you tomorrow." With that, Eric hung up and leaned over onto the work table. What the hell was that, he asked himself. At the same time, Christine hung up the phone and lit a cigarette. She wasn't sure what Eric was going to do, but she knew the wheels were turning in his head. Cole Julian wouldn't see a dime if Eric had anything to do with it. She took two drags, stamped out the cigarette and breezed to the kitchen and onto the next item on her agenda.

*****

ERIC pulled his cell phone out of his pocket as soon as he'd hung up with his grandmother.

"Dynex International. May I help you?"

"Reginald, please," Eric said.

"I'm sorry, but he is unavailable. May I take a message?"

"Please tell Reginald that the candidate is active."

"One moment, please. I'll connect you."

The phone clicked a couple of times and suddenly he was overcome with noise. "And what can I do for you?" Reginald boomed.

"It's after seven o'clock, Reginald. How long do you make that girl work?"

"Who?"

"The lady that answers your phone. The one with the sexy voice." Eric was bent over, looking at the underside of one of his chairs, inspecting it for flaws. "I mean, she sounds sexy. I'll bet she's smokin' hot, right?"

"Why thank you. I've been working out."

Eric stood up and looked at his phone. "You're a moron, Reginald. I was talking about your receptionist. What's her name? Is she single?"

"Reginald. And, no I'm not single." Reginald laughed and said, "That's me you hear on the phone. That's my voice. I'm the one that says, 'Dynex International.' I just got this new toy off the Internet. It's a voice reproducer. I take a random recording, like say somebody I taped walking down the street or that I was talking to, you know, having a normal conversation with, right? I take that recording,

Chief of Staff

convert the file on my computer, synch up the modulation and the intonation, put the sum of the parts through an analysis regenerative fragmentation processor using an algorithm I created…the one that comes with the voice reproducer was a bunch of crap. It didn't do nearly what I wanted it to. So, after the algorithm calculates the distance between the peaks and troughs in someone's voice, I'm able to digitally reproduce how they sound exactly, and I mean it's so good your mother wouldn't even know the difference."

Eric had put the phone down and picked up a piece of fine sandpaper. Reginald would be finished with whatever he was talking about in a minute.

"Eric? Are you still there? Are you listening to me?"

Eric picked the phone back up and said, "You are such a freakin' geek, Reginald."

"And you love me for it," Reginald said. You could hear him smiling through the phone.

"Listen, I need you to do something for me."

"Somebody messing with your senator?"

"No, nothing like that. It's my grandmother."

"Everything all right?"

"Not really. Somebody's trying to bilk her for some cash."

"How much?"

"That doesn't matter. The point is somebody's messing with my grandmother and I want them stopped. I want you to find out exactly who it is and what they're up to. Is that something you can handle for me?"

"Do you know who I am?" Reginald asked, chortling. "I'm the man, Eric. I can find out who took a crap in the Lincoln Bedroom of the White House at eight o'clock on a Tuesday four years ago. There isn't anything I can't find out. And especially for my most favorite client."

"You are also the man who, apparently, cannot find my father," Eric said calmly.

"Eric, there are some people who just don't want to be found. I told you that this guy's trail is stone cold. And it's been that way for about fifteen or twenty years. Cole Julian does not exist. If I ever find anything related to that man, trust me, you'll be the very first phone call I make."

"Good. Whatever. Back to my grandmother. Somebody's been calling her and trying to get her to pay up. Can you put somebody on her phone lines and whatever else it is you do?"

"Don't worry about the details. I'll take care of it," Reginald said. "What do you want me to do once I find out who this piece of shit is?"

"Once you find out who he is, I want you to put somebody on him. I want to know his movements, his favorite places to eat, his every habit, do you understand me?"

"This guy's got you up in arms, hasn't he?"

"You have no idea, Reginald. The one person you don't want to cross is my grandmother. I run a very close second."

"Understood. I'll start the process right away. I'll be in touch once I have some useful information for you. Oh, and my guy's almost got the encryption cracked on your flash drive."

"What the hell is a flash drive?"

"Boy, you are disconnected. It's the thing you sent me that you got out of the safe in your office. It's pretty rigidly protected. That's why it's taken this long to penetrate. I'll have something for you on it soon. And I'll find out who's messing with your grandmother. No worries."

"Thanks." Eric pushed a pile of sawdust with his finger, contemplating what he was going to say next. "Reginald?"

Chief of Staff

"Yeah? What?"

Eric closed his eyes and said, "Put somebody on my grandmother, too."

Reginald was silent for a moment. "And you're sure about that?"

"Do it before I change my mind. Something's going on with her and I'll be goddamed if I'm not going to find out what it is. Can you handle that?"

"Can I handle that? Do you know who I am?"

"Good-bye, Reginald," Eric said. What a night. Eric clicked the phone off, turned the stereo back on, and went back to work on Annetta's living room accent chairs for her new country house.

Chapter *23*

"GRANDMOTHER?" Eric walked in the front door of Dove's Nest bright and early that morning, keeping the promise he'd made the night before to visit his grandmother and appease her. He walked through the foyer to the living room, into the library and then into the kitchen. She was nowhere to be found. "Grandmother?" It was 9:30. Surely to God she was up and moving about.

"Master Eric, sir, good morning," Evan said as he rounded the corner. "I regret to inform you that despite your enthusiastic and indelicate warbling, she is not able to answer you."

Asshole. "Why not? What is she doing?"

"Mrs. Squire is not here." Christine's head butler greeted Eric with the half nod/half bow she had instructed him to perform in front of anyone with whom he came in contact.

"That's okay. I'll just wait for her and occupy my time until she gets back. How long do you think she's going to be gone?"

"If her itinerary is correct, and assuming she doesn't make any last minutes changes, she is scheduled to return Friday evening."

"Excuse me?"

"If her itinerary is correct, and assuming she doesn't make any," he repeated.

"No, no, I heard you the first time," Eric said, exasperated. "Are you telling me that she's out of town?"

"That is correct, Master Eric."

"And exactly when did she leave?"

"The car took her to the airport this morning around 7 a.m."

"You're kidding me!"

"I do not kid, sir."

"I told her that I would be coming by this morning to see her. I cannot believe that woman!" Evan looked as though he wanted to concur, but held his tongue. "Where is she going?"

"Let me see." He reached into his suit jacket pocket and produced a shiny iPhone. Perching his reading glasses just right on his nose, and extending his arm all the way out, he said, "Today, she will be going to her home in Marseilles. Wednesday morning, she travels from France to New York for a meeting with her attorney, Ms. Henderson. Thursday morning, she departs New York en route to the annual Alpha Kappa Alpha convention," he continued, stopping only to look over his glasses at Eric, "this year to be held in Denver, Colorado. She will give the keynote address and will return to Charlotte Friday evening, after a brief stop to check on some property she is interested in purchasing in Louisiana."

"That doesn't sound like a last minute trip."

"Certainly not, sir. I've been planning this over a period of two weeks." He put away his glasses and the phone and asked, "Is this the first you've heard of her recent travel plans? You seem a little out of sorts."

Eric grumbled that she had failed to mention any of that during their telephone conversation the night before. "I drove all the way up here and she's gone for the rest of the week. I am so irritated right now."

"Perhaps you would like me to connect you to the phone on the jet."

"No way," Eric said quickly, waving his hands. "I wasn't in the mood to deal with her this morning, and I'm certainly not going to deal with her now. Please just leave her a message that I came by."

Chief of Staff

"Of course, Master Eric. Shall I have her call you?"

"No." Eric started for the front door, consumed by his frustration with his grandmother.

"Good day then, sir," Evan cooed.

*****

IN the forty minutes it took Eric to get back to his house, he was amazed at the gall of his grandmother and it increasingly irritated him. He needed to get his mind going in another direction and decided the best thing to do would be to dive into work. Some vacation this was turning out to be. I'd rather be in Washington right now, he said to himself. At least Aunt Annetta's chairs were completed.

After a late breakfast, he grabbed the box of documents he'd brought with him and headed out to the back veranda and turned on the waterfall. That is the coolest thing ever, he said, like a teenager eyeing his father's fancy car or the latest electronic gadget. Eric sat the box on a table and began looking through it for something to catch his interest. As he leafed through the contents, he came upon the manuscript that Byrum had started writing.

"How did this get in here?" He must have slipped it into the box for some reason, maybe when he was researching his appearance on 'This Week'. "What the hell," he said, and pulled it out. Maybe a little mindless entertainment would be good right now. 'Betrayed', a novel by Charles Pinckney Byrum. Who in their right mind would name their child that? Eric imagined an old elementary school picture of Byrum, dressed in tights and those stupid knee-length pants, maybe wearing a funny hat and holding a swirled lollipop. He laughed out loud as he turned the first page.

Eric had always made a point of never skipping to the end of a book. It ruined the surprise, he told his mother once. What fun was there in that? He even went so far as to ignore the write up on the back covers, too. Byrum's manuscript was temporarily bound and, thankfully, there was no description of its contents. Stupid title. Hope it gets better on the inside.

He'd learned to quickly read and absorb material on the fly from his days pushing candidates. Eric breezed through the first 150 pages of the manuscript before he just couldn't take it anymore. The gist of the story was that some rich, mean old man had conspired to sell a bunch of land in the presumably fictional town of Cooperville. His daughter's husband died suddenly, which set off a mad grab for his company and all of its assets. It seemed like Byrum was trying to develop the story along a murder/blackmail plotline, but there wasn't a lot connecting the characters. He couldn't tell if Byrum intended for the old man to be a hero or a villain. The margins were dotted with Byrum's chicken-scratched secret codes, and Eric figured he was still tweaking the story. It certainly needed a lot more work.

"Well, there goes forty minutes I'll never get back," Eric said, giving up and laying the manuscript down on the divan. He sat back and closed his eyes, listening to the sounds of the waterfall, and drifted off to sleep.

Chapter *24*

"THE Prodigal Heathen returns," was Claudia's greeting as Eric walked back into the office Monday morning.

"It's lovely to see you, too, Bride of Blackula," Eric said as he walked past her desk and plopped down in his chair. Claudia followed close behind. "What happened with Lamprey and his press conference? Anything I need to do or did the senator take care of everything?"

"No, the senator's got it pretty well wrapped up."

"Where is he, by the way?" Eric checked his calendar to make sure their meeting was still on the schedule. Under the entry for his briefing with Senator Tanner was his 9:00 interview with Black Enterprise Magazine. He was particularly looking forward to the interview for several reasons. Eric had been profiled in Black Enterprise before, but this was a chance for him to show another side of himself to the readers. It wasn't about running his consulting firm, but his foray into politics as a player. The anxiety that had made it difficult to sleep the night before, had been transformed into a sense of urgency and extreme anticipation. Eric wanted everything to go smoothly. "I need to go over a couple of things with the senator before my day gets away from me."

"He went to the doctor."

Eric looked up wide-eyed. Only rarely had Senator Tanner ever gone to the doctor. He was scared to death they might tell him something he didn't want to hear. "Are you kidding me?" Claudia shrugged her shoulders. "That must be one hell of a cold he's got."

"Not sure what's wrong with him. He didn't look well at all after you left. Maybe he got worn down over this issue with Lamprey. I had to practically threaten him with a fate worse than death to get him to even agree to let me make the appointment for him."

Chief of Staff

"A fate worse than death? You know he'd never kiss you."

"Jerk. I'm sure that if he needs you to do something connected to Lamprey, he'll let you know."

"Keep me abreast of anything you hear, okay?" Eric was fishing through his briefcase for a file when he pulled out the manuscript and frowned.

"What was that for?" Claudia asked, and reached for the manuscript.

"Don't do that," Eric cautioned. "I don't know how Byrum ever got published in the first place. That is pure drivel."

"So you've read 'The Antihero', have you?"

"I don't think so. If it's as bad as that piece of crap, Byrum should have paid people to read it, not collect a huge advance and royalties. He was a horrible writer."

"What's this? 'Betrayed'? Never heard of this. Did Byrum write this?" Claudia flipped through and recognized the handwriting in the margins. "Where did you find this?"

"It was in the safe." Eric continued to look through his briefcase, not looking up at Claudia when he answered her question.

"You said there wasn't anything in that safe." She playfully tapped her fingernails on the end of Eric's desk and smiled. "Sneaky little critter, aren't you?"

"Well, I wish I'd never found it. In about forty-five minutes, I came to realize that any idiot with connections can get a book deal. I read the first part of it and put it down, bored and hating the literary world."

"What's wrong with it?" Claudia immediately flipped to the last few pages and started reading.

"What are you doing?"

"Reading."

"From the end?" Nails on a chalkboard.

"You read your way, I'll read mine. What's so bad about this? He seemed to be a very popular writer. Granted, he only had one novel, but sold it very well. People were always calling asking to speak with him about it."

"They were probably trying to get a refund. Ah ha!" Eric said, retrieving the file and grabbing his cell phone. "I don't even know where to start. The characters were totally unbelievable, the plot was trivial, the end of the first section, where I think he was trying to introduce some kind of murder and blackmail idea was stupid, and nothing tied together. Add that to the task of trying to decipher his dumb-ass coding and notes in the margin, and you'll understand the concept behind book burning parties."

"Harsh. Mind if I read it?"

"Suit yourself," he said. "But don't say I didn't warn you." He dialed a number on his cell and looked at Claudia as if to say, 'can't you see I'm on the phone?'

She rolled her eyes and got up. "I was going to say it's good to have you back."

"The day's not over yet. Close the door on your way out, please." The phone only rang once before Eric was connected to Reginald's voice mail. He didn't leave a message, figuring it would be best to try him back later. He still hadn't heard anything about the little device Reginald's NSA man was in charge of cracking and he was getting more and more curious.

Reluctantly, Eric went about the business of getting caught up on the emails and paperwork he'd ignored while he was in Charlotte. A quick thought about why Senator Tanner had actually agreed to go to the doctor, and he dove right into his day. He shivered when he thought about Claudia and the senator kissing. Total visual grenade.

*****

Chief of Staff

CLAUDIA walked into Eric's office to let him know that his interviewer from Black Enterprise had arrived.

"What happened to your using the intercom?" Eric asked, as he walked to his armoire to check himself out in the mirror.

"So that's why you wore your pink shirt today," Claudia said. "You knew the reporter they were sending was a pretty woman, right?"

"I can't help whom they send to interview me, Claudia. And, frankly, I'm offended at the suggestion." Eric turned and smiled at Claudia. "I wear this shirt on occasion when I have something important to do. It's my Lucky Shirt."

"I don't seem to recall you wearing your Lucky Shirt," she said with air quotations, "for your little television debut," again with air quotations.

"Poof. Be gone. Send in whomever it is, please." Eric sat back down behind his desk and tried to make it look like he was working, half anticipating the interview to come, and half to impress whomever they were sending to speak with him.

"Good morning, Eric. It's been a long, long time." Eric looked up and was completely in shock. "Wow, I haven't had that kind of response in quite a while. May I come in?"

Eric bolted up from his seat, almost too quickly, which unnerved him, and greeted his guest. "My, this is a genuine surprise. Kathryn Greenich. Black Enterprise sent Kathryn Greenich to interview me." Eric was still standing behind his desk, processing the woman he was staring at. His mind was filled with memories and the awkwardness he had as a young man.

"Shall we conduct this interview in the doorway?" Kathryn joked.

Claudia led her to the sofa and asked if she would like anything. Kathryn politely said no, and Claudia backed out of the room, mouthing to Eric, 'don't be a moron. Talk to her!'

Eric snapped out of his dream world and joined Kathryn on the sofa, shaking her hand as he sat down. "I have to say it's absolutely wonderful to see you, Kathryn, but I'm a tiny bit surprised to see you. I mean, not that it's a bad thing that you're here. Because it wouldn't be a bad thing. And it isn't a bad thing. It's just that I'm surprised to see you. Here. In my office. Wanting to talk to me. That's all. I didn't mean anything by what I said earlier about it being a bad thing that you're here. You know." Just like a tongue-tied teenager, Eric was mesmerized by Kathryn all the more as an adult. As usual, once he saw her, his mouth took over ignoring the 'DON'T TALK' signals his brain repeatedly sent out. Not two minutes into the interview and he was already making a fool out of himself.

Kathryn blushed slightly at Eric's fumbling. She had always found him to be attractive, but was wary of him when they were younger. Kathryn and Eric were in the same Jack & Jill group in Charlotte. Her father was a state Supreme Court judge and they ran in the same social circles. Kathryn was still gorgeous, even more so now that she was a woman. Light brown skin, hazel/green eyes, pouty lips and long black hair. Her face was slender, like her frame, but Eric could tell she was all grown up under her sleek business suit. Unconsciously, he scanned her from head to toe and marveled at her. Everything about her was classy, something she learned from her mother, and she took every advantage and used every trick she'd gotten from her mother as she sat on Eric's office sofa that morning.

For the entirety of his association with Jack & Jill, and beyond into the beginnings of his college days, Kathryn Greenich was the be all and end all as far as Eric was concerned. They flirted casually, but Eric was a seriously late bloomer, having zero confidence where girls and women were concerned. Oh, he could talk the ear off of anyone, charming and smiling as he went. But there was something scary about closing the deal; actually asking a girl out on a date was the most frightening thing he would have done as a teenager. It wasn't the rejection that made his mind go crazy. It was what he would do if one of them said yes that drove him insane. He'd have to kiss her and hold hands and do things that boyfriends do. Without a father to talk to, he didn't feel comfortable even broaching the subject. Yes, Senator Tanner talked to him a lot about girls and he got him to the point where talking to them was fun, and maybe even a little challenging.

But Senator Tanner wasn't exactly the model for how to treat a woman, especially for a teenager, love struck and chock full of raging hormones. They had the 'sex talk' a couple of times, Senator Tanner had supplied him with boxes of condoms and gave him advice on the best ways to, how do you say, pleasure himself, a conversation that will haunt Eric for the rest of his natural life. What Senator Tanner didn't tell, and what Eric didn't know to ask, was how do you have a relationship with a girl. How do you get comfortable enough to say something as dreadful as I Love You? To an introverted teen like Eric, that was the kiss of death. Many nights he'd dreamt of kissing Kathryn in some romantic setting, and then immediately exploding from embarrassment.

Jack & Jill parties, school dances, cotillions, and the like passed without Eric ever having the guts to ask Kathryn to accompany him to the events. For a time, Kathryn thought of Eric as cute and sweet, but because he always freaked out and walked away from her, she figured he didn't like her the way she liked him. Their friendship fizzled and their romance dissolved before it had the chance to ever really get started. Kathryn represented the one that got away for Eric. He learned a lot about girls and relationships in college, losing his virginity at the ripe old age of nineteen. But by then it was too late. Kathryn, he mused, had moved on with her life and he was but a distant memory of her past.

"You're doing that staring thing you used to do when we were kids, Eric." She smiled, but all Eric saw was the way her sexy mouth moved when she spoke. He hadn't heard a word she'd just said. "I said you're doing that staring thing, Eric." She reached out and touched his leg. "Earth to Eric?"

Pull yourself together, man! "Sorry. Sorry about that Kathryn. I was thinking about a proposal that's coming to the floor tomorrow morning. I didn't mean to get so lost." Always one for a quick lie, he hoped that worked. "God, it's wonderful to see you again. I've followed your career for the last five or ten years and you have been doing some great things."

"So you're a chief of staff and a stalker?" she asked, her perfect teeth brightening her smile.

His face dropped. "Uh, when I said that I've been following your career..."

"I'm joking with you. It's flattering that you've kept up with me, even though it was from a distance." Now she was doing it. This was all about business. At least that's what she was trying to tell herself over and over. When Kathryn saw the assignment on the Projects Board, she jumped at the chance. It had been more than five years since she'd interviewed anyone, but she wasn't going to let this chance pass her by. Not again.

"Why would Black Enterprise send out one of their contributing editors to interview me?" he asked. "I thought at the very least they would send out a rookie; at best a seasoned reporter. I certainly don't rank up there for a contributing editor."

"So you're saying I'm not good enough for you?" Kathryn raised an eyebrow and bent over to retrieve her briefcase.

"No, no, no! I'm not saying that at all." Eric saw the smile on her face and said, "Got me again, didn't you?" Kathryn shrugged her shoulders and sat up.

Chief of Staff

"When I saw this assignment on the board, I jumped at the chance. You've been in the magazine before, what with your consulting firm, of course, but this was a little different angle. I had wanted to get my feet wet again, to see if I could still write, and this was the best of both worlds. I'd get to see you and I'd get to put everything I have behind making this the best article we've showcased in quite some time. I hope you don't mind."

What Eric wanted to say was, are you crazy? I'd clear this coffee table and take you right here and now, you hot-ass, gorgeous, intelligent woman. I'd show you everything I learned in college and beyond. I'd make you do things you'd only read about in Karma Sutra books. I'd put my hand on the back of your neck and in the small of your back, pulling you toward me as I kissed you slowly and passionately and deeply until your knees quivered beneath you. I want you so bad I can't stand it. I'm not letting you out of my sight. Ever. "Of course I don't mind. This has already started out to be a wonderful day. And I'll do whatever I can to make it a great interview for you."

Claudia had left the intercom channel open on her phone to listen to the interview. She was sitting at her desk with her finger in her throat, pretending to make herself vomit.

"Great. I was a little nervous about showing up today. What do you say we get started?"

"Lead the way."

Chapter *25*

"THE readers of Black Enterprise are very interested in rags-to-riches stories," Kathryn began. Her tone was very professional and you could tell that she was concentrating on making this worthwhile and legitimate. "As our readers may know, however, yours is not such a tale. In fact the story of your life begins with your being born into a fabulously wealthy and privileged family in Charlotte, North Carolina. What triggered your desire to run in the political circles as opposed to joining your family business?"

"Wow, that's a great question, Kathryn. I would have to say that my late mother was the main driver in my forging my own path, seeking out that which made me happy and that which truly challenged me to give my best. I'd always told her that there was something about politics that intrigued me."

"And that must have been amazing in itself, because your mother passed away when you were young," Kathryn chimed in. She adjusted the recorder on the coffee table, angling it a little more toward Eric. When she leaned over, her shirt opened just enough to expose the most fabulous breasts, cradled in a soft lime green bra. Oh my. Concentrate! She was taking notes at the same time, but Eric couldn't see what she was writing.

"Yes. I was eight years old when she died."

"So it must have been deep within you, your love of politics."

"I don't know how to explain it, to be truthful. There is a complexity, a dance of sorts, to the world of politics. It was a realm in which I was totally comfortable. I learned every aspect and nuance that I could absorb as a child. I remember once," Eric laughed, "I even begged my parents to take me to the Republican National Convention so I could see the process up close and personal."

"And did they?"

Chief of Staff

"No," Eric laughed again, maybe a little too much, he thought. "I didn't have the opportunity to attend a convention until some time later."

"I understand that while you were in college, you ran the campaigns of classmates. Is that correct? How did that start?" Kathryn scribbled something and looked up at Eric who was, by all admission, staring at her.

"My first job, if you could call it that, actually came in high school, so it was a little before college. I was honing my skills. Never one to seek out political office, I thought the mystery and the art of the game lay in getting people elected. I actually had to campaign myself, in a way, to talk my first candidate into representing him and doing whatever I could to make sure that he won the election."

"And do you remember his name?"

"Absolutely! His name is Mitchell Goosmon. We still keep in touch. That's a picture of us over there on my shelf. We were celebrating his win as freshman class president at Andover."

Eric had gotten up, grabbed the picture and brought it back to Kathryn on the sofa. "This is the same Mitchell Goosmon who is currently the Lt. Governor of South Dakota?"

"The very same. Great guy."

Kathryn asked to use the picture for the magazine and Eric said yes, of course. "And from that point onward, you made it your business to get people into office?"

"That was my focus one hundred per cent. Not everyone I represented won, mind you. There were some extremely important learning experiences I had to have, sometimes at the expense of a candidate, but they brought me to where I am today."

"Before we jump ahead to your current role as chief of staff for Senator Scott Tanner, tell me, rather, tell our readers a little bit more about yourself. For example, how were you able to effortlessly run your consulting firm, travel the country, and do the myriad of tasks necessary to do what you do and keep up a family life. It must be quite the juggling act."

Leading question. Slow soft pitch. Whatever you want to call it, this was his in. "Oh, Kathryn, there's no way I could have accomplished any of my success and been able to hold down a relationship. I didn't have that ability back then. That's why I tremendously admire people like Jack Cyber and Samuel Boulevard, Bob Johnson and Magic Johnson, the list is one too long to recite. Those men are business titans and still, with little exception, they have found a way to intermingle their personal and business lives very well."

"Which means that you're single, divorced, what?"

"Single and looking. How about that?" Kathryn gave no visible sign that that was the answer she was looking for and that made Eric nervous. And a little mad. Was he playing into her request to interview him knowing their past? Or was he simply reading too much into the situation. Again, she scribbled something down that Eric couldn't read.

"So, we've got a general understanding of your family background. We know what drove you to the world of politics. Through your past interviews, which I plan to weave into this piece," Kathryn said, following some kind of outline she'd created, "we know the basics. Tell us about what propelled you to take this job and how you think you've done so far."

Senator Tanner walked into Eric's office from their adjoining side door and immediately apologized for the interruption. "Damn. I didn't know you had company."

Kathryn turned off the recorder and stood to greet the senator. "Good morning, sir. My name is Kathryn Greenich with Black Enterprise. It's a pleasure to meet you."

"Kathryn Greenich? Kathryn Greenich," the senator repeated. Eric was standing behind Kathryn slashing his throat and giving the shut up sign so only the senator could

Chief of Staff

see. This was about to get ugly. "Kathryn Greenich. I know you!" he said, clapping his hands together. He'd ignored Eric's pleas to stay silent. "You're the girl that Eric used to call me and run on at the mouth about. You certainly are a pretty girl. He was right about that." Eric closed his eyes and tried to wish himself to a distant, deserted island, trying to find his happy place.

Kathryn turned around and poked Eric in the shoulder, causing him to open his eyes and actually look at her. "Is that right?"

The senator walked to Eric's desk and pretended he was looking for something. "I can't tell you what kind of crush he had on you, young lady. I swear you must have been the hottest thing on the planet. I knew every fourth Sunday where he'd been. He'd call me from the car on the way back from a Jack & Jill meeting or a function." The senator took a blank piece of paper and folded it so neither of them could see what he had in his hand. "Scott, he used to call me back then. Scott, he'd say, she just looked so lovely today. So lovely. Why he never asked you out, I'll never know." Kathryn blushed further and Eric was still desperately trying to mentally escape. "It's probably too late now, right?" The senator walked to his door and said, "Pretty girl like you? Probably married or at least seeing someone. Right?" He looked directly at Kathryn, no hint of a smile at all.

"Well, no, actually," she started. "I'm not married."

"Seeing anyone?" Eric was in hell.

"No."

"Are you a lesbian?"

"Senator!" Eric shouted. "Go away."

Senator Tanner held up his hands in defeat and closed the door behind him. He died laughing and didn't make any effort to hide his delight.

Eric motioned for Kathryn to sit back down and apologized for the senator's behavior.

Chief of Staff

"That's okay," she said. "He's an interesting person. I can see why you like working with him." She reached over and turned the recorder back on, revealing those fabulous breasts again, and continued the interview.

For the next hour and a half, Eric Julian and Kathryn Greenich talked about everything the readers of Black Enterprise would be interested in. From his love of campaigning to his first victory with the Immigration bill, how making furniture helps him relax and even a little bit about his grandmother, they left no stone unturned. Along the way, they tried to contain themselves, but what with Senator Tanner's manufactured intrusion and his liberal retelling of Eric's childhood obsession with his interviewer, they both casually flirted back and forth with the other. The interview was all business, but there was an undercurrent of sexual tension and of discovery that neither had the strength to ignore.

When Kathryn clicked off her recorder for the last time, she thanked Eric for letting her take up so much of his time. They exchanged pleasantries and Eric walked her out. Kathryn turned to him as they were standing in the hall and gave him her card. On the back she had written: "Call me. Soon."

Eric and Kathryn shook hands and she walked away. He stared at her until she was absorbed by the other people on the floor and he could no longer see her. That was the perfect way to start the day. After seeing her again, nothing could go wrong.

Chapter *26*

ERIC popped back into the office and sat down in the chair next to Claudia's desk. She was reading the manuscript and put her hand in the air. "Wait just one second," she said slowly. Closing the manuscript, she turned to Eric and said, "What is it that you need?"

"We're going to lunch."

"When?"

"Today. Now."

"Is that right?"

"Yes."

"What did that pretty little reporter do to you in there?" Claudia asked. "You're in too good of a mood to have just given an interview."

"She's an old friend. That's all."

"Fine. If it isn't her fault, then what have I done wrong?"

Eric smiled. "Nothing. It's another part of my new kinder, gentler boss persona ideas I came up with on the George Washington that I'm implementing. I've got to get to know these people on a better level."

"These people?" Claudia asked, with that eyebrow arched. "Why not say something like peons, or maybe the help?"

"So," Eric ignored her, "I've decided to take everyone in the office to lunch, one on one. You're the first person on my list."

"I'm so overjoyed I might burst." She produced a tiny soft, pink cooler from under her desk and said, "Thanks so much for the offer, COS, but as you can see I brought my lunch today."

"Eat it tomorrow. I'm getting my jacket. We've got reservations at Lola's in fifteen minutes."

"Should I feel nauseous right now?"

In a flash, they were out the door and headed to one of Eric's favorite restaurants. He swore Lola's had the best soul food menu in Washington and he went there often enough to be on a first-name basis with just about everyone from the cooks to the hostesses. They were seated, ordered their lunch and Eric started the conversation.

"I'm actually nervous about this for some reason," Eric said, rearranging his silverware and unfolding his napkin. If this was going to be a good way to get to know his staff, Claudia was the best guinea pig he could have chosen. She was extremely direct and open, and whatever feedback he got would be useful. "So, Claudia," he began, "tell me about yourself."

"I'd rather not."

"Okay, then I'll start." Eric cleared his throat and started the getting to you know soliloquy he'd rehearsed. "I was born and raised in Charlotte."

Claudia stopped him abruptly. "I know everything there is to know about you that has ever been published, Eric."

"You're not making this very easy, you know. I'm trying to do something good and you keep shooting me down." This wasn't starting out so well.

She looked at Eric and sighed deeply, wishing she were sitting in the senate cafeteria with the other staff members, gossiping about somebody, anybody, rather than enduring this trumped up intelligence gathering joke Eric was passing off as good will. "You were born in Charlotte. Your mother died of breast cancer when you were eight years old. You went to Andover, Fisk and Hampton, and you have degrees in public policy and law. You owned a political consulting firm before you were surprisingly offered the position of chief of staff for Senator Tanner."

"Go on." Eric was intrigued and slightly caught off guard, but wanted to see how much she really knew about him.

"Your favorite color is blue. Not regular blue or light blue, but Duke Blue. You think mushrooms taste like dirt, and they do. You summered in Sag Harbor with your grandmother and other family members from the time you were little and return there on occasion. You cannot swim. You think that NAFTA was one of the worst mistakes in the history of free trade. You regularly returned to Charlotte when you were based out of D.C. to indulge in your passions for making furniture and to play golf. You need some serious help with your slice, which you lazily refer to as a draw, which it is not. You wear a size 13 narrow shoe, preferably Nike and anything Italian. Your grandmother has sheltered you your entire life and, in rebelling from that, you forged a semi-independence that you camouflage as confidence. Would you like me to continue?"

Eric was aghast. "How do you know all of that about me?"

"I read most of it over time. It's not like you and your family hasn't been splashed all over God and country in JET and Ebony and Black Enterprise and People Magazine."

"But how did you remember all of that?"

"There's more where that came from," Claudia said, nonchalantly. The waiter delivered their food and left them alone again. "Right now I'd rather eat my lunch than delve into the educational problems you've tried to keep hidden."

"Again," Eric asked, insistent on knowing her secret, "how do you know all of that?"

Claudia put her fork down and folded her arms. "Because I'm a genius."

"No, really."

Chief of Staff

"Really. My IQ, which I've had tested more than the normal person, is 147 – only 2% of the population have IQ's of 130 or higher. I have a partial photographic memory, which I use when it suits me. And since I know that you're going to ask, I'll tell you." This was certainly more than either one of them had bargained for, but what the hell, right? He might as well know at some point. "I was born outside Alpharetta, Georgia. I graduated from primary and high school early. At sixteen, I was the youngest person enrolled in Spelman College. I graduated in three years with a double major in Statistical Comparative Theory and Psycholinguistics. I taught at Spelman for two years before accepting a professorship at M.I.T. when I was twenty-three."

"You're kidding me."

Claudia shook her head no and continued. Eric dug into his pork chops and greens, staring at her while she spoke. "I left M.I.T. over a dispute with my mentor after a wonderful twelve-year career. I was fed up with his overtures and I had simply burned out on teaching. I needed to take a leave of absence. Had I done so, I was curtly advised, I would be forever blackballed from the university and he would see that my name was sullied at every college, university or trade school from coast to coast."

"Why would you just leave your professorship without putting up a fight?"

"I did fight, but nobody believed me. Let's just say that he was trying to take credit for my achievements and leave it at that."

"So ordered."

Claudia took a rather large bite of her meatloaf, and chewed it thoroughly, waiting an inordinate amount of time before continuing. "I came to Washington after my father died and got a job as a secretary working for Senator Tanner and Charles Byrum three years ago. And it is here where I remain to this day."

"So that would make you, what, a thirty-eight year old, over-educated, underachieving, sexually frustrated, bitter, evil genius, Russian, lesbian, African-American administrative assistant with a partial photographic memory?"

"You're a real clod, you know that?"

"That was a joke." His initial getting to you know you lunch wasn't working out how he planned.

"I mean it, Eric," Claudia said, pushing her plate away. "Sometimes you can be a complete and total asshole. God forgive me."

Why is this happening to me, Eric thought. I was trying to do something nice for her and I can't win for losing. "You've been busting my balls since day one. What in the world did I do to you?" He pushed his plate away, as well, ready for the ensuing argument.

"I don't want to talk about it."

"You don't have that option, Claudia. I want to know what it is that I've done to you that put me in the dog house."

"You took my job, that's what you did."

"What are you talking about? You're a secretary. How could I have taken your job?"

"Do you know who ran the office while you were on your little mental health sabbatical last week? I did. Do you know who ran the office after Byrum died? I did. Do you know who controls every aspect of what goes on in that office day in and day out?"

"Wait, I know this one," Eric said. His eyes were shut tightly like he was trying to concentrate on the best answer. "Uh, you do. Right?"

"Right. I was in charge before you got here and I'll be in charge after you leave."

"And what makes you think I'm going somewhere?" Eric pulled his plate back and started eating again. "Hope you don't mind, but my chops are getting cold."

Chief of Staff

"Forgive me, Lord, for what I'm about to do." Claudia at first hung her head and then looked at Eric with a seething hatred. "You think you've got it so easy, don't you? I've worked my entire life for the successes that I've attained, but you can just waltz in and take over at the drop of a hat."

"What makes you think I haven't had to work just as hard as you have to get where I am today? You think I just pulled my consulting firm out of my ass?"

"You people don't have to work at anything. Not like us black folks do. Everything you've gotten has literally been handed to you."

"You people? Christ, Claudia, who do you think you're talking to?"

"I know exactly who I'm talking to."

"You do?" Eric asked, leaning forward, head tilted. "This should be interesting."

"I've had to deal with smug assholes like you my entire life."

"Now I'm a smug asshole. Nice."

"Light is Right. My mother always told me that, but it took a long time before I realized what she was talking about." Claudia leaned in toward Eric. "Just because you're a house nigger doesn't make you any more worthy than me for the things you have. I've worked just as hard and just as long as you."

"Correct me if I'm wrong, but you're a secretary by choice. You and your mega brain could get a job doing anything, anywhere in the world. But you've chosen," Eric emphasized, "to lord over a senator and a chief of staff for three years. That's not my problem. And don't you ever call me a house nigger again."

"You get in where you fit in, COS," Claudia said. "When Byrum died, I just knew that Senator Tanner was going to make me his chief of staff. I had the job down cold. I knew everything there was to know about everything."

"Your fight is with the senator, Claudia. It's not with me."

"It most certainly is with you."

"Oh hell no, it's not."

"Since I was a little girl, a dark-skinned little rich girl growing up in Alpharetta, me and my family have always been treated like dirt by people like you."

"So we're back to that. I need a goddam map to keep up with you sometimes."

"It's all the same thing, Eric. What's worse is the fact that you either don't recognize the differences or you don't care to acknowledge them."

"I'm not like every other person in my position, Claudia. I recognize there's a separation in the black community between people with money and people without."

"That's not the point at all." Claudia was raising her voice and stopped to catch her breath and quiet down. "That's not the point at all," she said more quietly. "It's not the money. My father, Lawrence Eldridge, was the CEO of Progretta Foods, Eric. I was born with all the trappings and luxuries of wealth and privilege that you were. My family still controls that company and we are still richer than ninety per cent of the population of this country. For years, I was maligned by girls I tried to befriend because they said I was too dark. I missed out on opportunities like Jack and Jill and cotillions because I wasn't light enough."

"Again, that's not my fault."

"You know what? You know what I did, how far I had sunk?" She looked at the man sitting next to them who was shamelessly eavesdropping on their conversation and gave him the evil eye. He turned around and she looked back at Eric. "I wanted so badly to be accepted by the light blacks, the ones I saw who had all the chances and fun in life so I went to a beauty supply store. I bought a case of skin lightening cream and sat in my bathtub, covered in that stuff for hours. I did it every day for a week and nothing happened. I was still as black as I was when I started. Nothing changed for me." Claudia had started crying softly, tears rolling down her cheeks.

"So that's what this is about?" Eric said. "You've got to be kidding me."

"I'm not kidding one bit, Eric. I earned that job. When Byrum was killed in that crash, I had every reason to believe that I was next in line. I ran that office when both of them were gone, and I did a damn fine job of it, if I might say so myself."

"You forgot to save God forgive me for my language."

"And then there's that."

"There's what?"

"That attitude you ooze. You think you're so smart, so funny, so everything. You and everybody else just like you have got this superiority complex that I wish you would choke on."

"Everybody just like me?"

"Rich, bourgeoisie blacks."

"So now I'm the anti-Christ because I'm rich? Give me a break. People like you have no idea what I go through every day." Eric was fuming at the inference that he was somehow above everyone else.

"People like me? And what does that mean?" Claudia was trying not to raise her voice again, but containing her anger was trying.

"I don't want to even go there with you."

"Too late," Claudia said through gritted teeth.

Chief of Staff

Eric measured his words carefully before he spoke. "This is not the time or the place to have this discussion, Claudia."

"No, sir. You brought me here for this contrived little meeting to deepen your understanding of me and everybody else under your thumb. You asked the question and you're going to get the answer, whether you want to hear it or not."

"Whatever," Eric said.

"You are sitting in my chair in my office, telling my people what to do, and getting chummy with my senator." She looked at the blank expression on Eric's face and pointed at him. "That. That right there is the face you make when you know I've said something that's right on the money."

"I make this face all the time when I'm listening to a bunch of crap."

Claudia leaned forward and said, "Your entire existence has been predicated on judging people, black people, based on the color of their skin. Light is Right."

"Preposterous."

"Is it? You live in a world where you socialize, lift up, and benefit your own. You profit off of the backs of real black people, whether you know it or believe it. It is an insular, deranged and disgusting display of bigotry and self-loathing. It's not enough to just be rich. You have to throw your light skin, your good hair, your fancy colleges and your exclusive clubs in everybody's face. Bougie and privileged and sickening."

"You think I got this job because of all of that?" Eric had raised his voice and looked around to see if anyone was eavesdropping. "I got this job because I'm good at what I do."

"And bougie and privileged and light-skinned. It never fails. Fisk and Hampton may have educated you, but you've been stuck up since the day you were born."

Chief of Staff

"You went to Spelman. That's as bougie as it gets."

"And it was at Spelman where I truly realized how different I was; how different I am. It wasn't enough to be ignored and talked about because I was too dark. No, they had to take it further." Claudia was furious that Eric hadn't made the connection. "I've been rich my entire life. I was born with a platinum spoon in my mouth. I have everything you and your family have, with the exception of being included in your little club."

"What's your point?"

"You don't know what it's like being rich and black."

"Uh, excuse me? I'm most certainly tuned into that."

"I'm not talking about how white people perceive you. I'm talking about how black people look at you. They see your skin and your hair, your fancy suits and the parties your grandmother has at her estate. It's all over everything, Eric, and if you can't see that passing the brown paper bag test still gets you on the inside, you're deluding yourself. You are the worst kind of Uncle Tom. Yassa, boss man. What can I do for yuh, boss man? Is yuh hungry, boss? Oh thanks you so much fuh lettin' me come on the inside, boss. You don't give a damn about black people."

"How the hell did you go from lambasting me about my job to telling me that I'm a bigot? I got this job because Senator Tanner knew I would be great. He wants me to follow in his footsteps and take over his seat when he retires. I've known the man my entire life. He was, simply put, the father I never really had." Eric looked around again and lowered his voice. "It is despicable for you to say that I got this job because I'm rich and light."

"I'm rich and black and I'm just a secretary."

"You are choosing to be a secretary," Eric said loudly. "You can't use that argument."

"You still don't understand."

"I have no clue where this is coming from, Claudia. But I'm beginning to see why you hate my guts."

"I don't hate your guts, Eric. I hate what you represent."

Eric covered his face with his hands and exhaled deeply. "Claudia," he began, "I will not defend my life to you. I cannot help who I am. I only know how to be me and that's it. You think I'm obtuse and that I can't understand where you're coming from, but you're wrong. You're dead wrong. I'm not going to explain anything to you as your boss. But I'll clue you into what I go through every day as your friend." Claudia was very angry, and the frustration she had been keeping to herself was flowing freely. It scared her to be so honest with Eric.

"There isn't a single part of me that doesn't identify completely with what it means to be a black man in this country today. Yes, I am very wealthy and for the most part the money I have, I didn't have to work a day to get. We could both sit back for the rest of our lives and live off of our families' wealth. It doesn't matter to anybody that we're rich. The only thing that matters to many people, a number of whom are right here in D.C., is the fact that we're black. It doesn't matter how much money we have, how successful we become or what we do to help our communities, Claudia. We're always going to just be black. Do you think because I'm light that I get any less eyeballing when I walk into fancy stores or walk down the street in my custom-made suits? Do you think people don't do a double take when I'm cruising around town in a Ferrari or Porsche? I get all of it. I get what it's like to be oppressed and made to feel like a piece of shit. No matter my background, I took full advantage of my education so I could step out into this lopsided world, earn my respect and make a difference.

"I use my money and influence to do whatever I want to, taking great pride in pushing racism back in the faces of people who hate me for being black. I'm not a registered Republican because I identify one hundred per cent with their ideology and platforms. I chose to represent the party to smack the faces of assholes everywhere who try to categorize me and pigeon-hole me based on the color of my skin, not my competency. I made it my life's work so far to achieve things that my ancestors couldn't imagine. I am the puppeteer, making people do what I want because they think it's in their best interest. I move mountains to put people into office where they had absolutely no fucking chance and absolutely no fucking business in the first place because I can."

"And how many of those people look like me, Eric? How many of them were people of color? How many of them were women?"

"A handful, probably," Eric said quietly.

Claudia shook her head and looked around. "It's no coincidence that you brought me to a soul food restaurant in the middle of D.C. that's packed with white people. I can count, what, maybe fifteen blacks in this entire place. This is what you represent, Eric. This is what I'm trying to explain to you. Look around." Reluctantly Eric scanned the room. "Mocha is serving caramel. I have a serious problem with that."

"What are you doing about it sitting behind your desk, taking orders from me?"

"Someone once told me that you get out of your life what you put into it, Eric. I thought I had the job locked up and then you blew through the door. I had even planned to talk to Senator Tanner about taking over where Byrum left off. You don't remember but I was the person who called you the day you were playing golf because the senator wanted to set up a meeting with you. I knew exactly what it was about. And I was sick to my stomach. I thought I was going to be the first black female chief of staff for a United States Senator."

"I didn't know about any of that, Claudia. Maybe if I had things would be different."

Chief of Staff

"Would you have given up the chance to work with Senator Tanner had you known?"

"Probably not," Eric said. "This was an opportunity I couldn't pass up. There's a significant chance that I could become a senator." A tremendous sense of guilt overtook him and he couldn't believe he'd just said that out loud, especially given their argument.

"Then, no, things wouldn't be any different than they are now."

Eric's cell phone rang and he saw that it was Reginald. "I'm sorry, Claudia, but I simply have to take this call."

"Fine." Claudia stood, put her coat on and grabbed her purse. "You'll have my resignation on your desk when you get back to the office. Thanks for lunch. It was truly enlightening."

Eric's mouth fell open and Claudia walked away. By the time he'd answered the phone, Reginald had already hung up. Waiting anxiously, Eric dialed his voice mail immediately when the chime rang. The message wasn't very clear, and Eric could only make out Reginald saying that he'd found something, or was it someone, and that he had to rush out of town. Running to catch a plane. Call you when I have something. And then the line went dead.

Chapter *27*

"HERE," Eric said standing before Claudia's desk. She refused to look at him, only darting her eyes to the side to see what he'd put on her desk.

"What's that?" she asked, looking back at her computer.

"The last time I pissed you off, you told me to make it dark and expensive."

Claudia's face softened a little and she raised an eyebrow. "Is Denzel in that little box?"

"No, but it's the next best thing I could manage." Eric sat on Claudia's desk, forcing her to move over, and took her hand. "Claudia, I'm sorry for whatever part I've played in your being miserable here in the office. Know that I never meant to hurt you in any way. But also know I wouldn't change anything that's happened because it's brought us closer together." Claudia rolled her eyes and she fingered the wrapping on the box of chocolates. "Please don't leave. I don't know what I would do without you to run my life."

Very quickly and very hard, she elbowed Eric in the leg. "Don't you ever talk to me that way again. Do you understand me?"

Rubbing his Charlie Horse, Eric complied and apologized again.

"This doesn't solve everything, you know?" she said, easing a confection into her mouth. "I still have a huge issue with bougie black people, but I'll cut you a little slack."

"I'd appreciate that."

"And you're still taking me to lunch. Not Lola's, though." She fished out another chocolate and bit into it. "Agreed?" she asked, her mouth full.

"Agreed. You're a real piece of work, you know that?"

"Yes, I do."

Eric bent down and whispered into her ear. "I panicked today when I thought you were going to leave, Claudia. You mean a hell of a lot more to this office, and to me, than you realize. A hell of a lot more." Eric's office phone started ringing, lighting up Claudia's phone, in turn.

"Thanks, COS. I appreciate it. And I'm sorry, too. I'm sorry for the mean things I said like when I called you a house nigger. That was uncalled for and way out of character for me. I'll never do that again. Sorry."

"Apology accepted. Can we get on with our lives now?"

"Well, if you don't get out of my face and answer that phone, I'm going to put it some place you'll need a colonoscopy to find."

"That's the Evil Mistress I know and love."

"I finished the manuscript, by the way. What there was of it, anyway. There wasn't a real ending, so I don't know how it all ties together. He must have still been working on it when he died." Eric gave her his 'we'll talk about that later' look and limped back to his desk to quickly answer his ringing phone.

"Eric Julian." He grimaced in continued pain.

"I need to speak with you. The last time I called, you hung up on me. That was not a very wise decision."

"Who is this?"

"You'll find out soon enough."

Eric wondered why he was still talking to this man. "I'm not budging from this office until you tell me exactly who you are and just what business you have with me."

"Untrusting. Just like your grandmother, aren't you?"

Eric was silent. He didn't recognize the voice, but whoever this guy was, he was calm and collected. The phone number was unknown. Whatever he knew about Eric, he obviously either knew his grandmother or had some appreciation of who she was. Could it have been an old friend playing a trick? A weirdo who saw his name in the paper or a magazine and knew he was Christine's grandson? Eric sat back in his chair and looked at the phone again. "You know my grandmother, do you?"

"Meet me. Please. Lafayette Square, thirty minutes. If you're not there, I'll understand. I'll be disappointed, but I'll understand." The mystery caller hung up and Eric sat motionless behind his desk.

*****

THIRTY minutes later, Eric was sitting on a bench, searching the faces of everyone who walked past him. He hadn't thought to ask his peculiar caller what he would be wearing or what he looked like. He shook his head and wondered why he was sitting there, by himself, waiting for someone to come up from behind and do God knows what. He stood to leave when he heard the voice from the phone.

"Eric?"

He spun around and was greeted by the face he had never expected to see again. "Oh my God. Daddy?"

Eric's mind was flooded with what he wanted to say, but all he could do was stand there, mouth agape.

"Amazing," Cole said. "Look at you. You're all grown up."

Still unable to speak, Eric was numb and staring blankly. Was he dreaming? Could this actually be happening?

Cole stepped toward Eric, arms extended like he wanted to hug him, and Eric abruptly moved back. Cole retreated, as well – hands in the air - not wanting to force the moment. "I, uh, guess you're surprised to see me. After all these years and everything. Maybe this is more of a shock to you than I expected." Before Cole knew it, Eric had stepped up close, punched him in the eye, and dropped him to the ground.

"What the hell is going on?" Eric screamed.

Cole Julian had changed quite a bit from how Eric remembered him. He was still about medium height, with a high yellow complexion, but the athletic build Eric remembered had been replaced with sagging shoulders and the hint of a gut. His face was weathered and his hair was graying on the sides. He was a man that Eric had once admired tremendously. It was Cole who taught him how to throw a baseball and to ride a horse. Cole, with his light skin and wavy hair, had an impeccable style and always dressed phenomenally.

Perfectly articulate and brilliant beyond his formal education, Eric had always wanted to pattern himself after his father. That all changed when his mother got sick and Eric began to see a different side of the man.

Challenged by his only child to devote himself to his dying wife, Cole only distanced himself further and further from them both. Eric didn't know why, but he felt like Cole was scared. Hell, they were both scared, not knowing what was going to happen to the woman they loved more than anything. The sicker his mother became, the more Cole left them alone. He would disappear for days on end, no one knowing where he went or who he was with. Four months down the road, and Eric's move into Dove's Nest had become permanent. Cole Julian had dropped off the face of the planet. And now Eric was staring him in the face.

"You're not supposed to be here," Eric spoke, slowly and deliberately. It had been a long time since he'd punched anyone and his right hand throbbed from the pain of slamming it into Cole's skull. He looked around to make sure everything was as it had been when he got to the park. People were still playing with their children and dogs. The Immigration bill protesters were still chanting. He looked

Chief of Staff

across the street to the White House where the constant flurry of activity still moved at its usual pace. Birds and laughter filled the air and all was as it should have been. The notable exception, that is, being the man standing before him.

"Why not?" Cole asked, massaging his left eye. "Why am I not supposed to be here?"

"Because you're dead," Eric said.

Cole laughed out loud, looking Eric in the eye. "So is that what she told you? That I died?" Cole sighed and broke his gaze. Moving past Eric, he sat down on the bench, massaging his temples. "Maybe that was the right thing to do. Maybe that was the only thing she could have told you that would have made any sense at all. You were just a kid. I didn't know how to explain my actions or emotions to myself, let alone to you. I guess me being dead would finally allow her to get her claws deeper into you than they already were. What a wicked web we weave."

"My grandmother isn't the one who lied to me."

Cole looked up at Eric with a raised eyebrow. "Did she or didn't she tell you that I was dead?"

"Perhaps she did. Maybe you're still dead to me."

"Do I look at all dead to you? Jesus Christ, Eric, that woman could tell you anything and you'd believe it, wouldn't you?"

He didn't know what to say. Clearly, something was terribly wrong, but there was no way out. Somebody had indeed lied to him and he planned to find out exactly who it was. And why. "I'm done talking to you. I've got work to do." Eric turned to walk away from the man, the father, he hadn't seen in twenty-five years.

"Wait, Eric!" Cole spurted out. "Not yet. I'm not finished talking to you. There are some things that you need to know."

"About what?" Eric questioned, his back turned to his father.

"About your entire life, son."

"Don't you dare call me son!" Eric whipped around and stomped back to Cole, poking him in the chest over and over. "You lost that right the day you walked out on me. You left me to fend for myself. Mother was dead and you just fucking left me!" Eric was shouting so loudly that people were beginning to stare. Cole grabbed him by the arm and led him to the side of the fountain. "Don't touch me."

"Eric, I…I don't know what to say to you."

"Clearly."

"All I know is this." Cole bit his lip like he didn't want to say what was on his mind, like the secret he was harboring should stay locked in his brain indefinitely. Eric had regained his composure somewhat and waited for Cole to say something, anything, that would make sense of today. "Things are not what they seem."

Eric's jaw clenched, along with his fists, and he said, "That's it? That's all you got? Things are not what they seem." His voice began to get louder as he spoke, rising with his anger. "You are a piece of shit. Dead or not. I was a child. Without a mother. Left to be raised by my grandmother. Left by you. You left me!" Eric was beginning to cry, his eyes watering uncontrollably. The years of pain and disappointment were barreling out of him and there was nothing he could do to stop the torrent of emotion. "How can you stand there after all this time and simply tell me that things are not as they seem? Goddamit!" Eric stomped the ground much like a child would when throwing a tantrum and spun in a circle, head turned up to the sky. "Mother! Guess who I found! You'll never believe it!" Eric's cell phone rang, Cole jumping at the sound.

"Don't answer that."

"I'm done talking to you. After mother died, you were the only thing I had left. And you took that away from me."

"I had no control over that, Eric. I didn't leave you of my own accord." After three rings, the phone was silent.

"Right," Eric began, partly wanting to hear what he was about to say, and also to get this over with all the faster. "And, uh, who was it that made you leave?"

"Christine."

"Liar," Eric said, almost not waiting for Cole to finish the word.

"I'm not lying. Greedy, yes. But not a liar."

"What do you mean, greedy?" Eric asked.

Cole let the air between them get tense, taking further advantage of the situation. He called Eric out of the blue for the first time in God knows how long. He arranged a meeting over the phone to reveal the fact that he's not dead. And now, the piece de resistance in his battle against Christine Belmont Squire. "I was never the right man for your mother, that is, as far as Christine was concerned."

Eric's emotions had settled a bit and he had stopped crying. "Go on."

"You see," Cole said, moving to an open bench and sitting down, Eric securely in tow. "I was in the right place at the right time in your mother's life. Christine knew that and took advantage of my relationship with her daughter. We got engaged and married quickly. You were born. She got that awful disease." Cole dropped his head for effect, luring Eric to probe him further.

"And then what, you son of a bitch? You got scared and ran out? When does that part happen? When are you going to confess to that?"

"Before your mother died, Christine made it crystal clear that I would no longer be considered part of the family.

Chief of Staff

I wasn't blood. The only thing she wanted from her daughter was you." He raised his head to see the confused and questioning look on Eric's face and continued. "She told me the day your mother died that she had made a decision. I wasn't the best father in the world...you were really more of a surprise to me than anything. And I don't know that I really wanted children, but, by the time you were born it was too late. Anyway," he said and moved on quickly, not giving Eric a chance to interrogate him, "with the kind of money she was throwing at me to leave, I didn't know what else to do. I was young and foolish, you've got to understand. The choice seemed pretty clear to me at the time."

"Wait just a minute." He closed his eyes and titled his head the way he did when processing some strange bit of information or something that he believed he mistakenly overheard. "Did you just say that grandmother...? I didn't hear you correctly. Because if I had, it would have sounded like you just told me my grandmother paid you to leave. She paid you to desert me. That couldn't possibly be what I heard."

"A million dollars." It worked. Cole's next move would depend solely on Eric.

"One million dollars." Eric repeated the figure with the exact intonation Cole had used.

"She signed a check right there on the spot and told me to leave you and never see or contact you again."

"And you just did it? You just left me there?"

"Dove's Nest isn't exactly an orphanage, son."

The word 'son' hung in the air as Cole spoke it, lingering close to Eric's ear. It was a word that Senator Tanner used frequently in conversation either with Eric or about Eric. There was a simple appreciation for the word that Eric had never realized when it was spoken by someone other than Cole Julian. There was an elegance and a comfort in the word as he knew it, but not when it came from the mouth of the man who had left him to grow up on his own. Yes, the

Chief of Staff

friendship and very special bond he shared with Senator Tanner were fantastic in their own right. But what man can look back on his childhood and say that he wished someone other than his father had taught him the ideals and ethics of how to grow into a man?

Eric stiffened when he looked down at Cole, sitting by himself on the park bench in the most powerful city on the planet. He dared to call him son after what he just confessed to doing. His cell rang again and this time he answered it. When the short conversation ended, he turned to Cole and said, "I'm leaving."

Cole reached out and grabbed Eric's arm and held him tight. "Now you listen to me and you listen good. Christine is going to pay for everything she did to me, I'll see to it."

"It's you. You're the one who's been calling and blackmailing her, aren't you?" Eric shook free and stepped back again. "I thought she was out of her mind. I thought maybe that she was making it up. But it's true. She's not going to give you anything."

"I don't know what you're talking about," Cole said.

"She told me it was you. She said you called her and threatened her." Eric stared at Cole and considered hitting him again. His hand was still on fire from the first punch.

This was a flaw in the plan. Christine wasn't supposed to say anything to him. Cole had to recalculate and think fast. "You weren't supposed to get involved in this. You weren't supposed to be made a part of this. But, obviously, Christine took it upon herself to pull you in where you didn't belong." He looked at the ground and then back at Eric with a cold look. "She's an evil woman and she's put me through more than one man should have to endure. Make no mistake, she's going to give me exactly what I want and you, Eric, are going to see that it happens."

"Go to hell."

"After I left you, when your mother died, I got involved with some people I probably shouldn't have. Things got crazy. I started gambling again and my losses starting mounting faster than I could pay them off."

"That's not my problem. You got yourself into this mess and you're going to get yourself out of it. You leave me and my grandmother alone."

"I can't do that, Eric." Cole looked around at the people in the park and said, "I need to disappear quickly and for good."

"You can say that again," Eric spit.

Cole rolled his eyes and took Eric by the arm, holding him so tightly that he couldn't shake free this time. "Listen to me," Cole said in a menacing, low voice. "The people I owe don't want to hear that I can't come up with the money. They'll kill me just as soon as look at me. I need you to help me get them off my back. You've got the ability to influence that woman, to make it so these people get their money. And to see that I get mine, too."

"And then what? You disappear again? You steal from my grandmother to cover your debts and leave me alone again?"

"It doesn't have to be anything like that at all, Eric," Cole pleaded, still locked onto Eric.

"There's no way I'm doing anything for you." It took considerable effort, but Eric was able to pry himself loose from Cole's grip.

Cole's expression changed abruptly and he stared at Eric like he was trying to keep himself composed and refrain from yelling at his son. "You are going to help me do this or I will make your life very, very difficult."

Eric squinted at Cole and asked, "And just how do you plan on doing that? You're a nobody, a manic-depressive criminal low-life, and a thief."

Chief of Staff

Cole slowly interlocked his fingers and stepped even closer to Eric, whispering in his ear, "How would it look for a freshly-minted chief of staff, with visions of sugar plums and becoming a senator from North Carolina dancing around in his head, to knowingly have purchased – and to have retained possession of – several paintings of questionable background?"

Eric moved away from Cole and asked, "Excuse me?"

A very complicated and extremely well-rounded man, it was Cole who first introduced Eric to the world of art. Beginning with trips to museums and shows and select gallery openings, Cole instilled in young Eric what he used to call a 'painted passion'. The two of them could slowly meander through Impressionist and abstract displays for hours, their minds trying to soak up every brush stroke and interpretation possible before moving on to their next treat. This was a joy that Cole couldn't share with his distant wife or his evil mother-in-law. And since he didn't have any real friends, it was only Eric – even with his juvenile comprehension - with whom he chose to share his love of art.

Often, other patrons would either stare at this odd pairing and wonder what was going on, or just take the chance and ask Cole directly how he had woven his magical spell over Eric. A child who was that enamored with art? It simply couldn't be they told themselves. But it was true. And it is a passion that burns to this day.

"Since leaving you with that woman," he said with drawn-out syncopation, "I've watched you very closely. In fact, thanks to your grandmother's insufferable need to flaunt you in front of the world, I know quite a bit about you. I've learned new things about you over the years, of course, but some things never change. The need to buy and sell works of art, and to fully appreciate them, is in your blood. Naturally, I'll take the credit for that," Cole said, bowing mockingly in front of Eric. "I will also take credit for placing in your care some of the world's most rare treasures."

"My collection is probably priceless only to me, Cole, and it has nothing at all to do with you," Eric said, smiling slightly. "I buy things because I like them, because they speak to me. I don't buy anything, be it a painting or a sculpture or an antique, because of what it will say about me to people I don't even know."

"Perhaps not. But you are in possession of some things for which you have no appreciation." Eric gave Cole a blank look, wondering what he could have been talking about so Cole continued. "I know where some of those treasures came from; the very same treasures that hang in your little condo here in DC, and in North Carolina, both at your house and in the warehouse where you store your excess creations."

"Go on," Eric said, trying to see if Cole was making this up on the fly or if he was really on to something.

"Foulisetta, circa 1928, is an Impressionist landscape."

"Yes, I own that. So what? I bought it through a broker many, many years ago."

"Its real title is 'Migratelthia', and it once belonged to a prominent Jewish physician from whom it was stolen by the Nazis in 1939, and secreted around the world in black market sales for the past 60 years."

His eyebrows narrowed and he searched his memory for anything that could have validated this story, but could come up with nothing. Eric didn't quite know what to say.

"I believe you've also purchased a few other pieces with bloody histories."

"Such as?" Eric asked, trying not to let the emotion show.

"Well, I know you will recognize the titles, 'A Sunny Sunday' and 'Withering'. You took possession of them about ten years ago."

"Through a broker. The same broker I've used for years. They are reputable pieces, Cole, and I can assure you that I own them outright and legitimately."

Cole chuckled just a very little bit and cleared his throat. "Good evening, Mr. Julian," Cole said, altering his voice and accent to that of Sal Lichenstein. "I believe I have found for you some very intriguing pieces. Pieces I know you'll be very interested in seeing for yourself."

Eric was speechless. He ignored the consequences of his action, balled up his fist again, and in a flash he had clocked Cole in the eye very, very hard. Cole was knocked to his knee and sat there, motionless for a moment. Eric danced around, grimacing and holding his hand. For the last twenty years, off and on, he had had periodic but fruitful conversations about art with Sal. He had bought and sold a lot of art through Sal, without ever seeing him in person. When something came up for sale, it was always Sal who called Eric and gave him the tip. When Eric wanted to get rid of something, he called Sal and made arrangements. The intermediaries sent to Eric's home or office to deliver newly purchased paintings or to ferry paintings with which he was parting back to Sal's studio was the extent of their physical contact. Each of them would protest when a face-to-face meeting was proposed, saying that their schedules simply wouldn't allow it. Secretly, Eric decided that the cloak-and-dagger nuances of their relationship colored his transactions and heightened the excitement he felt when Sal would call with 'a find'.

Always - every time - they spoke over the phone, forging quite a relationship in the process. All along, Eric had been speaking with Cole.

"You son of a bitch," Eric said, winding up to take another swing at Cole, who had just stood up and looked his son up and down. With the exception of his being the target, Cole was impressed at how well his son threw a punch. He caught Eric winding up again and put his hand up.

Chief of Staff

"Hey, calm down! I let you hit me the first time," Cole started. "You got lucky the second time. But I swear to God that if you try it again and I'll put your ass on the ground." Eric let his fist unclench and Cole continued. "I want what I want, and I'm going to get it. Like I said, you will help me."

"And if I refuse?" Eric asked. "I have all of the receipts for everything I bought from you. You can't touch me."

"I wouldn't be so sure about that. You bought things that I got from clients who couldn't take the heat, you know, people who thought it would be cool to have something with a certain dangerous provenance. Three or four times I got something for somebody that we both knew was hot, and three or four times they freaked out about getting caught with it. I turned around and sold them to you. I changed the names and created some fictional stories about their origins. Before you know it, my son is harboring in his home the stolen artworks of the religiously persecuted – and no one's the wiser."

"Let's say I believe you. Let's say this stuff is stolen. All I'd have to do is turn you in as the guy who sold it to me and I'll be off the hook."

"If I can, and did, create histories for everything you bought that I knew to be stolen, don't you think I would also have created some record to show that you knowingly purchased the pieces? I'm not stupid. And without my connections, there's no way you'll ever find out where the paintings came from. It isn't like you can walk into a gallery with a painting under your arm and say, 'pardon me, but I think this was stolen from the Nazis and I think I bought it illegally, but can you tell me for sure?'"

"You might not be stupid, but you're evidently not that smart, either. One call to the authorities and this can be settled. You're a con artist, out to fleece me and my grandmother over gambling debts you couldn't repay. So I'd be out the money I paid for the paintings. That's a small price

Chief of Staff

to pay to make sure that you'll be in jail for a very, very long time."

"Eric, if you don't help me, not only will these people kill me, but they'll kill everyone I know. They know who Christine is. They know who you are. I've made sure of that."

"A true hallmark of great parenting," Eric said.

Cole simply raised an eyebrow and continued. "Once I'm dead and they rifle though everything I own, how long do you think it's going to take before they realize I sold you art that is quickly becoming priceless on the black market? Huh? How long do you think it will take before they've knocked in your doors, ransacked your homes and taken what they want? They don't care. They don't appreciate what they'll be ripping off of your walls. If that's one way for them to get their money back, then so be it. Whether we're all dead or alive, they won't stop until they get what they want. Help me get that money from Christine or you'll be signing all of our death certificates. These people are ruthless."

"You should have thought about that before you got involved with them. I hope they do kill you. Then you'll really be dead and you won't be able to bother me or my grandmother ever again."

Cole looked at Eric and calmly said, "I don't have a lot of time left. I don't have the luxury of arguing with you. This is going to happen. This has to happen. I'm going to be out of pocket for a little while, maybe a week or two, but I'll be in touch, son," Cole said as he stood, again with outstretched arms.

"Not on your life," Eric said. "I have nothing to say to you and I hope to God it will be longer than twenty-five years before I see you again."

Eric walked away and Cole sat back down on the bench. Smiling. Like a Cheshire Cat.

Chief of Staff

Chief of Staff

Chapter *28*

COLE Julian hadn't always been an unscrupulous person. In fact, he had enjoyed a rather idyllic childhood, complete with two loving parents and an older sister. He grew up in the mountains of western North Carolina, and was found at a very early age to have a propensity to calculate figures in his head with relative ease. Cole sailed through school, spending most of the summers of his youth at a mathematics camp of one kind or another. He decided that his future was going to be as a professor at the local university, shaping the minds of his young students, mathematically gifted or not. Everything was on track for him until he became a college student, himself.

He'd read a newspaper article one day about how a man had gotten caught defrauding a local bank. The formula in the article was simple, he thought, and he could see why the man had been busted. He got a summer job as a bank teller and put his plan into motion. A couple pennies here, twelve cents there, and so on, Cole was secretly diverting money from customers' accounts to one that he has established under a fake name. Because it was a small bank, he had to be very careful with the scheme. Typically, he didn't stay with any particular bank for more than a summer. But in that time, he had amassed a small fortune, at least as far as a college student was concerned.

Upon graduating, Cole moved to Charlotte and got another job as a bank teller. No one seemed to question why a twenty-one year old man, still a kid in the eyes of many, drove a moderately expensive car and wore the latest fashions, was perfectly happy as a bank teller. When he jumped from bank to bank, his trail had always gone cold by the time the nominal missing funds were discovered. Most of the time, the customers were simply confused by their checkbook or savings registers being off by no more than a dollar, an amount that was quickly and quietly refunded by the bank. As he became more brazen and more successful at stealing

Chief of Staff

from bank customers, Cole retooled his scheme, using the burgeoning technology of computers to construct complicated scenarios to hide his illegal activity. The amounts he funneled into his accounts were much smaller, probably no more than three or four cents. But in Charlotte, where there were many more banking customers than the western mountains of North Carolina, his balances quickly escalated. After only a year at Southern Banking and Loan, Cole moved to another, more tempting target, Community Savings & Loan.

Chapter *29*

WHEN Eric was certain Cole could no longer see him, he waved down a cab and made the short trip to his townhouse. Reginald had called while Eric was talking to Cole and said that he'd gotten some information Eric might be very interested in seeing.

Eric led Reginald into his townhouse when he arrived and they sat down at the dining room table. He was out of breath and shaking.

"This is a great place," Reginald said as he looked around. "I'm not much on the furniture or the paintings or the colors you chose, but the rest of it is great."

"You have no taste, Reginald."

"I know enough not to put an original Pochette on the same wall with what appears to be a very good reproduction of Elisebracht's 'Sunrise, Sunset'."

Eric was shocked. "How do you know about art?" he asked.

"How does one know about anything?" Reginald replied.

"Very existential of you. The Elisebracht is an original, by the way. I bought it in an estate auction three years ago." Eric walked over to the painting and adjusted its accent lighting.

"Original, you say. Well, one chooses to believe what they want."

"I don't have the stomach to talk about anything art-related. Let's change the subject, if you don't mind."

Reginald looked at Eric and noticed he was out of breath and a little distant. "Is everything okay?"

"Yes. Why do you ask?" Eric wasn't going to tell Reginald he'd just had a visit from Cole yet. There were

Chief of Staff

some details he had to work out in his head before he shared that information.

"You just seem harried, that's all. Did you not take a cab here?"

"I did, yes. Maybe I'm just nervous about what it is you have to tell me. I'll be fine in a minute." Eric went to the refrigerator and grabbed a bottle of water, draining it quickly.

"I promise you we'll get to the bottom of this. But first, I'm going to need you to focus on what I've brought you. Can you do that?"

Eric nodded yes and Reginald produced a large manila folder from his bag. He laid it out, unopened on the table. "You got all of that information from the time I put you on the case?" Eric asked.

"This stuff doesn't have anything to do with the blackmailing of your grandmother. Sorry, I should have made that more clear. These pages are printouts from the flash drive you gave me."

"Oh," Eric said dejected. "Sure. What did you find? What was Byrum trying to hide, if anything?"

"I'd say that he was certainly trying to hide something. He went to a lot of effort to ensure that only he could access the drive. The encryption was top-notch. I'm not quite sure how he did it, or if he did it himself, but getting through to the information proved a challenge. My guy at NSA said it is some of the best work he'd seen in a very long time."

"And? What am I looking at?" Eric asked, leafing through the folder. "This is just a bunch of spreadsheets, right? I can't make anything of them."

"If you look at them as they were arranged on the computer, you'll begin to see a very definite pattern. There were three tabs, and I've made screen shots of both to go along with what I've printed out for you. Tab one is titled 'Name', tab two is for 'Amount', and Tab three is 'Date Provided'. There was a back door on the spreadsheet and that was the hardest thing to get into. It is titled 'Information Provided'."

"It looks like all of tab one is only the initials ET and TE. Those are the same initials Byrum wrote in the margins of a manuscript I also found in his safe."

"You actually have the manuscript? And you're just telling me that now?"

"Sorry."

"I know you're trying to find out where this information came from, but it would have helped tremendously to have had access to the actual book. Don't you think?"

"Damn, Reginald. I'm sorry. But how was I supposed to know the book and this flash drive thing were connected?"

"I don't suppose you know anyone with those initials, do you?" Reginald pushed ahead.

"Not that I can think of off the top of my head."

"You'll notice as you compare all three tabs that there are thirteen rows each of information, segmented by month with hidden tabs for corresponding information provided. I wasn't able to get into Byrum's personal bank records, but I'm still working that angle. It occurred to me one night that maybe the money didn't come from his account, anyway."

"This is the part where I ask, 'so where else could it have come from', right?"

Reginald closed his eyes. "Just sit there and listen. I searched for any accounts tied to Byrum and Senator Tanner, along with any records related to Senator Tanner's last election campaign and you'll never believe what I found - an account with a large number of electronic transfers - over what looks like an eight to nine month period - to a bank in Canada, and then on to the Cayman Islands."

"Why would they have sent money to Canada and the Caymans from their campaign funds?" Eric asked, puzzled. "That doesn't make any sense to me."

"The money in that particular account was separate from any campaign contributions, Eric. From this effort, it doesn't appear Byrum was stupid by any stretch of the imagination. He knew that whatever this money was for in the foreign accounts, it couldn't be traced back to campaign fundraising because that would have raised some serious red flags. The money changed banks a couple of times before it was finally wired to this person on tab number one."

"That sounds like a lot of trouble to go through."

"Do you know what kind of money Grisham and Creighton generate from writing a best seller? The publishing game is a harsh and unforgiving gamble. People have been known to do things a hell of a lot more complicated than this to turn a buck."

"It's sickening the things people will do for money." Eric shook his head in disgust. "You said 'this person', but there are two sets of initials. What gives?"

"Not sure. There are two choices: either the initials belong to the same person, or there are two people, and one of them is working for free."

Eric sat and pondered the spreadsheet for a moment, thinking about the situation silently.

Reginald looked at his watch and said, "I've got to get back to my office, so if we could move this along that'd be great." He pulled out three more screen shots of the tabs and put them side by side. "The patterns on the spreadsheets didn't make any sense to me, initially, especially when you compared them with the transactions that culminated in the wires. And then I turned them upside down. More specifically, I sorted the columns in tabs one and three inversely. Which gave me this," Reginald said, pulling one more printout from the folder. "The amounts always stayed consistently low. Five thousand, thirty-five hundred, six thousand, and so on. Byrum was definitely paying somebody for information. Although you can see that there are quite a number of payments, there were never any payments above ten thousand dollars."

"Deposits above ten thousand dollars are supposed to be scrutinized by banks," Eric said, examining the sheet. "It's all part of this post-9/11 era and it deals with anti-money laundering and fundraising for terrorist groups. It's called the Patriot Act. And Senator Tanner was directly involved in crafting that legislation." Eric sat back in his chair and looked at Reginald. "He knows an awful lot about my family, Reginald. Do you think he could have been involved with this?"

"No. There wouldn't be anything for the senator to gain by funneling your family secrets to someone or paying someone to give him those secrets. He's already rich as hell. He doesn't care for Christine much at all, but you two are close. There's no way he would risk upsetting that apple cart. I just don't see it. Besides, the drive was in Byrum's safe. Had this been a plan they'd hatched together, I would have found some evidence of that in his office."

"You've turned his office upside down?"

Reginald smiled broadly. "And I didn't leave one thing out of place. I went through everything I could find and there was nothing, no disk drive, no flash drive, no journal, no ledger, no notepad of any kind that tied Tanner to the information here."

"It's Senator Tanner, and how did you get in the building?"

"The things people will do for money. Do you remember saying that a moment ago? You all aren't as safe as you think. Even a Capitol Police veteran isn't likely to turn down several hundred dollars to turn a blind eye. Trust me. Nothing at all links your man to the spreadsheet. Nothing."

"So who are these people?"

"Again, they could be one person, initials having been turned around to try and throw somebody off the trail should the drive have been compromised, or we could dealing with two individuals. If you look at them, there are only two sets of initials throughout the spreadsheets, ET and TE. My next task is to find out who belongs to these initials."

"Why can't you just look and see who the money was wired to? Shouldn't that give you a name?"

"The money was wired to a Cayman Bank account and from there the trail goes cold. I have never been able to break into any information on Cayman Bank clients. Never. People hide money there for a reason, Eric. Don't get me started on Canadian banking, either. That's just a mess. International banking rules don't always apply to Cayman Bank, and Swiss Banks, and the list goes on and on. At least we have some idea of the sophistication of the person we're dealing with. I don't know how those kinds of banks structure their security, but Cayman, in particular, is tighter than Fort Knox. And, no, that's not just a euphemism." Reginald raised a telling eyebrow.

"So what happens now? We know that Byrum was paying somebody for something."

"That's the last tab, the hidden section of the spreadsheet, but like I said, it is strategically tied to each payment amount. I'll let you read information on your own, but suffice it to say that it is all directly related to you and your family. Every last bit of it. It is personal and if it's the least bit accurate, it could be very damaging. I'll email the whole thing to you later today. I should think you're going to find yourself extremely livid at the contents."

Reginald's cell phone rang and he picked it up. "I'll be right back." He stepped out onto the balcony for a little privacy and left Eric sitting at the table, mulling over the screen shots and the intricacies of how Byrum's information had been scrambled for safety, when his own cell phone rang. It made him jump because he immediately imagined Cole was calling him. Thankfully the caller id displayed Dove's Nest.

Chief of Staff

"Eric Julian."

"Good afternoon, sir. This is Evan calling from Dove's Nest. I hope the day is finding you well."

"It is. What can I do for you, Evan?" The moment the name left his mouth, his heart leapt into his chest. Evan Trammel. ET. TE. Reginald walked back inside and sat down. Eric pointed at his phone and mouthed 'it's the butler'. He grabbed a pen and wrote Evan Trammel on a piece of paper. Reginald's eyes narrowed and he shook his head. It couldn't be that easy.

"Madam Squire has asked me to confirm your receipt of this year's commemorative Jewel Box gift. She hadn't received a thank you note from you and was worried it hadn't arrived."

"Yes, Evan. I received it." And threw it right in the trash just like I do every year, Eric thought. "Thank you for calling." He wished Evan a nice day and hung up. "You've got to be joking. The butler did it? I have always gotten a shady feeling from him where my grandmother is concerned. Do you think he would be capable of selling her out to Byrum for this book?"

Reginald gathered his documents and headed for the door. "We'll see about that. But first we need to switch gears for a second. That phone call I just took? We've got a lead on the mystery man who's been calling your grandmother."

"Do you know his name? Is it Evan?"

"I don't know any of that yet. This is something of an imperfect science." Reginald walked back to the table. "I've got to get out of here, but I want to show this to you first. At first blush, I doubt Evan is blackmailing your grandmother as well as trying to get rich off of selling your family secrets. It just doesn't compute. I think we're talking about two different people."

"Why do you say that?" Eric asked.

Reginald produced another manila folder and sat it in front of Eric. "You'd be surprised what I can find out. I don't normally share details with clients, but this is something of an exception to be sure. Digital telephone services, the Internet, email, etc., have made this business so much easier. And so much more costly for people who are trying to hide their secrets. After we spoke the first time, I digitally tapped your grandmother's phones. Here is the list of numbers I retrieved." Reginald opened the folder and pulled out a three-page listing of people who had either called Christine or to whom she had placed a call. "For the most part they are all fine."

"There must be fifty or sixty phone numbers here," Eric said, paging through the list.

"There are actually seventy-four. These two here," Reginald said turning to the next to last page, "don't come up under any of her previous phone bills. I had my source at the phone company check them out for me. It's unusual because there are no names attached to the phone numbers. It is something of an enigma. It only occurred twice in the last two months, and then again four or five times in the last week."

"Is this the guy?"

"That's what I plan to find out. My guy at the NSA was able to set up an alarm of sorts connected with the unusual phone numbers on the list. When these numbers hit Christine's phone line, the system automatically records two- to four-second snippets of the conversations. He's working on getting the complete conversations, but, again, that takes time, especially if you're trying to fly under the radar. There are a million scenarios, Eric. I've been doing this for a long time, and nothing would surprise me, but whoever is the one doing this, he's doing a good job of covering his tracks. I can't leave you with any kind of confirmation that you've solved the crime yet. I just can't do that. This whole manuscript scheme is our second issue, but I think we need to keep focused on the blackmail as our number one priority right now."

Eric slumped in his chair thinking about someone other than Cole targeting Christine and it made him ache. "You have no idea how much she means to me, Reginald. She's all I have left."

Reginald put his hand on Eric's shoulder. "We'll figure this out, I promise you. We're on the right track. Look at this. In one of the conversations, you can hear Christine's voice. You can't quite make out what she's saying, but voice analysis confirms she was the person on the other line. In another of the conversations, and subsequent emails confirming reservations, we now know that one of our mystery men had planned a trip to the mountains of North Carolina. He's going to be at a hunting lodge tomorrow. We're working on tracing the emails to a server, and that will give us more to go on, but that's going to take some time. Right now, though, this is a lot closer than we've been to him since we started."

"Great," Eric said. "He's got guns. I'm really starting to freak out here, Reginald."

"Don't worry. He's sneaky, but I'm sneakier. If it turns out to be this guy Evan – which I highly doubt, or just some schmuck from Nebraska, I'll know something soon. I've got to go buy a rifle. It looks like I'm going hunting."

Chapter *30*

"WHERE the hell is that woman?" Cole asked himself. Even before he popped back into Eric's life, he'd been calling Christine to set the next part of his plan in motion. Each time a maid or servant at Dove's Nest answered the phone, the response was always the same: "I'm sorry, but the Lady of the House is unavailable. May I ask who is calling, sir?" He'd hung up every time, not wanting to leave a message.

This time he changed his mind. "Yes, I would like to leave a message. Tell her I said, 'Honey pot, this is Big Bear. It's time for us to discuss the next round of talks between our two parties. To this point, you have been less than compliant. In case you didn't believe me in our first little chat, I have two words for you: Bryant Holdings. I expect to hear from you by the end of the day.' Did you get that?"

"Yes, sir."

"Good."

Cole hung up and decided that if Christine wanted to play the game like that, he would be just fine turning up the heat. Although he didn't much care for having to play the Bryant Holdings card so soon, he knew it would bring immediate results. Of the many skeletons in Christine's closet, Bryant Holdings would, at the very least, show her that he was serious. He was running out of both time and patience. Her obstinance had become tiresome and it had also pushed the timetable forward considerably.

"Wife, huh?"

Cole turned to see an incredibly large black man talking to him. How long had he been standing there? "No." Cole gave a deliberate but wary smile to the man.

Recognizing his intrusion, he introduced himself to Cole. He had a very southern drawl that became more pronounced the longer he spoke, which threw Cole off for some reason. "Sorry. My name is Reginald Dixon. I didn't mean to get into your business. It just sounded like what I go through with my own wife, well, ex-wife now. I'd swear she didn't listen to me half the time when I told her to do somethin'."

"No problem," Cole said, shaking his head. His left eye was still a little black and blue from Eric's punch.

"I've never been here before and I kind of started over your way as you were gettin' off the phone."

Cole stashed his phone in the pocket of his bright orange safety vest and went back to getting ready for the day. It was the first day of hunting season and he couldn't wait to get settled and in position. Reginald was standing next to Cole, waiting for the conversation to start up again. Cole saw him out of the corner of his eye and tried to wish him away. No such luck. "So, what now?" Cole asked, annoyed.

"What do you mean?" Affable and a little slow, Reginald acted like a confused puppy. Obviously his social skills were a little lacking.

"I presume by your extended, albeit silent, presence that there is something else I can do for you." Cole had turned around, leaving his preparation for the moment, and leaned against the open tailgate of his truck.

Reginald shuffled his feet and stammered an apology. "You're the only black guy I've seen here. I came up here by myself and figured maybe I'd try and make at least one friend while I was here. I'll leave you be." He turned to leave, head hung, apologizing once more.

Cole rolled his eyes and said, "Okay. Okay. My fault. I guess that was just me being an asshole. I'm not exactly a people person." Reginald stopped and turned back to Cole. "Let's, uh," Cole started. "Let's start over. How about that? Everybody needs a new friend once in a while." He stuck out his hand and said, "My name is Earl Tucker." It was a name he'd assumed as an alias in the past, never wanting to give

Chief of Staff

anyone he didn't know his real name. A long time ago, he'd bought the identity of the deceased Earl Tucker of Alabama, a vagrant without family or friends, who died in the shadows without anyone to miss him or investigate his death. Cole had a Social Security card and birth certificate forged and began living exclusively as Earl, in part to keep Eric from looking for him in case he ever learned the truth, and in part to completely start his life over after being run out of Dove's Nest.

"And I'm Reginald Dixon," he said, smiling broadly, revealing perfectly shaped and glaringly white teeth. "It's surely a pleasure to meet you."

*****

HUNTING had been a passion for Cole for as long as he could remember. Growing up in the mountains of North Carolina before going to college and settling in Charlotte just before meeting and marrying Eric's mother, it had been his experience that black hunters were few and far between. The thrill of stalking a deer or wild turkey, taking dead aim and firing was a feeling that he had never been able to duplicate. He'd hunted all over the country and had taken several trips abroad with his father when he was young. He'd formed an incredible bond with his father as they shared their experience and wanted to pass the exhilaration to his own offspring.

Soon after he married Eric's mother, Christine badgered him into putting down his obsession, saying it was cruel and tasteless to hunt innocent animals for sport. This from a woman draped in exotic leathers and floor-length furs. Under the spell of his wife's vast fortune that was at his disposal, he agreed to never hunt again. He didn't want to take the chance of losing the lifestyle to which he had very quickly become accustomed. It was worth the trade off. As soon as his wife died and Christine handed him his 'severance', he was back in the woods, making up for lost time.

He decided his first hunting expedition would be as grand as possible. He chose Chestnut Hunting Lodge in the

Chief of Staff

mountains of North Carolina. It was the very best way to get reacquainted with the love of his life and to sharpen his dulled skills at the same time. Boasting the largest hunting preserve in the state, Chestnut was an extremely rugged and, at times, unforgiving locale. It was also a Mecca for hunters of all skills and interests. Cole went back to Chestnut year after year, becoming a member of the Chestnut Deer Club, enjoying the creature comforts of a heated cabin replete with a kitchen, a comfortable bed, and a big screen television. Chestnut was his home away from home and his annual visit was arguably the best part of his year.

Usually, he kept to himself on his treks to Chestnut and that was just the way he liked it. People left him alone. Why Reginald really latched onto him, he wasn't sure, but he hoped it wouldn't last long. He was right when he said he wasn't a people person. Friends cause too many problems and that was definitely something he'd had enough of. Built like some kind of steroid-injecting super football player, Cole was struck at just how large Reginald really was. Black as coal, country as he could be, and probably stronger than a bear, Cole imagined Reginald running over quarterbacks, leaving them wilted and fractured. Sorry, Cole said mockingly to himself, likening his new friend to that idiot in Forrest Gump. Fried shrimp. Blackened shrimp. Shrimp taters. Shrimp gumbo. Reginald was a piece of work.

Hunts at Chestnut lasted a full six days, and in that time, you were able to take advantage of the incredible opportunities the outfitter offered. Over their six days together, Cole and Reginald had surprisingly forged a semi-friendship, hunting alone in the morning, and hooking up with a guide to hunt together in the early afternoon. They ate together and shared their stories about hunting and their lives away from the preserve. On one of the final days, Cole and Reginald sat down to a dinner of fresh venison steaks and huge baked potatoes. They innocently talked about the day's hunt, but Reginald was secretly setting a trap of another kind.

Chief of Staff

"I don't know that I've ever seen a buck that big, Earl!" Reginald exclaimed as they sat down. "It was almost as big as my ex-wife!"

Cole laughed and waived down the waiter. He ordered first, followed by Reginald who had a special request. "Hey, buddy," he asked, "have y'all got any of that Jaegermeister here?"

"What in the world is that?" asked Cole.

"It's some of the most rootin' tootinest alcohol you'll ever put your lips on. I'm gonna get us some so you can try it." He asked the waiter to bring them two Jaeger Bombs, a ferocious combination of Red Bull and Jaegermeister. He hadn't been able to successfully mine any information from Cole since they met in the parking lot, other than his name. It was a match to the initials on Byrum's electronic ledger, but if he was going to go back to Eric with anything, he wanted to make sure it was concrete. Jaeger Bombs had a tendency to uninhibit even the strongest-willed person. He and Cole would be parting ways in the next day or so and he had to push things ahead. The waiter brought the men their concoctions and gave Cole a look that said, 'I don't know if I'd do this if I were you'.

"Bottoms up!" Reginald shouted, tossing his drink back. Cole followed suit, coughing at the harshness of the taste, stomping his foot on the floor until the feeling returned to his mouth. "If that don't light your fire, there's something wrong with you," beamed Reginald. "Five or six more of those and we'll be just right."

"Five or six more?" Cole asked. The after taste was monstrous. "I don't know if I can do that again." The two men talked about their kills, their favorite kinds of guns and the different places they'd hunted and what kinds of prey they'd caught in the past. When their dinners arrived, Reginald dug in with excitement, even going so far as to tuck his napkin into the top of his shirt before letting loose a pig-out the likes of which Cole had never before witnessed.

"So what is it that you do, Reginald?" Cole asked. "I mean, what do you do for a living? It's crazy, but in all this time, I never thought to ask you that before."

Reginald shoved a hearty pile of food into his mouth and started to answer the question, food appearing and disappearing as he spoke. Cole's stomach turned and he forced himself to pretend he was looking at something over Reginald's shoulder. Please, God, Cole thought. Some manners, please!

"Well, I used to work my daddy's farm." He took a swallow of sweet tea, sucked his teeth for an elusive bit of something he'd already chewed and wiped his mouth. "I don't do nothin' now, though. Not since my daddy died."

"Sorry to hear that," Cole said.

"It's okay. He told me on his death bed he didn't want me workin' that farm no more. He told me, 'boy, when I'm dead, you sell this farm. Go out and get you a real life. Don't waste whatever time you got left doin' what I did."

"That's touching. Odd, but touching."

"Yeah. I guess." Another loaded fork shoved into his mouth. "I did some checkin' around and found this fella who said he'd buy it from me, lock, stock and barrel. So I sold the whole damn thing to him. That's been near three months ago. I didn't know what to do with myself after workin' that farm since I was knee high. I traveled around some, went to see my kids when their momma would let me, and decided I'd try some new things."

"Like hunting?"

"Naw, I'd been huntin' with my daddy and granddaddy forever. You know, down on the farm and on hunts with friends I knew who worked their daddies' farms." More tea.

"So what is new about hunting if you've been doing it all your life?"

"This place," Reginald said, his arms in the air, looking around. "I ain't never been huntin' at a place where I had to pay. And never at a place fancy like this. What better way to spend the money, right?"

"Good point." Cole took a sip of his tea and very smoothly asked, "So how big was your father's farm?"

"Two thousand acres. We grew tabacca, sweet taters, yellow and white corn, peanuts, had some hogs for a while before the government shut us down, and a couple other little crops."

Fried shrimp. Blackened shrimp. Shrimp taters. Shrimp gumbo.

Cole shook the image from his mind and moved deeper. "I'll bet that paid a pretty penny if you were able to come all the way up here and hunt, especially in a place as nice as this."

"Hell yes, it did!" Reginald exclaimed. "Twelve million bucks, to be exact."

Cole nearly choked on his steak.

"Now I just gotta figure out what I'm gonna do with it all. My deadbeat ex-wife ain't gettin' any of it, that's for sure. I do have this one idea, though."

"Yes? What's that?"

"I think I'm goin' take some of the money and open me a strip club. Real high class joint with foreign beer and all that." Reginald put his fork down and made a panorama in the air with his hands. "I'm gonna call it a Touch of Ass." He looked at Cole for a reaction. "You know, like a touch of class, but with ass. Clever, ain't it?" The blank expression on Cole's face said enough. "I mean, that's just an idea. You know, it's not somethin' I'm real set on just yet." He sat back in his ever-creaking chair and said, "Listen at me. Here I am rattlin' on and on about me and don't know nearly nothin' about you. What is it that you do, Earl? I mean, what do you do for a livin'?"

Clever, Cole thought, using the exact phrasing he had when he first asked the question. "I'm a day trader," he said.

"Uh huh. And what exactly does that mean? You ain't a communist, are you?" The dumbfounded look on Reginald's face was akin to an open door.

"It basically means that I take other peoples' money, invest it for them, and take a cut of the profits."

Reginald's eyes lit up. "No foolin'?"

"No, foolin'," Cole repeated. This was going to be easy as pie.

"Well, this is turnin' out to be an even better idea than I thought! It must have been divine intervention that I met you. I'm rich as hell and you're the guy who can take my money and make it do something. I always heard the rich get richer, but never thought that statement would ever stick to me. I'll be a monkey's uncle. What are the odds of that happenin'?"

"This is definitely your lucky day, Reginald Dixon, former farmer and newly minted millionaire," Cole said. "Rest assured that I'd treat your money just like it was my own."

One more loaded fork, followed too closely with what Cole hoped to be Reginald's last food-baring questions. "So how does this work? Is it easy?"

"Like taking candy from a baby."

*****

AFTER three more Jaeger Bombs, Cole was feeling pretty good, and they moved up to the bar to continue their conversation. "You said somethin' the other day about this bein' the first place you came back to when you hadn't been huntin' in a long time." Reginald had switched to beer, saying too much Jaeger gave him the craps, but encouraged Cole to keep on downing his 'new favorite drink'.

Chief of Staff

"Yeah, my bitch of a former mother-in-law made me quit. She said it was something stupid like it was immoral or something." His head was swimmy and he couldn't tell if he was slurring his words. Frankly, he didn't care. He was on vacation and relaxing with a friend for the first time that he could honestly remember.

"What a stupid thing to say. Huntin' people's immoral. Hell, if it wasn't for us hunters, the whole wildlife population would be bustin' out of the woods, takin' over everythin'. Immoral," Reginald repeated. "That's a crock of shit."

"Amen."

"So what was it about her that made you stop? It's not like spittin' out a piece of gum. Not for me any way. Huntin's a part of my childhood. I grew up on it. I don't know what could make me give it up."

"She was loaded. I mean she's still loaded. That witch pulled me to the side one day and said, 'you may have my daughter for now, but if you want to stay in my good graces, and have access to my money, along with a couple other items on my list, you'll do the right thing and put away your silly fascination with hunting.'" Cole rubbed his temples and said, "At least it was something like that. I don't really remember. All I knew was that there was no way I'd miss out on all that money. I could go hunting any time. If I got lucky enough, she'd die and I'd have the best of both worlds."

"Well, I figure since you're sittin' here with me, there's a couple ways to look at your little situation. One, she's dead and you can hunt all you want. Two, since I don't see no ring on your finger, I figure you're divorced and you can hunt all you want. Or three, you're up here huntin' 'cause you got tired of her mouth and decided to be your own man." Reginald took a long pull from his beer and eyed Cole. "Which is it?

Chief of Staff

"Sadly, she's not dead yet. I haven't given up hope on that one, though. And, no, I don't have a wedding ring because I'm not married anymore."

"She take you to the cleaners when she left?"

"Who?"

"Your wife," Reginald said. "She clean you out?"

"She died," Cole said.

Reginald looked like he'd just run over Cole's dog. "Sorry, man. I had no idea."

"She died and they put my money in the goddam ground with her," Cole said coldly.

"I don't follow."

"The day she was buried, my fabulous mother-in-law gave me my walking papers."

"Get the hell out of here!" Reginald said, slapping the bar. "You are one hundred percent shittin' me!"

"Nope. She gave me this little-ass check and told me to get the hell out of her life."

"I can't believe she kicked you out like that. Tell me y'all didn't have kids."

"One. A son." Cole took a deep breath and looked at Reginald. "I lost him, too."

"This is gettin' worse and worse. Sorry I brung it up."

"Don't be. One day I'll get my revenge on that crusty old hag. I just hope I get to her before she kicks the bucket. She gave me some money and I took off."

"How much did you get? Like a couple thousand or so?"

"One million."

"Dollars?" Reginald asked, mouth agape.

"Yeah. And she's got a hell of a lot more than that. Trust me. You want to know what the worst part is?"

"Did she keep your dog?"

Fried shrimp.   Blackened shrimp.   Shrimp taters. Shrimp gumbo.

"No. The worst part is that I actually took the money, which, yeah, was the wrong thing to do, but I didn't really have that much of a choice in the matter. I left my kid there with that viper. I did go back a couple of months later, you know. I wanted to make it right. I stood outside the gate and begged for somebody to let me in."

"They got a gate?"

"Reginald, they've got a huge mansion with anything you could ever imagine. Anyway, I stood outside the gate because she wouldn't let me onto the property. All I wanted was to see my son again. I even brought the check back to her to show her I wanted to be a good daddy to my kid."

"And?" Reginald was leaning in toward Cole, enraptured by the story.

"Nothing. I never heard from her again. I sent letters to her until I came to the point where I figured she'd never answer them. So I moved on. I thought maybe it would just be better to leave her and my son alone, let them get on with their lives, you know?"

"I can't even imagine that. What did you do with the money? A million bucks don't seem that crappy of a parting gift, if you ask me."

"I pissed it away, mostly," Cole lamented. "I got into some gambling problems and that ate it up. I bought some stuff, but nothing would have come close to having my son."

"That's a sure hard luck story, pal. When's the last time you saw your kid?"

"I saw him the other day," Cole said smiling a bit. "He didn't want anything to do with me. Hell, he's the one who punched me and made my eye look like it does. He's completely pissed and I don't blame him."

"You must have been crushed."

"Christine is the one who's going to be crushed," Cole said, his face folding with drunken anger. "She'll pay for everything she put me through if it's the last thing I do on this planet."

That was the smoking gun Reginald had been looking for. He tried to contain himself the best he could. "Is that her name? The bitch who took your kid?"

"Yes."

"Why not just go to the police to get Earl, Jr. back?"

"His name is Eric, actually." Reginald almost had a stroke right there at the bar. "Besides, he's like thirty-something now. He's grown. A real adult. And he's got this great job and everything. It's too late now." Cole picked a pretzel out of the bar bowl and smashed it between his fingers. "I'm going to squeeze her until she pops."

"And how you plannin' on doin' that?" Reginald asked, timidly.

"I had this guy, writing a tell-all for me, one of those scandalous books, you know? But this one...this one was going to be based on their family. He needed an idea and I needed money. It was a marriage made in hell." He shook his fist in Reginald's face and said, "I was going to shove this as far up her ass as I possibly could. I know all of her secrets."

"Dang, this sounds like a made for TV movie I saw once." Reginald looked at the ceiling like he was trying to think of the name of the fictional show. "When's the book comin' out?"

"It's not," Cole said, completely dejected.

"Why the hell not? I thought you and this guy were going to stick it to your ex mother in law. Why'd you stop?"

Chief of Staff

"It wasn't my fault."

"He get cold feet and quit on you?"

Cole started laughing, weaving back and forth on the stool. "Get this. Get this. The motherfucker died!" Again, he howled with laughter. "The motherfucker was in a plane crash. He got blown out of the sky right along with my plan!"

"Ain't that somethin'," Reginald exclaimed. "Just up and died?"

"Yeah," Cole said, "just up and damn died. And, poof, there goes my honey pot."

Reginald raised an eyebrow and looked at Cole. "You ain't funny, are you?"

Cole's neck snapped around at Reginald. "Honey pot is...no, I just meant that when this dude died, the money he was paying me for the information got burned up and sent to hell right along with him."

Reginald nearly passed out from exhilaration. He had just hit the jackpot! Earl Tucker is ET. And the proof was rock solid. "If you know all the secrets, why don't you just write the book, yourself?"

Cole looked at Reginald and said, "You ask a lot of questions, country boy, you know that?"

"Ah, hell, you try living on a farm with nothin' around you for miles. Nobody to talk to but yourself. I guess I got turned loose on the general public and can't keep my mouth shut from askin' questions and learnin' about people."

Cole shrugged his shoulders and went on. "No harm, no foul. Anyway, I thought about that, you know, writing it by myself, but then I thought against it. Besides I don't have that kind of time any more. I'm going to take from her what she took from me."

"Your kid? But," he said, scratching his head, "I thought you said it was too late for that."

"Not only am I going to get my son back, but I'm going to take her for a bunch of her dirty money. And there's nothing she can do about it."

"Oh, I love the sound of this," Reginald said, cooing excitement. "I love a good get 'em back and hit 'em low story. How much are you wantin' from her? Maybe you could be a partner in a Touch of Ass."

"For fifty million, Reginald, I can touch as much ass as I wanted to and never feel the same one twice."

Reginald rolled off of his bar stool, laughing uncontrollably. Fried Shrimp, Cole said to himself. Reginald stood up and ordered another round for he and Cole. "That calls for a toast. Bartender, set us up with a couple more of them Jaeger Bombs. We're celebratin' over here!" He stood up and loudly proclaimed, "Earl Tucker, may you swiftly and totally get everythin' you so richly deserve!"

Chapter *31*

"DO you realize it's been more than two weeks since you've called your grandmother?"

Eric shook his head, wondering why he answered the phone. "You seem to have gotten away from your usual phone manners, grandmother. Whatever happened to hello, how are you doing this morning?"

"Are you sassing me?"

"Of course not. And you're right, it has been a couple of weeks since I spoke to you last. Oh, wait a minute, I just remembered something."

"And what is that?" Christine said. She was sitting in the sunroom waiting for her breakfast to be served.

"I believe the last time we spoke I had promised to drop by Dove's Nest to visit you. I seem to recall that when I arrived, your insufferable butler told me that you had left for an extended out of town tour. Does that ring a bell for you?" Eric had just started working on an elaborate schedule of upcoming meetings for Senator Tanner. They needed to start the process of detailing a hate crime bill that was to be co-sponsored by Senator Tanner. Irony's a bitch, Eric thought, when the senator first came to him with the idea. The implications of this legislation would be sweeping.

Eric needed to concentrate, yes, but for some reason, he decided it would be more interesting to needle his grandmother for a couple of minutes. "There was absolutely no mention of that when you were berating me on the phone during my clandestine visit to Charlotte."

"Ah, yes, my trip. Did I not mention that to you? It must have slipped my mind," she said.

"It must have," Eric said coolly. "What is it that I can do for you this morning, grandmother?"

Chief of Staff

"I can't just call and say good morning to my favorite grandson?" Her breakfast was delivered and she instantly sent it back. The eggs were too runny and the orange juice wasn't cold enough. Good help is hard to find.

"Of late, dear, the only time you call me is when you need me to do something for you."

"That simply is not true."

"I'm guessing that the reason you've dialed me today is to tell me that Cole contacted you again. Is that correct?"

"Perhaps you should have been a police detective instead of a senatorial gopher."

"Perhaps you should tell me what you're calling about so we can both get on with our days, grandmother." Eric had started taking a tone with Christine that was very out of character for him. In the past, he wouldn't have dared to speak to her that way. But their relationship was changing. He had long known that not everything connected with his dear old grandmother was on the up and up. He couldn't shake the feeling that he was being cast in a role that let Christine get away with something. He didn't know what she was up to, but over the last several months, her behavior had become more elusive, more cunning.

Never one to be shy about expressing her feelings, especially where his career or love life were concerned, Christine took matters to heart and assumed the responsibility of being in everyone's business – for their own good, of course. She hadn't had any history of relying on anyone but herself to get through life. This whole business of her asking for Eric's help in dealing with Cole had taken Eric aback and he was determined to find the root of the issue. She was hiding something. But what?

"Although I don't appreciate being spoken to that way, I do need to speak with you about your father."

"I would ask that you not use that term with me when speaking about him, please." Claudia walked into Eric's office and sat down in front of his desk. Eric covered the phone and told her to come back. Please close the door on your way out. Claudia gave Eric an annoyed look and went back to her desk. "Call him whatever you want, but do not refer to him as my father."

"If you wish," she said. "Yes, he did contact me. Actually, he left me a message with one of the staff."

"What did it say?"

"Something about time was running out and that he expected to hear from me today."

"Did he call you this morning?"

"No. He left the message while I was out of town."

"And did you call him back?" Eric asked.

"I most certainly did not."

Eric sighed and asked her what else Cole had said in his message.

Christine's corrected breakfast finally arrived and after she inspected everything, touching the orange juice glass deftly to gauge its temperature, she dismissed the servant. "The only other thing that might have held any significance was something about Bryant Holdings."

"What about it?" Eric asked. He had gone back to working on the schedule for the meetings, trying to kill two birds with one stone. "Why do you think he mentioned the company?"

"I am not clairvoyant, young man. I have no idea what that is about."

"You are just not willing to put any effort into this are you, grandmother?" Eric asked. He laid the scheduling aside once more. "You are as helpful as a bag of wet clay. You called me, crying, and told me that Cole, whom I assumed was dead and buried, was trying to extort money from you."

"I said I believed it was Cole."

"A fact that we are going to assume to be true for the sake of this argument," Eric jumped in. "You asked for my help, and I told you I would do everything I could. I asked you to make sure that the next time he contacted you, to speak with him so as to get information out of him. I can't help you if you insist on playing this dumb cat and mouse game with me. If there is something you aren't telling me, you'd better fess up. Otherwise, what point is there in you calling me to rant and rave about him if there's nothing for me to go on in trying to put a stop to this? He wants money, grandmother. He is using some kind of information from either your past or his past to get you to pay up. Apparently you know what it is. Cole knows what it is, of course. I now know that it has something to do with Bryant Holdings, but since you aren't willing to extend that information to me, I'm afraid there isn't anything I can do for you to free you from this situation. Now, with that said, either you start being honest with me or I'm afraid this game is going to be over."

"This is in no way a game, young man. Cole Julian will do whatever it takes, including ruining my good name, if he doesn't get what he wants."

"If this were only about ruining your good name, grandmother, it would have been easier and a hell of a lot quicker to take whatever he's got on you and fax it to the New York Times and be done with it." Claudia walked back into Eric's office and he snapped his fingers, pointing at the door. Claudia mouthed, that's the last time, and left. "I have a tremendous amount of work to do, and if you don't mind I'd like to get back to it."

Christine's mind was spinning. She had to think quickly in order to come up with a good answer. Eric was right. She wasn't doing either of them any favors by being unresponsive. If she was going to get rid of Cole for good, there was only one thing she could do. "Fine. Yes, there is more to the story than I have divulged." Eric couldn't believe what he was hearing. Had he broken her? Surely not.

"However, this is a conversation that I intend to have in person."

"I'm not flying to Charlotte, wasting a day out of the office, to have you tell me what Cole knows that you aren't telling me."

"Then I'll simply have to come to you."

"When?"

"I have an overwhelming amount of planning yet to complete for the fundraiser I'm hosting here at Dove's Nest next month. I don't have the time to flit off to Washington today. I can, however, clear my schedule for tomorrow. Provided my morning goes smoothly, I should be there by lunch time. Does that work for you?" she asked, indignantly.

"Let me check my schedule." Eric held the phone close to his desk and shuffled some papers around to give Christine the impression that he was trying to find a slot for her. Truth be told, he would have cancelled his entire day to hear what she had to tell him, but she needn't know that. The proverbial ball was in his court and was going to take full advantage of it. "I have an opening between noon and 2:00 tomorrow. Shall I pencil you in?"

"Oh, please do," Christine dripped. The arrogance was something she would have to deal with if she wanted her latest problem solved. Once Cole was taken care of, she and Eric would have a long discussion about the proper respect one should have for his grandmother.

"Don't be late."

"I wouldn't dream of it."

They hung up and both of them wondered what the hell was going on. Christine thought back to the day when Cole came into her life and shuddered at the memory.

*****

AS clear as a bell, Christine sat back in her chair and as she pictured Cole Julian, sitting in her office with his smug

Chief of Staff

face and his wrinkled shirt, she knew this wasn't going to go her way. What the hell was he smiling about? He'd just been caught red-handed, a fist full of cookies from her jar, spilling onto the floor. And still he sat there with that goddam smile on his face.

"I wonder what it is about this situation in which you seem to have found yourself that you consider to be so amusing," she said, tapping her cigarette into the ashtray.

Cole shrugged his shoulders and said, "Amusing? I don't know about amusing. Interesting. Provocative. Unseemly. Perhaps even a touch of Hitchcockian macabre. But amusing? I wouldn't use that term, exactly."

Christine put out the cigarette and leaned forward. "You've been working here since we took over this bank." She paged through his personnel file and looked Cole up and down. "You would think that someone on your pay level wouldn't be so bold as to try and steal money from me."

Cole sat in his chair, looking at Christine as though she had yet to make her point. "I'm rather hoping this isn't going to take very long, ma'am. I've got customers out on the floor I need to help." And then he smeared that smile across his face again.

"You're fired."

"I don't think so."

"Come again? You don't think so? You're lucky I haven't had you arrested yet. I know what you've been up to. I figured out your little scheme and it's over. I've got you right where I want you and there's nothing you can do about it. You're fired."

"How can you do that to me?" Cole asked, setting her up. "You'd put me on the street? Like a common criminal?"

"That's exactly what you are."

"Oh, my dear, I'm much more than that."

Chief of Staff

"You will not address me as dear, not if you want to spare yourself...."

"Spare myself what?" Cole asked. "I know just what and who you think you are, Christine Belmont Squire. But there's something you don't know about me."

"And what is that?" The security guard knocked on Christine's door to make sure everything was alright. She dismissed him and turned her attention back to Cole.

"Family."

The very thought of Cole Julian being part of her family made Christine laugh out loud. "Now that's rich, young man. You? A part of my family?"

"What else do you call the father of your first grandchild?"

Christine had walked to the window, laughing, and turned around suddenly. "Excuse me?"

Cole's mouth was downturned and his expression was one of faked sadness. "Uh oh. You mean your darling little Evelyn hasn't told you yet?"

She cleared her throat as she sat down. Thinking she might pass out from the horrid surprise laid before her, the last thing she needed to do was hit the floor in front of Cole. "What are you telling me?"

"You're going to be a granny!"

"Liar."

"Come on now, granny. We both know the truth about your precious little Evelyn. Hell, I picked up on it the first day I met her. So soft and tempting, so young and full of herself. I know a slut when I see one."

"Shut your mouth this instant!" Christine yelled, prompting the guard to open her office door once more. "Open that door again and you'll be out on the street," she told him. He apologized, cursed her under his breath and closed the door behind him. "Cole," she said, with a look that

Chief of Staff

could have scared the devil, "if Evelyn is pregnant, I don't know what I'd do to you."

"Hell, granny..."

"Stop calling me that!"

"Grandma, then, whatever. Look, Evelyn gets around. It just happens that she got around once too many times. And Jesus, I'm glad the buck stopped here."

Christine was feeling faint. The fact that Evelyn tramped around was one of Charlotte's worst kept secrets. Christine told her time and time again that that simply is not how a young lady of her position acts. You can't go jumping into bed with every man you meet, she would say. Think about what you'd be doing to our family if something happened to you. What would people think about me, she would ask. Christine put her head in her hands and tried to take deep breaths. It had finally happened. Evelyn's luck had run out. Her own nightmare had begun and he was sitting in her office, staring back at her.

"Now, I figure you can fire me and call the police or whatever it is you thought you were going to do when you called me in here," Cole said, looking at his fingernails and picking gently at a hang nail. "But there are two, maybe three things that I bet will probably change your mind."

"And what are those?" Christine asked with her head still in her hands.

"I think the most important thing to think about is your social standing." Cole had Christine's number up one side and down the other. She may have cared for her daughter, but she loved the position she commanded even more. "It wouldn't do for you to have a slut, rather, a daughter give birth to a child out of wedlock." Christine groaned at the mere thought. "Secondly, it would be terribly embarrassing for your bank to have a scandal on their hands, you know, being the only black-owned bank in Charlotte. How much did I really take, anyway? What's a measly twenty thousand? That's a pittance, an extremely small price to pay compared to

Chief of Staff

the insurance claims and the lawsuits and the way your business is going to plummet once your customers find out and their confidence in your institution wanes and they take their business elsewhere."

Christine looked up at Cole and sighed. "And what is the third thing, Cole?"

"I know what you're planning to do with Bryant Holdings." Slowly, Christine's eyes closed to narrow slits and she could only stare at Cole. "I can tell by the rather stupefied look on your face that this is news to you. Yes, I know all about Bryant Holdings and the wards you and Mr. Tanner are planning to 'redevelop'."

Those were the worst three things Christine could have conjured up, and Cole laid them all out before her, like a tidy little battle plan he'd been working on in hopes of overtaking her in some twisted, apolitical coup. Right then she went into crisis mode, trying to work out the possibilities in her head. She stood to lose quite a bit if Cole was allowed to shoot his mouth off to anyone outside the family. He had suddenly become a very dangerous man. She looked at him and considered her options. It probably wouldn't be that hard to have him killed. That would at least preserve her bank's reputation and that of her social standing. But how do you explain the child he may or may not have fathered with her daughter? How could she be sure that he was telling the truth about that anyway? Waiting nine months wasn't an option. By then, the secret would certainly be exposed with no possible way out.

If she simply fired him, that still wouldn't keep him from running his mouth, and it wouldn't solve the problem of her daughter being pregnant. An abortion was most likely out of the question. Christine didn't even know how she could pull that one off. If you can't kill him, and you can't just fire him, what is the only alternative?

"I think I like where you're going with this, grandma," Cole said. "You're trying to figure out what to do with me, aren't you?"

"Perhaps I am."

"You know," Cole said, standing and walking toward the door. "I'd always wanted to have a big, pompous, over-the-top wedding. With a huge cake and tons of wedding gifts." He stopped at the door and turned to Christine. "Better make it snappy, though." He made a large arc from his chest to his crotch. "Time's a wastin'."

*****

THE untimely death of her daughter, although incomprehensibly painful, had given her the opportunity to relieve herself of Cole's presence. Now that he was back, and without any real leverage, short of complying with his outrageous monetary demand, Eric was the last hope she had of never having to deal with Cole Julian again.

But what would she sacrifice this time? Her reputation? No, that still wasn't an option. Her company? After what she went through to build it, Cole was not going to push her into a corner where Bryant Holdings was concerned. Eric? There were myriad possibilities there, ranging all the way from an interminable silent treatment to him never speaking to her again should he learn the truth. As she chewed the last of her eggs and swallowed her now room temperature orange juice, she decided that the only truth she could divulge would have to be one of convenience. But how far would she be willing to go to that end? She called her assistant to have her next day's appointments cancelled and contact her pilot. She only had twenty-four hours to get her story straight.

Chief of Staff

Chapter *32*

ERIC hung up and mulled Bryant Holdings around in his head. What does that have to do with anything, he asked himself. What is there about the family company that Cole Julian would have any interest in, let alone motive, to use against his grandmother? When he was little, like any child would have had, there was little to any attachment to the way his family made their money. His parents and grandparents went to work in the morning, he went to school, and at the end of the day, they all sat down to dinner. No one ever spoke to him about Bryant Holdings. He knew it was a conglomerate of different enterprises from which the Squire family made a tremendous amount of money, but even as a young man growing up and moving in the direction that took him away from the family business, it never really held any significance for him. Eric's dream world had always been politics, and the idea of sitting in a boardroom discussing Profit & Loss statistics or how to better engage management in order to increase their Return on Investment was as enticing to him as a root canal. He had no idea what his grandmother was going to tell him, but it had better damn well be extraordinary.

Claudia entered the office once more and stood there, waiting for Eric to glare at her or send her off like a peasant girl. "Yes, Evil Mistress, what do you need?"

"I told you the other day that I'd finished the manuscript you found in Byrum's safe."

"Bless your heart. You read the entire thing?" Eric pulled his schedule out again, working as Claudia sat down. He looked up at her and eyeing her he said, "You don't look any worse for wear. What did you think about it? Horrible, right?"

Claudia tilted her head and smushed her lips around like she did when deciding whether or not to say what was on her mind. "You want the truth?"

"Give to me straight. I could use a good laugh after that last phone call."

"I liked it a lot. I mean, for what it was intended for. I was thinking, though, and call me crazy, but that story has your family written all over it. I mean if you look at it creatively, that is." Claudia leaned back in her chair, anticipating Eric's reaction.

"And how's that?" he asked, as he continued working on the schedule, crossing out names and penciling in others. First his grandmother and now Claudia. He was half listening to her, but wasn't really invested in their one-sided conversation.

"Well, the story was kind of unbelievable at first, I'll give you that. The characters are crazy and the plot was a little undefined. I don't know, maybe he was working on that part. You know I remember once when he was writing the first novel and asked me to review it for him. He knew about my photographic memory..."

"Partial," Eric said, smirking.

"...And he wanted to have it read and critiqued quickly. I told him that I didn't have time to get into it right then, but that I would check back with him later. I don't remember what I had to do that day, but it must have been daunting. You know how this place can get."

"You're rambling. How about skipping ahead to what you think I'm interested in hearing about."

"Anyway," she started again, "I applied that whole Byrum writes things backward principle and it just kind of worked out that he kind of sounded like maybe he was writing a story based on your family."

"Kind of sounded like maybe. Quite the theory," Eric said. Reginald's research had proved that point conclusively, but Eric wanted to see if the point of view was the same from an outsider. He remembered that Reginald was supposed to email the spreadsheet and he checked his In-Box. Nothing.

Chief of Staff

"Whatever. If you don't believe me that's fine. You asked me what I thought about it and I'm telling you. It wouldn't be that hard to do, you know, write a book based on the mighty Squire family. The old man is your grandmother. The husband that died is your mother. I mean some of the things don't match up exactly, but enough of it is possible for a person to say to you what I said. It could be based on your family."

"Or maybe even some other wealthy family." Anybody in his family was probably more than capable of blackmailing someone, especially Christine. But Eric couldn't picture a murderer sitting down to holiday dinners at Dove's Nest. Byrum had obviously taken a little too much artistic liberty where that was concerned. Whatever it takes to sell books.

"Some of the stuff he obviously embellished to give the characters depth, like the part about the daughter tearfully promising her dying father under the star-filled midnight sky that she would grow up to be a world-famous doctor and find a cure for cancer so her daddy didn't have to die and leave her alone." Claudia pursed her lips together and rolled her eyes. "Give me a break. What eight year old is going to say something like that?"

Eric put his pencil down and looked at Claudia.

"What? Why are you looking at me like that? You're giving me the creeps."

"Was that really in there? I never read that."

"It was toward the middle, probably after the point you got lazy and stopped reading. Why?"

"Tell me that part again."

"What part?"

"What did you just say about what the kid in the manuscript said?"

"I said what eight year old is going to tell their dying parent that they would grow up to find a cure for cancer?"

Eric leaned back in his chair and looked blankly around the office. "I did." If he had said that to his mother, alone on the sun porch, how did that get into the manuscript? Who the hell was feeding Byrum information? Evan Trammell was the only person he could think of.

Chapter *33*

LATER that morning, Claudia dropped Byrum's manuscript on the edge of Eric's desk on her way out to run a quick errand for Senator Tanner. "Here you go. I'll be back in about twenty minutes. It's probably, and this is going to sound just awful, especially coming from a Christian...."

"Especially," he mocked.

"...but it's probably a good thing that Byrum wasn't able to finish this."

"Why is that?" Eric asked.

"If it really is based on your family, or some family just like yours, and if the truth ever got out, I'm sure it would cause a lot of people harm. That kind of thing shouldn't happen to people – whether they're evil or not."

"So now my family is potentially evil?" Eric asked, with a sarcastic smile.

Claudia rolled her eyes and said, "I'm sure whoever else was involved in writing this thing feels the same way, or at least they should. That book was a bad idea."

"I thought you liked it. You're changing your mind?"

"I'm not changing my mind. It was a good book."

"If you're a crack whore," Eric said.

"I just had a change of heart concerning what could happen to the people he was writing about, that's all."

"You do, in fact, have a soul," Eric said.

No matter her opinion and her newfound sense of compassion toward his family, and his kind of people, and certainly not to try and prove her wrong, Eric desperately wanted to read the manuscript from cover to cover, but he simply didn't have the time. He also wished Byrum had not only lived to finish the book, but lived to regret writing and having it published. He refocused on the spreadsheet as Claudia stood to leave. The deadline for the schedule was charging at him and the impending visit from his grandmother only compressed his availability that much further. "I'll look at it a little later. Where are you off to?"

"I've been dispatched to pick up some medicine for Senator Tanner," Claudia said.

"What for?"

"It's for my cold," Senator Tanner said walking into Eric's office. "Is that okay with you?"

Claudia quickly left, sticking her tongue out at Eric behind Senator Tanner's back.

"I'm going to have to put a Lo-Jack in your suits, Senator," Eric said. "Where have you been? I understand you missed the meeting with the Judiciary Committee this morning. Care to explain that?"

"No, I do not. But, since you are going to dog me until I give you an answer, I was at the doctor."

"Again?" Eric sat forward, motioning Senator Tanner to sit. "You're starting to worry me with this going to the doctor constantly stuff. I thought you just had a cold."

"You'll find, young sir, that the aging process is not kind to everyone." He laughed and tried to change the subject. "What are you working on?"

"Not so fast. I'm serious. I'm worried about you. What gives? What is Claudia running to the pharmacy to get for you?"

"I don't believe that is any of your concern or your business, Eric."

"Dead wrong. Everything about you is my concern and it is most assuredly my business. I exist to make sure things run smoothly for you, within this office and without. You can be straight with me or I will indulge myself to pry out of you what I want to know by any means necessary."

Chief of Staff

"Good God, Eric," the senator smiled. "Squire DNA runs so completely through you it's scary. You win. If you insist on embarrassing an old man, I'll tell you what you want to know. For the past several months, I have had trouble getting and maintaining an erection."

"Whoa! That is seriously too much information." Eric turned his head and closed his eyes. "That's what visual grenades and nightmares are made of."

"You asked."

"Against my better judgment."

"Are you through interrogating me?"

"That still doesn't answer the question. You've been sickly for what, two weeks now? You looked like hell when you came back to the office from your self-imposed exile and I retreated to Charlotte for my mental retrofitting. You look a little better, but not by a whole lot. You're still kind of yellowish."

"That's nice. Yellowish."

"What gives? And, please, don't mention your manhood again. What else is going on with you?"

Senator Tanner looked at Eric and opened his mouth like he wanted to say something, but chose to leave the mystery between them. "What I'll tell you, Eric, is that I hadn't felt well for a while, but now I feel better and better every day."

"What does that mean?"

"It means simply that." Senator Tanner waited for Eric to say something. He didn't like lying to Eric, for any reason, but when he did it had always been for a very good reason. This latest secret was one he would have to hold close to the vest. There was no reason to reveal anything to him, not at this point, anyway.

Eric, too, searched for something more to say, but it was clear the senator had said all that would be offered up on the subject. "Whatever. Just get better."

"I'll give it that old college try." Senator Tanner peered over the pictures on Eric's desk and pointed to Byrum's manuscript. "What's that?"

Instinctively, Eric reached out and picked it up, trying to nonchalantly pull it toward him. "It's nothing. It's the manuscript Byrum was working on, I guess, right before he died."

"I hope it's better than that first shitbag he wrote," Senator Tanner said, frowning in disgust. "What's it about?" He took the manuscript out of Eric's hand and started paging through it.

"I haven't had a chance to read the whole thing. Being chief of staff doesn't lend much time to leisurely pursuits, sir. It's definitely on my to do list, that's for sure. If there are any revelations about a certain southern senator, I'll be sure to mention them." Eric suddenly tensed up, imagining that Senator Tanner would know exactly what it was about as he looked through it. He then remembered that until Claudia gave him her expert analysis that morning, even he didn't know exactly what it was about. And he still didn't. Claudia could have been completely off base, but until he found out for himself, he wouldn't know for sure. There was no way the senator would make the connection in the ten seconds he had it in his hands. "I'm not really sure what it's about."

"You already said that."

"Yeah. Maybe I'm getting old and forgetful. It has something about an old man and his crazy family. Blackmail is thrown around in there, I think." He reached for the manuscript and put it back in its place on his desk. "Like I said, I've only read the first little part. Sorry but there's not much more I can tell you about it past that."

Senator Tanner shrugged his shoulders and stood to leave. "Maybe I should have written a book. I think

Chief of Staff

I've got a pretty interesting story to tell. Don't you?" He winked at Eric who wagged his finger at him.

"I don't know about telling that story, Senator. And, hey, once you retire, you'll have all the time in the world to write. Sit back on Trinity, sail around the world, and write the Great American Novel. Sounds absolutely delicious to me."

"Two things, Eric. You never have as much time as you think you do. And never, ever, say delicious in a sentence to me again." They both laughed and Senator Tanner turned to leave.

"Oh, before I forget, as though I ever could," Eric started. "My grandmother is going to be here tomorrow."

Senator Tanner whipped around. "Excuse me?"

"My grandmother is coming to visit me tomorrow."

"Christine? Is coming here? Tomorrow? When?"

"This feels like the L.S.A.T. Yes, Christine. Yes, she is coming here, as I've already said twice. Yes, tomorrow. And," Eric said, actually writing it in his calendar, "she should be here about noon."

"Thanks for the warning. Please extend my warmest regards," Senator Tanner said, walking backward as he spoke. "I, uh, I've got a meeting to get to."

Eric checked the calendar. "No. No, you don't. There's nothing on your calendar until tomorrow morning's meeting with the Joint Chiefs. And after that, you don't have anything until a dinner meeting with Senator Fasciolo to talk about the highway improvement bill she wants your support on."

"No," Senator Tanner said, searching for a way out of seeing Christine, "I distinctly remember Claudia making an appointment for me. It's probably going to last all day. I may not even have the chance to come into the office tomorrow."

"A pity," Eric said, sarcastically.

Chief of Staff

"Okay, gotta run. I'm off. I'll see you in the morning. Have a pleasant evening! Enjoy the book!"

And with that, he was gone, leaving Eric sitting alone with an unfinished manuscript and an unfinished schedule of senatorial meetings to keep him company. "What a day."

*****

THAT night after he left the office, Eric toted Byrum's manuscript back to his townhouse. Armed with a bottle of very dry red wine and Four Play's 'Elixir' on the stereo, he settled on the sofa and started reading. The first part of the manuscript hadn't gotten any better since he'd read it on his veranda in Charlotte. This is still horrible, he told himself. He was very curious, though, to understand how Claudia could have tied the characters and the plot back to his family, and that alone spurred him to keep turning the pages.

When he'd finished the first section again, he got up to change CDs and that's when it hit him. The familiarity with the characters was beginning to feel like someone had, indeed, recorded his life, his experiences, his family's interactions. The notes in the margin still didn't make any sense to him, though. He still didn't have that email from Reginald with the mystery tabs detailing the information that had been passed to Byrum and that frustrated him. Normally, Reginald was on top of things. Byrum's shorthand was indecipherable at times and maddening at others. Eric poured another glass of wine, hunkered down again, but soon found his eyelids drooping. It was almost eleven o'clock and the wine, combined with a ridiculously busy day, started wearing him down. He flipped the unread sections through his fingers and wondered if he should read the rest of it in the morning. There was no good reason he should be losing sleep over the ramblings of a dead man, no matter the connection it may have held to his family. He thought about it for a second and decided he had to finish it, corroborating evidence from Reginald or not. He uncorked the wine, poured another glass, and started the next chapter. By the time he'd read the very last page, he was both drunk and mad as hell, as he fell into bed.

Chief of Staff

*****

"HELP me, Eric," Christine pleaded. Her face was grotesquely distorted and her voice was shaking. Fear gripped her face, eyes open wide and begging for him to come closer, to save her. Fire burned around his grandmother searing her flesh, singing her hair and clothes. She would cry, then laugh, then cry again. Her arms and legs were tied as she lay on the ground, a dirt floor that crawled with snakes and spiders. They slowly criss-crossed her body, encircling her neck and disappearing into her nostrils. As she spoke, an acrid smell came from her mouth, streams of green-hued steam belching from her gut.

"There's nothing I can do for you now," Eric replied. He wasn't angry or upset, but he heard in his own voice something raw and uncaring. It was though he enjoyed watching her writhe in pain. It felt comforting to him that he did nothing to ward off the evil that had possessed her. He stood above her, floating perhaps, looking down over this woman, this caregiver who bent him and shaped him into her own image.

Eric felt his face and as his fingers traced the heavily wrinkled and melting flesh, he realized that he, too, was somehow grossly disfigured. Looking down, he noticed that his hands were bloody and beginning to stick together, but he didn't know why. He fell from the sky, landing next to her. At once, he and Christine slowly melded into one being, fantastically evil and now frantically clawing at each other for freedom, each willing to sacrifice the other for their misdeeds.

In the distant, graying skies looming over the mountain range far away, light broke through the clouds. A mysterious figure was approaching Eric and Christine, drifting ever closer until it was as if he were standing atop them both. Hidden in the eclipse of light, Christine couldn't bring herself to focus on their visitor. She had stopped asking Eric to help her, stopped fighting him, instead straining to free herself from her entanglement. A snake slithered gracefully toward her mouth and down her throat, making it impossible for her

Chief of Staff

to breathe or even to speak. A hand broke free of its shackle and Christine reached deep into her mouth, searching her stomach for the intruder. Eric turned from his grandmother back toward the man in the light. The fire had abated and his face was smooth again. The man reached out, and grabbing Eric's hand, separated him from his grandmother. As he opened his mouth, the wind howled in Eric's ears, cold enveloping him and caused him to shiver violently. A shadowed finger pointed toward Christine, struggling to breathe, consumed by fire once more.

"Blessed is the man who does not walk in the counsel of the wicked!"

Eric looked back at Christine once more, and just as her body exploded in a ravenous ball of flame, the alarm clock blared in his ear, shocking him out of his nightmare and back to consciousness.

Chief of Staff

Chapter *34*

"GOOD afternoon, young lady. My name is Christine Belmont Squire. I am here to see my grandson, Eric Julian. Would you please let him know that I have arrived?" Dressed in a full-length black fur coat over a beautiful burgundy dress, with diamonds accenting her ears and wrists, Claudia was face-to-face with the woman she had read and heard so much about. Trying as best she could to discreetly check her out, Claudia marveled at the elegance and poise of the matriarch of the Squire family. Everything about this woman was perfect, Claudia said to herself. Not a hair out place. Exquisite 3-inch peep-toe Stuart Weitzman slingbacks. Flawless polish on her nails. And that wonderful creamy skin. There was no way this woman could even be close to ninety years old.

The day before, Claudia had told Senator Tanner that Eric's grandmother was going to be in the office and that she couldn't wait to meet her. Be careful what you wish for, the senator said. She is wickedness personified. Jesus is my protector, Claudia said. He watches over me and keeps me from harm. Under that slick persona is a werewolf just waiting to be unleashed at the flick of a switch, the senator replied. Not even Jesus can protect you from that.

"Yes, ma'am. I'll tell him you're here. Please have a seat and I'll be with you in just one moment." She certainly doesn't seem like any werewolf I've ever seen before, Claudia thought.

"There's no need to sit, grandmother. Thank you, Claudia," Eric said as he emerged from his office. "Please do come in."

Christine flowed past Claudia and into Eric's office. "She's certainly a nice girl, Eric. A little too dark to be sitting out front like that, and I'm not sure what to make of her fingernails, but she seems fine." Eric closed the door behind her, making sure to mouth the words sorry and help to Claudia before turning his attention to his guest.

Chief of Staff

"Well, what do you think?" he asked, showing her around his office.

Slowly, Christine scanned the room, moaning with that mix of displeasure and suspicion she was so good at. "It's no Dove's Nest, but I guess opulence wasn't what you were going for then, was it?" She stood in front of Eric with her arms open. "I've missed you."

"And I you, grandmother." He took her fur and they sat down on the sofa. "Can I get you anything?"

"I've already eaten, but if that girl wouldn't mind, I would love to have some coffee."

"She's not a servant, grandmother. I've got a coffee pot in the break room. I'll make some and bring it in here for you." When Eric returned to his office, his grandmother had vanished. "Grandmother?"

"I'm in here, Eric," she said, calling out from Senator Tanner's office.

"What are you doing in here?" Eric took her by the arm and led her back to his office. "You can't just roam around."

"Why does he have bloody tissue in his wastepaper basket? That is a little unsanitary, don't you think?"

"Grandmother, it doesn't pay to be nosy. He had a bloody nose this morning and he threw the tissues in the trash, where they belong. What would you have him do with them? Wrap them up and take them to the bathroom?"

"I'm just saying," Christine responded. "I also noticed there are several pictures of you in the senator's office."

"And?"

"Nothing. I know you're close and I just find it interesting that he feels comfortable enough displaying candid photos of the two of you." Christine fixed her coffee and returned to the sofa.

Chief of Staff

242

"I've known the man my entire life, grandmother. Those pictures are just memories of the times we've shared together."

"I have no problem with the pictures, Eric. I was just making a point." After a liberal sip, she said, "I notice the senator isn't here at the moment. He wouldn't be avoiding me, would he?"

"He is most assuredly not avoiding you, grandmother. In fact, he asked me to send his regards."

"Did he now?" she asked, subtly shaking her head.

"He had an all-day meeting," Eric said, wondering why he was covering for the senator's absence when even he had no idea his boss had gone and why he didn't want to see Christine.

"Perhaps he will be free the next time I make the journey here to visit my grandson."

"I'll make sure to pass that along, grandmother." Eric took a deep breath and instead of belaboring the point, he moved on. "Tell me about Bryant Holdings, please. What is it that Cole seems to think is so important that you'll pay him to keep quiet?"

"Well aren't we Mr. Get Right to the Point?" Christine sipped her coffee and cleared her throat. "This may take a while. I want to make sure that I get everything correct." What she meant was that she wanted to make sure she didn't confuse the story in her head. Eric was a sharp young man, so she had to be one hundred per cent certain that what she was about to say made sense in his mind.

"You have two hours, grandmother. May I remind you that I have a two o'clock appointment."

"Then, since I am constrained by your schedule, I will simply start from the beginning." Sitting her coffee cup down on the table, she said, "Where do I begin?"

Eric leaned over and picked up the pad and pen he was going to use to take notes from their conversation. "Start wherever you need to."

"As you know, your grandfather was an attorney and very intuitive businessman."

"Yes, I remember that. He died when I was around six or seven, but I remember my mother telling me stories about him."

"Well, when we came to Charlotte, we weren't like a lot of the other families. We had no children at the time and we were focused on trying to grow your grandfather's law practice. A rather clever move on his part, he befriended black community and business leaders just the same as he befriended white community and business leaders. Mind you, it was much more difficult for him to get in the door of the white folks, but never the less, he introduced himself and told every one of them what he could do for them. His law practice began to thrive very soon after we moved to Charlotte. I was very proud of him and, naturally, our standing in the community began to rise.

"Times were very different in Charlotte in those days than they are right now. Yes, your grandfather and I had money and nice things, but at the base of it, we were black people. In those days, Charlotte - and more specifically, downtown Charlotte - was made up of wards, much like it is today. Early in its history, Charlotte had been a melting pot of black and white communities, each sharing the richness of their experiences and existing in a way that was simply unprecedented for the times. At some point, however, and this was long before your grandfather and I moved to Charlotte, there came a change. Blacks and whites began to segregate and they became more inward, not feeling comfortable with the open relationships between the races that they had once enjoyed. Times and attitudes changed and there developed a caging, of sorts, where blacks and whites didn't intermingle.

"That was the beauty about what your grandfather did, Eric. Even though there was a tenseness permeating Charlotte where race and class dominated every nuance of life from where you were allowed to live to what high school you would be allowed to attend, to what restaurants you could freely patronize, your grandfather found a way to bridge that chasm."

Eric stopped taking notes and decided to simply listen, fascinated by this story. Of all the years he'd lived in Charlotte, he had never taken the time to understand any of its beginnings, passions or drama; any of the ideology that gave his hometown its character. "Excuse me, grandmother," he said as he went to the door of his office. "Claudia, cancel my appointments for the rest of the day, please." With that, he returned to the sofa and his now smiling grandmother. "Please continue."

Christine touched Eric's leg when he sat down and thought about his mother. "You've turned out to be quite the young man, Eric." He nodded his thanks and asked her to continue. "What was I saying?"

"You were talking about grandfather bridging a chasm."

"Ah yes, that's right. Now back then, it wasn't accepted that a woman have a formal place in the business world. Our opportunities were limited, to say the least. It was our place to keep the home, to raise the children, and to make sure that the needs of your husband were met. You can imagine how that sat with me."

"I believe I have a clue, yes, grandmother," Eric said, with a knowing smile.

"As a graduate of Spelman, I hadn't intended on sitting back and letting your grandfather reap the glory for the family, so I took action, behind the scenes, of course. God knows what would have happened if word got out that I was whispering ideas in your grandfather's ear that proved beneficial to both the business world and the social

Chief of Staff

community we enjoyed. I had made it a point to reign supreme socially in Charlotte, and I was bound and determined to function as both a matriarch and a businesswoman simultaneously, even if under the cloak of secrecy.

"In bridging the chasm between races, your grandfather was able to garner the respect of white and black business leaders. He knew that in order to make money in the legal world, you had to seek out your clients. And not just any clients, mind you, but those who would provide a level of service and income necessary to improve the bottom line and lead to an increased social standing. That last part was my idea," she said, winking.

"Imagine that."

"As part of the plan, your grandfather targeted what were known as black businesses. You know, funeral homes, family-owned grocery stores, other small businesses like clothing stores, beauty- and barber shops. The list goes on and on. Well, at the time, all of those black businesses and owners lived in one of the four wards of downtown Charlotte. And let me tell you that they were thriving. When business was good for them, it was doubly good for your grandfather. He began making large sums of money on both sides of the fence, as it were. His stature in both the white and black communities was growing by leaps and bounds every year.

"By the time we were able to afford to build Dove's Nest, your grandfather was something of a Charlotte legend. His law practice was exploding and my ability to influence the Charlotte social calendar was also becoming something of a coup. Of course, with there not being more than a handful of our kind of people in the surrounding area, it took longer for me to establish myself, and our family, socially. The main areas where we were concentrated were Atlanta, Memphis, Maryland, Rock Hill, and a few other southern cities. So," she said, rolling her eyes, "you can see what I was up against.

"Anyway, one day while we were sitting on that bench by the pond at Dove's Nest, I turned to your father and told

Chief of Staff

him I had an idea. Actually, I had two ideas, but they would have to come one after the other, in succession, for them to work. The first idea was that he should start his own bank." Christine poured another cup of coffee and stood up to walk around the office. Eric kept his seat, but watched her as she spoke. "The reasoning behind that was very simple, if you ask me. The fifties and sixties were taking a toll on everyone in Charlotte. Segregation was entrenching itself and, it seemed, affected more and more sections of life as we knew it. Now, your grandfather and I were insulated from all of that nonsense, for the most part, because we were out of the city by that point. Dove's Nest was, and still is in many respects, a sanctuary, cut off from the rigors of everyday life, and the problems of everyday people. In that way we were very lucky. It was a wonderful place to raise your late mother and her brother.

"But because times were changing and people, especially blacks, were more and more distrustful of whites, the only logical idea was to open a bank they could believe was their own, that acted purely in their best interests. Give them savings accounts, fund loans for college and whatever else they needed, offer low-rate mortgages, etc. It was most brilliant on my part, if I do say so myself."

"Brilliant, perhaps," Eric interrupted. "But how did grandfather go from being an attorney to owning a bank? That seems quite the leap to take given he didn't have any experience in that regard."

"You're right. It was something of a leap of faith. But the one thing your grandfather had always been good at was meeting and charming people. He made a contact with a local businessman, Lauren Tanner."

"The senator's father?"

"Yes."

So that was the connection, Eric said to himself, remembering the conversation he had with Senator Tanner on the yacht the night his world unfolded. "How did they hook up?"

"In the late sixties your grandfather represented Lauren in a case, the details of which escape me at the moment. Lauren owned a construction and demolition business and was quite well off. After I put the seed in your grandfather's head about starting up a bank, we realized that we needed much more capital than we had. Yes, his law practice had done well, and we were very wealthy by that point already, but to fund a bank it was going to take much more than we originally estimated. Your grandfather and Lauren proposed a deal whereby he, and a couple other investors, would put up the money and we would run the bank. Money in, money invested, money out. It's simple economics, mixed with a tremendous amount of government-derived rules and regulations."

"Grandfather wasn't the majority owner?"

"Not in so many words, no."

"So it was only a black-owned bank in principle?"

"Our names were on all of the documents, of course. Lauren and the other investors gave their money to us and we created a corporation to handle the assets. The bank was established and we hung our shingle. In all reality, we had bought a small, local bank and renamed it, forming Community Savings & Loan."

"Sounds a little shady."

"I assure you that everything was legitimate, Eric."

"Right. Continue."

"Well, things were going extremely well for us. The bank was a lightning rod for blacks and their wealth, at all levels." Christine sat back down on the sofa and poured herself another cup of coffee. "You see," she said, slowly stirring in the creamer and sugar, "Charlotte was something of a rough hewn city, progressive though it was, mind you. There were still some facets of the population and the layout

Chief of Staff

that weren't very attractive to the civic leaders. In the middle of the sixties and into the early seventies, a period of redevelopment was spawned. I believe it was an attempt to freshen Charlotte, to modernize and liven it up in hopes of attracting businesses and to spur economic growth."

Eric's phone rang and he excused himself. "This won't take but just a moment, grandmother. I'm sorry." He listened intently to whomever it was, intriguing Christine, and hung up after a very brief conversation.

"I don't suppose that was the president, was it?" she asked.

"No, ma'am. Just someone who's doing a little research for me, that's all." He sat back on the sofa and gave the floor back to his grandmother.

"As I was saying, there was a period of upheaval in Charlotte and one of the areas of focus was downtown. Remember that it was casually divided into four wards."

"Right."

"Well, the leaders of the time decided that it just wouldn't do for that area to remain dilapidated and run down because it was beginning to become an eyesore on the map toward progress. It was going to be razed and replaced with more upscale housing and the entire area was to be revitalized to attract businesses and other types of entertainment."

"But weren't those primarily black neighborhoods?"

"Yes, they were."

"And the city was going to tear them down to make way for economic growth?"

"Again, that is correct."

"Is that where Bryant Holdings comes into play?"

"I'm getting to that. Hold your horses." Christine put her hand on her chin and wondered how she was going to craft this next part of their talk. "What is important that you keep in mind, Eric, is that your grandfather and I were making

Chief of Staff

every attempt to ensure that the future of our children and grandchildren would be taken care of. It was crucial in our eyes to provide for the next generations as our parents had provided for us. Life can be difficult if you aren't associated with the right parts of society. Do you understand what I'm trying to say?"

Eric nodded yes, but wasn't exactly sure where she was going.

"Okay. Bryant Holdings was a corporation we established separate from the bank, and completely separate from your grandfather's firm. The city put out bids to companies who were interested in doing the demolition and rebuilding of the four wards of downtown. Because of his contacts in the business and legal world, and along with Lauren Tanner, we, meaning Bryant Holdings, won that business."

"And Cole was a part of that somehow? I still haven't heard you make the connection to anything illegitimate."

"Cole had quickly moved his way up the bank hierarchy and by this point he was a vice president, deeply involved in the accounting and managing of the bank's assets. He was also married to your mother at the time, something that brings chills to my spine when I think about it. Bryant Holdings was a depositor, of course, in our bank, and all of the funds generated from the reconstruction were deposited with us. Everything was going smoothly. Lauren and we made a ton of money from the city, we earned government contracts from the state, and our depositors were reaping generous interest rates on their savings and other interest-bearing accounts. As Cole was more or less in charge of the accounting for the bank, I put the blame squarely on his shoulders for what happened."

"Which was what? The pace of this tale is coming to a screeching halt, grandmother."

"You're just like your mother, impatient; a quality which is very unbecoming," Christine said with a raised eyebrow. "You asked me for a causal link and I'm providing it to you. Don't critique me on the delivery."

"I apologize most profusely," Eric said.

"As well you should. Now, once everything was over, all of the wards had been rebuilt, a process that took about five years, by the way, Cole and your grandfather sat down with Lauren and audited their records. It turned out that somewhere along the way, Bryant Holdings had collected more from the city and the state than we were actually owed."

"How much?"

"Around five million dollars."

"That's not a lot of money. What did you do about it?"

"Nothing."

"Nothing? You didn't tell anyone? No one became suspicious and came looking for the money? I find that rather hard to believe."

"It's not a lot of money now, but back then it was a windfall. Lauren and your grandfather decided to keep the secret, only fessing up should they be questioned about it. And no one ever did."

"You basically stole five million dollars. Is that what you're telling me Cole has on you?"

"Young man," Christine said, exasperated, "we did nothing of the sort."

"But you didn't give it back, right?" Eric asked, smiling, unable to hide the guilty pleasure of catching his grandmother involved in something so very unseemly. "You kept the money and never said a word to anyone."

Christine poked the side of her mouth with her tongue and bit her lip. She blinked quickly and shook her head. "No, I wouldn't say it like that."

"But it's true."

"Again, the times were different back then."

"You're a crook," Eric teased.

"Stop it! Stop saying that," Christine said, smiling and embarrassed and trying her best to fake remorse. "You don't understand."

"Oh, I understand perfectly. I'm guessing that Cole's idea was to give the money back, right? And then maybe my mother got sick, he couldn't handle it, ran away from the family, remembered the banking scandal and figured this would be the best way for him to squeeze you for money." Christine never said a word. Her grandson was clever and if this was the story he wanted to go with, she'd play right along with him. "I guess Cole thinks that five million dollars you stole is now worth fifty million. That must be where he got that figure from."

Eric put his head back on the sofa and thought for a moment. By coming forward and making a pre-emptive strike announcing the accounting scandal that happened eons ago, Cole's blackmail attempt would fizzle and he would, hopefully, go away. On the other hand, telling the world about what happened would go a long way in destroying not only Christine's reputation, but it would also sully the fond memories many people held for his grandfather.

Of course, layered on top of that was Senator Tanner's father and his reputation. Media speculation automatically put into play Senator Tanner, even though he had nothing to do with the scandal at all. That, in turn, would strike up controversy around Eric representing the state of North Carolina should the time come. The son and grandson of thieves who ripped off their city and state sitting in the catbird seat of the United States senate. The more he thought about it, the more ghastly the scenarios became. Was his chance of becoming a senator worth $50 million? Would exposing the scandal be the end of his dream?

"Grandmother, we've got to find a way to either give Cole the money, or make him think he's got the money.

We've also got to get from him every stitch of information he has that links you and grandfather and whomever else to what happened. It may not have been a big deal when it happened, but the consequences have multiplied exponentially for everybody."

"As you may remember, we sold the bank when you were younger. The bank's records were analyzed thoroughly by government agencies I didn't even know existed. No one found anything, Eric. Because we really didn't do anything wrong. The assets have been sold several times since then, and everything that once existed as Community Savings & Loan lives under the Wells Fargo corporate umbrella. It's out of my hands and has been for quite some time."

"That still leaves the matter of Bryant Holdings and whatever records exist from that time period as they relate directly to the company today, though, grandmother." Eric looked at Christine and throttled back. "Don't worry. This is all going to go away."

Christine leaned over and hugged Eric. "I knew you were the right person to come to. I'm sorry for involving you, but I didn't know where else to turn. I wish your grandfather were still with us."

"I do, too, grandmother," Eric said. He pulled away and took her hand. "Why don't you stay in D.C., tonight? We could go to dinner and talk some more."

"I'd love to, really I would," she said, rising from the sofa. "But I simply have to get back home tonight. Along with the fundraiser, I'm in the midst of putting together a birthday celebration for one of my dear friends and I'm getting farther and farther behind with every precious moment I spend with you." Eric knew a back-handed compliment even before it smacked him in the face. His gesture, however sincere at first, was a ploy. Washington never held any fascination for Christine at all. He knew she'd never spend any more time there than she had to, but manners dictated that he make the offer. Dinner with his grandmother was actually the very last thing on his mind.

Chief of Staff

"Well, maybe another time then?" he asked.

"I'd like that very much." Eric helped her into her fur and walked her out. "It was very nice to meet you, dear," Christine said as she walked past Claudia, not stopping to look at her or shake hands. She turned to Eric and kissed him on the cheek. "I know my way out. Have a nice day, dear. Thank you so much for spending time with this old woman. I love you."

"I love you too, grandmother. Have a safe flight back home." Eric watched her walk down the hall, discreetly escorted by a senate page. When she was gone, he dashed back into his office and got on the phone.

"Yes, she's gone. I can't talk here, though. I'll call you from my townhouse in thirty minutes."

Chapter *35*

"WELL, what did you find out?" Eric asked, out of breath. He'd flown out of his office, jumped in a cab and practically knocked his front door down getting to the phone. His stomach was churning and his heart felt like it might explode. The excitement and anxiety together were killing him. "What's this guy's name? Was it Evan? Was I right?"

"Speedy Gonzales didn't talk that fast, Eric. Slow down. We've got a lot to talk about. I've found out more than I expected, to be honest with you."

"Just start at the beginning. I want to know everything." Eric had popped open a bottle of water and sat down at the kitchen table. Hmm, that's strange, he said to himself. He could hear Reginald speaking, but nothing he was saying registered. Eric got up from the table and walked into the living room. He was staring at two things: an abstract painting on the south wall, and a sculpture of Nasiteen on a pedestal right below the painting. Each of them had been moved just slightly, but how? His cleaning lady hadn't been there that morning and he was quite sure he would have noticed something so peculiar before he'd left for work. He scanned the room and noticed that several more pieces were out of place. A chill ran down his spine just as Reginald began to yell at him.

"You're not going to believe this, but I found him! We've got this guy by the balls, Eric. To begin with, our guy isn't Evan, the butler. I knew that was too easy. His name is Earl Tucker."

"Who?" Who was Earl Tucker? Cole had confessed to the blackmail that day in the park. Earl Tucker was a name Eric had never heard before. He continued to walk around his townhouse, looking for things that were out of place, but couldn't find anything else. "Are you sure that's his name?"

"Am I sure that's his name? I believe I've just been offended."

"Shut up, Reginald. Are you sure his name is Earl Tucker? I mean, the initials match the spreadsheet, but how do you know?"

"That's where this gets interesting." Reginald clapped his hands together and opened his file folder. "When I got to the hunting lodge, I asked around and introduced myself to everyone I could find. From the desk clerks to the guests, I left no stone unturned. I ran into this guy on the phone in the parking lot on the first day we went out to hunt and he gave me his name. I was running out of people to question and this was the break I needed.

"I pretended to be an idiot farmer, flush with a bunch of cash, who wanted to hunt at an upscale lodge. We struck up this weird friendship and I started the process to pump info from him. Let me tell, you, Eric, this guy was an extremely tough nut to crack. He damn near ran me off the first time I met him. He was on the phone with somebody and was pissed that I'd interrupted whatever the hell it was he was doing to get ready for the day."

"Sounds like a prick if you ask me," Eric said.

"At first, yes," Reginald said. "But for whatever reason, he changed his tune and was…"

"Was what?" Eric asked, drinking another bottle of water.

"Never mind. Lost my train of thought on that one," Reginald lied. "We'd decided to keep to ourselves for the morning hunts, and then we'd meet up and go out with a guide in the afternoon. I didn't bag anything, but Earl was a pretty aggressive and very skilled huntsman. I was quite impressed."

"I don't care. Tell me what I want to know."

"It's your dime. I ran a pickpocket game on him the second night we were there. The bar was packed and he

Chief of Staff

didn't even feel me take his wallet. I grabbed a credit card and used that as a jumping off point. You know you can find out anything you want just from somebody's credit card if you know how and where to look. Here's the part where we ran into a little drama. From his credit card, we mined his social security number, address, date of birth, and so on and so forth. I had my people check into any- and everything they could find on our Earl Tucker. I did the same thing on him that I do when you've got a candidate you need me to scope out. I ran a complete background check on this guy.

"Now, normally, you'd find things like voter registration, spousal information, stuff on their jobs and all of their past residences, any known aliases, criminal records, professional groups, credit history and the list goes on and on. What I found when searching for Earl Tucker was quite a bit different. It's good news, bad news kind of scenario. Bad news: It turns out Earl Tucker died about twenty years ago."

"Come again?" Eric was puzzled.

"All the information I have leads me to believe whoever this guy is, he either stole or bought the real Earl Tucker's identity."

"How do you know all of this?"

"Do you remember the voice mail I left you several weeks ago? I told you that I'd found someone and that I needed to check him out. I was on my way to the airport to jump on my plane for a quick flight out of town to follow him. Does that ring any bells for you?"

"You have an airplane?" Eric asked, caught off guard.

"Yes."

"I pay you way too much money. I don't even have my own plane."

"I have a King Air 350. Does your grandmother not have her own Boeing Global Express?"

"She does."

"And do you not have unlimited access to it and the other company planes?"

"Yes, I do."

"Then we can either debate my soon to be increasing fees or the fact that not only do you have one private plane, you have a veritable fleet of private planes." Eric said nothing in response. "As always, silence is golden. You were saying about my voice mail?"

"I remember the voice mail, but to be honest, I couldn't quite make out everything you were saying."

"Well, it turned out that time we had the wrong man. We started all over from scratch and it was during our last meeting at your place I got the call that broke the case wide open. We accessed his phone records and found out that he was going on a hunt. It seems Earl is some kind of expert big game hunter. I left you and raced to this hole in the wall, pretended to be said idiot farmer and got in his good graces."

"This is shaping up to be a fantastic story. When do you tell me the part about shooting laser beams out of your eyes? What's the good news?" Eric was hugely disappointed that Cole wasn't the person targeting his grandmother. He noticed a bright light, like some kind of reflection, coming through the window and got up to see what is was. When he pulled the curtain aside, his jaw dropped. That goddamn stalker in that goddamn hooded sweatshirt was standing outside, on the curb, bouncing sunlight off of his watch and into Eric's home. He waved when he saw Eric and dashed off. Eric ran out the front door, looked left and right, but he couldn't find a trace of him. He'd simply vanished. "What in the hell?!"

"Like I said," Reginald continued, "he was a tough nut. It took almost four days before he felt comfortable enough to share even the most-minute of details about his life with me. Over dinner on the second to last day, he told me that he was some kind of day trader and I played along, asking him how he could make some money for me. His face lit up

Chief of Staff

when I told him I'd sold my father's, or rather, my daddy's farm for twelve million. Very quickly, he offered to help me invest the money and make it grow."

"Earl Tucker, huh?" Eric was writing down the name over and over again in the margins of a magazine as Reginald spoke. "What do we do now? How do we prove that he's trying to get money for telling my family's history?"

"There's a great deal more to this story. So after dinner, we moved to the bar. Oh, before I forget. At dinner, I introduced my new friend to Jaeger Bombs and he sucked them down like a bum does cheap red wine. Before long, he was inebriated to the point where I could set him up with questions to whatever I wanted to know."

"Jaeger has a tendency to do strange things to people, Reginald."

"Well, what it did to Earl Tucker was propel him to drop more than 'F' bombs. While I was there, I took some pictures of this guy. I'm sending them via secure email. Let me know when you get them."

Eric walked into his home office and sat behind his desk. It looked as ridiculous as his desk in the senate building. Piles of documents, voting records, research on what seemed like a thousand agendas, and there in the corner, the manuscript. He brought his computer back to life and said, "Yeah, I'm here. Go ahead and send what you've got."

Eric pitched forward in his chair when his In Box chimed, quickly opening the folder and clicking through the first grainy images. As the pictures opened, ten in all, and he realized who he was looking at, his blood ran cold.

"Oh my God. That's my father. Cole Julian and Earl Tucker are the same person!"

"I know."

*****

"LISTEN to this. It's the best part. So we're sitting at the bar and I could tell he was drunk out of his mind. I started with one simple question, something about why he'd come up to hunt. He told me that his former mother-in-law was some crazy mean old lady who banned him from hunting if he wanted to continue to enjoy the family fortune."

"Cole told me about hunting when I was a kid. Said he loved it, but that he'd given it up. He never told me why, though. That makes complete sense."

"Maybe to you, but I didn't know that." Reginald's voice was as shrill as it could be, given his deep voice, and he was bubbling over with excitement. "So then I asked more, not really knowing what he was going to tell me. And he unknowingly confessed to everything. And when I say everything, it was like I'd hit a three-run homerun in the bottom of the ninth to win by one. I couldn't stop him if I'd wanted to try. And I didn't."

"What did he say? Did he tell you what he was up to?"

"Not only did he tell me, he slammed the bar and cursed Christine. He said that he was going to crush her in his fingers. He copped to the blackmail and the manuscript! He told me about his gambling problem, how the guy who was paying him for his inside secrets died in some freak plane crash, the staggering amount of money he wants from your grandmother, and every little gem in between. He was fired up, drunk as hell, and on a roll!"

"You're kidding!" Eric was still studying the pictures Reginald emailed, not believing that they had caught him red-handed. "Is that it?"

"He talked some about you, too, the son he was forced to leave behind."

"He wasn't forced. The jerk took my grandmother's money and ran."

Chief of Staff

"I don't know. He sounded completely remorseful. He said he'd written letters she didn't answer and even went back to the house once but he couldn't get in. Nobody would let him through the gate. All he wanted to do was be a good daddy to his kid."

Eric couldn't believe what he was hearing. "I know you're not defending him, Reginald. Is that what I hear? He's a grade-A piece of shit. I was abandoned. He got a million dollars to walk away. And he did it."

"Hey, man, you're preaching to the choir. I'm just telling you what I heard and what I saw in his face when he was telling me that stuff."

"So one minute he's a conniving bastard, out to ruin my family's good name, extort millions more from my grandmother, and then he turns on the charm and says that the only thing he wanted was to be a daddy?" Eric scoffed and said, "That's the biggest pile of horse dung I've ever heard."

"I don't get paid to argue with you, Eric. I get paid to bring you results and that's what you've got. Interpret it however you want to, but don't murder the messenger."

"My fault, Reginald," Eric said, apologizing for his emotion and outburst. This was way more than he could handle. "And you're absolutely positive that Cole is the one trying to extort my grandmother?"

"Technically the term is ransom, as he claims to have something belonging to your grandmother that he's willing to exchange for money."

"Whatever."

"I'm one hundred seventy-five thousand percent this is the guy. I was secretly taping not only that conversation, but all of the chats we'd had together. At the end of every day, I sent them back to my lab for them to be analyzed, just like we did with your grandmother's voice. With the exception of his slurred soliloquy we never got less than a ninety-eight percent positive correlation. This is most definitely our guy. We've got him, Eric. We've got the bastard right where we want him." Reginald beamed from ear to ear. He didn't know if he was happier with himself for finding the elusive Cole Julian, or knowing that his favorite client would soon be rid of his problematic father.

"So what's next?" Eric wanted to know. "Where do we go from here?" His heart was still pounding in his chest. He was thrilled and scared at the same time. Or maybe he was nervous and nauseous, he wasn't sure.

"He mentioned that his timeline was running short and that he needed to make something happen fast. I've got a pretty good feeling he's going to be getting in touch with you real soon. I've got a meeting set up with him next week to bring him a suitcase full of money that he's going to invest for me. About five hundred grand."

"You're going to give him half a million dollars?" Eric asked, startled.

"I've tried in vain to catch up to him, to get a physical location on him, but he's sneaky. I don't know if he assumes somebody's following him or what, but he never takes the same route twice, and he's ditched more than a couple of the people I've put on him. If I get a solid lock on his office or his place of business, that's going to give me a strong lead on how to take him down. If this guy is worth to you what I think he is, that's a drop in the bucket."

"Future business, right?" Eric asked. Reginald wasn't stupid. He knew very well that helping Eric solve this would mean a constant stream of business for a long time to come.

"I told him we'd start small and see where the situation goes from there."

"Reginald, I can't thank you enough for all of this. I'm going to make this worth your while in a big, big way."

"I'm just glad I was the one you called to help. I'll do whatever else you need me to."

Chief of Staff

"Actually there are a couple more things I need you to do for me." Eric drew a line through one of the scribbles of 'Earl Tucker' in the magazine margin. "How hard would it be for you to figure out who he owes money to?"

"Let me work on that."

"Good. I think I've got an idea to remove Cole Julian from the picture."

"And how is that, exactly?"

Eric reached out and picked up the manuscript. "I'm not sure. But it's going to be a page-turner for sure."

When they hung up, Eric sat back in his chair going over the conversation. If Cole is blackmailing my grandmother for money, and if Cole was the person who was getting money from Byrum to write that piece of shit tell-all about my family, and if Cole and Earl Tucker are the same person, who is stalking me and who the hell is TE?

Eric bolted out of his chair at the sound of his doorbell. He walked past the kitchen and was about to open up the door when he thought maybe he needed to have a weapon or something in his hand. He grabbed a knife from the block on the counter and held it behind his back. He couldn't see anything as he looked through the peep hole, and, quite honestly, had second thoughts about opening that door. His heart beat wildly and he took several deep breaths.

Yanking the door open quickly, he scared the crap out of his neighbor, a little old woman who lived next door. She looked at Eric like he was crazy, but started talking anyway. "The nicest young man was walking down the street a moment ago and asked me to help him find your home." The little old lady peered around Eric, like she always did, to see if anything had changed inside. Eric subtly moved over to block her view and asked what else he'd said. "Nothing. I told him we were neighbors and that I would walk him here, but he just handed me this." She stuck a note out and Eric grabbed it quickly.

"Sorry. Just a little excited. I've been expecting this for...uh...quite a while. Thanks so much for brining it by, Mrs. Thomsburry. Have a lovely day!" Eric spoke quickly, thanked his nosy neighbor, closed the door, and ripped open the note at the same time.

It read: "You have a very lovely home. Watch your back."

That afternoon, Eric had his security system upgraded. And thanks to the NRA's lobbying for Instant Background Checks – against his better judgment – he'd bought a gun.

Chapter *36*

"WELL don't you look like a stud," Eric said as Senator Tanner walked into his office. Senator Tanner had on a tuxedo and sat down in front of Eric's desk, futilely trying to adjust his bowtie. "You got a hot date tonight or something?" The mid-afternoon jaunt to his townhouse, not to mention dealing with the security company and buying a goddam pistol, had put him behind schedule and there were a number of things he still needed to complete before going home again.

"Nothing like that," Senator Tanner replied, smiling. "I got roped into going to Pam's niece's first grade celebration about something. She said something about a song she'd been practicing. I was in another world when she asked me and without thinking I said yes."

"That's nice. I'm sure Pam's niece will find it charming that a big senator came down to hear her sing, even though he got roped into it by a staffer he can't stand."

"Funny," he said, looking at his chief of staff with suspicion. "You kind of went radio silent this afternoon. I couldn't find you anywhere. Anything I should know about?"

"This afternoon?" Eric asked, thinking quickly. "Oh, no, I just had to go back to my townhouse. They're repairing a pipe or something. You know how old homes can be. Nothing major." Moving back to the senator's evening he said, "First graders, huh?" He wanted to tell Senator Tanner what was going on, but there had to be a better place and time. Eric didn't want to ruin the man's evening.

"Yes. And let's hope they can sing. There's nothing worse than a multipurpose room full of screaming children."

"Agreed." Eric looked the senator up and down. "You think a tux might be a little over the top?" Eric sat back in his chair and put his arms over his head.

"The tux isn't for the performance or whatever this is. I'm going to the opera right afterward and I don't think I'm going to have time to scoot all the way back here to change."

Eric smiled and asked, "So, again I ask, you got a hot date? Nobody goes to the opera by themselves. And, by the way, I know that you had Claudia order two tickets for something. You're meeting someone, aren't you?"

"I am not having a rendezvous, if that's what you're trying to get me to confess."

"Whatever," Eric said, putting his hands up. He smiled and said, "I'm just looking out for you. Do we need to have 'the talk' before you head out? Do you have protection?" They both laughed at the thought of Eric giving Senator Tanner, a formerly notorious ladies man, advice on sex.

"You missed your calling. You should have been a comedy writer," the senator snipped.

"Perhaps, perhaps." Eric leaned back toward his desk and resumed his latest project.

"You do know that it's 6:30, don't you?" Senator Tanner asked. "Everybody else has gone home for the night. You should do the same."

"The senate doesn't run itself, now does it," Eric said, focused on what he was doing.

"I just don't want you to burn yourself out. You've been working like a dog. You've been here for almost six months and the amount of work you've been able to pump out is astonishing, it's ridiculous, even. In fact, I was talking to Governor Lewis about you just this morning."

"And how is the dear Governor Lewis?" Eric asked.

"Fine."

"And I came up in the conversation how?" Eric questioned. He stood and walked to his filing cabinet, pencil gritted in his teeth, holding a notebook. He rested the notebook on the filing cabinet, with Senator Tanner facing his back, and started digging for some unknown treasure.

"We were talking about people with enormous heads," the senator said.

"Uh huh." Eric continued to comb the cabinet.

"And then he said that if you ever wanted to do a threesome with him and his dog that you should give him a call."

"I'll make sure to get right on that in the morning, Senator." He found what he was looking for, made a couple of notations in the notebook and walked back to his desk.

"And then we said that with the global modernization of the third world and the way Paris Hilton won the open House seat in California meant that there was probably going to be an alien invasion and everybody on earth would either be eaten alive or strung up by their pinky fingers and salt cured for later."

"Right," he said, not looking at the senator. "Salt cured. I understand. I'll make a note of that for in the morning."

"You haven't paid me one bit of attention, have you?"

Eric looked up, briefly, and then went back to work. "Of course I heard you. Something about the Governor and salt curing something or other. Right?" He scratched out whatever it was he had previously written and went back to the filing cabinet.

"Come away with me, Eric," the senator said.

"Uh huh." He looked around and stared at Senator Tanner. "What? I'm sorry. Say that again."

"I said come away with me."

"Like our own little hot date?" He smiled, closed the cabinet and sat back down.

Chief of Staff

"Funny."

"What?"

"You're going to drive yourself crazy with all of this work, Eric. You need to take a break. Let's go on vacation somewhere. Get your mind off of whatever has been dragging you down for the last month - or two. I don't remember it's been so long."

Eric clasped his hands together, leaned onto his desk, and rested his chin on his knuckles. "You haven't the slightest idea what it takes to run this place from day to day, do you?"

"That's why I have a chief of staff." And a senator-in-training, he said to himself.

"Not only am I the chief of staff, but I am the senator in proxy. I am the daycare teacher. I am the problem solver. I am the social committee president. I am the…"

"I get the point," the senator said, holding his hands up. "I get it."

"I don't think so. While you're out doing whatever it is that you do when you're not here, I am, in effect, you. I go to meetings in your place. I speak with constituents in your place. I reach out to senators and their chiefs of staff – in your place. I am obliged to opine on matters of influence where you would normally have a voice. I research voting patterns on upcoming legislation, not to mention recording your voting history on every subject under the sun. I make sure that the words that come out of your mouth, the limited number of engagements wherein I am not a surrogate mouthpiece, are not only eloquent, but that they make sense to the media and that they can be readily absorbed by the voters of North Carolina who steadfastly and passionately eat up everything that you tell them. Do you see this desk?" Eric asked, slowly waving his arms over the piles of minutiae before him. "This is what I do. These piles are my To Do list. This is the responsibility to which I devote my entire energy six and seven days a week. Between my obsessive-

Chief of Staff

compulsive grandmother, a personal matter I neither have the time nor luxury to talk about, and playing the formidable role of Senator, I don't have the ability to take a vacation. The only thing I don't do around here is vote on bills, which, by the way, might be easier said than done because senators and their chiefs of staff know my face a hell of a lot better than they know yours these days."

"Hello. My name is Eric Julian. And I'm a work-a-holic," the senator said. His bowtie had mysteriously come loose and he fumbled with it again.

"I'm a work-a-holic because my boss isn't."

Senator Tanner all of a sudden got that look on his face. The look that meant, in no uncertain terms, that he was quickly becoming pissed. Eric looked at him and was about to ask what his problem was when the man exploded. "Do you have any idea what it is I'm doing for you?" Eric started to respond but the senator cut him off. "Don't even open your mouth. Don't even say one word to me. I'm trying to position you for greatness, Eric Norman Julian. And you could care less. All you do is complain about one thing or another. You've got too much responsibility. Your time is no longer your own. There are too many things for you to focus on at once. Blah, blah, blah! Shut up and take a look at the big picture, please."

"Fine. What is the big picture?" Eric was used to the senator's outbursts, but they were normally directed at someone other than himself. He was taken a little off guard, to say the least.

"The big picture is that you are doing things that other chiefs of staff can only dream about. They don't have the access you do. They don't have the ability to network with senators and senior government officials the way you do. They aren't crafting legislation and controlling the processes that make senators who they are. They don't have the talents you do and they don't have me in their corner. I told you that I was going to make you into a senator and that's exactly what I'm doing."

Chief of Staff

"Some kind of education in absentia, I presume?"

"Call it whatever you want, but when I'm gone, you're going to be the man."

"There's no guarantee for that, you realize."

"What I realize is this: you have to know this place, my job, and the way you're going to fit into it like the back of your hand. If you want to succeed me, there are a whole hell of a lot of things you're going to have to swallow begrudgingly and say thank you for at the same time. You're going to have to kiss asses and babies and old women. You're going to have to deal with pompous assholes you wouldn't hire to clean your house who think they're better than you because they're white, and because they believe they're entitled to their position for no other reason. You're going to have to jump into situations where you know you're the smartest person in the room, listen to the bullshit people are spewing to get votes, and realize that when it's all said and done, your position has not only been heard, but taken as the Gospel.

"In the next eighteen months, your sole job is to make sure that every fucking registered voter, republican and democrat, knows that you would kick in your own grandmother's teeth to make sure they don't lose their jobs because their textile plant went out of business, or that you'll do whatever you can to get whatever agenda item that's stuck in their sweaty panties to the floor of the Senate, voted on, and passed under the twenty-five goddam pens the president is going to use to sign it into law. You have to be sweet and rude and genuine and sarcastic and every adjective in between, and you have to do so without so much as a peep of complaint or remorse. You're going to be a United States Senator, Eric. It's time you started acting like it. Wouldn't you rather be prepared for it now as opposed to falling on your face after you're sworn in?"

Eric let out a long breath of air and looked at Senator Tanner. He knew he was right, but it hadn't dawned on him

Chief of Staff

that the senator was putting him through his paces for a genuine reason. "Okay, so now I feel like an ass."

"Apology accepted."

"Hey, I never apologized," Eric said, smiling.

"Are you sure? Because to me it sounded a lot like you said you were sorry."

"I'm even more not sorry now than you thought I was."

The two men smiled at each other and the nonsense that just fell out of Eric's mouth. "Please God don't ever put that in one of my speeches. Come on, Eric," the senator said, abruptly changing the subject again. "Take a tiny break."

"Who are you now, Jekyll or Hyde?"

"I'm serious. Go somewhere with me. Like we used to in the old days. All of those pictures of us in my office take me back to a time when we could just jet off some place and have a great time."

"I know," Eric said with mixed emotion. They always had a fabulous time wherever they went, be it Fiji, the Grand Canyon, or just taking a quick hiking trip to the High Country. "I just don't think I have the time."

"There it is right there," the senator said quickly. "You don't think you have time. But you do. There's a long weekend coming up. Let's get out of town. Trust me. It's going to be a great adventure."

"Oh no!" Eric said, waving his hands frantically. "The last time you used the words 'trust me' and 'great adventure', I found myself in a Canadian jail cell."

"Ha ha! That's right! I totally forgot about that! God that was a good time."

"Said the man who wasn't in a Canadian jail cell."

"Oh come on. Once I talked to the Royal Mounted police and told them that you weren't actually trying to steal that statue, they let you go. And, really, you were only in jail for like, what, two or three hours?"

"Try six."

"Did you make any nice friends while you were on the inside?" Senator Tanner howled and quickly grabbed at his side, grimacing in pain.

"You okay?" Eric asked. "Looks like that hurts."

"I'm okay, really. Just a cramp from the gut laugh." He rubbed his side until the pain subsided and resumed his assault. "Seriously, let's take advantage of the free days."

"Can't be done."

"Why not?"

"I've already formulated a strategy for tackling some of these agenda items. I'll be here most of the day Saturday and Sunday. I'll be working from home on Monday if I can find a way to take everything I need from the office and store it in my townhouse."

"Pish posh."

"Pish posh? Who says that?"

"Pish posh," the senator repeated. "Life is too short to worry about all of this nonsense. We're going away this weekend and that's that. This stuff," he said, poking Eric's stacks of work, "will be here when we get back. It's Wednesday. We're leaving Friday morning. You've got two days to do whatever it is you do – in my place. And, hey," he said, pointing his finger at Eric. "Don't bring a bunch of crap. It's just you and me. No fashion show. Got it?" He stood to leave, and right when he got to the door his bowtie came loose once more. "Dammit! I hate these things!" he said to no one in particular and left for the night.

"Have fun at the opera," Eric said to himself. "While I sit here. Alone. Working." He rolled his eyes, picked up his pencil and notebook, walked back to the file cabinet and started digging once more for his elusive treasure. "Alien invasion, my foot."

Chapter *37*

SHORTLY after the senator left for his night out, the silence of the empty office started to get to Eric. It hadn't typically bothered him to be alone in the office, as there weren't any side conversations or staffer phone calls or Claudia to distract him. But for some reason he started thinking about his stalker and couldn't get him off of his mind. Every little sound made Eric lose focus on what he was doing. "This is useless," he said, and packed up for the day.

When Eric left the office, he realized that he was now extremely nervous. He stepped lively from his office, through the corridor and onto the elevator. When the doors opened up and he walked into the parking garage, he eyed everyone who passed him. Nobody he saw was wearing a tacky hooded sweatshirt, but that didn't rule them out or cancel any invented suspicion Eric might have had about them. It wasn't very late, a little after eight o'clock, and the garage wasn't empty by any stretch of the imagination. Eric would never know how many people who parked in this garage laughed at him, or thought he was crazy, and talked about him behind his back. Each morning and almost every night of the week, on the way to and from their own cars, they walked by either the black Mercedes-Benz or the red Mercedes-Benz in his reserved spot and shook their heads. He was always the first person to get to the office and he was always the last person to leave.

He wasn't accustomed to seeing so many cars, and so much activity in the parking garage and it had begun to make Eric a little edgy. He could hear his shoes clicking against the pavement as he walked. The sound of car tires inadvertently screeching as cars rounded the garage corners made him recall those old murder mysteries on AMC. He picked up his pace when he remembered the gun lying on the floor of his car, and wanted to get to it as quickly as he could.

Eric looked up to see a man sitting on the back of a car, about half-way between him and his car, and immediately tensed up. He wasn't wearing a suit or a police uniform or anything else that would have signaled he belonged in the underground garage of the senate complex. He was just lazily leaning against the trunk, loitering for all Eric knew. He remembered Reginald saying something about how people weren't as safe as they thought they were. Great.

Moving slightly to the left, Eric didn't look at the stranger until they were parallel to one another. His heartbeat quickened a bit when the man looked back at him and smiled ever so slightly, and stood up. This guy was enormous, wearing jeans and some kind of bomber jacket. No doubt under that jacket, Eric thought, were massive arms ready to choke the life out of him. He sped up.

Eric tore open his car door, threw his briefcase inside, slammed the door shut, and locked it. He reached under the passenger seat and fished out his gun, clicked off the safety, and laid it on his lap. As he was backing up, he fumbled with the gun, not sure how he was going to drive and shoot at the same time. He threw the transmission into gear and stomped on the gas. He zoomed toward the guy that was staring at him, ready to shoot him if he 'made a move'. Suddenly, his focus changed when he saw something out of the corner of his eye. He looked quickly to the right and stomped on the brakes as hard as he could, braced for impact.

Like some kind of grotesquely huge cat, the enormous man leapt off of the trunk and jumped in front of Eric's car, putting his body between Eric and the little girl who had literally come out of nowhere. Thank God he yanked her out of the way. Eric's car stopped quickly, but when it finally came to rest, it was clear he would have killed that little girl. Numb, Eric looked in his rearview mirror at the man who had turned around and was glaring at him. He was saying something but Eric couldn't hear anything other than his heartbeat slamming into his ears over and over and over. Eric put the gun back under the passenger seat and got out, ready

Chief of Staff

to apologize for being so careless. He looked to the right and a woman carrying a car seat and baby was running between the parked cars. She looked like she was screaming or had screamed, maybe at the little girl who had run out into the path of Eric's car. The enormous man turned away from Eric and scooped up the little girl who had started crying. He comforted her and the woman with the car seat and baby hugged the little girl. And then the enormous man walked over to Eric. He grabbed Eric by the shirt, pulled him up and close to his body, shook his giant fist in Eric's face and screamed, "Slow the fuck down! You almost killed my little girl! Fucking rich bastard."

Eric stuttered and stammered an apology and offered whatever assistance might have been appropriate, but the enormous man had started to walk away, turning back every so often to curse and glare at Eric several more times.

Eric stood there with his head in his hands, not sure what he should do next.

Maybe a vacation wouldn't be so terrible after all.

*****

BY the time he'd pulled onto his street, Eric was out of his mind. What had he just done? His office was about five miles from his townhouse, and since he had a reserved spot in the garage, he drove to work. Meetings and lunches and various appointments required he be able to travel at a moment's notice. And he certainly wasn't going to take public transportation if he could help it.

His townhouse was on 28th, between O and P Streets. Corny as it may have been, when he first bought the place it made him think of Opie Taylor, the son on the 'Andy Griffith Show'. He dove into a spot in front of his townhouse and just started crying. It was getting darker and nobody could really tell what he was doing, sitting by himself, sulking. Six months ago, had anyone told him that his life would be what it was right then, at that instant, he would have told them they were crazy. But it was true. His life had been turned upside

Chief of Staff

down in a way that even Byrum clearly couldn't have imagined. Eric tossed his head back and closed his eyes. He wiped the tears from his face and tried to relax, tried to get away from everything. "Christ," he said to himself, "I almost ran over a little girl and shot her father. Something is seriously wrong with me."

Eric's thoughts shifted quickly to Cole and he felt his face get hot. He opened his eyes and sat bolt upright in his seat. Eric banged the dashboard and screamed, "You son of a bitch! You're the reason all of this is happening to me! I swear to God, Cole Julian, that this will stop…one way or another. You will not do this to me again. I will never be your hostage again!" Impressed by his own passion, Eric was about to launch into a tirade against the man who left him so many years ago when somebody ran up to his car and banged the passenger side window, scaring Eric to death. He leaned over and his stalker was staring at him. Not flinching one bit, Eric looked down at his gun sitting in the floorboard and back at his stalker. "I've got you now, motherfucker," he said, slowly dipping down for the weapon.

The stalker saw what Eric was reaching for and took off. At first, he ran toward O Street, but turned around for some reason, and ran right toward Eric, who had jumped out of his car. He firmly believed he was ready to shoot this guy dead in the street, but thought better of that stupid idea at the very last second, and tossed the gun back into his car. He stood there, hunched over and readying himself to tackle this guy. With an unexpected speed, the stalker got closer and closer until he bent down and threw his shoulder into Eric's chest, knocking him backward against his car and then to the ground.

Eric grabbed at this guy's clothes, but he slipped away again. Eric got up, snarled at the huge gash in his suit, and took off after him. Running as quickly down the street as he could in dress shoes, Eric knew he was at a severe disadvantage, but he wasn't going to let this guy get away again. He could see the stalker turn right onto P Street so Eric cut right, too, jumping through the back driveways and yards of neighbors he barely knew. He stopped for a second when he reached P and looked around a townhouse to see if he could locate his prey. Nothing.

"Hey!" Eric poked his head out and saw the stalker standing there, taunting him. "Catch me if you can, pretty boy!"

With that, Eric took off down P Street, re-energized and not feeling the pain that throbbed in both of his feet. Whoever this guy was, he knew where he was going. He ran up P Street and darted to the right, and onto the softball field, bolting through a game in process. They were only a block from Eric's townhouse, but encumbered by his business attire, it felt like he'd been running for miles.

Eric ran up to the little four-foot fence surrounding the field, but instead of jumping it, simply trotted along the first-base line, watching his stalker and trying to predict his next move. Most of the players moved out of the way when the stalker ran through, until Eric shouted, "That guy just stole my watch!" At that, several of the more brazen, but ill-prepared players tried to tackle the stalker, only to be stiff-armed and left in his wake. There seemed to only be one way off the field, but this guy was anything but predictable. With seemingly no other choice, Eric, too, jumped the fence and ran toward the back of the field.

The stalker ran to the back of the field, jumped the fence again, and to Eric's amazement, ran through the woods and onto the Rock Creek & Potomac Parkway. Eric gave chase until he got to the edge of the road, cars and trucks flying past him. There was no way he would attempt to cross. He bent over, hands on his knees and tried to catch his breath. The traffic broke when he stood up again and his heart stopped. The stalker stood across the highway, staring back at him. And with the passing of a transfer truck, he disappeared.

*****

Chief of Staff

ERIC walked back to his townhouse, grabbed his briefcase, the gun, and a couple other things from his car and climbed the steps to his front door. Normally, he'd have pulled his car around back to his garage, but he didn't have the strength or interest to move it right then. It could wait.

Dropping everything as he walked through the door and into the kitchen, he had every intention of grabbing a beer and slumping down into his sofa to ponder the low-speed chase he'd just been on when he stopped in his tracks. Eric was scared at first, and instinctively reached for his gun, until he recognized the silhouette of the man standing in his living room. "What the...? How the hell did you get into my house?" First a marathon chasing a stalker, and now this.

"Your mother's birthday," Cole said as he slowly turned around to face his son, "is a clever security code. I'm guessing you're probably going to be changing that now. This isn't the first time that I've been here, of course." He walked over to the sculpture of Nasiteen and said, "I see you've moved it back." He smiled that evil little smile and waited for Eric to make the next move.

Trying to process the fact that his father had broken into his home for a second time, Eric took a deep breath and walked over to the refrigerator. He pulled out a beer and leaned against the counter, staring at Cole and wondered what he was supposed to do. Calling the police wasn't an option. The news report of Senator Tanner's chief of staff having his con artist, risen-from-the-dead father arrested would spread faster than wildfire. He took several long pulls from his beer and set the bottle on the counter, still not saying a thing, only staring. Shrugging his shoulders, Cole turned back around and continued staring at a painting on the wall above the sofa. "This is 'Sunrise, Sunset', is it not?" When Eric didn't respond, Cole walked quickly to the kitchen, which unconsciously prompted Eric to stand up.

"If this is how you want to play the game, boy, then that's exactly how we can do this." Cole's voice was evil and angry. Eric had never heard that tone directed at him before and at first he was scared, a little boy being dressed down by his father. And then, instantly, he bounced back to reality. "Oh," Cole said, seeing Eric stiffen up. "You think you can take me?"

"I think I can do a hell of a lot of things you'd never count on," Eric growled.

Cole put his hand through the pavement-torn sleeve of Eric's suit and ripped it off. "I want you to consider something," Cole said as he slowly wrapped the material around his fist, ignoring Eric's dropped jaw. "I am more dangerous than you might understand. I have been backed into a corner, Eric, and you will do whatever it takes to get me out of it." Like a flash of lightning, Cole punched Eric hard in the ribs. Eric fell back onto the counter, grimacing. Cole slowly stepped toward him again, rewrapping his hand. "If you wrap your fist, there is less chance of bruising. Did you know that?" he asked, swiftly punching Eric again, incomprehensibly in the exact same spot.

Eric tried to stand but the pain was too great. He felt like an anvil was sitting atop his chest, making it impossible to breathe. He slumped to the ground, his brain screaming at him to get up, to kick this man's ass, but there was nothing he could do. Mind and body had been disconnected save for the signals from his brain detailing his excruciating pain. "Breathe," was a command he had to reiterate to himself, rather than a natural reflex to stay alive. Cole stood over him, unwrapped his fist, and threw the material onto the counter.

"I don't care what happens, son," Cole said. "I don't care what you have to do to. I figure in about ten days, either you'll come through for me – or..."

"Or, what?" Eric asked, squinting at Cole.

No matter how mean we was, or to what end he would go to pay off his debts, Cole had selfishly put his son's life in jeopardy and it was too late to turn back time. He prayed Eric was smart enough to play along. His face softened for a split second and then instantly hardened again. "Get that money

Chief of Staff

from Christine, or I promise I'll pull you right down into the grave with me."

Chief of Staff

Chapter *38*

ABOUT fifteen minutes after Cole left Eric's townhouse, slamming the door violently behind him, Eric was able to raise himself up off of the floor. Breathing was torturous and he battled through the pain as best he could. It'll go away, he argued with himself. Just like that time he went on a passing route across the middle against South Carolina State and got positively brutalized by the defense. The feeling in his ribcage was exactly the same. Just give it a little time.

Hobbling back to the refrigerator, Eric pulled out another beer and planted himself on his sofa. He popped four Tylenol and gulped his beer until it was gone. And then it started, the uncontrollable laughter. Eric laughed until he cried and cried until the only thing left to do was stare blankly ahead. There was no emotion at all running through him. Eric was numb.

Six months ago, he was on top of the world. Granted, he was as busy as ever, but he was happy. Things were going well for him, and at the time, he didn't think life could have gotten any better. He was running the campaign for now-Governor Lewis. His consulting business was booming. Even his grandmother seemed be on her best behavior. "Now look at yourself," he spoke out loud, still staring blankly ahead. A chill overtook him and he shuddered for a moment. How quickly things can change, Eric thought. Sitting there on his sofa, Eric felt like some kind of freak circus performer, forcing himself to contort and twist his body into unimaginable positions. Nothing was the same as it had been such a short, sweet time ago. Eric drummed his brain and wondered if it ever would be again.

Quickly, he stood and walked into the living room. Entering the combination into his safe, Eric could only half-smile at the irony. It had been Byrum's safe that he pilfered in search of secrets and other such private information. And

Chief of Staff

locked behind the doors of his very safe, Eric hid an enormously expensive and decidedly dangerous secret of his own. With gloved hands, Eric rolled them out onto his living room coffee table and sat back to admire them. Simply glorious.

Eric had lied to Cole the day he supposedly found out that he'd purchased Holocaust art. There was something odd about the deal his art broker had put together for him, not the least of which were the secluded meetings, and the insistence on the money being wired to an off-shore account. Eric had a feeling something was hot about his new purchase, but he couldn't put his finger on it. The second time his broker came to him, with similar demands of covertness, Eric asked no questions, and quickly took possession – undocumented possession – of his prizes and tucked them away.

In the ensuing years, each time he would add a new piece to his collection, or rotate pieces from either his safe or his warehouse, he would think about his art noire, as he liked to call it. When the mystery had finally overtaken him, Eric took it upon himself to research his treasures. He went to college libraries and combed through stacks of information, rolled through what felt like a mile of microfiche, and scanned innumerable periodicals. He went online and talked with Holocaust survivors in chat rooms, always with a fake name and history, to find out if anybody knew anything about the existence of a painting his 'Bubbe' said had been in his family for generations before being stolen by Nazi soldiers. It was priceless, he would always say.

The art world, as superficially glamorous and pretentious as it was to the uninitiated, was actually a cess pool of the greedy, egomaniacal, and the filthy filthy rich. As it were, Eric's history of making major purchases put him on the radar of brokers around the world. Cole had always been a part of that world, but his ability to chameleon himself into a prestigious broker of expensive paintings and sculpture was beyond Eric's comprehension. It would have been easy enough for one of Cole's clients to pass the paintings through him and onto Eric. It wasn't unusual for Eric to wire millions of dollars for a piece that he simply had to have. Like any investment, the concept was 'Money in, Money out'. Unlike stocks or bonds or property, he could actually appreciate these investments on a personal and intimate level. His passion for art beautified his home and since it didn't put any appreciable dent in his wallet, it was a passion he allowed to flourish. Once it became dangerous, though, everything changed.

When he found out the history behind two of the paintings he bought through Cole, immediately he panicked. They had been locked in his safe for ten years and only now, sitting alone in his living room, laid out of the naked glass of his living room table, could Eric fully appreciate what it was he looked on with wonder and amazement. And fear.

Someone died for these paintings. If he wasn't careful, he might be next.

Chapter *39*

SENATOR Tanner's driver picked Eric up at his townhouse that Friday morning and headed to Murkoff Proper, a tiny out of the way airport that the rich and famous had used for two decades to ferry them out of town on private planes. It was secluded and very well guarded. "I'll have you at Murkoff before you know it, sir," the driver announced.

"Excuse me?" Eric said to the driver. "I thought we were supposed to be going to the marina."

"My directions are to take you to Murkoff. From there, you'll be flown to Miami and then transferred to Trinity where you'll be joined by the senator."

Miami? Eric knew he should have asked the senator for more clarification when he said, don't worry about a thing. I've got everything under control. Just get in the car and you'll end up in paradise sooner than you can blink. Sarcastically, Eric sat in the back of the car and blinked hard several times. That didn't work. This was going to take forever and the only thing on Eric's mind was the mountain of work molding on his desk.

Like he promised, the driver had Eric at Murkoff in short order and he was on the senator's jet inside of thirty minutes. This was going to be a fast flight, no more than an hour or so, he figured. Once he settled into his seat and went through his pre-flight routine, Eric pulled out his cell phone and his briefcase. He thought about Senator Tanner calling him a work-a-holic, rolled his eyes, and started dialing.

The flight to Miami was a little quicker than he counted on, but even that short journey gave him the chance to reach out to a number of his peers and line up several very critical meetings. The pilot thanked Eric after they had taxied and come to rest saying that the next leg would be aboard a helicopter, ferrying him out to Trinity.

"A helicopter?" Eric asked. He took a deep breath and tried to relax. Never one for helicopters, he avoided them at all cost. The whirling and the noise and the fact that if the engine died, the whole damn thing would crash into the sea, made Eric nervous just thinking about it. If the senator hadn't made him agree to take this vacation, there would have been no way in hell he'd have gotten on a helicopter. And why wasn't Trinity docked at a marina in Miami, Eric wondered. The ride across the airport to the waiting helicopter gave him a quick moment to catch his breath. He shook his head when the driver pulled up to the gate, waved a credential and stopped on the tarmac next to a gleaming burgundy machine of certain death.

"Right this way, Mr. Julian," the pilot said. "I'll have you on Trinity before you know it."

"Just don't kill me," Eric said. "That's all I ask."

He buckled up and the death trap took to the air. He was now Senator Tanner's prisoner for the next three days. He'd better start enjoying himself.

*****

THE pilot touched down on the Trinity's aft landing pad with extreme precision, which Eric appreciated more than he could express. "Thank you for not killing us," he said, shaking the pilot's hand and jumping out. The pilot gave him a wink and a thumbs up. Eric cleared the helicopter and watched as it took off again, zooming out of sight. He pulled out his cell phone to take care of one last agenda item when the senator walked up to him. He grabbed the phone, hung up, and handed it to a steward.

"Lock this in the safe," he said, pressing the phone into the young man's hand. "If he gets this back, for any reason, before this vacation is over, you'll be fired on the spot. Do you understand me?" The steward nodded, smiling at Eric, and disappeared. Eric turned to see the last glimpse of the helicopter, and surprisingly, begged for the pilot to come back.

Chief of Staff

"That wasn't so bad, was it?" Senator Tanner asked, pulling Eric on the shoulder and turning him around. "I know you're no fan of helicopters, but it just made more sense for you to join me out here. Trinity was sailing from Charleston Wednesday on the way back to North Carolina. When I informed the captain of our vacation plans, he said it would be just as easy for us to meet him in Miami."

"No phone, huh?" Eric asked, irritated, ignoring Senator Tanner's explanation. "Lovely."

"Forget about the phone. And forget about work. We're all about enjoying ourselves this weekend. It's going to be…"

"I know, a great adventure."

Senator Tanner shook his head and sighed. Another steward had taken Eric's bags and struggled to get them inside the yacht to take them to his stateroom. "I thought I told you to pack lightly."

"What are you talking about?" Eric pointed at the steward and said, "That is light. I've only got two bags. You said this was going to be casual."

Senator Tanner looked at Eric and laughed. "You're worse than a woman!"

"You should know!" Eric followed the senator through the yacht to the upper deck.

"So where are we, exactly?"

"Right now we're just off Miami. Over there," he pointed toward the coast in the distance and, apparently a perfectly good marina which would not have required a helicopter ride, "is where cruise ships depart."

I'm going to spend three days trapped on a yacht in the middle of nowhere when I could be getting work done, Eric thought to himself. What a colossal waste of time.

"I can see what you're thinking, Eric. Stop it," the senator said.

"Who are you? Master Yoda? You have no idea what's going through my head right now, Senator."

"You're wondering why the hell you're out here with me when you could be working. Am I right?" He was holding a very cold, very refreshing beer that Eric kept staring at.

"That is dead wrong."

"I know you better than you know yourself." The senator waved down a steward and inquired about lunch. Thirty minutes and everything will be set. He dismissed the steward and started in on Eric again. "I didn't ask you out here to lament about your not being able to stick your nose into a folder."

"If you'll recall, Senator, there wasn't a whole lot of asking going on. I was more or less told that I would be coming out here, work be damned."

Senator Tanner walked to the bar and asked for another beer. He had pulled Eric with him and they sat down on the stools. "What's happened to you?" the senator asked. "Where did the fun loving Eric I knew and loved go?"

"He got sucked into a black hole called the Senate." Eric looked out over the open ocean and took it in. The horizon went on forever as he swept back and forth. The sun was shining and it was still warm, even with the wind slowly whipping around. Eric slid his sunglasses on top of his head and walked to the railing.

"What is it that you love so much about the sea, Senator?"

"That's something many people have asked me, Eric." He was still sitting on the bar stool, peeling the label off of his beer bottle. "And, honestly, I don't know that I have one, all-encompassing answer to give them. I imagine I love the sea for a number of reasons."

"Like what?" Eric returned to his stool and sat down. "Tell me."

Chief of Staff

Senator Tanner looked around and filled his lungs with sea air. "Smell that? It's glorious. That's the smell of freedom, Eric. That smell is what brings me back time and again. That smell is why I built this floating mansion."

"How you managed to keep this thing a secret from me for so long is an achievement in itself," Eric said, smiling.

"This was a labor of love," Senator Tanner said, stroking the bar. "It took two years to go from concept to what you see before you. My love of the sea is like your love of making something out of a piece of wood. The rush I get from the salty sea air is, well, it's kind of like your saw dust." Eric smiled because he could relate to what he saying. "I still have the first thing you made me - that disjointed, lopsided cabinet. Do you remember that? You were eleven years old, I think."

"I can't believe you kept that thing. Throw it out and I'll make you something else," Eric said, prideful that the senator had kept that hideous example of woodworking.

"I'll keep it for the rest of my life, Eric. Since the first time you made a chair or a table and showed it off to me, there has been something that's drawn you to making furniture. Maybe it is the smell, I don't know. That's singular and personal and it's something you cannot attempt to define." He walked to the railing and opened his arms. "This is serenity and confinement for me all at the same time. I can go wherever I want to, any place in the world, but I always want to escape to the sea."

"And where are we going?" Eric asked, taking a long pull from his beer.

"That I'm not sure about."

"You told me you had it all figured out. That we were going to paradise." Eric looked around and all he saw was water. "This ain't paradise, Senator."

"Maybe we'll just float right here for the whole vacation. Maybe we'll just troll back and forth up the

Chief of Staff

coastline. It doesn't matter. Whatever we want to do we can do because we're not in the office." Senator Tanner snapped his fingers and wheeled around to face Eric. "I know! I know exactly what we can do. Why didn't I think about this before?" Eric sipped his beer, waiting for the 'revelation' to be revealed. "Key West!"

"Been there. Done that," Eric said.

"I know. But this time it's going to be different. In fact, let's make this trip totally different than what we've ever done before." Senator Tanner was mouthing something to himself and pacing in circles, thinking as he went. "What are we used to, you and me?"

"I have no idea what you're talking about."

"We're both the victims of our background."

"You know I'm a pretty good swimmer, right?" Eric looked over the railing and figured the drop to the water might not be that painful. "I'll jump off this thing if I have to."

"Blah, blah, blah. Whatever. Listen, we've both become accustomed to the finer things in life, right?"

"And?" Eric winced because he didn't know where the senator was going with this.

"What if we vacationed like regular people?" the senator asked.

"Did I ever tell you how much I don't like regular people?" Eric joked.

"What if we took a trip the way normal people do?"

"Like a private plane taking us to a helicopter that, in turn, takes us to a two hundred foot yacht floating off the coast? That kind of normal trip?"

"Okay, okay, so there's going to be some excess involved."

"Some?" Eric was smiling and started to laugh. He could see something come over Senator Tanner, a giddiness

Chief of Staff

he hadn't seen in a while. "I'd say the excess is already off the meter for a 'normal' vacation."

Senator Tanner walked up and grabbed Eric by the shoulders. "From this point forward, we're going to be regular people. I'm not a senator and you're not a chief of staff."

Eric jumped around and asked, "Ooh, I know, can I change my name to Skippy and can we go to Sam's Club and buy folding beach chairs and garish beach towels, and can I talk with a fake accent?"

"You're ruining this. Shut up and listen." Senator Tanner put his hand to his chin and said, "How do regular people go on vacation? Minus the plane and the helicopter and the yacht?" He sat down on a chaise and pursed his lips together.

Eric sat down beside him, mocked the senator's pose and said, "What would Jesus do?"

They both rolled with laughter and the senator snapped his fingers again. "Ah ha! Nothing fancy."

"With the exception being the private plane, the helicopter and the yacht, right?" Eric asked. "There's a theme here, I just know it." Senator Tanner rolled his eyes and let Eric continue. "I appreciate the enthusiasm, Senator, but if you don't come up with something soon, I'm going to do a Greg Louganis off this thing and swim back to my office."

Senator Tanner got up and walked inside the yacht. A couple minutes later, he returned, beaming at Eric. "It's all set."

"Dare I ask?" Eric had returned to the bar and was snacking on the shrimp cocktail one of the stewards had brought from the galley.

"Here's the plan. The captain is going to sail us to Key West right now. We'll hang out there for a little while, depending on what we find to do and what kind of trouble we can manage to get into. Then we'll leave Key West and steam right back up the coast to Myrtle Beach."

Eric choked on a shrimp because he was trying to object just as he started to swallow. "Myrtle Beach?" He washed the shrimp down and asked, "Isn't that kind of, uh, how would one put this? Pedestrian?"

"You are such a snob," the senator said. He pulled up next to Eric, smiling wide, and said, "This is the first vacation we've taken in a while. Let's make it memorable. We have no idea when we'll be able to do this again."

"With as little as you work, we can do this any time we want. Why do we have to devolve just for the sake of being on vacation?"

Senator Tanner picked up a shrimp and smiled at Eric. "This is going to be great."

Eric felt the yacht shift and looked at the coastline, as the captain pointed them south toward Key West. "Yeah. This is going to be just great."

Chapter *40*

BY the time they arrived at the marina in Key West, the sun had started to dip in the sky. Along the way, Senator Tanner napped and Eric enjoyed the magnificence of the yacht. His first visit to Trinity had been at night, and shrouded in secrecy. During the party, also at night, Eric was more concerned with making sure people were having a good time than his location. Now, though, he was able to fully investigate every nook and cranny he could slip into.

Each of the four main decks were outstanding. While the senator rested, Eric changed his clothes and toured the floating extension of a penis his grandmother had so brusquely derided. Everywhere he turned, his eyes popped even further out of his head. From the theater to the gym; the observation decks to the Jacuzzi; the beautifully-decorated guest staterooms to the main lounge and all the way in between, Eric knew that yacht like the back of his hand. He closely examined all of the furniture – deep, lustrous, dark wood bed frames and dressing tables in the staterooms; light and airy stains on cabinetry in the galley and several common areas. He stood for a moment in each room, wondering if the designs met his satisfaction for craftsmanship and whether or not they complimented or detracted from the décor. With fresh flowers and wonderful art on the walls, surely the senator had an interior designer, Eric mused. There was no way he could have put all of this together by himself.

Along the way, stewards greeted him and asked if there was anything they could do for him. Eric stopped to talk with each of them, like a politician, learning their names and prying tidbits from them about their families and what it must be like to work for the senator on his grand yacht. They were all very nice, and pleasantly surprised at his asking questions of them and taking an interest. He'd counted fifteen people, never seeing the same one twice during his two-hour jaunt. They were all dressed very sharply in white and red outfits and you could tell they were accustomed to dealing with the

Chief of Staff

wealthy. How many more were on board, hidden in the engine room and asleep in the crew areas, he could only guess. The captain came over a very discreet intercom system and announced their arrival. Eric thought it was strange to be aboard such a huge vessel, just the two of them, and that they were the only passengers who cared that they'd arrived at their destination.

After they docked, the newly-refreshed senator dispatched one of the servants to a local store to pick up some 'touristy' clothing for him and Eric. When he came back, purchases laid out before the two of them, Eric nearly fainted.

"I am not wearing that."

"Shut up and change your clothes, Skippy," the senator said. He was thoroughly enjoying this and he was determined to make the most out of it. "I think the pattern suits you. And don't forget the hat."

Eric closed his stateroom door and reluctantly changed. He stared in the mirror at the hideous ensemble he had somehow forced himself to put on: A floral shirt boasting what had to be four hundred separate and distinct colors; blue madras shorts that fell below his knees; green flip flops; and a white mesh trucker hat festooned with 'KEY WEST ROCKS!' in bold red lettering.

Senator Tanner opened Eric's stateroom door and they both fell on the ground. "Oh my God! You look horrible!" Eric yelled. "What the hell are you wearing? Is that pink?" He laughed so hard he got a cramp and was curled into the fetal position on the ground.

"Key West Rocks!" Senator Tanner yelled at Eric. He, too, was laughing and he had begun to tear up. "I'm crying I'm laughing so hard!" He stood up while he continued to laugh and turned around so Eric could take in his complete outfit. "What do you think about this? I'm going to start a whole new trend." He turned to show his very own floral shirt, the majority of which was a crude pink color featuring what appeared to be hand-drawn sea shells strewn

Chief of Staff

about between badly drawn flowers. The pale green shorts didn't really match anything on the shirt, which was a miracle given the rainbow with which it visually assaulted anyone who dared look at it. And then there were the shoes. "I think these are great," the senator said. "And they're so comfortable."

Eric walked over, bent down and touched the sandals the senator had put on. "Is that plastic?" he asked, his face twisted in disbelief.

"I believe it might be. Comfortable as hell, though."

Eric made his way to the top of the senator's head and asked, "You aren't really going to be seen in public wearing that...are you?"

'Don't Hate the Playa...Hate the Game' had been woven above the brim on the senator's white faux fedora. "I think it's fitting, don't you?"

"I think we're going to get killed. We look like idiots." Eric and the senator stood in front of the floor-to-ceiling mirror and studied each other.

"This is fine. No, this is fine. We look like regular people."

"Regular people wear Ralph Lauren and Dolce and Gabbana, too."

"Not when they're on a normal vacation with us. Let's go."

Eric and the senator walked off the yacht and quickly hopped in a cab to take them to the heart of Key West, Duvall Street. Eric knew it was a bad sign when the cabbie did a double take as they got in. Senator Tanner couldn't wait for their adventure to begin and smiled the entire five minute drive to their destination.

The two of them, spectacles in their own right, mixed in with the tourists and it didn't seem anyone else gave them a second thought. Instead of La Trattoria, Eric's favorite Key

West restaurant, they waited in line for a cramped table at Jimmy Buffett's. Senator Tanner joyfully ate every last bite of his Cheeseburger in Paradise while Eric struggled to finish some of the 'most rubbery and tasteless' calamari he'd ever attempted to eat. To dull his pain, Eric ordered shots of Tequila and chased them with Coronas. Senator Tanner had gotten a little crazier and decided to drink only shots over dinner. The first one was called a Gorilla Fart, equal parts Wild Turkey and 151. Now that's pedestrian, he told Eric. After the Cement Mixer and the Blue Motorcycle, the senator changed his mind and went with Johnnie Walker Red over rocks. By the time they left the restaurant, they were on their way to becoming stumbling drunk.

"Are you having fun yet?" the senator asked Eric in a loud voice, screaming over the mass of people walking up and down the street.

"Why are you yelling at me?" Eric stood on the sidewalk outside Jimmy Buffett's and closed his eyes. "I think I'm drunk."

Senator Tanner slapped him hard on the chest and said, "You're not drunk! The night is young! We've got more drinking to do!" The streets were crowded with all walks of life that night. Senator Tanner and Eric started walking back down Duvall Street in the direction of Mallory Square and blended in with everyone else. The great thing about Key West is that within reason you can be and do whatever the hell you want. Gay men and lesbians walk hand-in-hand. Transvestites walk among families of four on vacation from Middle America. The elderly party with college students in bars on every corner. The police ride around in their little electric vehicles and on bicycles, watching to make sure that nothing gets too far out of hand. It's a party every night of the week and no one leaves Key West unhappy.

"Let's get tattoos!" Senator Tanner said, and yanked Eric into a Head Shop. Eric scanned the walls and tried to focus. There were black and white samples of tattoos, and

Chief of Staff

pictures of fresh tattoos on biker dudes and fat girls and weirdos, mixed in with various images of pot and pipes and skeletons plastered everywhere. Black lights accentuated psychedelic colors and Eric's head started to spin.

"Hell no," Eric said. "My grandmother said that if I ever got a tattoo…"

The senator covered Eric's mouth and sat him down on the chair. "Pick something out," he said, and pointed to a huge 3-ring notebook of the artist's work. "I'll be right back. I'm going to get us some beers." And with that he was off, leaving Eric to ask himself if he was really going to do this. Faster than he thought possible, the senator was back, thrusting a cold beer into his hand. "Find what you want?" he asked, taking an extended sip of his beer.

"You're serious, aren't you?" Eric took the beer and flipped casually through the notebook, not really concentrating on any of the designs.

"I already know what I want. Move over if you're not ready." The senator patted the tattoo artist on the back, moved Eric out of the way, and sat down. He pulled up the back of his pink floral shirt and said, "I want a big fucking tiger going across my entire back! Can you do that?"

The tattoo artist smiled and with dollar signs in his eyes, of course, said yes. Eric's eyes got wide, he gulped down his entire beer, pulled the senator's shirt back down, grabbed him by the arm and jerked him up. Senator Tanner laughed and laughed as they ran. "You crazy old man!" Eric was yelling and laughing. "You crazy, crazy ass old man!" They stopped running after a block or two, but they couldn't catch their breath from the laughter.

"You should have seen your face!"

"You have lost whatever tiny bit of a mind you had before we got here, Senator!"

"No, remember you can't call me that. At least not while we're on our normal vacation. Just call me Scott. You're still Skippy, by the way."

"Joyous rapture."

"Come on, Skippy," the senator said, looking up at the sign above them and smiling wide. "College girls, wet t-shirt contests and dollar draft awaits. The night is young and we're on vacation!"

*****

FLASH bulbs. Cold beer. Large breasts. Medium breasts. Small breasts. Screaming. Cheering. Boos. Tongues in mouths of strange women. Breasts of strange women cupped in hands. A blowjob in the alley between the restaurant and the stage. Vomiting in the same spot twenty minutes later.

Senator Tanner's eyes opened and those were the only things he could remember. He had zero recollection of how he had gotten back to his yacht. He had zero recollection of how he'd gotten into bed...naked. He had zero recollection of the name of the gorgeous, twenty-something blonde girl in bed with him. She woke up with him staring at her and, without speaking, rolled over and they had some of the most mind-blowing morning sex he'd ever experienced. If this was anything like the sex they'd had when they got back to the yacht, he was sorry he'd never remember it. The girl had skills.

Ever the gentleman, Senator Tanner walked his guest to the dock after she'd showered and gotten dressed. Standing at the bottom of the gangway, after deeply kissing a magnificent brunette goddess, Eric smiled at the senator as he and his still unnamed conquest descended to meet them. "It was a pleasure, ladies," Eric said. "The prince and I thoroughly enjoyed your company." Senator Tanner looked at Eric as if to say, 'Prince? That's awesome'! The ladies got into a waiting cab and drove away.

Chief of Staff

"A prince?" Senator Tanner asked as they walked back to the rear deck and sat down to breakfast. "Superb."

Eric couldn't help himself and said, "Key West was a great idea! It was a fantastic idea!" He was yelling as loud as he could, not embarrassed a bit by who might hear him. "Do you know what we did last night?" he asked the senator. "We turned ourselves into legends. We're fucking legends, you and me!"

The steward plated their breakfasts and handed Senator Tanner a note letting him know that the captain would be ready to sail to Myrtle Beach at whatever point the senator was ready. Let's go now, the senator replied and turned his attention back to Eric. "I woke up this morning and it felt like my head was ripped open. I really only remember something about a whole hell of a lot of breasts and screaming."

"That was the wet t-shirt contest we judged," Eric said, smiling and chewing at the same time. "I've totally never done that before in my life! We were on fire last night! Everything we touched turned to goddam gold, Senator!" What Eric kept to himself was the vague memory of some tall, brooding guy who walked up to him in the middle of the wet t-shirt contest and stood a little too close to him. They exchanged pleasantries and smiles and Eric left it at that, and they both joined the rest of the crowd chanting at and taunting tender college girls to take off their tops. After a couple of minutes, this guy took Eric lightly by the arm, and over the thumping bass and loud music leaned down to his ear. He very quickly said, "Your father is worth lot of money to the man I work for. If my boss doesn't get his money," stopping only to take Eric's face in his hand and move in closer until their mouths were mere inches from one another, "I am going to kill you both. And enjoy it." Eric was now supremely intoxicated and his vision was blurred, but the chill that ran down his spine told him he'd gotten the gist of what his close-talker had said.

"Were those girls the winners?" Senator Tanner popped some Tylenol and gulped down his entire glass of orange juice. "My God, I don't even know their names!"

Eric shook his head and looked out at Key West as the crew made ready to sail. This mess with Cole and people threatening his life had to stop one way or the other. He looked around and wondered who could be watching him now. Was there somebody on the yacht who had been paid to keep tabs on him? He focused on the senator pouring a liberal amount of salt onto his plate and sighed. "The blonde was Teresa and the one with me was Georgia. They weren't contestants, just some girls in the crowd. They're students down here from some college in Texas, hell if I know which one. After they found out we were judging the contest, they came up to us."

"Buck up, son. This is supposed to be a happy story." Eric agreed and smiled, while the senator continued peppering him with questions. "So exactly when did I turn into a prince?"

"You talked them into coming back here with us and I panicked! I told them you were a Norwegian prince to explain the yacht. What was I supposed to say, 'excuse me, but he's actually a United States Senator and we're trolling Key West for single women who want to go back to his gazillion dollar yacht for a Bacchanalian festival of love'?"

"I probably would have gone with the Bacchanalian thing, myself." He opened a small plastic box labeled for every day of the week, palmed what Eric quickly counted to be about seven pills of various sizes and colors, and chased them with his tomato juice. He looked at Eric and explained, "I normally take these in the morning. I don't see you in the morning. Close your mouth."

"First you're going to the doctor. And now you're popping pills? What's changed?"

"Nothing."

"Liars go to hell," Eric teased.

Chief of Staff

"I hope they have an Immigration plan," he said, laughing. He stopped and, as he picked up his fork, asked, "Did I hurl at some point? Why do I remember that?" Senator Tanner began devouring his breakfast of scrambled eggs and lightly toasted English muffins. As always, he segregated the fruit salad for later.

Eric smacked the arm of his chair. "That's right! You disappeared on me for like fifteen minutes! Here I am, in the middle of a wet t-shirt contest, hosing down girl after girl, fondling multiple sets of boobs, and I look up to see you aren't anywhere to be found. You stumbled back to the stage and told me you'd gotten the best Lewinsky 'in the free world'. And, yes, you did the whole air quote thing," Eric said to an unbelieving senator. "About fifteen or twenty minutes later, you disappeared again and came back to the stage in a different shirt. You said you'd hurled in the alley and somebody gave you a shirt to wear. You were absolutely fubar. I introduced you to Teresa and Georgia, we bought them some beers, I gave you some breath mints, and we wound up back here, screwing two of the hottest women on the Key in our staterooms until early this morning."

"I think you owe me an apology, young man," Senator Tanner said, slowly sipping his espresso.

"For what? I got you drunk last night. Because of me, you got more action last night than you've had in over a year. And I got you laid, Mr. Norwegian prince. Why am I apologizing to you?"

"I believe you scoffed at the phrases 'trust me' and 'great adventure'."

"I'll make a deal with you," Eric said, pointing his egg-laden fork at his boss. "If, in two weeks, neither of us has crabs or some other nasty STD from those two smokin' hot girls, I'll apologize up one side and down the other. How 'bout that?"

Trinity powered her way out of port with Eric and Senator Tanner trying their best to recall the events of the night before. The sun was high in the sky and the breeze felt great as it danced across their skin. Key West got progressively smaller and smaller until the marina was out of sight completely. Both men smiled, each wondering what the next leg of their 'normal' vacation would bring and talked and talked until their breakfasts were gone and they each retired to their rooms to recover. Before they knew it, they would be docked in Myrtle Beach, ready for Round Two.

Key West Rocks!

Chapter *41*

"RISE and shine, Sleepy Head!" Senator Tanner shouted as he burst into Eric's stateroom Sunday morning. They'd spent all day Saturday relaxed at sea, and sailed through the night to reach Myrtle Beach. He hit the button for the automatic curtains and the room was flooded with light. "Come on, get up! I've got something I want to show you."

Eric groaned and pulled the sheets up over his head. "I'm not ready to get up yet, you crazy bastard!" he said through the sheets. His voice was muffled, but Senator Tanner heard him plainly enough. "Leave me alone for another hour." He peeled the sheets back, peaked at the clock and couldn't believe his eyes. 6:30? In the morning? Weren't they on vacation? There's no way I'm getting up at 6:30, he said to himself, and disappeared again.

Senator Tanner walked to the bed and gave Eric one warning. He counted to ten and, in one swift motion stripped Eric and the bed of its covers. "Get up." He was smiling at Eric who returned a glare. "We've got a huge day ahead of us and I'm ready to get rolling. The captain told me that we should be docking shortly. We don't have much time. Get dressed and meet me in my office. I want to show you what we'll be up to today."

After an hour and a half, Eric casually walked into Senator Tanner's office and sat down on the sofa. A steward asked Eric what he would like for breakfast and left the two men alone.

"What?"

"I woke you up at 6:30. It is now 8:00."

"I am aware of that. I've been able to tell time since I was five years old."

"What the hell takes you so long to get ready in the morning, anyway?" Senator Tanner was paging through some

Chief of Staff

website, and attempting to have a conversation with Eric at the same time. "You don't look any better now than when I pulled the covers off of you."

"You'd better be glad I don't sleep naked," Eric said.

"You'd better be glad I don't collect tiny things," the senator shot back, glancing at Eric's crotch and laughing.

Eric picked up a magazine from the side table and threw it at the senator because he couldn't think of anything funny. "Ha Ha. Besides, I'm just not one of those people who can pop out of bed and instantly be ready to tackle the day. There are quite a number of steps in the process that lead to me looking the way I do. I have to shower, shave, decide what I'm going to wear, make sure it doesn't need to be ironed, brush my teeth…"

"Jesus. Maybe your mother should have named you Erica."

"Maybe you should learn how to work an iron," Eric said. He'd gotten up from the sofa and stood behind the senator as he poked away on the keyboard. He pinched the senator's shirt and said, "How old is this rag?"

"This is my favorite vacation shirt, thank you very much."

Eric didn't argue with the senator about his clothes because his complaints fell on deaf ears. Most of the time he was able to dress himself appropriately, but there were days you could tell he just didn't give a damn about what he had on. The senator wasn't as concerned about his fashion sense as Eric thought he should have been. In every picture ever taken of the senator, Eric could pick out at least one thing that needed to be fixed or a trend that needed to be retired. If he wasn't wearing a Madras shirt or sandals, the collar was wrinkled. Maybe the length of his pants was too short or he was wearing pleated pants when he should have been wearing flat-front. And forget about taking the man shopping. It was as pointless as arguing with a rock.

Chief of Staff

Eric continued his mental nitpicking over the senator's clothes and peered over his shoulder, as he hunted and pecked his way around a website. "And what are you looking at? What are you going to get us into today?" Just as Senator Tanner was about to launch into their agenda, a steward announced that breakfast was ready. The printer spit out a couple more pages and the two men went out to the aft lounge to eat and discuss their plans.

"Look at this," Senator Tanner said. His face was lit up like a child's at Christmas. "This is what we're going to be doing today."

"The Pavilion?" Eric asked, searching the picture on the print out. "Tell me you aren't serious." It was colder outside than Eric expected. He hunched over a bit at the table trying to keep warm. There wasn't a cloud in the sky and he could hear the sounds of the marina mixing together in the background. Children and gulls shrieked. There was the constant din of the engines on the yacht, softly vibrating the hull and up through Eric's seat at the breakfast table. Trinity was the largest craft currently docked and there were the inevitable sightseers ambling by trying to take pictures and to see who in the world was on board. His breakfast of Belgian waffles and 3-minute eggs was getting cold and he wasn't at all interested in being captured on film, with a mouth full of food no less, by some nosy tourist. This day wasn't starting out very well at all.

"Oh, there's a lot more there than just the Pavilion, although the people in the picture look like they're having a great time. Look at this," Senator Tanner said, snatching the information from Eric and turning the page. He downed his motley assortment of pills, got up from his seat and saddled up next to Eric. The enthusiasm on his face was infectious, and it softened Eric a little bit. It had been a while since Eric had witnessed the senator enjoying himself so obviously, so unrepentantly. He didn't know why or what had caused his exuberance, but the senator was having the time of his life. Eric loved spending time with him; their excursions were

Chief of Staff

always a blast. It had been a long damn time since he'd allowed himself to step away from his job and just enjoy life. He watched as the senator delightedly turned every page, and he listened to his voice as it rose and fell during his descriptions. Eric couldn't help it and just smiled. He was truly glad to be there, sharing every minute of their bizarre vacation experience.

"And there's golf, and we can go to one of those medieval shows for dinner maybe, and we can play the video games in the Pavilion Midway, or we can shop for whatever we can find on this Grand Strand whatever that is, or we can play putt-putt and, ooh, look at this place I found online," he said, grabbing another print out from the table. "This place has bungee jumping! Ever wanted to do that? I think I might give it a try. It looks very scary!" His barrage of information was only briefly halted when he looked at Eric for a response and, without so much as a breath, went right back to it.

"Whoa, slow down, Senator," Eric said, putting his hand on the senator's, preventing him from turning the next page, assaulting him with even more ideas.

"I'm a little out of my mind, I guess," Senator Tanner said. He gathered up his information and went back to his chair.

"You're fine. Trust me. But listen, we've got all day. We've got plenty of time to do whatever it is you want to do. I'm good with whatever you want to do." He dug into his waffles and hoped there wasn't a telephoto lens trained on him.

"Are you sure?"

"I'm sure," he said, with a mouthful. Christine would have slapped him silly.

"And we can do whatever I want?"

"We can do whatever you want." Eric pointed at the senator's bowl with his fork to let him know his breakfast was getting old.

Chief of Staff

"This is going to be an awesome day, Eric." Senator Tanner shook his head, grinned broadly.

"Since when do you say 'awesome'? Eric chided.

"Since when does it take a man an hour and a half to get ready in the morning?" Senator Tanner raised an eyebrow and poured milk into his cereal bowl. "It's going to be an AWESOME day."

*****

AROUND 5 am Sunday night – or, Monday morning, however you look at it - Eric was running ragged. It had been almost twenty-four hours since his rude wake-up call that morning. Senator Tanner had dragged him all over Myrtle Beach, and as far as he could tell, the rest of South Carolina, as well. They started out by playing a round of golf at an extremely nice course. My first ex-wife's cousin owns this place, the senator explained. He hated her guts almost as much as I did. After our divorce, he said I could come down whenever I wanted and play for free. Game on.

Senator Tanner beat Eric handily, and without compromising, waited for his winnings.

"I am not going to do that. Not here," Eric said, looking around. They were standing on the 18th green after the senator tapped in for a round of 78.

"Drop 'em," was all the senator said. As was standard, if one of them lost by more than ten strokes, the loser had to stand in the middle of the 18th, in full view of the clubhouse, and drop their pants to their ankles. They had been doing this for years, ever since Eric started learning how to play golf. It was an incentive the senator drummed up to help Eric get better at the game. Teenage boys don't want to drop their pants in front of anyone, let alone a golf course full of strangers. It worked to perfection and Eric was soon taking the senator for ten and fifteen strokes at a clip. The senator tried to change the bet after Eric began to beat him easily, but Eric would hear nothing of it. What's good for the goose, he said.

Chief of Staff

"I will not."

"Excuse me," the senator said to the foursome coming up to the green. "Sorry to be in your way but we've got a bit of trouble here." He explained the bet to the gentlemen and, to his absolute astonishment, they all agreed. Drop 'em was the command.

"No."

"The longer you protest, the more people I'm going to call over here. A bet's a bet." Senator Tanner winked at one of the strangers, who was trying to stifle his laughter. "Drop 'em."

That's when it happened: they started to chant. Drop 'em. Drop 'em. Drop 'em. Drop 'em. Drop 'em. The chanting had soon drawn several more people to the green, and Eric was mortified. He poked Senator Tanner in the chest, said this is what you get, turned around to face the clubhouse and dropped his pants to the ground.

The crowd gasped because along with his pants went his boxers. Eric leaned over slowly, spread his cheeks and farted. It was deep, long, and crude. And it smelled. The men in the foursome fell over laughing, but most everybody else who had gathered quickly ran away to safety.

Senator Tanner hurriedly grabbed for Eric's pants, pulled them up awkwardly and yanking Eric off the green, rushed to their golf cart. Eric couldn't breathe he was laughing so hard. Senator Tanner's face was a brilliant shade of red.

"That wasn't funny, Skippy," he said loudly, making sure everyone could hear Eric's vacation-only alias. "That is not the way we act in public." He turned around to see that some of the people were still doubled-over, laughing hysterically.

"First of all, I'm not a senator," Eric replied. "And secondly, you know that was funny as hell. Don't lie. Don't try to hide it. And don't even think about trying to scold me

Chief of Staff

like a child again." Senator Tanner mashed his lips together and turned his head away from Eric. "I see you, old man. I see you trying not to bust out laughing."

He couldn't hold it any longer and laughed so hard he almost drove the golf cart into a pole. "I couldn't help it. That was probably one of the funniest damn things I've ever seen you do! I loved it!"

"Then why did you yank me away? I still had a little more ammo built up."

Senator Tanner stopped laughing long enough to take a couple of deep breaths, rub his side and say, "I didn't yank you off of the green because I was embarrassed. Do you know who was in the crowd?"

"Who?" Eric sat forward, still putting himself back together, and prayed it wasn't someone who would have recognized him.

"George Greenich."

"Judge George Greenich? Father of Kathryn Greenich?"

Senator Tanner was forced to take quick breaths to ease his laughing-induced cramp. All he could say was, "Uh huh," before he started howling all over again.

"Shit. And shit again."

*****

SENATOR Tanner had planned for the two of them to have dinner at one of those medieval knights performances with jousting and food served on metal plates and such. But the second they entered the building, the sound of screaming children and the rather distant, although still malodorous stench of dirt and horses had them bolting right back out the door. That was a little too normal, they reasoned. "What's your second choice?" Eric asked, still pinching his nose.

Chief of Staff

"We could always go to this place," he said as he produced his trusty Myrtle Beach Tourism Guide from his back pocket. "It's called Dick's Last Resort."

"Is it Pedestrian?"

"From what I can tell, it might be more pedestrian than anything you've ever witnessed." They looked at each other, back to the medieval nightmare and, in sync, said let's go.

Walking into Dick's Last Resort was an experience in and of itself for Eric. The walls were covered with memorabilia, there seemed to be some kind of reptile tank out back and it was loud as hell. The hostess greeted them with, "What do you want?"

"Excuse me?" Eric asked, his inner Christine charging forward.

Senator Tanner pulled him back and said, "I forgot to tell you about this place. You kind of sit back and get swallowed up doing things you wouldn't normally. The joke is that although everybody is kind of rude, people come back year after year just for the great time they have. At least that's what the guide says."

Eric rolled his eyes and followed the tiny big-haired hostess to their table, dodging children running about and adjusting to the sensory overload. There was an enormous neon Bud Light sign hanging behind the stage presently occupied by a band doing a talentless cover of Eric Clapton's 'Layla' – and a striking, tall blonde bombshell wearing the slightest hint of a silver string bikini. It was unclear why she was on stage, gyrating to the rhythm, but no one seemed to question her, either. Balloons and strings of every color were dipping from the ceiling for some reason and almost everybody in the joint was laughing, smiling, or singing along with the band. Senator Tanner looked at Eric like, we're going to enjoy the hell out of this place, and Eric reservedly agreed.

"Welcome to Dick's Last F'in Resort," the waiter said as he strolled up to their table. Eric had been checking his

Chief of Staff

silverware and when he found an identifiable spot encrusted on his fork, asked for a new one. "Don't think so. That would require me walking back to the wait stand. And I'm not in the right frame of mind to do that." Eric stared at him blankly. "So, now that we've moved past that, my name is Jimmy, and it would appear that you're sitting at one of my tables. I'm so happy." Jimmy was a six foot four inch white guy with jet black hair and a fluffy handlebar moustache, and a very deep voice. Eric and the senator had to crane their necks to look at him. The expression on Jimmy's face was dour and his down-turned mouth only lent to his expression. "If you want something to drink, you'd better tell me fast because I've got to go pee."

Eric looked at Senator Tanner who quickly stymied him. "I'll have a Michelob Light," he said, turning his attention to Jimmy. Eric ordered the same.

"And what are you two doing in Myrtle Beach? Here for a convention or something?" Jimmy hadn't bothered to write down their drink order.

"No, we're just here traveling," the senator said.

"Together?"

"Yes."

"And not on business?" Jimmy raised an eyebrow and checked them both up and down.

"We're kind of partners," Senator Tanner said.

"That's sweet. I wouldn't have put you two together." He looked at Eric and took in his outfit. "He's a little more uptight that you are, isn't he?" he asked the senator.

"You could say that!"

"And how long have you been together?"

"Pardon me?" Eric had started looking over the menu, trying to find something he thought was edible and due to the raucous noise level, hadn't clearly heard Jimmy's question.

Chief of Staff

"I said, how long have you two been together? Oh wait, I love playing this game. Which one of you is the top and which one of you is the bottom?" He playfully tapped a finger to his mouth, looking back and forth at the senator and Eric.

"Top or bottom of what?" Eric asked, leaning forward and turning his ear toward Jimmy. The senator knew what Jimmy was getting at, but sat back to watch the fireworks display.

"Which one of you is the catcher and which one of you is the pitcher?"

Eric looked at the senator with an inquisitive look and then it hit him. Broad-sided him, in fact. "I'm not gay!"

"Right. Just your boyfriend is, I presume." He winked at the senator who, just to make Eric more upset, returned an overly enthusiastic wink of his own.

"I'm not gay!" Eric repeated.

"Whatever. I'm not here to judge."

"Not that there's anything wrong with gays or lesbians or whatever. I'm just not one of them. I'm as straight as they come." Eric was sinking in a moral quagmire and the senator wasn't doing anything to help free him.

"It's always your own people, sometime's it your own people."

"What does that mean?"

"Mos Def? Talibe Quali? Black Star Productions?"

"Speak English," Eric commanded.

"Sorry. They're rappers." Jimmy shrugged his shoulders and dug in the knife. "You're supposed to know who they are. I guess I was wrong, but I thought you were black."

"Get up!" he said to the senator, standing. "We're leaving."

Chief of Staff

"Hold onto your panties, honey," Jimmy said. "The night's still young." Senator Tanner calmed Eric and sat him down. "I'll be right back with your dainty little light beers, ladies."

Even though his experience didn't start out the way he would have imagined – in his lifetime – and even though the food was tepid by his standards and the loud-ass atmosphere and the never-ending torturous renditions of classic rock songs never ceased, Eric started to really enjoy himself. It could have been the sixth Tequila shot he was intimidated by Jimmy into ordering, switching from his dainty little light beer. He wasn't sure. What he knew was that he was now standing on the stage, in front of God and every last drunk in Myrtle Beach and their trailer-trash children, screaming the lyrics to "Mustang Sally" and holding the aforementioned blonde bombshell around the waist. Senator Tanner screamed right along with the rest of the crowd, refusing Eric's pleas to join him on stage. What Eric didn't know was that the paper hat Jimmy insisted he wear, and not look at while they were in the restaurant, was emblazoned with the hand-written phrase: "I'm Not Gay…. But My Boyfriend Is." He was having the time of his life.

Chief of Staff

Chapter *42*

THE last stop on their tour turned out to be a TGI Friday's restaurant they were driving past in a cab on their way back to the marina, and some well-deserved rest. It was 2 am and they had just left Dick's Last Resort. Tired and partied out, they were ready to call it a night. Or so Eric thought. The senator and Eric were tanked, and Eric was still wearing his paper hat. "Stop the car!" the senator screamed at the driver. "I'm in the mood for a night cap."

The cabbie pulled over, Eric handed him twenty dollars - more than he should have for the short three-block drive and he sped away. They straightened themselves up as much as possible, and sauntered up to the bar. It took a couple of minutes before they realized that everyone in the restaurant, except the wait staff, was dressed exactly like Mark Twain. Confused and wondering what Jimmy had snuck into their drinks, they looked at each other and scanned the patrons again.

"There's a Mark Twain convention in town this weekend," the bartender said, unfazed by the circus of men and women, alike, dressed in starch white suits and white wigs, and slowly wiped off the bar in front of them. He placed those little drink napkins down on the glossy wood and asked, "What'll you have, boys?" He looked at Eric's hat and restated his question. "What'll you and your boyfriend have?"

Eric noticed the bartender looking at his hat and jerked it off of his head to read it. "Son of a bitch," he said, smiling and shaking his head.

"I've have a double Jose Cuervo Tradicional," the senator said.

"Me, too," Eric said, putting his hat back on. Oh, the things drunk folks will do.

"Most people don't know that I was a great person and a great American." Senator Tanner turned to the man next to him, wondering why he was speaking so loudly and wondering if he actually thought he was, in fact, Mark Twain. The senator leaned back a bit to adjust his focus on the man and said, sure, whatever you say. "I was a man, both complicated and simple at the same time."

Senator Tanner looked at Eric, who shrugged his shoulders, and then back at Mark Twain. "Pardon me for asking, good sir. But do you believe you are Mark Twain? I mean, if you were, that would mean that either I'd be dead or the afterlife is treating you better than I expected." He laughed at himself and tossed back his double shot of Tequila.

"I am no more Mark Twain – or Samuel Clemens – than any of these other fools," he said with an air of self-deprecation and a wide, alcohol-tinged grin. "We all just enjoy what he represented and wonder how delightful the world would have been had he lived to enlighten our day and time."

"And you fools get together and do this every year?" Eric asked, leaning forward on the bar to look around the senator.

"Every year. Of course, this is our first time coming to Myrtle Beach. But, yes every year we pick a destination and we all meet up. My friends think I'm crazy."

"Perhaps you should begin to agree with them," Senator Tanner said. "You're all a bunch of freaks." His eyelids were starting to become heavy and he knew it wouldn't be long until he was passed out drunk. He hoped to God he wasn't going to fall out at a bar of TGI Friday's in Myrtle Beach surrounded by a surreal collection of Mark Twain impersonators and impressionists.

"You know, Mark Twain, or maybe it was you," Eric blurted out, inserting himself back into the conversation, "once said, 'The trouble is not that the world is full of fools; it's that lightning isn't distributed right'." He chuckled to

Chief of Staff

himself and raised his hand to flag down the bartender. "I should know because I work for a fool, a United States Senator, at that."

Senator Tanner's eyes somehow opened more fully, though still barely above a wide slit, and he punched Eric in the arm.

"A senator, huh?" Mark Twain asked. "Which one?"

For the first time, Eric noticed that Mark Twain was a lot taller than he remembered from the pictures of his advanced literary class at Fisk. And never, he thought, would Mark Twain be drinking a Cosmopolitan. That was most certainly a woman's drink, light of flavor and absent any sign of masculinity. For a man to drink a Cosmopolitan without apology meant certain flaws in his character were evident and, brazenly, on display for anyone to critique. "You like Cosmopolitans, do you?" Eric asked with a raised, you're a sissy, eyebrow.

"Yes," Mark Twain said. "Which senator do you work for?"

Senator Tanner punched Eric in the arm again and closed his eyes. "Lamprey, republican asshole from California." Senator Tanner reached out, eyes still shut, felt around and patted Eric on the back. "I think what you said about politicians rings true in most cases, especially for my boss."

"And what is it that I said?" Mark Twain had put down his drink and subtly asked the bartender for something a little stronger, perhaps more manly, like a scotch, please.

"He said that Congress was the grand old benevolent asylum for the helpless." Eric slapped the bar and threw his head back laughing. Instantly he got dizzy and grabbed for the bar. Once he settled himself he said, "And not only that, but he, I mean you, I mean he, whatever, one of you said, 'Imagine that you were an idiot. And then imagine that you were a member of Congress. Wait a minute. I repeated myself.'" Again, he tossed his head back to laugh, but this

Chief of Staff

time he lost his balance and slipped off of his stool, falling to the ground, still laughing.

Several Mark Twains, including one with large breasts and silky smooth hands, which even in his stupor Eric found to be quite a disgusting and contradictory combination, helped him to his feet and placed him back on the stool. The bartender walked away, wishing to himself that he'd taken that job over at the Pavilion passing out game tokens to angst-ridden teenagers.

"You seem to know a great deal about Mark Twain," said Mark Twain.

"I know a lot about a lot of things, sir." Eric flagged down the bartender again, intending to order another shot, but forgot what he was going to say. Never mind, he said with a wave of his hand. It'll come back to me. "I know a lot about a lot of things," he repeated.

"You already said that."

Eric shrugged his shoulders and looked at Senator Tanner, seemingly asleep where he sat. Eric fished through the senator's jacket pocket until he found his pack of cigarettes. He'd lit two before he realized he was lighting the filter end and not the tobacco end. His third try was a success. "I know a lot about a lot of things, sir." He blew a shoddy smoke ring into the air and scrunched up his eyebrows like what he had said was oddly familiar to him.

"Well, I must say that I'm quite the historian, myself. Did you know that Mark Twain was quoted as saying, 'I suppose an honest man shines more in politics…'"

"…than he does elsewhere," Eric interrupted, continuing the quote himself. "But shouldn't a senator keep his word? Or a president? Should he set a high example? Is keeping one's word so extraordinary a thing when the person achieving that fete is the first citizen of a civilized nation?'" Mark Twain, clearly irritated that he was being shown up by a stranger at his own Mark Twain convention, snatched up his manly scotch and stormed off.

Chief of Staff

Eric flagged down the bartender once more, remembered what he was going to ask and tried as hard as he could to focus on the newly poured shot before him. "That is the oddest thing I've ever seen," Eric slurred to absolutely no one, tossed back the Tequila and got up to mingle.

Without any warning, Senator Tanner suddenly shot up, sitting bolt upright and looking around like it was the first time he had realized where he was. Just as suddenly, he broke into song. "I want my baby back, baby back, baby back, baby back, baby back. I want my baby back, baby back, baby back. I want my Chili's baby back ribs. I want my Chili's baby back ribs." And in the lowest voice he could muster, from the deepest part of his body he said, "Barbeque sauce."

Eric had walked over to, and had started rather successfully chatting up, the buxom Mark Twain who helped him up from the floor and whipped his head around when he heard the senator's voice carrying across the restaurant. He looked around and saw that he wasn't the only patron in awe. The manager went over to Senator Tanner and, with a polite hand on his shoulder, seemed to be asking him to calm down and to, please God, stop singing the competition's jingle, catchy though it were. Senator Tanner nodded with matching politeness, seemed to apologize, and waited for the conversations to resume.

"I want my baby back, baby back, baby back, baby back, baby back," he started again, louder and more distinctly than the first time. He had this shit eating grin on his face and as he held onto the bar with all of his strength, he stood up from his stool. Tottering back and forth, now with both hands in the air, like some drunken philharmonic conductor, he goaded the crowd into joining him. You could tell that the collection of Mark Twains had never come across anything like this before, odd as that may sound, but like a domino effect, one after the other, in large groups and small, they all started singing right along with Senator Scott Tanner.

"I want my baby back, baby back, baby back, baby back, baby back. I want my baby back, baby back, baby back,

Chief of Staff

baby back, baby back. Chili's baby back ribs. I want my Chili's baby back ribs." And from the bowels of the restaurant, a large black man resembling Michael Clarke Duncan squeezed into a white suit and white wig, put forth a guttural, "Barbeque sauce." The entire restaurant erupted in laughter. Over and over again, to the complete dismay of the now not-so-polite manager, the annual Mark Twain conventioneers sang about their love of Chili's baby back ribs at the tops of their lungs. Even the bartender snuck in a timid "barbeque sauce" when his boss wasn't looking.

Have you ever seen two hundred people dressed as Mark Twain kicked out of the TGI Friday's in Myrtle Beach? Eric, hand-in-hand with the buxom Mark Twain, Senator Tanner, aka 'the Conductor', and the rest of the choir were immediately asked to leave. They all filed out, still singing the jingle, and walked down the street to destinations unknown to continue the party.

Chapter *43*

WHEN Eric and Senator Tanner returned to Trinity, the sun was just beginning to rise. They barhopped a little longer with the assortment of Mark Twains and ended their day by hitting a local Waffle House, giving Eric his first taste of the greasy and over salted breakfast concoctions that had fed college students' post-party appetites for generations. The senator borrowed a cell phone and asked Trinity's Captain to have the yacht ready to sail for Wilmington once they were aboard. After the obligatory exchange of phone numbers and the 'I promise I'll call you' line, everyone parted ways.

Both Eric and the senator had pounded cup after cup of weak Waffle House coffee in an effort to sober up, and as a result, they were both too wired to sleep. Eric was standing on the aft deck watching as the marina slowly slipped into the background. The sun's light was dim, but you could tell that once it had fully risen, it would be another glorious day in the very pedestrian, very exciting city of Myrtle Beach, South Carolina.

"What are you smiling about?" asked the senator as he handed Eric a blanket and some hot chocolate he'd fumbled around in the galley to make. "Here you go. It's a little chilly out here."

Wrapping himself up and taking the drink, Eric said, "I was thinking about my mother just then, actually."

"Ah, I see. I'll leave you with your thoughts then."

"No, no," Eric said, reaching out and stopping him. "Sit down with me." They moved to the side of the Jacuzzi and sat on its cover. They both bundled up in their blankets and sipped their delightfully non-alcoholic beverages. "She was a really special woman, you know?"

"One of the best. I really miss her. I miss her a lot. She was a very, very good friend to me, Eric."

"And she was a great mom, too." Eric looked up to see the last grouping of stars he could make out and closed his eyes to say a hello prayer. "I don't know where I would be or how my life would have turned out had it not been for her. It scares me to think about it sometimes."

"The beauty of that is you don't have to think about it. You've grown into a wonderful and very responsible young man, Eric. You have a great head on your shoulders. You're smart and you're a nice person, to boot. She can see that. She's probably smiling right now, herself, looking down on you."

"There are some things I hope she wasn't a witness to this weekend," Eric laughed, prompting the senator to do the same. He looked into his mug and pushed around a couple of the marshmallows. "I just hope she's proud of me, you know?" Eric turned to the senator who was tearing up. "What's wrong?"

"Son," he started, his voice wavering, "if she's half as proud of you as I am, the way you've turned out and dealt with so much drama in your life, you've got nothing to worry about." Eric started crying, too, but he didn't know why. Intense emotion overtook him and he couldn't stop it. They hugged for a long time, each thinking about the mother and friend they lost, thankful for their strong relationships.

Senator Tanner broke the grip first and walked to the railing. "Come over here. I want to show you something." Eric wiped his eyes and stood. He was still a little intoxicated and the subtle swaying of the yacht caused him to stop momentarily and regain his balance. "You asked me when you came aboard what it was that I loved so much about the sea. Do you remember that?"

"Yes, I remember."

"Look out there, into the distance. We aren't that far out, but from here things like the coast and buildings and whatever else are kind of mixing together, becoming a totally different image in your brain than the detail you see when

Chief of Staff

you're right up close, right on the marina and everything is exploding in your face; the colors and smells and sounds are bold and dramatic up close." Eric took in the panorama and turned up his mug to get the last, resistant marshmallow wallowing at the bottom. "Turn around and tell me what you see."

"The sea and the horizon," Eric said, both of them leaning their backs against the railing.

"Between somewhere and nowhere," the senator said. "This is what I love about the sea. I exist on a completely different plane, some different level of consciousness when I'm at sea. I'm between somewhere and nowhere and it's the most comfort I have experienced. This feeling is like a paradise I've never found anywhere else on the planet and I don't think I ever will."

"It's certainly serene," Eric said, noting the silence. The only true sound he could hear other than the hum of the yacht's motor and the churning of the waves, was the breeze as it softly rolled by his ear. The sky was that amazing mix of new colors that you can only see when day breaks, and Mother Nature repeats the lunar cycle all over again. He took a deep breath and let the smell and taste of the sea air, the salt in the air, wash over him. Calm. He felt calm and, strangely, something he simply couldn't define. Maybe that was what the senator couldn't explain to him before. Maybe Eric wouldn't be able to explain his connection to the sea for many more years. But right now, at that moment, he understood completely what Senator Tanner was talking about.

"Will you promise me something?" Senator Tanner was starting to cry again and had a hard time asking his next question. He didn't look at Eric, only stared out over the horizon, tears falling past his nose and dripping from his chin.

"Anything," Eric said. He'd turned to the senator and rested a hand on his shoulder.

"This is where I want you to put me when I die."

Eric was silent, not because he didn't know what to say, but because he was taken by the enormity and directness of what he'd just heard.

"Can you do that for me? If you want to put up a marker somewhere in a graveyard or whatever, I don't care." He took Eric by the hands and squeezed them when he said, "Please just don't let anybody put me in the ground. Please, Eric. This is where I want to be when I die. Cremate me and bring out here between somewhere and nowhere."

Eric was crying now, too, and grasped the senator's hands tightly. "I promise. I promise you I won't let anyone put you in the ground."

"Because I couldn't stand that, Eric," the senator pleaded, his nose running and words jagged from not being able to fully catch his breath.

"I know."

"Swear it. Swear to me you won't let that happen. I have to hear you say you swear, Eric. I have to hear you say that to me."

"I swear," Eric said through rushing tears. "My God, I swear, Senator."

Senator Tanner grasped Eric by the back of the neck and kissed him on the cheek. He paused long enough to feel his warm breath as it rebounded from Eric's skin, walked away without saying another word, and vanished into Trinity, leaving Eric alone with his thoughts

All Eric could do was stand there, holding his empty hot chocolate mug, wondering what in the world had just happened.

*****

"HELL no," Eric said as he pushed open Senator Tanner's stateroom door. "Hell no." He'd stood out on the aft deck trying to process his directive to cremate his best friend and decided that it wasn't going to end there. Senator

Tanner was sitting on the bed, wiping his eyes when Eric burst in. "We're not done with our conversation."

"Yes, we are."

"What's wrong with you? And don't give me that same song and dance because I don't want to hear it." The senator looked at Eric and shook his head, no. "Unacceptable. Something is wrong with you and I demand to know what it is."

"You demand?" the senator questioned. "You don't have the right to demand anything of me!"

"The hell I don't!" Eric shouted back. "I love you. I am concerned about you. And I want to know what is going on. Now!"

"Fine! I'll tell you!" Senator Tanner shouted back, not knowing why they were yelling at each other. "I'm going to die! Are you happy?" His face contorted again and he started to cry. "I'm going to die."

"We're all going to die, Senator." Eric sat down on the bed and put his arm around Senator Tanner. "Man, we're all destined to die. And unless you know something I don't know, there's nothing we can do about it. Is that why you're all twisted up? Is that why you've been shoveling vitamins and all of those pills in your mouth every day?" He gave him a one-arm hug and said, "I thought something was really wrong with you. You're getting older. It's not a bad thing. You're just getting older."

"I have what my doctor called liver cirrhosis."

"What?" Eric let go of the senator and sat back more fully on the bed. Something inside of him had deflated. He could feel himself becoming pale and a little short of breath. His night had just gone from bad to worse with one very short sentence.

"Liver cirrhosis."

"How long have you known?"

"About seven months. I was diagnosed just before Byrum died." The senator sat back on the bed and both men leaned against the head board, propping themselves up with pillows. Their voices were low and cautious, one not wanting to scare the other more than necessary. "My doctor didn't want me to fly to California, so Byrum went by himself."

"Thank God you didn't go."

"I would have died on that plane, too."

"Count your blessings that you're alive."

"Sometimes I think it would have been better that way."

"Don't say things like that. Everybody's better off with you being alive. Don't forget that. Don't forget what you mean to everyone, what you mean to me."

"They can't treat it anymore," the senator said, taking Eric's hand. "There's nothing more they can do for me."

Eric was trying very hard not to cry, not to break down in front of the senator. "With today's modern medicine? Come on," he said, playfully punching the senator in the arm. "There's nothing money can't buy when it comes to your health. We're gonna beat this, you'll see. We're gonna make you better...no, even better than before. You're gonna be great. I promise."

The senator squeezed Eric's hand tightly. "It's too late, son. My blood is being poisoned. That's what the liver does, it takes toxins and other shit out of your blood, not to mention a laundry list of things my doctor told me that is too long to repeat right now. My body has already started to change and it's on a course that, I'm sad to say, simply cannot be reversed."

Eric jumped up from the bed, and bounded around the stateroom. He was scratching his head and rubbing his face and thinking out loud. "No way! There must be something that we can do." His voice was higher, like he was excited or maybe just trying to mask his pain. He had to be upbeat, not only for his sake, but for the senator's, as well. "I know there's something that can be done. When we get back to Washington, I'm going to start making some calls. I know doctors, Christine knows doctors, I know people who know doctors. Somebody has to be able to tell us something that can be done to make you well. You said it was your liver? Easy fix. I'll just give you part of mine. It'll regenerate or whatever it does inside you and everything will be fine."

"Everything isn't going to be fine," the senator said. The tenderness of his words would have made you think that Eric was the one with the disease, that the senator was comforting him and telling him that he would be alright. "The pills I have been taking aren't vitamins. They're some pretty powerful drugs that, to now, haven't done anything for me. I have all of the symptoms and none of the progress in fighting what's killing me."

"You're not going to die," Eric pleaded. "There's a way out of this."

"Jaundice, nail changes, fluid retention, easy bruising and nosebleeds, and on and on. I have all of it. That's what I deal with every day; what I've dealt with for the last seven months. It's not getting any better and it's not going to change. They call it end stage, and although a liver transplant may work in some or most people, I've done too much damage."

"We spent the whole vacation drinking!" Eric realized. "You've been drinking ever since I came to Washington. We toasted my first win with champagne. We got blitzed on Trinity that same night. If you've got this disease, why are you still drinking?"

"I've probably got twelve to eighteen months left, son," the senator said, avoiding Eric's question.

"You knew you were going to die when you called me to Trinity and asked me to be your chief of staff, didn't you?"

"I didn't know then. I mean, I knew, yes, but I didn't have a time frame. My doctor didn't tell me that until

Chief of Staff

recently. He put me on this course of treatment that included the pills and eating right and other stuff."

Eric walked into the bathroom and came back out with the senator's pill bottles. "Water tablets, laxatives, some of kind vitamins and calorie supplements, green pills, red pills, tiny pills." He tossed them onto the bed and said, "If this stuff isn't going to keep you alive, then what will?"

"Nothing," the senator said quietly.

"Come to Washington. Be my chief of staff. Let's put you in position to become a senator when my term is over. Do everything I'm supposed to do as a senator to get practice for the job you may or may not take over once I'm gone. And oh yeah, I forgot to tell you. I'm going to die. Have a nice life!" Senator Tanner stood and walked to Eric, but Eric turned to walk out. He kept his back facing the senator. "My mother left me. My father left me. And now you're going to leave me. That's just beautiful. All I want right now is to get off this damn boat and back to Washington. I have to learn how to become a senator," he said, walked out and closed the door behind him.

Chapter *44*

THE instant Christine picked up the phone, several things happened simultaneously. The mousetrap Reginald's guy at the NSA had created tripped and started recording. Reginald's own phone rang, having been surreptitiously linked to Christine's phone system, and allowed him to listen to every word of the conversation. Lastly, the intercept Reginald personally attached directly to the phone system at Dove's Nest switched on and provided a secondary recording should Reginald not have the opportunity, or desire, to listen to each and every one of the constant calls that either came into or originated from the mansion.

Reginald was particularly proud of himself for tapping Christine's phones, himself. Yet again, Christine was hosting a party and the flurry of activity on the grounds gave him the perfect cover. He snuck onto the property and blended in like just another one of the other worker ants, did what he needed to, and slipped out.

"Christine Squire," she said, introducing herself to the caller. Normally, she knew everyone who called Dove's Nest. There were times, though, when a reporter or inquiring long-forgotten acquaintance called 'just to say hello'. That meant they really wanted to get on the guest list for one of her shindigs, most notably Jewel Box. Evan or another servant would hand her the phone and, without thinking, she automatically answered, "Christine Squire." People of certain upbringing, she would explain often to Eric, should always use their most courteous phone manners at every occasion. "To whom am I speaking?"

"I just love the way you answer the phone, Honey Pot."

"Cole."

"Ooh, and the way you say my name brings a joyful tingle to my spine." He chuckled and said, "And how are you?"

"What do you want?" Christine was reclining by the pool, under a patio umbrella to ward off the sun's rays. She'd already been to church, made several phone calls checking on her business interests in France and potential land deals in the mid-west. The next item on her schedule that morning was a briefing by her son, and the rest of the board of directors for Bryant Holdings. It wasn't unusual for Christine to call a meeting on a Sunday, as it was her most productive day out of the week. Until now, everything was running smoothly and this was an interruption she didn't care to have.

"I pity the elderly," Cole nipped. "The memory seems to simply slip away from you all, doesn't it? Perhaps your doctor might suggest a little Ginko. I hear that will do wonders for staving off the interminable effects of senility that accompany you on the jagged walk to your grave."

"That was neither clever nor amusing. I am very busy."

"You're never too busy for me, Honey Pot."

"Good day, Cole."

"I would like to point out something extremely important to you, Christine."

Silence.

"I have done a little research and I have the phone numbers, fax numbers, and email addresses of every editor of every magazine and newspaper that has a circulation over five people in this country. Several of them are published abroad, but I don't think I'll do anything with them." Cole didn't really have that information, but he figured it couldn't be that hard to obtain. Hell, spend a day in the library poking through periodicals and he could find whatever he was looking for.

"And what are you planning to do with that?" Christine asked. Eric told her that the next time Cole called, she was to play dumb, to ask questions in order to obtain more information. What did he actually have on her? Was he making the whole thing up? Was there a way to make Cole stick his foot in his mouth and run away with his tail between his legs? No way was Christine going to give up any money to Cole - not five dollars, not fifty dollars, and certainly not fifty million. Cole was lying somewhere, Eric told her. It would just be a matter of finding the weak link in his story.

"I don't have time to play games with you. I told you as much the first time I called. You owe me some money and I will get it."

"That's right," Christine said, pretending she had forgotten. "Fifty million. I really must be losing my mind. I'm just an old, frail, helpless woman."

"Old? Absolutely. Frail? Maybe. Helpless? I don't think so. Get a pencil and write down this account number." Christine told him she was ready, but instead sat there looking at the way her gardener was incorrectly pruning her roses. When Cole was satisfied, he started again. "You've got five days to deposit my money into this account. If on the sixth day I don't see the money, I'm going to bring you down."

"And God rested on the seventh day."

"That was neither clever nor amusing," Cole teased.

"You know, Cole, I have a question for you." Christine stood and walked to one of the gardeners, motioning to him and instructing him on the correct way to trim her roses. "Why should I give you anything? I mean, you're nothing to me. I could step on you like a piss-ant little bug, wipe you off of my very expensive shoes and keep walking like nothing ever happened."

"Bryant Holdings."

Chief of Staff

"What about it?" Christine taunted. "It's just a company. Companies have histories. Companies keep records. Companies make mistakes."

"And the press eats up stories about companies with histories who keep records and make mistakes but go to extreme lengths to hide what they've done. You forget that I used to handle your books. I know your secrets. I know about the real estate and the collusion and the illegal business transactions. I know the truth about Charlotte's first supposedly black-owned bank. I know about all of the money you defrauded from the state, and oh my, never saw fit to return."

"All of which can be easily explained away by accounting errors, Cole. You'll have to work a hell of a lot harder than that if you want me to continue this game. In truth, you are tiring me and I've decided that this is no longer fun. In the beginning, I thought I'd play with you, like a cat plays with a mouse. But you have proved to be no match for me. I've lost interest. There are no skeletons in my closet that would bring me to supply you with a ball of lint, let alone my hard-earned money."

Cole's face reddened and his face felt hot. How dare she speak to him that way? How dare she treat him like some common thief bearing empty threats. "You have five days, Christine. I will bring you down and savor every delicious phone call, each sumptuous fax, and every tantalizing email I send out decrying your foul play."

"I don't think so, you son of a bitch!" Christine screamed. The gardener snapped his head back to Christine and then to the rose bush. "I will not be spoken to that way."

"You forget who you're dealing with," Cole said, cutting her off and impersonating her gravelly voice and stiff upper lip attitude. "I'm the magnanimous Christine Belmont Squire."

"Go to hell!"

"I'll do you one better, old woman. You think you're so untouchable? You think you can weather a public scandal regarding your company? You think your snobby little friends won't care that you're a thief and slum lord? That's fine. That's cool." Cole wound up and delivered his knockout punch. "What do you think Eric is going to say when he finds out that his mother was manipulated into marrying his dear old dad just so his grandmother could avoid the social indignity of having an illegitimate grandchild? Do you think he's going to be overjoyed to learn that he was an unwanted, unloved, bastard child? How about the fact that his mother was forced to marry someone she didn't love, and forced to give birth to and raise a baby she hadn't had any intention on keeping? All of that happened just to save his grandmother's reputation? Maybe Eric will finally understand the source of your guilt, and why you've created this world of overcorrecting what you did. The gifts, the money, the lavishing of attention on the one thing you never wanted to deal with.

"You manipulated and coerced everything connected with him to fit the mold of what you thought it should be, how you thought your friends and business associates perceived you to have the perfect little family. Your daughter wasn't going to screw that up for anything, and you definitely made sure of that. And God rested on the seventh day, indeed," Cole spat. "Ha, ha, I wouldn't blame Eric if he hated you for the rest of your brief, natural life."

Reginald was actually listening to this call, and his mouth hit the floor.

"Please, Cole," Christine said, sobbing with real emotion and authentic tears. "Please don't do that. Please leave him out of this. He is the most precious thing to me on the face of this planet. Don't do that. Don't ever let him know the truth. Don't ever let him know what I've done."

He recited the account number one more time. "Five days. Fifty million." And he hung up.

Chief of Staff

Christine was screaming and crying into the phone, not realizing that Cole had already ended the conversation. "Don't do that, Cole! Don't tell him anything, Cole! Are you listening to me? Cole? Cole?!" Silence was replaced with a dial tone and she knew then that he was gone. "God-damn you, Cole!" she screamed, and threw the phone into the pool. She stormed into the house quickly, much faster than a woman of her age might have moved. Under the circumstances, though, time was of the essence. There was only one thing left for her to do. It was the ultimate last resort, but she was Christine Belmont Squire, and if anyone could pull it off and get away with it, she was the one.

She slammed the door to her study and picked up the phone. "I need you to do me that favor we spoke about some weeks ago," she said to the person on the other end of the line. "No trace of him should be left. None. And trust me…if this gets linked to me in any fashion, you will regret it."

Christine hung up, took several deep breaths to calm herself, and walked down the hall into her bathroom. She stared at herself in the mirror and slowly reapplied her lipstick and touched up her eye make-up. She combed the hair over her ears ever so delicately with her pinky and, after several more deep breaths, called for Evan. "Bring the car around, please. I do not want to be late for my board meeting."

Chapter *45*

"GOOD morning, Evil Mistress," Eric said as he walked into the office Tuesday morning. Claudia was on the phone when he came in and tried quickly to end her call. Eric strode past her desk, grabbing his mail on the way, and walked into his office. "Hey, Zeke," he said. Eric stopped in his tracks, looked over at the sofa and walked back out.

"I was going to tell you about that, COS," Claudia started to explain, "but I was kind of stuck on the phone."

"Uh huh, right. Why is Zeke sitting on my sofa in my office?"

"His mother got stuck working and since she didn't have anybody else, I kind of agreed to watch him."

"Where's the boy's father?"

"He died when Zeke was eighteen months old."

Eric suddenly hated that he'd asked that question, especially since Zeke could hear everything they were saying. "Shouldn't he be in school?" Eric asked, turning back to his office. Zeke waved and smiled at Eric, who instinctively smiled and waved right back.

"Today is a teacher work day. Zeke's school is closed and she didn't have anybody else who could watch him. If it's a problem, I can try to think of something. We literally just got here about ten minutes ago. I sat him in your office while I took care of some morning business. If it's a big deal, I can bring him out here to sit with me." Claudia realized she was pleading her case poorly because Eric was still staring at her. He didn't look pissed, but she could tell he wasn't happy. "Look, I can try and find somebody who can sit with him until she gets back."

Eric turned around again and looked at Zeke. The vacation he'd taken with the senator put him off schedule and even though they'd had a ton of fun, his plan was to dive back

Chief of Staff

into the craziness of his world this morning. "Didn't his mother know she'd have to work today?" Eric asked.

"She's an emergency room nurse at Memorial. Somebody quit and she was pretty much forced to pull a double shift. It's over at 3:30. She's going to come get Zeke right afterward. He's as silent as a church mouse, I promise." Claudia walked into Eric's office and told Zeke that Mr. Eric had a lot of work to do and that he'd be sitting with her for the day. Eric knew the sofa in his office would be much more comfortable than the side chair at Claudia's desk and started feeling bad about the whole thing.

"He's as quiet as a church mouse, you say?" he asked, walking into his office and looking at Zeke. Claudia said absolutely and Eric reluctantly agreed to let him stay. As long as you know, Zeke, he said with a fatherly tone he pulled out of thin air, that I'm a very busy person and I need to have quiet time to think and get things done. Zeke looked at Claudia and then back at Eric and nodded his head wildly. He was smiling and his eyes were beaming. It's just an office, Eric thought, and got ready to tackle his day.

"You ready, girl?" Eric, Claudia and Zeke looked at the doorway to find Richelle Chapman, the executive administrative assistant for the Senate Majority Leader, standing there, notepad and pen in hand.

"For what?" Claudia asked.

"The seminar. We've got the Ethics seminar today. You forgot, didn't you?" Richelle was smiling and when she saw Zeke, walked into the office and shook his hand. "Good morning, Zeke. It's nice to see you again."

"And you, as well, Ms. Richelle." Eric wondered how this kid knew everybody in the free world. The manners, though, were extremely impressive.

Claudia turned to Eric with a panicked look. Today was simply not the day for her to have forgotten something, let alone for her to have Zeke stuck in Eric's office without her all day. Eric saw the pained expression on her face and said, "No. No way. You've got to be kidding me."

"I don't really have another choice, COS."

"You're serious, aren't you? Why don't you take him with you?"

"To a seminar on Ethics? Really. Please?" Eric thought she was about to drop to her knees and beg. "I'll do anything. I've been waiting on this seminar for two months. I never would have agreed to keep him if I'd remembered I'd already paid to attend. No offense, Zeke."

"That's okay."

"Fine. Go. But I swear, Claudia," Eric started.

"Momma says you aren't supposed to say that, Mr. Eric."

Eric took a deep breath, apologized to Zeke, and pointed Claudia and Richelle toward the door. "You'd better be back as soon as this thing is over, do you hear me?"

"Loud and clear. We'll be back around 3:00."

"3:00? It's only 7:15 right now! We all know that an Ethics seminar for anyone working with the government should only take about twenty minutes. Accept this kind of gift, give this one back. Don't take money from shady lobbyists or send dirty text messages to underage pages. It's elementary. Nobody pays attention to that shit anyway." He closed his mouth and shut his eyes because he knew what was coming.

"Momma says you aren't supposed to say that, either, Mr. Eric."

Another apology. When he opened his eyes, Claudia was already grabbing a notepad and pen and giving Eric instructions on how to care for Zeke. "He's not allergic to anything. He's got coloring books and crayons in his bag. He's had breakfast, but he'll probably want a snack in a little bit. He's O Positive. His mother's cell phone number is on

Chief of Staff

my calendar on my desk. You've got my cell phone number programmed in your phone. Call me if you have any questions or if anything goes wrong. Thanks, COS! I appreciate this more than you'll know." And she was gone.

Eric sat down at his desk and stared at Zeke. Zeke stared back. What the hell am I going to do with this kid today, he asked himself. Good thing Zeke didn't hear that because he would have gotten another Momma-said-you-aren't-supposed-to-say-that mini lecture. "Do you want some coffee?"

"I don't drink coffee, silly," Zeke said, laughing. Eric could see that he'd lost his two front teeth since the last, and hell, the only time he'd ever seen him. He made a huge deal out of it and Zeke soaked it up. It was the same way when he'd lost his own front teeth. Eric got up from his desk and sat next to Zeke on the sofa. He reached into his pocket and pulled out two dollars, one for each tooth. Zeke was overjoyed at having his very own two dollars and stuffed them into his jeans pocket. "Do you have any milk? I love to drink milk."

Eric smiled at Zeke's complete and utter excitement and said, "I think we can handle some milk. You know they say milk does a body good."

"What does that mean?" Zeke asked, moving over closer to Eric. It was weird, or strange or whatever the feeling may have been, but there was a comfort that came over Eric in knowing that Zeke was his responsibility that day. He'd always thought about having a child - or kids - of his own, maybe a son or twins or an entire basketball team, but work came first; it was always paramount and everything else was relegated to the background of his life. Christine chastised him about it relentlessly, telling him that she wanted to see him happy and married and a parent before she died. He'd gotten very good at both avoiding the subject and dodging the question when he was asked. The surprise of seeing a six year old sitting on his office sofa first thing in the morning was hard for him to take. But now, as Zeke was sitting next to him, reliant on him to make sure he was kept safe and fed and, honestly, entertained until either Claudia returned from her stupid seminar, or his mother got off work, Eric wondered if this feeling he had was what it was like for fathers around the world. His mind wandered to thoughts of Cole, but he quickly banished them from his head.

"Really, I don't know what it's supposed to mean. I just know that milk is good for your bones and if you drink it, it helps you grow big and strong."

"You must have dranken a lot of milk when you were little like me."

"It's not dranken," Eric said, correcting him. "It's drank. And, yes, I did."

"Neat. Maybe if I drink a lot of milk, I'll be as tall as you one day."

"Maybe," Eric said, smiling and nodding his head.

"So what do you do, Mr. Eric? My Aunt Claudia says you talk on the phone all day and that you go to meetings a lot. She didn't tell me what else, but I figure there must be something with all of that stuff on your desk."

"Your aunt? Ms. Claudia is your aunt?"

"No, silly," Zeke said, laughing again. "She's not my for-real aunt. I don't have one of those. She's my pretend aunt. Momma just says that I'm supposed to call her that."

"Hey, I've got a pretend aunt, too!" Eric said. The excitement is his voice startled him. "Her name is Aunt Pat and I love her very much."

"But she's a girl," Zeke said, twisting his face up at the thought of girl cooties.

"One day, Zeke, you'll..." and then he stopped. That was a conversation he needn't get into with a six year old. The topic of girls and love was best left to his mother. "To answer your question, I work for a man named Senator Tanner."

Chief of Staff

"What does he do?"

"Not much," Eric said with a wink, prompting more laughter from Zeke. "I make sure that people know he's working to bring good changes to their cities and towns and that he helps make the laws that will help all people get signed by the president."

"The guy that lives in the White House?"

Zeke seemed to skip everything Eric had just explained and focused solely on the White House. "Yes, that guy."

"That's what I want to do when I grow up. I want to live in the White House."

"You want to be the president?"

"No, I just want to live in the White House. Momma said one time that when I got old enough she'd take me, but then those therapists ran planes into some buildings in New York and into the Pentagon, and she said nobody could go to the White House anymore."

"Terrorists. Those are the people who did all of that bad stuff. A therapist helps people."

"Oh," Zeke said, not really caring about the difference between the two. "Well, I want to be a doctor when I grow up. Or maybe a therapist or a trash truck driver or an astronaut or a fisherman. They all get to do neat stuff and they help people, too, just like the guy you work for."

"You know, you're pretty smart for a six year old." Zeke's ear-to-ear grin said it all.

Time for an executive decision. The piles of work calling Eric's name would have to wait yet another day. He couldn't put his finger on it, but there was something about his conversation with Zeke that spoke to him. He imagined that he'd had the same kind of innocent talk with Senator Tanner years and years ago. This wasn't something he wanted to ignore, no matter how much work he had to do.

Chief of Staff

Eric got up from the sofa, grabbed Zeke's mother's number from Claudia's calendar, and made a couple of phone calls. Permission granted. Time to have some fun.

"So what are we going to do today, Big Guy?"

Zeke walked over and leaned on the arm of Eric's desk chair. "I don't know, Little Guy. What do you want to do?" Clever, Eric thought. Maybe this kid's smarter than anybody knows.

"I've got a couple of ideas I think you're going to like. Grab your coat and let's get out of here. Adventure awaits."

"What about my milk?"

*****

FROM the moment the guard let them pass through the huge black wrought iron gates, all the way through the bowels of the mansion, Zeke's mouth never closed. There were people everywhere and the sights and sounds of the White House had him turning this way and that, making sure he didn't miss anything at all. "Momma said we couldn't come in here."

"She's right. Most people can't. But I know the guy who lives here." Eric was too proud of himself. This was awesome. Zeke was overjoyed and that made Eric really happy. Zeke could care less that this was the seat of the most powerful man in the world. It didn't matter one bit to him that kings and queens and presidents of other countries had visited this historic home and office complex. All he knew was that Mr. Eric had given him the best surprise of his six year old life.

"He'll see you now," the president's assistant said, winking at Zeke. Of course, Zeke winked back. Player. The door to the Oval Office opened and Justin Burnette, a very well connected Washington politico, and the senior senator from South Carolina, Steve Canosa, who seemed visually relieved, walked past. Neither of them took the opportunity to speak to Eric.

Chief of Staff

"Zeke, do come in," President Brown said.

Thanks for doing this for him, Eric whispered to President Brown as they shook hands. No problem, he whispered back.

"I've only got about five minutes, son, but I wanted to make sure I got a chance to meet you." President Brown walked up to Zeke and shook his hand.

"Wow, you really live here?" Zeke asked, still clutching the president's hand.

"I sure do. Maybe one day when I have more time, I can take you on a tour. How would you like that?"

Zeke let go of the president's hand and started jumping in the air, squealing, and abruptly stopped. "Wait. Can I bring my momma, too?" Of course. With that he started jumping around again. Completely counter to the fear and anxiety that gripped adults when they were in the presence of the leader of the free world, Zeke's exuberance and uncontained joy hit both Eric and President Brown in the heart. Eric was thinking of his future; the president of the son he'd lost too soon into his life. A man in a dark suit took a couple of pictures of Zeke and he grabbed for Eric's hand. "Who is that?" he asked.

"Oh that's one of the White House photographers," President Brown answered. "Don't be scared. It's his job to take pictures of me and everybody that comes in here."

"Why? Don't people remember what you look like?" Zeke questioned.

"That's a great question, Zeke. I don't know why they take so many pictures of me and my guests," he said and winked at Eric. The president sat down behind his desk and gathered some papers. "And what is it you gentlemen are going to do today?"

"Well, one of the things Zeke wants to be is an astronaut, so I thought maybe we'd go to the Smithsonian and

Chief of Staff

check out all of the rockets and planes and spaceships. What do you say, Zeke?"

"Yes! Yes! Yes! This is the best day EVER!"

President Brown's assistant poked her head in to tell him that the car was ready. "You know, Zeke, it was great meeting you. I've got an appointment I need to get to, but I have an idea." President Brown bent down to Zeke's level and said, "Guess what?"

"What?"

"I believe I'm going to be driving right past the Smithsonian." Eric closed his eyes and prayed to God he was going to hear those magic words. Big kids like toys, too, and this one was a real piece of work. "How would you boys like a ride in my limo?"

"Yes!" Eric yelled, and then realized the question was meant for Zeke. Sorry.

"In your limo? Are they going to turn the lights on and have the motorcycles and the other stuff?"

"You betcha they are."

"Really?"

"I'm the president. I can do whatever I want. And if that means taking my newest bestest friend to the Smithsonian so he can see spaceships and airplanes and rockets, then I'll do just that."

"Promise?" Zeke asked.

"I swear."

"Momma says you aren't supposed to say that." Eric couldn't help but smile.

*****

WHEN the motorcade stopped at the front entrance to the Smithsonian, and after the Secret Service agents had cleared a path, Eric and Zeke thanked the president for their once-in-a-lifetime ride and got out. Everybody wondered

Chief of Staff

who they were, but nobody knew for sure. The motorcade zoomed away and the boys went about their day

At 3:45, Claudia and Zeke's mother walked into Eric's office. After a full day of visiting the White House, riding in the president's limo, walking around the entirety of the Smithsonian, eating lunch in the senate cafeteria, and having a snack of ice cold milk and chocolate chip cookies, Eric and Zeke had crashed on the sofa. They were both exhausted, each for different reasons.

Zeke's mother carefully packed up his coloring books and crayons. There was an envelope marked 'From the Desk of the President' with his name on it and she peeked inside. She was shocked to not only see a picture of her son standing in the Oval Office with the President of the United States, but what appeared to be a handwritten invitation for him to come back any time he wanted – "and make sure to bring your mother, too." She showed it to Claudia whose mouth fell. Still in shock, Zeke's mother picked him up and put his backpack over her shoulder. She wrote out a thank you note for Eric and left.

Claudia gently put a blanket on her boss and very quietly, closed the door behind her as she walked out.

Chapter *46*

WHERE was that ringing coming from? It was muffled and distant, but Eric knew he heard something. There it was again. The same sound. But what was going on? Slowly, Eric opened his eyes and looked around. He was in his office, that he knew. But the lights were off. And where did this blanket come from? Oh my God, he said out loud, sitting up quickly. Zeke? Where was Zeke? The last thing he remembered was the two of them sitting on the sofa watching The Wiggles on television. And now he was gone.

He stood up, still groggy from his over-extended nap and his right leg seized from an enormous cramp. Massaging his leg, he called out, "Zeke? Hey, Big Guy, where are you? Are you hiding from me?" Please God, let me find that boy. Claudia would be pissed. Not to mention his mother. He'd told her expressly that Zeke would be just fine in his care. And now look what he'd gone and done. I've lost a six year old. Dammit.

Limping around his office, Eric flipped on the lights and threw open the door. "Zeke?!"

"Good Lord, what's your problem?" Claudia asked. "Stop yelling."

"Uh, hey, Claudia," Eric said. "How was your seminar? Learn anything interesting?" As he spoke, Eric tried to casually look around the cubicles, searching for any sign of his elusive charge.

"It was fine," Claudia replied. She figured Eric had been dead asleep when she and Zeke's mother came to collect him. He looked tired when he walked into the office that morning, and Claudia figured he could use some rest, especially after chasing a child all day. She'd cancelled his appointments and forwarded his phone directly to voice mail. She knew he was looking for Zeke, but this was too much fun for her to let slip away. "What did you and Zeke do today?

Chief of Staff

His mother's going to be here in a minute or so to pick him up."

"Uh, we just kind of hung out, that's all." By now Eric had started to walk around the cubes, smiling politely at the staffers and inspecting their desks. "Nothing major. Just regular guy stuff."

"Interesting." She quickly stopped smiling when Eric turned around. He was almost panicked, but trying hard to hide it. "So can you go get him? I want to make sure he's packed and ready when his mother gets here."

"Right. Well, that's the thing," Eric said, an overwhelming feeling of terrible guilt coming over him. How do you explain that you've lost someone's child? Their keys, maybe. Even little things like their phone number or an invitation, whatever. But a kid? This was going to be bad. "I don't, uh, actually know where he is." He stepped back and squinted, readying himself for Aunt Claudia's imminent tirade.

"That's because he left about two hours ago."

"What?" Eric looked at Claudia and asked her to repeat herself. "You mean he's gone? With his mother? I didn't lose him?" Oh thank God.

"Is that why you were walking around like that?" Claudia asked, smiling fully now.

"Yes, it was," Eric said, catching her smile. "Now that simply was not funny, Claudia. Jesus, I thought I'd lost that kid." He bent over, his hands on his knees, and blew a sigh of relief. Claudia picked up the note Zeke's mother left and Eric read it aloud. Thanks so much for watching Zeke today, Eric. Claudia was right...you are a wonderful man. Eric looked up at Claudia who denied ever saying that. The note went on to say that any time he wanted, Zeke would be more than welcome to hang out with him. And the visit to the White House, picture with the president, and the limo ride were nice touches. Zeke will be talking about that for a long time to come. Thanks so much. Patricia. Eric looked at his watch and panicked all over again.

"Don't worry. I know what you're going to say," Claudia said as she walked back to her desk. "You looked awful this morning and I figured that since you and Zeke were knocked out on the sofa, you must have really needed the rest. I would have gotten you up sooner or later. To be honest, the peace and quiet was refreshing." Eric was still trying to fully wake up and he was still processing the information that he hadn't actually lost someone's child. Claudia's dig went right over his head.

"I guess I was more exhausted from my trip with the senator than I thought," Eric said.

"And what exactly did you do?" Claudia asked, handing him the messages from people who didn't want to leave a voice mail for Eric.

"Never mind that. Let's just say we had a good time and leave it alone." He leafed through his messages and found one from Reginald. "Hey, when did this guy call?" he asked.

"Well," Claudia said, taking the message out of his hand and pointing to the top. "It says that a Reginald called you at approximately 4:45, and then again at 5:00, and then again at 5:30, and then again at…"

"Thank you for pointing that out, Dark Princess." Eric turned to walk into his office and stopped. "Claudia," he said, turning back to face her. "I'm kind of glad you forgot about your seminar. I really enjoyed hanging out with Zeke today. I don't know how to explain it. It was just really neat." He smiled at Claudia, closed his door and went right to his desk.

"Come on, Reginald. Pick up the phone."

"Dynex International." The sultry voice of a woman had been replaced with a man with a heavy Scottish accent. Who was he really talking to, Eric thought.

"Reginald, please," Eric said.

Chief of Staff

"I'm sorry, but he is unavailable. May I take a message?"

"Please tell Reginald that the candidate is active."

"One moment, please. I'll connect you."

While Eric waited for Reginald to answer, he heard that ringing again. He thought it was a dream before, but now that he was awake, he was certain he heard something. Opening each of his drawers, he finally found the source: his cell phone. Why was it in a drawer? Zeke, he said, smiling and shaking his head. Or Claudia? No matter. The phone beeped and the voice mail indicator lit up. As he was about the check his messages, Reginald picked up.

"Where in the sam hill have you been?"

"And a fine Howdy Do to you, too, Reginald."

"We've got some serious business to talk about. You're not going to believe what I have to tell you."

"About our current case?" Eric asked.

"Right on the money."

"What's going on?" Eric was sifting through his desk drawers to make sure Zeke hadn't hidden anything else.

"I've got two things. The first thing is that I found out where he operates. Remember I told you we were going to meet to so I could give him some investment money?"

"Yeah. How'd that go?"

"I flew out last week. I tried to call you, but your cell service wasn't working."

Eric thought back to the steward who had confiscated his cell phone on Trinity. The one time he actually needed his phone and he was without it. "I was on vacation."

"Whatever. I met him in at a farm in some place called Marion, just outside of Asheville. I gave him the cash, he told me what he was going to do with it, we had a couple of drinks and I left."

"Sounds simple enough."

"Before I left, I took the liberty of placing a tracking device on his car and marked the exact location of the farm using some GPS coordinates. Now that I know where he's going to be, assuming he takes the only vehicle I saw on the property, it'll be no problem to turn the place upside down looking for more evidence."

"Cool. Get that done as soon as possible and keep me posted. What's the other thing you had to tell me about?"

"Before we get into that, I did some digging and found out who's hounding Cole for money. It's not good."

"Who does he owe?"

"He's in about two million to the Petronovanich brothers."

Eric was dumbfounded. "Did you say the Petronovanich brothers? The hoteliers?"

"Yep. Hoteliers, casino operators, real estate, whatever. They've got their hands in a lot of places. And from what I understand, they're not the kind of people you want to mess with. I found out that he got a marker at a casino they own, lost it at the Blackjack table, got another one, lost all of that one, too, and tried to skip out without paying them back."

"How much were the markers for?"

"Not sure what the initial amounts were, but I'm figuring the interest blew up. Add in the fact that he's running from them and things generally tend to go from bad to worse."

"When did this all start?"

"About a year ago."

"A year? That's how long the payments from Byrum go back, right?"

"Exactly," Reginald said. "How he's stayed in one piece this long remains a mystery. There's no way he would have been able to pay back two million on the scraps he was getting from Byrum. I'm guessing that's why he came up with this scheme to squeeze your grandmother for millions. Pay off the Petronovanich brothers, grab some extra cash for his gambling habit or whatever, and ride off into the sunset again. Eric, man, I've heard some pretty scary stuff about those guys and they even scare the shit out of me."

Eric wrote 'Cole owes the Petronovanich brothers $2 million' on a piece of paper and continued checking out his desk drawers. "Is that it? You said we had something serious to talk about."

"It's your grandmother."

"What about her?"

"She got a call from Cole yesterday morning."

"Yesterday? And you're just telling me now?"

"I had to check something out first so I didn't call you yesterday. And I've been calling you for over two hours, both on your office phone and your cell. Would you like to rephrase your question?"

"No," Eric said. There was no telling how many other people had tried to reach him, and there was no point in arguing with Reginald. "What's going on?"

"Cole called your grandmother Sunday morning and gave her an ultimatum."

Eric closed his drawers and sat up in his chair. "I'm listening."

"He told her that she had five days to put the fifty million in his account or he was going to ruin her in the press."

"Go on."

"He gave her an account number for her to deposit the funds into. And it matches the account number I have for the mystery account at Cayman Bank."

"Oh my God."

"There's more. If, in six days, the money is not in his account, he's going to unleash some kind of public relations nightmare on your grandmother, the likes of which should be, at the least, extremely devastating."

"That son of a bitch!" Eric roared. Claudia threw open the door and Eric apologized, asking to her to close the door on her way back out. "That son of a bitch," Eric repeated, more quietly.

The other part of the conversation, about Eric's mother being a whore and sleeping around wasn't anything Reginald felt comfortable getting into. If Eric found out, so be it, but that information wasn't coming out of his mouth for any reason. "That's not exactly the bombshell of the conversation, though."

"Don't tell me he's threatened her with something else, Reginald. I'm ready to kill him right now as it stands."

"You might not get that chance."

"What are you talking about?"

"It seems that your grandmother has some friends in very, very low places. The kind that, for the right price, would do just about anything she paid for."

"What are you telling me?"

"She's put a hit out on him."

"On Cole?" Eric couldn't believe what he was hearing. "A hit? Like a murder hit? Like somebody's going to kill him? That kind of hit?"

"Precisely. It would appear that whether you do it, or your grandmother's henchman takes care of it, inside of five days, this being Monday....Cole Julian is going to be a dead man."

Chief of Staff

Under his breath Eric said, "And he might not be the only one."

Chapter *47*

ERIC hung up with Reginald after they'd hashed out their ideas and thrown together an extremely rough blueprint of how everything was going to go. Christine's plan could already be in motion for all either of them knew. If Eric was going to take Cole down, he had to act fast. What they didn't discuss, Eric would have to fluff as well as possible. He leaned back and took a very deep breath, exhaled slowly and counted to ten. His grandmother had hired a hit man to take out his father. Incredible. He shook his head because although he knew very well that she was cunning and deceitful, there was never a moment that he imagined she would stoop to this level. Whatever Cole was using to blackmail her had to be more substantial than the story she told him about Bryant Holdings. And in order for her to want Cole dead, that information had suddenly become priceless to Eric in more ways than one.

Eric figured he'd only get one chance at this and it had to be spot on. It had to work flawlessly and Cole couldn't be allowed to sense even the slightest apprehension. But how? Talking it over with his private detective helped, but there were too many holes, too many things that had the potential to go wrong. Give me Cole's phone number, he had commanded of Reginald. Yes, I know it's risky that I contact him directly, but I have no other choice. When Reginald questioned him about what he was going to do, Eric didn't have a response. He could only hope that the power of quick thinking suddenly came upon him once Cole picked up. The part of the plan they couldn't finalize would have to simply come to him while he and Cole were on the phone. Otherwise, he'd be stuck, foot in mouth, with no promise of exacting his revenge on Cole before his untimely, albeit second, death.

Eric stepped out to Claudia's desk and asked that he not be disturbed for any reason until he came out again. You know, lots of work to do on this hate crime bill. Lying to

Chief of Staff

Claudia was not what he wanted to do, but it was necessary. Maybe, just maybe, she would stay out of his office for the next twenty minutes or so.

"Do what you want, COS," she said. "It's 6:45 and I'm leaving."

Thank God, Eric thought. One less distraction, and one less pair of ears to hear what he was about to do. Sitting back down at his desk, he dialed the number Reginald had given him. Quickly, he hit the cancel button. Loosening his tie, Eric sat back in his chair and thought for a second. Claudia had cleverly listened to conversations on his office phone before, even though she didn't know he knew that, and this was one conversation he needed to keep as secret as he could. He wished he had remembered that ten minutes ago when he was running off at the mouth about their plan using that same office phone he now wanted to avoid. If she had been listening, she didn't give any outward signs when he stepped out and she told him she was leaving for the night. Give it fifteen minutes, make sure she's gone and then I'll call. Better yet.... He pulled out his cell phone and dialed the number again.

When Cole answered, Eric's heart leapt into his mouth.

"Hello?"

"Cole. I need to speak with you about something." His mouth was dry and he almost felt faint. Power of quick thinking, he prayed.

"Who is this?" Cole asked. There were only a select few numbers he'd memorized that had a D.C. area code, and Eric's cell phone wasn't one of them. Even still, he knew exactly who was calling by the sound of his voice. The cat and mouse game was on.

"It's your son. It's Eric," he said, catching himself and making the correction.

"How did you get this number?" Cole thought for a moment and couldn't remember giving this cell phone number to Eric, or anyone he didn't trust, for that matter.

"Working for the United States government, and having certain contacts wherein, provides me advantages the average person doesn't enjoy," Eric said. No, really, the guy I've been paying to spy on you gave me your phone number that he stole from you while the two of you were on a hunting trip in the mountains of North Carolina. "I need to speak with you."

"You do, do you? Well, sorry but I don't seem to have time in my schedule right now. I wish I could accommodate you, but it doesn't appear that's going to be possible." What the hell did Eric want, Cole wondered. And how in the hell did he get this number, government contacts or not?

"Make it possible."

"The child giving the parent a directive?"

"The shoe is now on the other foot, isn't it?" Eric asked. "You'll do this for me. You'll meet me because you owe me. And you know it. You deserted me. I've never in my life asked anything of you but for you to love me, and you bailed. You mentally left my mother long before she died, and when she finally succumbed, you weren't there to comfort me and make me feel better. Twenty-five years later you show up in D.C., tell me you want my help in sticking it to my grandmother for the way she treated you. I was irate at the suggestion that somehow I was expected to help you exact revenge on her."

"And now? What are you trying to say to me now? That you've changed your mind?"

"There's no love lost between us, Cole. I've got the bruised ribs to prove it. I'll always see you as a coward and runaway parent."

"You know you get more flies with honey than vinegar."

"Shut up. This isn't a comedy hour." The balls on this kid, Cole thought. Christine must have done something right. "It turns out, unbelievably, Cole, that we both need each other. We both have something the other wants and we both need it to move on with our lives."

"And what is it that you think I want so desperately that I can get only from you?"

"Money."

"I have that bird well in hand."

Eric stood up from his desk and paced around his office. "You know she's not going to give you a dime of that extortion money."

"Extortion? That's harsh and so, well, illegal," Cole said. Where was Eric going with this?

"In five days when she hasn't put that money into your bank account, using the number you gave her, whatever public relations war you are attempting to wage against her will backfire in your face."

Cole rolled his eyes and pushed his dinner plate to the side. "That woman can't keep anything to herself, can she?"

"My grandmother, for better or worse, has only had my ear since I was a child. She confides in me more than she should at times. Yes, I know about the ultimatum you gave her. I also know that Christine Belmont Squire will not go down without a fight. Go ahead and send your press releases and emails. They won't get you anywhere. And who's going to believe a dead man, anyway? Right now, she's probably got her people working on every different angle she can use to spin this story, this ranting that is to be anonymously sent to editors around the country. Again, from a dead man. This isn't a war that you can win."

Chief of Staff

"It's not going to matter where the information comes from. The only thing that will matter is the fact that your grandmother's secrets will be exposed, spelling the end of her supreme reign."

"Where will that leave you?"

"Extraordinarily pleased."

"By toppling an old woman who, as you say, scammed the government out of five million dollars?"

"It goes deeper than that, Eric. It goes much deeper."

"So, if she doesn't pay the money, and you expose her as a fraud to her friends and business associates all over the world, how is that going to solve your other dilemma?"

"What other dilemma?"

"That day in the park, you told me you had some gambling debts, that you owed some dangerous people a lot of money. And if said debtors didn't get their money, they'd kill you, me, my grandmother and anybody else they felt like."

"True."

"There are quite a number of reasons I would rather not be murdered in the near future, but the most important is that I stand to become a United State Senator very soon."

"Ah, there it is."

"There what is?"

"You're not out to protect your wicked grandmother, you're looking out for yourself. Let's see," Cole said, looking at the ceiling and ruminating about the possible scenario in Eric's head. "How would this go? For the sake of everyone involved, we'll leave out the part about murderous thugs tracking the three of us down and doing whatever it is they're going to do. Say Christine doesn't pay me and I go ahead and put all of her business out in the public. She's got less than five days to comply. After those five days, when she's been stripped of her reputation, which will eventually lead into conversation and speculation about her loyal grandson, poof,

Chief of Staff

there goes any hope you had of ascending to the throne as it were. Christine will have gone down in flames, and your senate dreams will be incinerated right along with her."

Eric truly wished he'd thought of that angle, but now that Cole had introduced it, he picked it up and ran with it. "It pains me to say this, but you are absolutely correct. But what you haven't considered is that I am in a much better position to bring her down than you will ever be. I'm not part of the family company, and I can insulate myself to the extent that I need to – but I have to know what I'm dealing with first. My grandmother crossed the line and I intend to see that she pays dearly for underestimating me and disparaging the memory of my mother. I found out something about Jewel Box and the money she....," he said, stopping, hoping Cole would take the bait.

"That she, what?"

"I'm not going any farther with this until you agree to meet me."

Cole was intrigued by the call and Eric's bravado, but he wasn't hooked just yet. "You still haven't gotten to what it is that I'd be getting out of this deal."

"Money."

"You've said that before."

"A million should be enough to cover your gambling debts and get those people off your back."

"That doesn't even scratch the surface," Cole said. "The figure is fifty million."

"Another ten million should give you reason to divulge what you've got on my grandmother and leave us alone for the rest of our lives."

"Fifty million. And don't pretend that you don't have it. Your trust fund alone has to be more than that. Jesus, when you were eight years old, you inherited more money from your mother's estate, about which I will be eternally pissed, than most people will ever earn in a lifetime. Your grandmother's got it, you've got it, and no matter where it comes from, I'm going to get what I deserve."

You'll get more than that, you asshole, Eric said to himself. "Time and place, Cole."

"There's a gas station off of Highway 40 toward Asheville. Take the Marion exit."

"I'm not sitting in a gas station parking lot and handing over fifty million dollars to you."

Cole's eyes jumped out of his skull. Did Eric just agree to the fifty million? Don't question him. Move on. "And I wouldn't expect you to hand over that kind of money. You already have the account number. Wire it."

"Not an option. Not all of it, at least. I need to know that the product I'm getting from you is worth the money."

"How much does a senate campaign cost these days?" Cole asked flippantly.

"Ten million up front, wired from my personal account, in person and in front of you so you'll see I'm serious about this. Becoming a Senator is the most important item on my agenda."

"More important that the relationship you have with your grandmother?"

"More important than even that. I don't expect you to understand my ambitions or my motives, Cole. The only thing that makes any sense to you, obviously, is easy money. And after I get the information I need to bring her down, it'll just be a matter of hitting the 'send' button again and the remaining forty million will magically appear."

"Meet me at the gas station. Tomorrow at midnight. I'll drive you to a place where we can talk."

"If I think for a second that you're bullshitting me, Cole, I'll pull the plug and choke you until you die in my hands."

Chief of Staff

"Don't even try to threaten me with that, kid. I showed you in your townhouse that I could kick your ass if I needed to. That was just a prelude. Besides, kill me and there goes your little senate job."

"With my grandmother's considerable assistance, I've been able to get away with more than you'll ever imagine. I could probably even get away with murder. She's done it before. And for her favorite grandson in the whole, wide world, the possibilities are endless. Do not fuck with me."

"Come alone."

Chapter *48*

ERIC hopped into the elevator and pressed the button for the parking garage. He had a nervous smile on his face, delighted at how he'd commanded the conversation between himself and Cole. But he was also dreading the events to come. He decided to put them in the back of his mind and soak up the feeling of getting over on Cole. A little dinner, maybe a nice bottle of wine, and he'd come in fresh the next day, anticipating their rendezvous.

Eric pulled out of the parking garage onto Constitution for the ride home. He'd long stopped fuming in the morning and accepted the fact that it was going to take him an hour to drive five miles to work. The drive back home in the evenings was better, but not by a lot. He merged into traffic, playing with the radio, and never noticed the black Range Rovers following behind him.

At 1st Street, the first Range Rover pulled out, sped up, and tucked itself neatly in front of Eric's Mercedes. They passed under I-395 and a short hop from Pennsylvania Ave back onto Constitution, and Eric thought nothing of it. When they both turned right onto 23rd Street, and the second Range Rover pulled out of line and pulled next to Eric, matching his speed, he looked at the SUVs and laughed. "Idiots. How about a little originality." The fire engine red, $200,000 CL65 under Eric's rump had originality, and exclusivity, in spades. Even among the jaded and uber-rich in Washington, D.C., this car stood out. When he looked in his rear-view mirror and saw a third black Range Rover, he began to get the sense that something was wrong. Quickly, and in a very coordinated motion, all of the Range Rovers closed ranks on Eric's Mercedes, and forced him to the side of the road.

In a flash, a thug with a crowbar jumped out of the lead Range Rover, stormed back to Eric's car and rared back like he was about to smash the window and stopped. "I can break it or you can get out on your own," he commanded.

Chief of Staff

Eric didn't know what to do. He'd left his gun at his townhouse after realizing what a stupid move it was to buy the damn thing in the first place. Now he wished he'd brought it with him. Apparently, his thought process took too long. Before he could do anything to stop it, glass from the shattered driver-side window was raining down on him and the street. The thug with the crow bar unlocked the door, cut Eric's seatbelt with an enormous knife, yanked him out of his car, and threw him against the Range Rover.

Even with everything moving so quickly, Eric recognized the guy who'd just vandalized his car from the parking garage and outside his townhouse and from the steps of the Hart building. "You!" Eric screamed as he was shoved backward into the open door of SUV that was along side.

Another thug in the back of this SUV grabbed Eric's hands and zip-tied them together. "Stop struggling," a voice said from the front seat. "It won't do you any good. And you're getting glass all over the place."

"Who are you and what do you want with me?" Eric asked, scared out of his mind. "What are you going to do with me? You don't want to hurt me. I've got powerful friends and they'll see to it that you're hunted down and brought to justice." He was talking rapidly, and for whatever reason noticed that they hadn't taken off with him. They were still sitting there.

"Shut him up," the man in front said.

As the thug pulled back to punch him, Eric screamed out, "Not in the face! Not in the face! Please, God, don't hit me in the face!" He had balled himself up as much as he could, what with his arms restrained, and turned his head toward the window. The thug looked at the man in the front seat not knowing what to do. Nobody had ever said that before. The two men had a good laugh at Eric's expense until some silent signal unleashed a three-punch flurry into Eric's ribs and stomach, doubling him over further.

"I am here to collect a debt, Mr. Julian."

Chief of Staff

"I don't owe you any money, you motherfucker." Another two quick punches to the gut.

"You might not, but your father does." Eric could hear cars driving by, but no one stopped to see what was going on. He could see his window was busted, and the scene on the side of the road obviously had the look of an accident, but still no one was coming to his aid. "I want my money."

"Get it from my father!" Eric yelled. He flinched when the thug pretended to punch him again, but sat back in his seat. "He's the one who owes you, not me."

"Ah, but you are the one with the ability to repay my boss what he has borrowed and not seen fit to repay."

"I don't even know who you are! Who's your boss?"

The man smiled slyly and said, "I'm not at liberty to divulge that information. I'm sure you understand."

Eric knew the Petronovanich brothers were behind this, but part of the plan in playing dumb was to get as much information from this guy as possible. "Fine, then...then what's your name? Maybe we can come up with a way to fix this mess, whatever it is Cole supposedly did."

"Names are of no consequence to you, Mr. Julian. The only thing my boss wants is his money."

"Cole doesn't need to squeeze me for money because he's got plenty of his own, I'm quite sure. Leave me and my grandmother out of this."

"What does your grandmother have to do with anything we're talking about?" The surprise and interest in his voice was genuine, but Eric couldn't hear it.

"Right. And I'm sure you know nothing about my paintings, either. Let me out of here!"

"Are you also a painter, Mr. Julian?" he asked, beginning to laugh again. "Aren't we just well-rounded." At that, the driver, who had been completely silent, laughed along with the two other men. Eric closed his eyes and

Chief of Staff

chastised himself. That day in Lafayette Square when he saw Cole for the first time and found out about the extortion and the gambling debt, Cole was lying the whole time. The threat behind exposing his possession of holocaust art and this guy killing his grandmother were fabrications. Cole knew how much each of them meant to Eric and he used them to his advantage. Obviously, since he'd just been kidnapped, Eric was, himself, a target, but that must have been where it stopped. Eric could have kicked himself for believing Cole.

"Why are you coming after me?" Eric asked, trying to stall for more time. "I haven't done anything to you or your boss."

"I guess it's that whole sins of the father thing. You're going to pay for his mistakes."

"The hell I am!" Eric screamed.

"Besides," he said, unfazed and with his voice trailing off a little trying to his embarrassment, "You're much easier to track down than he is."

"You grabbed me because you can't find him?"

"You needn't worry about details, Mr. Julian. I'm only interested in recovering the money owed. It's either going to come from him or you. And I've got you. From what Cole tells," he said as he pointed at Eric's car, "you've got more than enough to make good and never see my bright, smiling face again."

"My father is a lying piece of trash. What makes you think I'd do anything to help him?" When he got no response Eric screamed, "The very fucking least you could do, sir, is look at me when I'm speaking to you!"

The man in the front of the SUV whipped around in his seat and looked at Eric. It was the same tall, brooding guy from the wet t-shirt contest in Key West. Eric remembered the way his captor's hand felt rough when it squeezed his face, and how his breath had an odd minty smell as he threatened Eric's life two inches from either kissing him or biting his lips off. "Please pardon me for not addressing you properly," he said with supreme sarcasm. "Is this better?"

Eric had to get out of this situation and threw himself into fire control mode, like he used at his consulting firm. "I'll get you your money," he started.

"There, that's nice," he said. "I knew you'd come around."

"I can get you your money," Eric started again, "but you have to follow my orders to the letter."

"Perhaps you are unaware of something." He turned to face the front of the SUV again and said, "You are in the back of my vehicle. My people have already cleaned up the glass from your window and one of them is prepared to whisk your car away at my command, disposing of it in a manner that is not befitting a machine as glorious and wonderfully overcompensating as it is." He let that hang in the air for a moment. "You could disappear tonight and no one – I mean absolutely no one – would ever find you again."

"I've got a plan," Eric blurted out. "Kind of. But you have to trust me. I'll get you your money."

Once more his captor turned around to face Eric. He studied his face a long time and gave yet another signal to the thug in the back seat. Eric flinched when the thug whipped out a massive knife and reached for his arms. The zip tie was quickly cut off and Eric massaged his wrists. "I know where you are at all times. Double-cross me and you will die."

"Kill me, idiot, and you won't see a dime."

"You'd be surprised how much murder can motivate an individual. You'd also be surprised at how one's statements made under duress can change things. I believe you mentioned something about a grandmother." He eyed Eric, raising one eyebrow and waiting for Eric to say something.

"I'll get you your money."

"In that, I have no doubt."

"Does that mean we have a deal?" Eric asked in his best good cop/bad cop voice, trying to reclaim the masculinity he'd lost, and attempting to mask the incredible pain shooting through his ribs and gut.

The doors unlocked and Eric reached for the handle and his escape. The thug in the back seat grabbed Eric and jammed him between the front seats for his final admonishment. "You've got three days." The door whipped open and Eric was dragged out of the Range Rover one last time, and slammed him against it. His stalker smiled at him, slapped him playfully, but hard, in the face and got back into the lead vehicle. Eric stood there next to his battered car and watched as his assailants drove off into the night. He massaged his ribs and thanked God he hadn't gotten punched in the face. You've got three days.

"I only need one."

Chapter *49*

"YOU'RE late."

"I realize that," Claudia huffed.

"Didn't you tell me something about having a hot date last night?" Eric asked, playing with her.

"I did."

"Will miracles never cease?"

"Shut up."

"I'm assuming it went well?"

"It's none of your business, but, yes, it went very well."

"And she's a nice Christian girl?"

"For the last time, I am not a lesbian, Eric. I had a date with a man. If you must know, he's an accountant with the General Accounting Office. And he's hot."

"Is he good in bed?"

"I'm not that kind of girl, Eric."

"Right." His body ached when he attempted to stifle a laugh, still smarting from his pseudo-abduction the night before.

"Why I'm explaining this to you, I have no idea, but we were up later than I had planned, which threw my morning out of whack, and that's why I'm late. Are you finished interrogating me?"

"For now." Eric smiled and sat there staring at her.

"Thank you. And why is it, exactly, that you're sitting at my desk?" Claudia asked. She put down her bag and hung her coat on a hook on her filing cabinet. "Get up, please."

"I was leaving you a note," Eric said. He stood and leaned against the side of her desk.

"You don't have a pen and a piece of paper in your nice big office?" Usually Claudia was already in the office and settled by the time he arrived. He marveled at the efficiency and the obvious repetition with which she started her day. He wondered if she always did the same things, in the same order.

"Got a little OCD, huh? That was funny. Got a little OCD, huh? That was funny. Got a little...," Eric started laughing out loud, but stopped when his ribs began to ache. "Ooh, ooh, I'm sorry," catching his breath. "I couldn't resist."

"You shouldn't make fun of the handicapped, Eric. It's not nice." She noticed that he had disturbed her pencils and right before she began to put them back into a neat, tidy row just the way she liked them, she caught Eric out of the corner of her eye waiting for her to put them back in order. "Stop it. I don't have OCD, but I can't help it. I just hate messes."

"Right." He reached over and turned her 'I'm the Queen – Deal With It' coffee mug one-quarter turn to the left and waited. Two seconds later, as if driven by some irresistible impulse, Claudia snapped her hand out, turned the mug back and rested her hand back in her lap. "OCD. But I love you anyway."

"Shut up." As she logged onto the network, she asked Eric just what it was he had decided to leave her a note about. Couldn't it wait until I got in today?

"Well, I guess it could have. The note was about getting you to do something for me."

"For some reason you think I don't have enough to do around here?" She was still rearranging her desk, moving her sticky notes and scratch paper and pen holder back to their normal positions. Evidently, in the three minutes Eric had occupied her desk, he disturbed more than he thought. Either

Chief of Staff

that or Claudia was the most anal person he'd ever met when it came to her workspace. "What is it? What else can I put on my already heaped plate?"

Eric swung Claudia's side chair around and sat very close to her. He laid out a document on her desk, shifting her keyboard. "My fault. Do you want me to move it back?"

"If you did that on purpose to further aggravate me and get your jollies at my expense, it wasn't funny," she said moving the keyboard back.

"Sorry. I'm done. I'll leave your OCD alone until another day. No more messing around with your stuff." He cleared his throat and smoothed out the pages. "Let's get down to business. This is your new baby."

"I don't recall agreeing to anything yet, COS."

"Remember our disastrous lunch at Lola's?"

"I do."

"Well, out of that explicitly miserable experience, I remember you telling me that you wanted to be a chief of staff, that you want to have my job – or at least a job like mine."

Claudia squinted her eyes and said, "Go on. I'm listening."

"Well, I can't make you a chief of staff, but I can do my best to put you on that track, to make sure your career path gets you where you ultimately want to be. Of course, that's only if you're still interested."

A wide, and from what Eric could tell, involuntary smile crossed Claudia's face. "Are you serious?"

"Dead serious. If you repeat any of this, I'll not only disavow the statement, but I'll turn everything on your desk backward and upside down for a month. Deal?"

"Deal."

Eric leaned in a little closer so those staff members who were passing by couldn't hear what he was about to say. "You are really an impressive young lady, and I think that your talents are so under-utilized it's ridiculous. You are fast on your feet, you have a great work ethic and you are one of the smartest people I've met in a long time. You can do this job with your eyes closed and your hands tied behind your back. And I trust you."

Claudia was listening to him, but she was taken by how wonderful he smelled. Eric was an extremely handsome man, and though she had smelled his colognes du jour before, she hadn't been this close to him. What a delicious man you are, Eric Julian, she was thinking to herself. Simply delicious.

"So what do you think about that?"

"I think that's great. Everything except for the last part," she said, covering. "Can you tell me that once more?"

"Partial photographic memory, did you say?"

"Shut up. I was distracted by something...on my desk."

Eric shook his head and reiterated the last part of his statement. "You are a wonderful person and you're ready to move on."

"Thanks, Eric. That's very nice of you to say. And I won't tell anyone for at least twenty minutes." They smiled and she asked about the document he'd put on her desk.

"This is a rough draft of the legislation, at least our part of it, that I want to you look over, correct, and where you see fit, add whatever you think would strengthen it. Is that something you think you'd want to do?"

"Oh my God! Yes! Of course! Yes!"

"Whoa, Trigger!" Eric said, playfully reeling back a bit. "It's just a little assignment. You're not solving world peace here."

"I know. It's just nice to be valued enough and for you think highly enough of me to ask me for my help. Thank you so much."

"Wow. If you weren't so damn dark, I'd assume you were blushing."

"Don't ruin the moment, COS," Claudia said and smiled.

"I won't. And you are more than welcome. It's only a little gesture, and a little start on your way toward ruling the universe, but I'm glad that I can help...and I'll continue to help in any way that I can."

Over the next thirty minutes, Eric gave Claudia some background information on the hate crime bill and what they were hoping to accomplish in crafting the legislation. They were huddled together more closely than they would have been in his office or sitting on his sofa, each paying careful attention to the other, and Eric trying desperately not to move anything on her desk for fear of reprisal. In a point-for-point debate, Eric would say something to gauge Claudia's understanding of a particular aspect of the text, and Claudia would immediately respond with a barrage of ideas. This was going to work out just perfectly.

"Excellent," Eric said when they'd gone over every nuance they each could think of related to her project. "This is going to be a piece of cake for you. I can't wait to see what you come up with. Do me proud, okay?"

"You bet."

Surprising them both, they actually sat at Claudia's desk for a little bit longer and had some non-work-related conversation. They smiled and Claudia even told a joke – it wasn't funny, but it was a joke, nonetheless.

"Aren't y'all just peas in a pod," Senator Tanner said strolling into work.

Eric and Claudia sat up like they'd gotten caught doing something they shouldn't have been, even though

Chief of Staff

everything was on the up and up. They looked at each other because not only was he an hour earlier than normal, but he was in an extremely good mood. That hadn't been the case for a couple of weeks and they were puzzled.

"A little later on you could do each other's hair and talk about the boys in school you think are cute." Senator Tanner cackled loudly and walked into his office. Eric and Claudia raced after him.

"Why are you in such a good mood?" Eric asked.

"I can't just be in a good mood? Have I been that much of a tyrant lately?"

"Yes," they said in unison.

The senator didn't say anything in response. He just looked at them and sighed. As he logged onto his computer, Eric noticed that his left hand was bruised. He didn't want to say anything in front of Claudia because he didn't know how much, if anything, she knew about his condition. "And what were you two dishing about when I walked in?"

Eric looked up, and when the senator realized Eric had been looking at his bruised hand, he quickly folded his arms and asked the question again.

"It's nothing. Well, I shouldn't say that," Eric said, looking at a still-smiling Claudia. "I've got her working on the hate crime text. I want her to start taking a more active role in the things we do in the office."

"Like she doesn't already have enough to do around here?"

"That's what I said, Senator. But this is an opportunity I have to take."

"And what is she going to be doing to the text?"

"Right now she's just going to go over it, make sure it says what we need it to, and make any changes or additions that she thinks would strengthen the language."

"That's the job of the chief of staff. Am I not correct?"

"You are," Eric said. "We had a lunch meeting a little while back and one of the things Claudia told me is that she wanted to be a chief of staff. I can't do it for her now, but when the time comes, when there's an opening with one of the senators or even congressmen, she needs to be in the best position to capitalize on it. We're starting small, but we'll get her there." Claudia's phone rang and she excused herself to answer it.

"No offense to your plan, Eric, but she already knows how to do the job."

"That's what I hear."

"Did she tell you she was pissed when you got the job over her?"

"I'm not at liberty to discuss that," Eric said with a slight grin.

"Understood. Did you tell her why I hired you and not her?"

"I told her you thought I was a qualified candidate and, with my political connections, I was a logical choice for the role."

"Liar."

"Whatever. It sounded good."

Claudia stepped back into Senator Tanner's office and said, "Excuse me, Eric, but your grandmother is on the phone."

"I'll call her back."

"I don't think that's an option. She said she'd hold as long as it took."

Eric rolled his eyes. "Why me? Fine. Can you send her to the senator's phone?"

"Actually, I have some calls to make, Skippy. Sorry."

Chief of Staff

"Skippy?" Claudia asked.

"Forget you heard that," Eric said. He and Claudia left the senator to get ready for his day and Eric picked up Claudia's phone. She sat down in her chair and made no bones of hiding the fact that she was intent on listening to his conversation.

"Good morning, grandmother. How are you today?"

"I am so happy that you're coming to Charlotte today. I can't wait to see you. What are going to be doing?"

"I've got to visit one of Senator Tanner's supporters. I'm really just flying in and flying right back out. Wait a minute. How do you know that I'm going to be in Charlotte today?" Eric asked. Claudia looked at her calendar and pointed to today's date. It was blank. Eric waved her off.

"The fleet manager just called me to get my authorization for your plane."

"Since when do I need authorization to use one of the company planes? From the time I turned sixteen, the deal has been that I can go anywhere I want as long as I pay for the jet fuel. Has that changed?"

"Oh no, it hasn't changed. I think there was just a mix up. He wanted to make sure that I was okay with it. I'm taking the Global Express to Marseilles tonight. He knows I love that plane and was checking on its availability."

"I know full well that's your favorite plane, grandmother. All I told him was that I needed a plane for tonight. Whichever one he picked was out of my control."

"Pay it no attention, Eric. I've handled the situation, telling him in no uncertain terms that you are not to be questioned again with respect to using one of the planes. As long as it isn't my Global Express, of course. There's no reason to be upset. Water under the bridge."

"I'm not upset, it's just odd that he would call you."

"That's fine. Let's move on. Now, let me see, who did I see that asked me about you?"

"I don't have time to talk, grandmother. You know I could sit on the phone with you for hours," Eric said, winking at Claudia who was mock-barfing. Stop it, Eric mouthed and smiled. "I've got a million things to do before I leave tonight. I promise I'll see you very soon, though. I love you."

Eric hung up, dodged Claudia's evil look and stood up to get his own day started.

"A Senator Tanner supporter, you say?" Claudia asked.

"I know why you were late today." Eric quickly took the focus off of himself and tried to keep a blank look on his face.

"Why is that, Inspector Clouseu?" Claudia asked.

"This is just a guess, of course, but I figure you spent the night at your new man's place, got your groove on, woke up late, maybe had a little morning booty – I'm not sold on that yet - got dressed out of the overnight bag you hung up when you got here, and shot over to the office."

"Untrue."

"Like I said it was just a guess." Eric stood waiting for Claudia to dismiss him and grinned.

"What?"

"It would seem that in your haste to put your clothes on this morning, you missed two buttons on your shirt and you put your sweater on inside out."

"Jerk."

Eric started to walk away and over his shoulder he said, "Dirty girls have all the fun."

Chapter *50*

ERIC was a machine the entire day, completing a bunch of the items on his To Do list. He hadn't been that focused in a while, but every now and again, he would think about what it was he was going to do that night and it made him nervous. He allowed himself a couple of minutes to agonize over the many things that could go wrong, but then redirected his energies to the pile of work on his desk. At 9 pm, well past the time when everyone had gone home for the evening, Eric left his office and drove to Murkoff to board a Bryant Holdings jet.

A quick stop at his house in Charlotte to pick up a car and some other items and he shot right back out the door. The drive up Highway 40 gave him some time to himself. There were no distractions other than the stereo. He'd brought along his newest favorite CD, 'The Evolution of Robin Thicke', and jammed to every track. When 'Cocaine' came on, he thought about irony of the situation. The last time he'd heard a song by that title, it was at Dick's Last Resort and he was singing along with the cover band and that outrageously hot girl in the silver bikini. He was sure Clapton would have rolled over in his grave had he been dead. He remembered the senator sitting at their table, refusing to come on stage, and frowned. How pissed he would be if he ever found out what Eric was on his way to do. Maybe he wouldn't tell him. He didn't know. With all of the other stresses in the senator's life, it was probably best that he held this secret close to the vest, anyway. Huh, Eric thought. Perhaps I really am destined to be a true politician.

The Marion exit sign came up a lot faster than he anticipated and, suddenly, he got a very nervous feeling in the pit of his stomach. Pulling off the interstate, he found the gas station and pulled into a parking spot on the far side of the building. His hands were very cold and clammy. It was 11:50. Was Cole already there? Waiting for him? Was he sitting somewhere Eric couldn't see, deciding whether or not

Chief of Staff

to go through with the whole thing? Eric opened his bag and took out his laptop. He switched it on and made sure there was enough battery left. God, how bad would it be to come all this way, to lay so much of the plan out, only to have the transfer to Cole's account fall through because of a lowsy low battery. He was reassured when the icon showed a full charge and put it away.

Feeling it coming on quickly, Eric popped out of his car and ran to the bushes where he threw up. Why do I do that every time I get nervous, he thought.

When he got back into his car, his cell phone rang, scaring the daylights out of him. He'd expected Cole's call, of course, but hearing that ring meant this was really going to happen; he was going to be face-to-face with Cole Julian again and it was his only chance to save his grandmother from what even he couldn't imagine. No matter what she'd done in the past, there was no reason for her to have been put in this situation. Eric was determined that it would end tonight.

"Yes?" he asked, answering the phone.

"I'm here. Where are you?"

"I'm in the black 911 to the left of the building, back by the bushes."

"You drove a Porsche to Marion, North Carolina? Way to be inconspicuous," Cole said. "I'm in the green Ford pickup." He flashed his lights and got out. As he walked to the car, Eric popped a breath mint and counted to fifteen; ten wasn't going to get the job done.

"Get in," Eric said and motioned Cole to the passenger side.

He got in and said, "Ten million up front and then we can get on with this." Eric pulled the computer out again, turned it toward Cole and logged on. "Ain't technology grand?"

Eric didn't speak and went about transferring the money. "There. It's done. Ten million in your account."

Chief of Staff

Cole figured there was no reason to hide his pleasure at this point and gave Eric a huge grin. "I've got ten million dollars now. What makes you so sure that what I'm going to tell you is worth the other forty, or that I'm even going to tell you truth at all?"

"Like I said, if I think you're giving me the run around, you'll be dead before next week. This can work out to the benefit of us both if you're willing to play the game like I need you to."

"Honor among thieves, huh?"

"Something like that. Enough chatter. Let's go. I'll follow you to wherever it is you're going to hand over what you've got on my grandmother."

"No, sir."

"Excuse me?"

"You're coming with me. I'll take you there, I'll give you what you want to know and then I'll bring you back here." Eric processed the fact that he'd be Cole's prisoner for a moment and agreed to go with him. "Wish you hadn't brought this fancy car with you. I'd hate for anything to happen to it while we're gone. It's not every day you see one of these things around here. People can get curious, you know."

"This isn't going to take very long. I'd like to get this over with as soon as possible. Come on." Eric and Cole got out and as they walked to Cole's beat up truck, Eric chirped his alarm for good measure. "You can never be too safe, can you?" he said smartly.

At midnight in the mountains, it's very difficult to make out where you are. Given the fact that there aren't a lot of street lights, and no discernable landmarks, Eric knew that if he had to escape and run for his life, there was no way in hell he'd be able to get back to that gas station on his own. It seemed like Cole had been driving forever, winding up and down curvy roads, maybe even taking an extended route to throw off Eric's sense of direction. Eric kept checking his watch to see how long they'd already been gone.

"Fifteen minutes," Cole said, looking straight ahead. "We've been gone for fifteen minutes. Looking at your watch for any reason in particular?" Eric didn't say anything. "Fine, be that way." They were alone together for the first time since Eric was a child and they both felt very uncomfortable. Had it not been for the classic R&B station playing softly on the radio, there wouldn't have been any sound between them at all.

Finally, Cole put his blinker on and turned onto a dirt road. It was absolutely pitch-black. "Where are we?" Eric asked.

"In the middle of nowhere."

Between somewhere and nowhere, ran through Eric's mind.

"I live in a little house I rent from a farmer. It's not much to look at, but that'll change soon. I pay him cash under the table, I don't make any fuss, he leaves me alone and I leave him alone."

"Sounds like quite the arrangement," Eric said. "Where is the farmer's house?"

"He lives on the other side of the ridge, about a mile that way," Cole said, pointing to some unseen spot in the blackness. They pulled up to a tiny two-story wooden house and Cole stopped the truck. How could anyone live here, Eric thought. And how did he pass himself off as being an investor when Reginald came up here to give him a pile of money the other day? The two halves didn't equal, but Eric let it go. They got out of the truck and went inside, where Eric was even less impressed.

Spartan wasn't the word. You could tell the house was old and maybe even built by the farmer who rented it. It looked like a dimly-lit creation of Dr. Frankenstein, himself, oddly built and horribly decorated, cobbled together from spare parts. The first floor had a miniscule dining room and a kitchen that blended into what Eric assumed was intended to be a common area. A television, sofa and some chairs were the only furniture he could see. Every wall was covered in wood paneling. The hardwood floors creaked a bit as Cole lead Eric to the den, a room that seemed to have been added as an afterthought onto the back of the house. The entire inside of Cole's house was visually blistering.

"You can wipe that look off your face, Eric. I swear you and Christine are the same person."

Eric sat down in the chair in front of Cole's desk, some kind of ghastly amalgamation of wood and metal and said, "Start talking."

"Oh, I can do better than that," Cole said opening his desk drawer. Eric wasn't certain, but he thought he saw the glint of metal. A gun, perhaps? That wasn't part of his plan. "I've got everything you will need to ruin Christine right here in this folder." He dropped a large, bound, accordion-style folder onto his desk with a thud.

Chapter *51*

"YOU may think you know your grandmother, Eric, but you don't," Cole started. "There's a lot hidden beneath her shiny façade. From the first moment I met her, I knew that the feeling I had where she was concerned was genuine."

"And what feeling was that?"

"That she would do whatever she wanted, to get whatever she wanted, for whatever purpose suited her. Back then, I didn't trust her as far as I could throw her, and nothing's changed my opinion one iota."

"When did you meet her?" Eric asked.

"She and your grandfather bought into the bank where I had just started working, and successfully passed it off as a black-owned business. I'd been there maybe five or six months. I was a teller back then. For a couple of years I had worked at little banks, and I had this scheme were I would deduct small amounts from customers' accounts, padding my own."

"A thief to the core," Eric said.

"And a very good one, at that. By the time they bought the bank, I was moving toward a promotion which would have taken me off the teller line and away from day-to-day access to clients' accounts. I was able to stall long enough to make a little bit more and then Christine came into my life."

"This already sounds like a bad dream."

"Yes and no. Along with your grandmother came a beautiful girl, your mother. I fell all over myself the first time I saw her. I can't say for sure whether Christine had gotten into her head or not, but it took me a long time to win her over. She was one of those girls who liked to play hard to get, but I saw through her games and waited patiently.

Chief of Staff

"Now you've got to understand that your mother and I came from vastly different sides of the tracks. She was a debutante, sorority girl with fancy parents and fancy friends. I'm from right here," he said, waving his arms, "the mountains of North Carolina. And the Squires were unlike any family, especially any black family, I'd ever encountered. I saw the way they lived and dressed and spoke. I committed myself to one-day becoming like them."

"Like the Squires or a part of the Squires?" This was taking far too long. Get to the damn point, Cole, Eric thought.

"Initially it was just to be like the Squires. My scheme was working and I figured nothing could stop me. In the three or four months after they took ownership and I had won over your mother, my luck changed."

"How's that?"

"She got pregnant. Boom, that was my 'in', if you will."

"So you never really loved her?" Eric was beginning to get hot under the collar. "You wanted the money over my mother?"

"At first, yes."

"You're a son of a bitch."

"Hold on. I fell in love with her. I honestly did. After we got married, I honestly felt some kind of kindred connectedness with her. Sadly, I don't think your mother ever felt the same way about me. It was an unrequited love, to say the least." He put his hands up and took a step back. "I'm jumping ahead. Okay, so one day I got called in Christine's office. She looked pissed, more so than I'd witnessed. She lit a cigarette right there in the office, something I'd never seen her do before and she launched into me. I'd been busted stealing from the bank. By God's own grace, she didn't arrest me."

"Why the hell not? I would have thrown you under the jail, myself."

"You're the reason I didn't go to jail."

"Excuse me?"

"That's the $40 million dollar question, isn't it? I'll get to that in a moment. There's another part of this that you need to hear first. Somehow, some way, Bryant Holdings, the company that your grandparents established after buying the bank, was born. The reason for its inception, from what I have read, stems from a relationship they had with Lauren Tanner."

"The senator's father, I know. My grandmother told me all about that."

"Did she tell you that she and the senior Tanner were lovers?"

"I've never heard of anything like that, Cole." Eric was getting geared up to take the folder, knock Cole out and make a run for it, but he remembered the gun, or what he assumed was a gun, in Cole's desk. He sat back and, biting his lip, allowed Cole to continue.

"He owned a demolition company."

"Right."

"When the city of Charlotte, and those powers that be, decided to raze the poor, predominantly black parts of downtown – or the uptown, however you call it, Bryant Holdings came through with the winning bid."

"That's not news to me."

"Lauren Tanner silently owned twenty-five per cent of Bryant Holdings."

"That I didn't know. I thought it was considerably less than that."

"It may have been a pure stroke of luck, or something sinister, but Bryant Holdings won the bid, Lauren's company won all of the demolition. At the same time, they gathered together some folks, a lot of whom, I discovered, owned small parts of your grandparent's bank, and formed a construction

Chief of Staff

company. Bryant Holdings, et al, knocked down and rebuilt the wards of downtown, Lauren Tanner pocketed a shit ton of money, and your grandparents did the same. As word spread to other cities about Charlotte's revitalizing of their eyesore, city governments around the country contacted them. Bryant Holdings was consistently the lowest bidder, went through run down areas, displaced the residents and rebuilt whatever the city contractors wanted. From the money they made, your grandparents bought land all over the country, put rental houses and apartment complexes on them, and raked in money hand over fist."

"None of that is terribly offensive, Cole. They were businesspeople. They were making money."

"The land they bought, Eric, is now full of tenements; run down apartments and below-poverty level housing complexes. The very same people they displaced, generations of them, are still trapped there, living like animals, while Christine sits back in the lap of luxury. Bryant Holdings has deals with every city and state in which they operate. On paper it looks like the city is in control of the housing and the land and making sure everything is properly maintained, let alone livable. But the truth of the matter is, Bryant Holdings controls all of that, and they aren't doing what they're supposed to. Those people live in horrible conditions. Complaint phone calls the residents think are going to a government hotline are funneled to a third party answering service run – and owned - by Bryant. The whole thing is a shell company, under which she operates a large number of real estate management companies. They were slumlords. And your grandmother still is.

"What does any of that have to do with me and the reason I kept you from going to jail?" Eric asked. Had this all been a ruse? Had he been conned into giving his deadbeat father ten million dollars for something he already knew?

"Evelyn had gotten pregnant. With you. And I used that to my advantage. I told Christine when she'd caught me for skimming money that she could certainly throw me in jail, never to be seen or heard from again. But that complicated her life too much."

"I don't follow."

"Your grandmother has been concerned with her image probably from the time she realized she could manipulate the world around her with her actions. Have you ever seen your grandmother upset in public? Has she ever cut anyone down in earshot of others? What is it about your grandmother that most irritates you, but attracts others to her like flies to horse shit?"

"She thinks she's perfect," Eric spit, as convincingly as he could.

"Not only that, but she exudes that perfection and parades it in front of anyone who wants to benefit from her connections and social status. At home, inside Dove's Nest, she's a completely different woman. I remember how she used to scream at and verbally abuse the servants for the slightest error in judgment or mistake. My God," Cole said, thinking back, "I remember once she took off one of her shoes, you know those fucking three-inch heels she's always wearing, and beat the fool out of a maid for putting a silk sweater in the dryer and ruining it. That poor girl was black and blue. Christine could have easily sent someone out to any one of a hundred stores and gotten another sweater, but it made her feel better to beat the crap out of that girl." Eric was sickened by the story, but didn't believe it was impossible.

"The perfection with which she masqueraded around town and across the country in front of her fancy black friends would not have allowed an illegitimate child to cloud what she had taken significant steps to create. Not to mention her little white boyfriend."

"I was a bargaining tool?" Eric asked, focusing on himself. "She would rather have you as her son-in-law, someone she hated and whom she knew stole from her, a man who had fathered a child out-of-wedlock as opposed to sullying her reputation?"

Chief of Staff

"This was the seventies, Eric. Not only that, but her world was such that shame would have been brought on your family if Evelyn had been allowed to have that kid, you, and not gotten married to his father. And that comes even before my having been less than wealthy. You could say that I wasn't the ideal candidate for your daughter's hand in marriage. And your birth wasn't exactly out of wedlock. Evelyn had just told me that she thought she was pregnant a day or so before."

"My grandmother didn't know?"

"No. She assumed she knew everything about her children, but she didn't. Evelyn was a little flirty back then. Don't get me started about your uncle, Clarence."

Unexpectedly, Eric laughed – and he was genuine about it – because everyone knew how inept Clarence was.

"Christine doesn't have everything as closely guarded as she thinks. If anyone found out that she used you, her favorite grandson," he said with those damn air quotes, "as a way to keep her from falling from grace, in effect bartering with me so I would stay out of prison, there'd be hell to pay. It's not that she didn't want you, not as you grew older, that is. It's just that you were a kink in her plan, whatever that might have been. I truly think that she panicked when I told her Evelyn was going to have my baby. She arranged a quickie marriage, after parading me around town, of course, and made up some story about how I came from a long line of educators and civil rights pioneers to make it look like I actually belonged in her circle."

"I can't believe this."

"Believe it."

"You're saying she didn't want me? When did that change? When did I become important to her?"

"You don't want to hear that, Eric."

Eric considered moving on, but there was no way he could do that now. "No, Cole. I have to know. Tell me, please."

"I think it might have been around the time you were seven or eight."

"Seven or eight? What? Just before my mother died?"

"Christine was never really fond of children. Well, that may be a rough statement. She had Clarence and Evelyn because that was what she was supposed to do. It was what women of her generation did, I guess. A governess, and then eventually a nanny raised them both. Same thing with you. But there again, we have her insane obsession with appearances to consider. She was always kind and gentle with you when I was around or when other people were around, but in private and in conversations I overheard - more than once – she expressed a different opinion."

"Which was what, that she didn't want me? That I was a black mark on the family?" Eric wasn't sure whether or not he could believe what Cole was telling him. On the one hand, he'd already gotten ten million, more than he imagined he would have gotten from Christine. So why not spill his guts? On the other hand, there was four times that much waiting for him, based on some bombshell he was keeping from Eric. If his grandmother really hadn't wanted him, that would change things considerably. He stopped his mental chess game because he needed to focus on Cole again. A show of outright anger, though, would prove to Cole that he was serious about destroying his grandmother and keep the ruse going.

"To the extent that I can, I'll say that when you were a little boy, she would have just assumed you weren't around. From the time I told her about Evelyn being pregnant until your mother was diagnosed with breast cancer, you could have been invisible to her. Your very birth under the wrong set of circumstances would have been socially debilitating for someone in her position."

Eric stood up and walked around Cole's tiny den, his arms folded tightly against his body. He remembered growing up and visiting Dove's Nest often as a child. It was one of the best places in the world, like Disney World or some fabulous amusement park he had all to himself. Cole taught him to ride horses on the property and taught him how to swim. They went skeet shooting and played video games and pool and watched movies in the bottom floor entertainment room. Eric and his parents would have sumptuous dinners and attend glamorous birthday parties on the estate. He could recall a lot of his childhood memories with the exception of his grandmother. When she was around, she seemed distant, but still loving. Was that part of her façade? Why couldn't he remember just hanging out with her, like most little kids remembered about spending time with their grandmothers? He sat back down and didn't speak for a moment. This was a lot to take in all at once.

"Are you saying that I replaced my mother?" Eric asked, completely confused.

"I wouldn't say replaced. I would say that you gave her the chance to start over, to do a better job raising a child than she had done with Evelyn or Clarence, both of whom she considered to be complete failures." Cole patted the large folders. "She kept everything, Eric. The proof is right in here. When your mother died, your grandmother was the center of attention."

"My mother was the center of attention."

"No, sir. Everything revolves around that spider of a woman, Eric, no matter what. Even your grandfather wanted out of their relationship. After an eternity cow-towing and acquiescing to her demands, he ended it."

"What do you mean?"

The color drained a little from Cole's face because he realized this was something no one had ever told Eric. "Shit. You don't know this."

"Know what?"

Chief of Staff

"Uh, dammit, how do I tell you this?" Cole looked directly into Eric's eyes and said, "Your grandparents weren't married when he died. I mean, they were married, but they had totally separate lives. Dove's Nest is a very big place, and it was all-too easy for them to live apart. A year or so after they 'separated' I guess he couldn't take it anymore. Given their living arrangement, again with an eye on her public perception, Christine wouldn't allow him to divorce her. He was aging and he probably figured it wasn't worth fighting. Let's see, you're thirty-three now, which means he would have been about sixty-eight or seventy when he died. Imagine being tied to Christine for that long."

Eric playfully shuddered, but he was trying to play the game and deal with what he was hearing at the same time.

"He didn't have to give up half of his fortune and they left each other alone. It seemed like an amicable situation. Something changed one day, and he took a bottle full of pills."

"He killed himself?"

"Yes. His suicide note said that he couldn't go on any more. He was depressed and tired of living a lie. He was a very proud man, Eric. You have to know that. But he'd reached his breaking point. He probably even knew about Lauren and your grandmother. His heart stopped from the massive amount of drugs he'd swallowed, but Christine paid somebody to leave that out of the coroner's report. She couldn't let the word spread that she had a husband who'd killed himself just to escape her. That wouldn't do at all."

Even though Eric didn't know him very well, and his memories of the man were fleeting, he felt a deep and palpable sorrow for his grandfather. Catching his breath, Eric asked, "And what changed where I was concerned? Why did she turn around and decide that I wasn't just some accident?"

"I can't answer that. I was out of your life by that point. I don't know what changed. Maybe she understood that she had been wrong to treat you the way she had for so

Chief of Staff

long. If she has a soul, something in her must have been triggered. I really can't say. And that's the God's honest truth."

Eric pondered his grandmother's feelings for him but couldn't discern anything, any experience he could point to and say, 'ah ha, that's where she started treating me differently'. He was bothered by that in a lot of ways and Cole could read the conflicting emotion in his face.

"Let me explain something to you, Eric," Cole said, leaning forward onto the desk. "This should give you a much better understanding of your dear grandmother and what she values in her life. Now, after your mother and I were married and we moved into Dove's Nest temporarily, I had moved up the ranks of the bank. Mind you, Christine never told your grandfather what had transpired between us, never told him that his daughter was pregnant and that I was guilty of larceny. He had no clue. Things went along smoothly for a while and then came the Bryant Holdings deal. Soon after that, your grandfather died, and then your mother died. In between that time, the three of us had moved into a home of our own and then back into Dove's Nest so your mother could be cared for. It was a quick turn of events."

Eric was still a bit unsettled at the news of his grandfather's passing and was trying to pay close attention to Cole. "Go on."

"I got kicked out of Dove's Nest when your mother died, put out on my ear, straight away. Christine told me the day we buried her that with the death of her daughter she was finally rid of me. I said, fine, whatever. I started to pack our things and get us the hell out of there for good. She followed me upstairs, told me in no uncertain terms that I was leaving by myself and waved a check for a million dollars in my face. We argued back and forth about you and she fired me from the bank. I knew that was coming, quite honestly. I mean, how could it not, right? Next thing I know, she threatened me."

"How?"

"She said that if I didn't leave, gift and hat in hand, she would be forced to go to the police and tell them that I had stolen money from the bank."

"That was eight years prior. There had to be a statute of limitations. You didn't think about that?"

"She had taken it upon herself to frame me, Eric. There was an account that she'd opened in my name, from the looks of it right after I married your mother, and for eight years, she had had money transferred from her personal account into this secret account to make it look like I had been stealing from her all along. She told me it was her plan to get rid of me a while back, before Evelyn got sick. But when she fell ill with cancer, she couldn't bear to see her daughter in further pain. Like I said, I knew she didn't love me. We both played the game in front of Christine, but your mother never once told your grandmother that she was unhappy. Everything she sacrificed in her life was for you. She had you and that was, apparently, all she ever needed."

"So she was making it look like you had been scamming her? When, in fact, you hadn't? That bitch."

"Right. She said once a thief always a thief and that if I said anything to anyone about it, she'd not only tell the police about this scam, she would bring up past indiscretions related to the bank's customers. I would never have seen you again. And there was nothing I could do about it."

"So instead of fighting back, you took the money and ran. You're both to blame here, Cole. Very honorable."

"I was very ashamed of that, Eric. I was ashamed that I'd taken the money. You've got to know that."

"Why not just leave without the money? Take me and run."

"Because I had gotten used to a certain standard of living."

"That standard of living included a son, you asshole."

Chief of Staff

"I left, but I went back. Over and over again for several months, I went back for you. I'd stand outside the gate and beg somebody, anybody through the intercom to let me in. I considered showing up at your school and just taking you, but she was thinking two steps ahead of me."

"So that's why I went to Andover? She was hiding me?" Eric couldn't help it now. His anger at both Cole and his grandmother was rising continuously. He wanted to out of Cole's rickety little house so badly he couldn't stand it. A confrontation with Christine was quickly rearing itself over the horizon, and it wouldn't be pretty.

"I think that's right. How better to hide you than ship you off to school?" Cole leaned back and cracked his neck and knuckles. "You know, I wrote that woman letter after letter telling her I'd made a mistake. I told her how desperately I wanted to have you back in my life, to be a father to you. But I never heard from her again."

"And you gave up."

"I did. And I'm sorry."

"And the extortion?"

"I lost a good bit of the money she'd given me and then I got involved with the wrong people. I'd borrowed some money from them and couldn't pay it back. The only way I could think of to get the money was to do this."

No mention of the manuscript, Eric thought. Why was he holding that back? "And that's it? You've told me everything?"

"Your grandmother is hiding something, a secret she's more than willing to take to the grave, Eric. It's larger than Bryant Holdings. It's larger than her unfortunate, late-in-life realization that she loved you. It's larger and more damaging than you could be expected to comprehend."

"That's a little hard to believe, given how you've dropped my whole life into the toilet."

"It's sitting right here. In this little folder."

"What is it? What could be worth $40 million more?"

"What I've got in here is enough to prove, without a shadow of a doubt, that she had Lauren Tanner murdered."

Chapter *52*

"OH my God, tell me you're lying."

"Afraid not," Cole said casually.

"Can you really prove it?" Eric asked. If he could, and if Cole was telling the truth, should anyone ever find out about this, his dream of becoming a senator was truly going to remain just that, a dream. And what would happen to his relationship with Senator Tanner if he ever found out the truth? Hell, the way things were going, he probably already knew what Christine had done to his father, adding yet another secret he was keeping from Eric, protecting him from his grandmother and her wicked history.

"I can. And it's bullet-proof. I have a letter, written by Christine, herself, implicating her in the murder. I swiped it when I was at Dove's Nest right before Jewel Box this year."

"You were there?"

"For about thirty or forty minutes, but that's all it took to copy her hard drive and jimmy the lock on her desk drawers."

"I want to see it. Show me the proof."

"Show me the money."

Eric's heart was racing. His grandmother, instead of just putting a hit out on Cole had actually done the very same thing in the past. But for what? She'd killed the father of the man he loved like a father. She'd changed the lives of people she'd never know. And for what? That was what Eric had to find out. That was what drove Eric to do it, to pull out his computer, punch in the numbers, and hit the send button.

Immediately after the transaction was complete, Cole's phone rang. "Excuse me, Eric. I don't know who the hell is calling me this late at night, but I'll get rid of them."

"Cole."

"Yes?" Cole tried to control himself the best he could, but that was hard to do considering Christine Belmont Squire was on the other line, and his son, who had just transferred $40 million dollars into his offshore account, was sitting in front of him. He didn't speak her name, more to keep Eric from freaking out than revealing who he was talking to.

"I have changed my mind." Christine's voice sounded a bit off, but that was of little concern to Cole.

"Pardon?"

"I had decided that there was no way I would have paid you a dime of that money, you greedy bastard. I was going to sit back and wait for the authorities to pick you up and take you to jail and let you rot with the other criminals."

"And?" Cole looked at Eric and said, just a minute longer.

"And then I thought about Eric. He's too important to me to lose. I couldn't bear for him to know the truth, that early on I didn't care for him; that he was being used for a social purpose I'd rather not go into again. I have the account number and I'm going to transfer the amount you have requested. Eric can know nothing about this, Cole. Do you understand me? If he does, if something goes wrong and you double-cross me, you'll pay with your life."

"I believe you more than you know." If the threat of exposing Bryant Holdings hadn't worked, he had Lauren Tanner's murder to fall back on. That little piece of information would now be tucked right back into his pocket. So what if Eric knew the truth. As far as he was concerned, it was only speculation. He would never get his hands on the proof.

Cole excused himself and went upstairs. He turned on his computer, logged into his bank account and there they were: two transfers from Wells Fargo. Eric's two transfers were listed first. A second later, his system updated and to his amazement, another $50 million, courtesy of his nemesis, flashed 'Pending Transfer'. Cole almost passed out.

Still talking to Christine, Cole walked back downstairs to rejoin Eric. "Thanks, honey pot, for your donation." In his rush to get upstairs and check his account when Christine called, he'd totally forgotten about the folder and the gun in his desk drawer. Both of them were now sitting in front of Eric who'd gotten up from his seat and was now sitting in Cole's chair, watching him walk back into the den.

"I believe the terms of our deal have changed, Cole," Eric said when he saw the bewildered look on Cole's face. "Everything I need is right here." He tapped the folder and the gun and signaled someone Cole couldn't see. Cole heard a voice he thought he recognized, one that was much deeper than Eric's. He turned to the left and Reginald was standing there. Cole was so shocked, he couldn't move. "Reginald?"

"You know me as Reginald Dixon, but my name is actually Reginald May." Eric stood up and Cole realized he wasn't at all shocked to see Reginald or whoever he was. He didn't know what to do. The only thing that could have gotten him out of this situation was the .40 caliber Desert Eagle sitting in front of his estranged son.

"There's still the matter of the manuscript that we need to discuss," Eric said.

Reginald stepped forward and punched Cole Julian hard in the face, knocking him to the ground, unconscious.

*****

WHEN Cole woke up, he realized he couldn't see out of his left eye. He tried to move, but his arms and legs had been tied to his desk chair. "What the hell is going on?" he screamed.

"Temper, temper, Earl."

"Who is Earl?" Cole protested, and wrestled with the ropes tying him down.

Chief of Staff

"It's better if you just relax." Eric had propped himself up on Cole's desk, his foot resting on the arm of the chair, slowly rocking it back and forth. "You've been a very bad boy and it's time we had an honest chat," Eric said.

"I told you everything I know," Cole begged. He could see a massive, though hazy figure across his desk, as he squinted with his right eye, and figured it was his new hunting buddy. "What are you doing here with my son? If you aren't Reginald Dixon, just who the hell are you?" he asked Reginald.

"That's an interesting question," Eric said, quickly pushing the chair back with his leg, knocking the back of Cole's head into the wall. "His name really is Reginald May. And he works for me. You probably remember him as an idiot farmer you tried to scheme out of his money. Come to think of it, if your name isn't Cole Julian just who the hell are you?"

"It's a pleasure to meet you, Cole," Reginald said with a smirk.

"Fuck you," Cole shot back.

"Your arms and legs are bound. Should you get too mouthy, the bandana around your neck can be easily converted into a gag. If I were you, I'd watch my tone." Eric knelt down, eyelevel with Cole and said, "You have severely underestimated me. I am not like my grandmother. Oh no. I'm much, much worse. And you have done yourself an extreme disservice in trying to play me against her, let alone trying to ruin my family."

"Everything I told you is correct. You've got my folder. You'll read everything I've told you about. Just open it up and see for yourself."

Eric pulled out several sheets of paper that had been stapled together and read to Cole. "Earl Tucker, born August 26th. Interesting, because that's not your name or your birthday, yet you had this man's identification in your wallet. A wallet that Reginald stole from you..."

Chief of Staff

"I would have said, 'borrowed'," Reginald interjected, smiling.

"Ah, of course, 'borrowed' from you," Eric turned and winked at Reginald, "during your visit to Chestnut." Cole glared at Reginald who simply shrugged his shoulders. "Let's see what else we have here. Wow, you've been a very busy man, Earl. Or do you prefer Cole? Or my loyal art broker, Sal Lichenstein. That one still pisses me off, by the way. Hell, I'm not sure what to call you, to be honest. Do you have a preference?" The syrup in Eric's voice sickened Cole, but there was nothing he could do about it. "Okay, well, with your silence, I'll presume you don't care what I call you. I want you to tell me about Byrum and the manuscript."

Cole didn't say anything for a moment. "I don't know what you're talking about, Eric. I don't know anything about a manuscript. And who the hell is Byrum?"

Reginald leaned forward and placed a tape recorder on Cole's desk, ready to play back their entire bar-side conversation. "You have one more chance to tell me the truth," Eric said, rolling up his shirt sleeve.

"And what do you think you're going to do?" Cole asked, laughing at the suggestion that his son was going to beat him up to make him talk.

"Ever been punched in the ribs?" Eric asked, making Cole laugh, mocking him.

I've got more money sitting in my account than I'd counted on, Cole said to himself. Tell him what he wants to know and they'll leave me alone. Even if they beat the living shit out of me, I'll still have the money. "I think I'm starting to remember something about that deal."

"I thought so."

"I met Byrum by accident about a year ago. We were at the hunting lodge."

"Chestnut?"

"Yes," Cole said, looking at Eric, with his one good eye, wondering how he knew that.

"Don't look so surprised. You'll recall that's where you met Reginald the first time."

Cole tried to open his left eye, but it was still tightly shut and swollen. "That's right. The rich idiot."

"That rich idiot sitting over there is my private detective. The same idiot to whom you confessed conspiring against my grandmother."

"Clever," Cole said, looking at Reginald, who was smiling back at him. "Byrum was some kind of writer, mysteries or something, I don't remember. He was talking to somebody on the phone and I happened to hear what he was saying. It might have been an editor or agent or somebody. He was telling them that he had a framework for a book, but was having trouble coming up with real ideas." Cole looked at Eric who had sat back down on the desk and was thumbing through the folder, seemingly not paying attention to his story.

"I'm listening," Eric said.

"Anyway, when I saw him later in the day, I told him that I might have a story idea for him. But that if he was interested, he'd have to pay for the information."

"And I'm assuming he agreed."

"Not at first, but when I told him who was involved, and that they were linked to Senator Tanner, he all but jumped me. He kept saying, 'if this is going to work, we've got to do things my way'. I had no idea who he was, let alone that he worked for the fucking senator."

"And I'm sure you wouldn't have gone along with the whole idea had you known that little bit of information, right?" Reginald asked.

"I needed the money."

"That's a good reason," Reginald said. "That's a great reason."

"Hey, give the man a break," Eric said, looking at Reginald with a fake expression of sincerity. "He is my father, you know. And family helps out family in time of need." He turned to Cole, pushed his chair back a little and asked, "Isn't that right, Daddy?"

This will all be over soon. Just keeping feeding them the answers they already know and you'll be off to the Caymans before you know it. Cole repeated that to himself over and over. Without so much as a sign, Eric closed the thick folder and slammed it across Cole's face, bloodying his nose and mouth. Then he slammed it back in the opposite direction, breaking open Cole's swollen eyelid, blood trickling down his face. Some blood had seeped into his eye, causing an unbearable burning. Reginald had never seen Eric's temper and although he was impressed at the fury with which he was interrogating Cole, he made a mental note to never piss him off.

"Talk to me about why you had the right to do this to my family!" Eric screamed. He pulled the manuscript out of his bag and motioned like he was going to hit Cole again, making Cole wince and shrink as far down in his chair as the ropes would allow. Eric came within a half inch of Cole's face and stopped. "Who gave you the goddamed right to do this? To my grandmother? To me? To the memory of my mother? You piece of shit!" he screamed, this time whacking Cole in the head so hard he almost blacked out again.

"Your mother, that's who!" Cole screamed back at Eric. "She's the reason I did it. She's the reason I got the idea in the first place. She gave me the idea to ruin Christine!"

"Bullshit!"

"I don't give a damn if you believe me or not, you ungrateful excuse for a child!"

Eric picked his leg up and stomped on Cole's crotch. "You say one more disrespectful word about my mother and I'll kill you right here!" Reginald stood up and was about to

Chief of Staff

tell Eric to just calm down when he saw him reach for Cole's gun on the desk. "One more word and I'll empty this thing into you and never look back."

"Your mother was a whore, Eric. Just like your grandmother!" Reginald immediately reached out and snatched the gun from Eric's grip. It's not worth it he motioned, holding his hands up. It's not worth it.

Eric turned back to Cole and kicked him in the chest.

Spitting blood as he spoke, Cole spilled everything. "Your mother was a whore from the day I met her until the day she died." Eric started screaming for Cole to stop. Anger had welled up in him to the point that he didn't think he could control himself. "She was a good little piece of pussy and everybody knew it. I had her over and over again while I worked for your grandmother. That's why she got pregnant. In the closet, in the break room, on top of my desk. Men screwed the living shit out of her like the sun rises and sets!" Cole's breathing was belabored from the kick to the chest, but he kept talking.

"Not only that, but after we got married, she kept it up. She knew I was only in that marriage for the money!"

"You told me you loved her! You told me that!"

"I was lying, you moron! Why else would I marry a whore? It was an arranged marriage. I told you that, too. Christine arranged for your mother, the whore, to marry me, the fake socialite, in order to save her shiny reputation and your mother hated Christine for it. She taught her how to be a slut, but didn't give her the right to marry who she wanted."

"Stop it!" Eric said, covering his ears. "Stop it!"

"Your precious grandmother was nailing Lauren Tanner like it was going out of style. That's how they got the winning bid and that's how their bank and real estate businesses shot through the roof. She was giving him that old smelly snatch in return for aggressive rates on the money he had in her goddam bank. And she didn't do it once, or every

Chief of Staff

now and then, she was giving up that ass to Lauren every dirty little chance she got."

Eric's cell phone rang and he jerked it out of his pocket. "What?" has asked without looking to see who was calling.

"Eric, it's me," the senator said. "I've got to tell you something. Tonight. Can you come to me at the...?" he asked when Eric cut him off.

"I don't have time for you right now. I'll call you back." He hung up the phone and put it back in his pocket. It rang again and he ignored it.

"I swear you're going to die tonight," Eric said enraged, pacing the tiny den. Cole had flipped a switch in Eric when he started saying those derogatory things about his mother

"And when he told her he wanted out of the deal," Cole kept talking, "that he felt bad about virtually imprisoning thousands upon thousands of black folks in the areas around the country that they had torn down and shuffled the residents into public housing, she had him killed. Your mother knew every last bit of it. And that's exactly where I got the idea from. Don't pin this on me. I just took your slut mother's idea and ran with it." Cole spit blood onto the floor and said, "And I'm not the only one who knows what's going on with your grandmother."

Eric closed his eyes, balled up his fists and said, "Who the hell else was Byrum paying?"

"Hell if I know," Cole said. "And if you think I'd tell you, you're crazy." He started laughing at Eric and said, "Christine is going down. I know for a fact that the second person on Byrum's payroll won't stop until that happens. He told me, himself. The Squires can kiss my black ass."

"Who is the other person?" Eric screamed. Cole smirked at Eric and said nothing. In a flash, Eric jumped across the desk and began to pummel Cole in the face, both of

Chief of Staff

his hands becoming slick and bloody from the repeated punches.

Reginald came up behind Eric and struggled to pull him away, to stop the beating for fear that he really would have killed Cole as he sat tied up in that chair. "Eric! Chill out! Stop it!" he said, tossing him to the side and putting his body between Eric and a badly beaten Cole.

Eric was trembling and trying to understand what was going on. He looked at his father, tied up and unable to defend himself. His face was disfigured from the punishment and his head was slumping as he was too tired to hold it upright on his own. And then Eric looked down at his hands and saw them bloody and sticking together. It was the same image he had seen in his dream. Eric stepped out of the den and got a towel to wipe off his hands. His cell phone rang again when he returned. The caller id displayed 'unknown caller' and he put it back in his pocket. "I'm getting some air," he announced and walked out.

*****

AFTER about twenty minutes, Eric walked back in. Cole was grimacing from the pain Eric had inflicted, but sat up quickly when he saw who was behind his son.

"I would introduce you to Brett," Eric said, "but I believe you've already made his acquaintance." Eric's mouth was drying out and he made a concerted effort to speak clearly. "I understand from Brett that he works for a man by the name of Goran Petrovanich, the same man from whom you absconded with around two million dollars." The only thing Reginald could do was stare and hope to God Eric knew what he was doing.

Cole's heart beat so rapidly now it might very well have burst through his chest. He struggled against the ropes anchoring him to the chair until Eric reminded him that he wasn't going anywhere – not at least until he said so. "I can't say it's nice to see you again, Brett."

Chief of Staff

Brett nodded to Cole and sat down. The brute with him stood faithfully and silently by his side.

"How do I know that you aren't scamming Petrovanich, yourself?" Cole asked Eric, trying to buy some time, and hopefully talk his way out of the situation. He turned to face Brett and asked, "How do I know you aren't going to beat the hell out of me, finish the job my worthless and ungrateful son started, take the money and disappear?"

"Because he understands that I would have him tracked down and killed, just like you." Cole nearly passed out when Goran Petrovanich walked into his home office. Eric and Reginald whipped around, not at all expecting to see or hear him. Regal wasn't even close to describing this man. Tall and slender, even his hair looked perfect. He looked like somebody's wealthy grandfather, not a businessman with an enviable fortune and a shadowy reputation. Goran walked over to Eric and apologized for showing up unexpectedly and then turned his attention back to Cole.

"Good evening, Earl. Your son tells me, though, that your real name is Cole. I find that somewhat amusing."

The second, and larger, goon trailing Goran squeezed himself through the doorway and stood next to Cole. "You see," Eric said, "I told you that you underestimated me. This was a set up from the beginning. The money you think you have in your account will be sucked back out once I make a call to my bank, having them reverse the wires that I initiated online." Cole opened his good eye as far as he could, and with both eyes, darted back and forth from Eric to Goran and back to Goran.

"Additionally, the money you think you got from my grandmother came from my account, as well. Reginald, my good friend here, was simply posing as my grandmother using a fancy little gadget he found online. It enables him to sound like anyone of whom he has a clear voice recording."

In his own voice, Reginald repeated part of his conversation with Cole. "And then I thought about Eric.

Chief of Staff

He's too important to me to lose." He couldn't have known about that unless he really was the person to speaking. Cole's bladder emptied.

"You have nothing." Eric's voice was low and shaking. He spoke slowly and deliberately to make sure he got through to his father. He had waited for this moment for almost his entire life, and now that it was upon him, Eric couldn't contain himself. He bent down to Cole until their noses touched, and an unrehearsed soliloquy started flowing from him. "I...hate...you. With everything that makes me who I am, every bit of me that is good and evil, every part of me that lives and will die, I...hate...you. I hate how you destroyed the life of a little boy whose mother died and left him alone. I hate how you carelessly and despicably stayed connected to me and in my life without my permission. I...hate...you." Eric trembled as he spoke and he swallowed intermittently, causing flecks of his spit to pelt Cole's face and mouth.

"I hate knowing that I came from you, that I was the product of a loveless union between you and my mother." Eric gripped the arms of Cole's chair and squeezed them tightly. He had long since become the only other person in the room with Cole, ignoring his audience. "I hate that your blood runs through my veins and that God above allowed you to be a part of me, with no possible way to divorce me from you." Eric closed his eyes just as tears began to slowly run down his face. "I hate that you coerced me into buying that goddamed Holocaust art. And I hate myself more for not getting rid of it, even though I knew the truth about its origin. For that, and God knows what else, Cole Julian, you will most assuredly burn in hell for eternity."

Eric stood up and sat back on the desk, and looked at Cole for a long time, not saying anything at all. He rubbed his mouth and he ran his hands over his face and his head. A deep breath. Count to ten. Relax, Eric was telling himself. He opened his eyes and he saw how Cole was looking both at him and Goran and explained their connection.

"You can't bullshit a bullshitter and you shouldn't try preachin' to the choir. But, clearly, you can con a con artist." Cole's nose started to run and you could tell, even with one eye swollen shut, that he was crying. His lip trembled. "I'm what they call a back room politician. I make a living manipulating people into doing what I want. I get people elected because people believe what I tell them to say and how to say it. I help people achieve their goals. And if I have to beg, steal, lie, cheat and borrow to make that happen, then so be it."

Eric looked at Goran, who had removed his overcoat and gloves, and sat in a chair that goon number two had retrieved for him. "You should have paid more attention to me all those years you claimed to be keeping tabs on me. Had you done so, you would have realized what a very poor choice it was to target me and my grandmother. That, father, was a fatal mistake."

Cole looked at Eric with a questioning face and asked, "What does that mean? What does that mean, a fatal mistake?" He squirmed in his chair more than he had, and looked at everyone standing around him. "What are you going to do to me that you haven't already? I'm sorry. Is that what you want to hear?" Cole pleaded out loud and begged for mercy, looking at each man until they turned their gaze away from him. "Don't do this!" he screamed. "Don't let them do whatever it is they're going to do to me! I'm sorry! I'm so goddamned sorry, Eric! I'm sorry!"

Over his father's voice, Eric pulled out a duffle bag and handed it to Goran, saying only, "Here. You'll find the two million, in cash, that he owes you in this bag. His debt is now repaid."

Goran studied his surroundings and thought for a moment. "I think I'll ask you to keep your money, Mr. Julian," he said to Eric and stared at his captive. "What I have in my possession now, after a long and fruitless search, is much more valuable to me." He waved his hand and the large goons removed their jackets and rolled up their shirt sleeves, revealing muscled and tattooed forearms.

"I don't understand," Eric said. "We agreed that I'd bring you the money and that you'd leave everything else to me. We're done here." Brett stood and stepped close to Eric until he was called down by his boss. Unsure of what was happening, what had gone so wrong with his plan, he looked at Cole who begged him for help. He'd slumped in the chair again, the ropes tugging at his wrists. His voice was quieter now, but Eric could still hear him begging through slobber and slurred words. Cole was asking for compassion from his persecutors, looking into his only son the way that innocent man must have looked into Senator Tanner so long ago. "What are you going to do with my father?"

Goran squinted at Cole and twisted his mouth into a devilish smile, like he'd just come up with the most demented idea he could have imaged. He then turned to Eric and Reginald and said, "I think it's best, for you, that certain questions not be answered. I also think it's time for you to leave."

Moving like a man on fire, and without speaking another word, Reginald quickly grabbed the folder, the gun, the laptop, the bag of money and dragged Eric Julian the hell out of that house.

Chapter *53*

IT should have only taken Eric about two hours to drive from Marion back to his house. Two and a half hours after he and Reginald scrambled out of Cole's house, he finally pulled into his driveway. Reginald had followed Eric home because he looked awful. Several times, Eric pulled over on the side of the highway intending to vomit. But since he had been too nervous to eat much of a dinner, combined with his earlier nausea while waiting for Cole, he was besieged by painful and irritating dry heaves.

"You didn't have to follow me all the way back here, Reginald," Eric said as he walked into his house. "I know you've got better things you could be doing right now."

"After what we just went through?" Reginald asked. He propped himself up on the island in Eric's huge kitchen and watched him fumble around for a moment. Reginald was mentally exhausted and sat there, massaging his temples and rubbing his face. Although he was too tired to function, he realized that his friend and quasi-employer had just taken an emotional punch in the guts. "There's no way I'm leaving you alone tonight, man."

Eric stopped puttering around the kitchen long enough to thank Reginald profusely for everything he'd done for him. The surveillance, the secreted information, the clever computer gizmos and their seat-of-the-pants plan; none of it would have been possible without Reginald's immeasurable assistance.

Reginald graciously accepted the thanks and said he was glad he could help, let alone glad they made it out of there alive. I'm here for you any time, he promised.

"You okay?" he asked Eric.

"Yeah, I'm fine. I'm dealing with everything that Cole told me tonight – and the way it all ended - but I'm fine." Eric assumed Reginald knew he was lying, but what was the point now? Even if he had told the truth, that he was destroyed beyond comprehension, that he didn't know what he was going to do about his grandmother, let alone the rest of his life, there wasn't anything Reginald could do about it. They certainly weren't about to hug it out. "I'll get through this."

"You know you can call on me if you need to."

"You're the only person I can trust now. Do you realize that? Everybody else in my life has lied to me about one thing or another."

"It's the money that's keeping me honest." The joke was intended to lighten the mood, but it didn't work and Reginald regretted saying it. Eric was standing there with a blank look on his face, staring at the stove and hadn't seemed to be listening to Reginald's poor joke. "I'm gonna bug out, man."

Eric snapped back to reality and said, "Christ, it's what…four o'clock in the morning? To hell with you leaving. Pick a room, Reginald. You can crash here tonight. It's the very, very least I can do."

"Thanks, man. I appreciate it."

They went their separate ways, Reginald to a guest room on the second floor, and Eric into the master suite on the main. Too keyed up and wired to sleep, and how could they be expected to, they both laid in bed staring at their ceilings and going over the unbelievable night they had just had. Reginald finally drifted off to sleep, but Eric was still wide-eyed at seven a.m. when his cell phone rang. He contemplated not answering it until he remembered Senator Tanner calling the night before and saying he needed to speak with him. He didn't recognize the number on the caller id, but answered it anyway.

"Eric Julian," he said, again with his standard ambivalence.

Chief of Staff

"Eric, thank you for taking my call. I've been trying to reach you."

"Who's speaking?" he asked, wondering why people never took the time to announce themselves. Maybe they needed a good dose of Christine's Charm School. Then again, maybe not.

"My name is Dr. Michael Traynor. I'm calling from Presbyterian Hospital in Charlotte."

Eric's heart leapt into his throat. "What can I do for you, Dr. Traynor?"

"I'm afraid I have some bad news for you, sir." Eric could hear the doctor shuffling some papers in the background and covering the mouthpiece to speak to someone. "How quickly can you get to Charlotte?"

"I'm in Charlotte right now," Eric said, becoming worried at the somber tone in Dr. Traynor's voice. "Does this have something to do with my grandmother?"

"No, sir. I'm afraid it's your father. It seems he has taken a severe turn for the worse. He's asked for you. Whatever you have to do to get here, do it. Do it and do it quickly."

"Wait a minute. Are you telling me that my father is there? In the hospital?"

"This is difficult for me to tell you over the phone, sir." Dr. Traynor wasn't sure how to respond to the question, leaving far too pregnant a pause in the air. "I'm assuming you haven't been notified, but, yes, he was brought in very early this morning. Your father is gravely ill, Eric. I don't think there is much time left, to be quite honest. That's why I'm calling you now. He has listed you as his only next of kin. It is imperative that you get to the hospital as quickly as you can if you…" he trailed off, rethinking his words as he spoke.

"Is he going to die?" Eric asked, standing quickly, ready to run out the door.

"Yes," Dr. Traynor said.

"How long does he have?" Eric asked.

"Days, perhaps. His condition continues to worsen by the hour. It may be less than that, to be brutally honest. I'm so sorry. I'll explain more when you get here. He's on the tenth floor, the Belk wing. Hurry."

"Thank you, doctor. I'm leaving right now." Eric hung up the phone and dialed the office. He didn't know why, but Claudia was already at her desk. "Claudia, I'm still in Charlotte. Something's wrong with my father. I'm going to be out of the office for the next little while. I have to run to the hospital right now. I'm not sure when I'll be back. If Senator Tanner calls in, let him know he can reach me on my cell." And with that, he hung up leaving Claudia to process the whirlwind of information that was just dumped in her lap.

Eric ran upstairs to let Reginald know about his phone call and that he had to leave. Reginald asked if Eric wanted him to go, too. "With what went on last night, there are bound to be people there asking questions about how Cole got injured. If he's talked, and if the police are there, it wouldn't make sense for both of us to be arrested." Reginald agreed but decided to trail Eric just in case. Once Eric was gone, he jumped up and left, too.

Presbyterian Hospital, a private hospital on the outskirts of downtown Charlotte, was about twenty miles from Eric's house by the way the crow flies. But in Charlotte, where it can seem to take forever to drive even a short distance, the drive was unbearable. His brain was a mess of emotions and he questioned everything he had allowed himself to do where Cole was concerned. He wondered why the doctor wouldn't tell him about Cole's condition. He asked himself if Goran Petronovanich's thugs had intended to beat Cole to the point of death, and if he had somehow, miraculously, escaped from them only to find his way to the hospital? But why Presbyterian? Why not a hospital in Marion? How did he get all the way down here? Hell before he and Reginald left, Cole was only semi-conscious and there

Chief of Staff

was no telling what kind of brutality befell him once they had run out on him. The guilt in his heart was deeply entrenched. No matter their icy and indifferent relationship, how could he have done something so awful to his own father?

Half way there, Eric called Christine to let her know something was wrong with Cole. Not surprisingly, she didn't have a lot to say. I'll be extending my stay in Marseilles she told Eric, but she said for him to call her with any news and to come by the house the first chance he got once she returned. When he reached the hospital, he jammed his car into a parking space and raced through the hospital following Dr. Traynor's directions.

His anxiety was out of control as he ran through the hospital toward the Belk wing, finally pushing the button for the tenth floor and whatever destiny awaited him. It was at that moment that he pictured his dream of becoming a senator slip away. It had only been something of a pipe dream, implanted in his head by Senator Tanner, but over time he came to envision himself in the role and he relished the opportunity to make that dream a reality. Depending on what was going to be waiting for him on the other side of the elevator doors, the police he figured, it had all gone up in smoke.

The elevator ride was painfully slow, but it gave him a moment to try and relax. Senator Tanner hadn't called him on the drive, but Eric had checked his schedule before he left for Charlotte and saw where he had crossed out the entire week and wrote, 'vacation' in large red letters across the pages. He was probably somewhere out of the way. Senator Tanner always liked to keep his personal vacation plans to himself, and delighted in finding tiny out of the way locales to spend a week or two decompressing. Now that he had Trinity, more often than not, those vacation destinations were accessible by yacht. He bypassed Senator Tanner not calling him, and as he was trying to calm down and breathe normally and find Cole all at the same time. The elevator chimed and he stepped out.

Chief of Staff

A nurse noticed he looked lost and asked him if she could help.

"Yes, ma'am. My name is Eric Julian. Dr. Traynor called me this morning."

Whether she meant to do it on purpose or not, her face fell. Obviously, the situation was much worse than Eric had imagined. Her cheery smile had been replaced with a compassionate pursing of the lips, and she instantly went into support mode with Eric. "Ah, yes. He's been waiting for you." Just then Dr. Traynor rounded the corner. "Doctor," the nurse began, "this is Eric Julian."

The doctor's face fell as well, and he extended his hand to Eric. "Hello. I'm surprised, but very thankful, that you made it here as quickly as you did."

"Of course, of course." The only thing Eric wanted right now was to see his father. An unbelievable number of emotions coursed through him as he stood there, taking in the sterile white environment and the awful smell of disinfectant and the low volumes of televisions in patients' rooms meant to give something to distract them from the pain and inevitability of their deaths. It reminded him of the scant few times he visited his mother in the hospital before she was transferred to Dove's Nest. That memory almost brought Eric to his knees and his eyes began to well up with tears. "Can I please see my father?"

"Oh yes, forgive me," Dr. Traynor said. "I fully believe that some people hold on as long as they can, just to see their relatives one more time before they pass. I think the senator has been holding on, waiting to see you."

"The senator?" Eric asked, genuinely confused.

"You are Eric Julian, are you not?" the doctor asked, praying that he hadn't made a terrible mistake.

"Yes, I am." Eric dabbed his nose and the corners of his eyes with a tissue the nurse handed him.

"And your father is Senator Scott Tanner, is he not?" the doctor asked, still praying.

Eric felt his knees weaken and he began to collapse. The doctor caught him and with the nurse's help, sat him down in a nearby chair. The color was draining from his face. A cold compress and some juice revived Eric to the point where he could speak. "Did you say Senator Scott Tanner?"

"Yes. He listed you as his next of kin." The doctor was feverishly flipping through his chart, searching for the form Senator Tanner had signed just before he was admitted. "Yes, right here. Next of Kin: Eric Julian. He wrote your phone numbers and addresses right here. You are his son, aren't you?"

For the first time in his life, he didn't know what to say. All of the years spent growing up and being impacted by this man, never knowing he was his real father. Never knowing the joy of being able to celebrate his life's milestones. Never being able to steal away those intimate details that truly melded father and son. Eric thought about all of the times Senator Tanner told him he loved him. And he thought about all the times he called him son. Often people would say they had a slight resemblance...their thin noses and the shape of their eyes, the way they both walked and their odd senses of humor. When they heard these things and were together, the senator would instantly say that Eric had known him since he was born and that, maybe, he'd just rubbed off on him. Squires genes run deeply within you, Eric, he would quip. But was there another explanation?

He began to sob uncontrollably again, his nose running and tears obscuring his vision. This man had meant more to him - and done more for him - than was possible or necessary. The guidance and the scolding; the amusement and the long talks about life; the lessons and commitments and achievements they celebrated together. Through everything, not even once, had Eric fathomed that this man could have been his father.

Chief of Staff

Byrum's manuscript had been the key to it all. It was the map that would have led to the truth, but it didn't register as he read it. Why hadn't he been able to see through to the truth? What reason, if any, would he have had to even fantasize about Senator Tanner being his father, whether he had been provided the clues in Byrum's tale or not? Why hadn't Senator Tanner ever said anything to him? What was holding him back from embracing his son and, together, building a life based on the truth? With the events and the lies of last night, the only question Eric had right then was, can it be true?

Eric thought about his grandmother and her role in staging this hoax that was now his life. The character in Byrum's book resembled her, but, again, there had been no reason to link fiction with real life. Byrum had cleverly disguised the details, giving his characters just enough realism to sell books, while hiding the truth from everyone but those who were entitled to it. But how? How was the information in the manuscript, however massaged, so accurate, so reflective of Eric's life? Now that he knew of Cole's hand in creating the book, questions still lingered. If Cole supplied all the inside information, who contributed the other, small details, the ones that most people would miss and not think twice about carrying around in their head for fear of wasting precious brain matter?

Eric wished Byrum hadn't died for two reasons: first, he would have killed the son of a bitch, himself, for what he was planning to do to his family; secondly, the book wasn't finished.

There was no ending to the misery he'd crafted. The story of Eric's life had died with Byrum. Some of the things he'd written simply couldn't have come from Cole. They happened too far after Cole had left him, stranded and alone, at Dove's Nest. Byrum was writing about dates and events Cole couldn't have witnessed, he couldn't have been a part of. It was clear that someone had taken great pains to accurately and correctly chronicle his entire life, to time-sort the

Chief of Staff

triumphs and tragedies of thirty-three years based on lies and God knows what else. Instantly Eric became incensed all over again, his blood running cold. Who in the hell was helping Cole Julian and Charles Byrum?

Of little consequence now, he would deal with all of that later. His emotions were a mix of explosive rage at being kept in the dark by the senator and an extreme love for the man who was losing his battle with life. Tightly closing his eyes and wishing to God that he would awaken from this nightmare, the only sound he heard was the soft voice of the nurse, calling to him and asking him if he was okay. He slowly opened his eyes and thought about the senator, the father he never knew he had.

He was dizzy and fighting the nausea as best as he could. There he was, sitting in a hospital with a doctor and a nurse, crying without the pretense of knowing people were staring at him, whether or not they were silently sharing his pain and anguish. He sat, hovered over by a doctor and a nurse, trying their best to console him as he processed his feelings. He was eight years old again. Eric wanted to crawl into the same dark, lonely, comforting place he had gone to as a child when he saw his mother's body in her room at Dove's Nest, just minutes after she had died. Only the doctor's voice kept him from retreating inward.

"Eric?" the doctor quietly asked. "Is Senator Tanner your father?"

"Yes," Eric said slowly, his eyes reddened and tear-sopped, his mouth quivering. "Yes, he is my father. And I would like to see him now. Please."

Chapter *54*

"ERIC," Dr. Traynor said, as he helped Eric stand and put his hand on his shoulder. "You need to know that he is in extremely bad shape. He will not look like you are used to seeing him. He was brought into the hospital last night by one of his household staff. He is experiencing some very traumatic complications from the treatment he's under for his liver disease."

Eric listened to the doctor as best he could, but a lot of what he heard was simply noise. Hospice and imminent death were the only things that registered to him. "What happened to him?" Eric asked. "He told me that he had more than a year, and that that was conservative."

"It was an estimate, Eric. What I told your father was that he might have up to eighteen months, provided he did exactly as I said and followed the treatment I prescribed to the letter."

"The pills and the other stuff?"

"Yes, but there was more to it. Your father has a drinking problem. I don't know that he's an alcoholic, but there's something that drives him to drink. Some people are compelled by family history, others are held prisoner by their emotions like guilt or complex feelings they can't emote. They find emotional release in a bottle...of whatever. And that's why I think your father has dipped so sharply, negating the treatments he was on. With liver disease, or cirrhosis, Eric, there can be a chance of living an extended life, beyond the time frame a doctor can tell you."

"Like a liver transplant? Would that have helped?"

"His body was too badly damaged for that to have even been a remote possibility. His other organs were being compromised and his continued drinking didn't help him in any way, shape, or form." Dr. Traynor looked at Eric and said, "You need to be so very thankful that you were able to

Chief of Staff

spend so many quality years with your father. A lot of people can't say the same thing. For the entire time I've known this man, he has talked about you with a shine in his eye I don't know that I've seen in any father, before or since. And I've known the man for twenty years. He loves you more than you will ever know. His body has started shutting down. Death is at his doorstep, Eric. Get yourself together and go in there to be with your father. You're all he has left."

Eric's mouth crinkled like he was about to cry and again and he forced himself to take a deep breath. He nodded at the doctor when he asked Eric if he was ready to go in and opened the door.

"Hey, old man!" Eric said, trying to hide his pain. How could someone have changed so radically in twenty-four hours? When he walked into the office yesterday morning, he was chipper and upbeat. He didn't look bad at all, discounting his all-too-familiar jaundice and the bruised hands and forearm. "What are you doing in the hospital? We've got a hate crime bill to get to the floor."

Chapter 55

SENATOR Tanner looked at Eric with sad eyes as he walked through the door. The last time he had seen him, he and Claudia were huddled together at her desk, working on some project. Before he walked into the office, he'd overheard them talking to each other and they actually seemed to be accomplishing something. Together.

He was in so much pain that morning, but the last thing he wanted to do was let Eric or Claudia know what terrible shape he was really in. He woke up at some point Sunday night in excruciating pain. It wasn't the first time it had happened, but this round was more painful than any time before. It was though he was on fire internally and there was nothing he could do about it. The senator rolled into a fetal position and rocked himself back and forth, eventually crying himself back to sleep.

He woke up Monday morning with dried blood on his face and matted in his hair. There was also dried blood on his sheets and pillows, the result of an overnight nose bleed. The screaming pain that woke him up during the night was now at a low rumble; still very present, but manageable. He slowly sat up in bed, cringing, and asking himself what had happened. He didn't remember a thing. The empty bottle of Chivas on his nightstand told it all – but still, he had no recollection of anything that may have happened as he downed the bottle. He limped to the bathroom to shower and get ready for his day and gasped as he passed the mirror. His hands normally hurt when he woke up, but this pain was different. Bruises covered the backs of his hands from his knuckles and just past his wrists. The blood on his face and in his hair made it look like he'd been a fight, and somebody had gotten the better of him in a hurry.

Showering was a chore because he didn't have full range of motion in his hands and his entire body still ached from his mysterious pain. He cleaned himself up as best he

Chief of Staff

could, trying to remain upbeat and determined to get through this. Getting dressed turned from a quick process to one that was drawn out and required frequent breaks to rest his hands. Every fiber of him was in pain. Was this the beginning of the end, he asked himself. Should he have gone to the hospital last night? So bad were his hands that couldn't possibly endure opening nine pill bottles, and skipped taking them all – except for a double-dose of his pain pills.

When he got to the office and stood outside listening to Eric's and Claudia's conversation, he decided the only thing he could do was lie. He plastered a big smile on his face, gripped his briefcase with authority and strode through the door, cracking jokes.

Lying in a hospital bed twenty-four hours later, time was indeed running out for the senator. The phone calls he'd made when Eric was talking to his grandmother were to his attorney and his doctor. He'd written 'vacation' on Eric's calendar, but had planned to fly to Charlotte later that morning to see his physician, Dr. Traynor. Seeing Eric now, wasn't as comforting as he'd hoped it would be. He could see the questions in Eric's eyes and prayed that he would have the strength to answer them.

Eric's eyes began to water as he sat down next to the senator's bed. He was so frail, Eric thought. Not the vibrant man who burst into the office telling jokes yesterday. "Hey, Senator," he said softly. Senator Tanner was wearing an oxygen mask and started to remove it so he could speak. "No, buddy, I think it's best you keep that on for right now." He pulled the senator's hand down and just held it at his side, gently stroking the top of his hand. "I'm sorry I didn't have the chance to talk to you on the phone last night. I was in the middle of something that, at the time, was very important. You must have been calling to tell me you didn't feel well." He looked around the hospital room and said, "Had I known you were in this kind of shape, I'd have dropped everything and come to be with you. I'll never forgive myself for that."

Senator Tanner took the mask of with his right hand and very quietly said, "You look like warmed over ass." Eric was still wearing the clothes he had on from the night before.

"I had a pretty rough night, but nothing compared to you, huh?" Eric said.

"I'm sorry, Eric," Senator Tanner said. His voice was raspy and Eric had to lean close to the senator to hear what he was saying. "I'm sorry you had to find out this way, that I wasn't able to tell you the truth before now. I'm sorry you had to learn that I'm your father from the doctor who called you and not from me. I should have done that. I should have been the one to tell you, but I didn't. I'm so sorry."

Eric shook his head and said, "Don't you ever apologize to me for that. Don't do that. I'm confused and a little overwhelmed and I'm mad at why you had to lie, why my mother and everybody I love had to lie, but don't you lay there feeling sorry for yourself. And don't feel sorry for me. We're going to get you through this and you can beg and beg for my forgiveness once you're out of here." There was no way to cover up the trembling and hurt and disbelief in his voice. He knew his father was never going to make it out of that hospital alive.

"Eric," the senator started, again low and raspy, "I need to explain something to you."

"No, save your energy and put it toward getting better."

"I'm going to die, Eric. You're so sweet for trying to fool me, but I'm going to die and we both know it. God only knows how long I have left, but before He takes me, I need to explain things to you." Eric's lip quivered when he heard the finality in the senator's voice. Eric squeezed his hand a little tighter and agreed to sit there and listen. The nurse came in to check on the senator, made sure the I.V. was dripping pain medication at the appropriate rate, wrote a couple of things down on his chart and left.

Chief of Staff

"In all of my years on this planet, there have only been two people whom I have truly loved: your mother and you." Tears were softly rolling down his face as he spoke, staring into Eric's eyes. "Never in my life could I have imagined having a better man for a son. Never in my life could I have pictured how much the love of one person could have changed me so profoundly, so magically. I used to tell you that you were the son I never had, and in some ways that was true. It was true because I'd made a promise to your mother that I would never, ever, reveal to you the truth. I promised her that I would keep her secrets until the day I died. It's hurt like hell to not be able to sit you down and explain how all of this craziness unfolded. I can't find a way to erase the pain that hearing this is going to cause you; what pain you've already suffered just in the last five minutes has been so hard to swallow, I can only imagine what's going through your head."

"Senator, there will be plenty of time for you to tell me all of this," Eric argued. "You need to rest."

"That's just it, son. I can't rest until you know the truth. I know I'm breaking my promise to your mother, a promise I worked so hard to keep, but I don't want to die with this on my heart." Both men were crying now, holding onto each other, ironically, for life.

Helped by Eric, Senator Tanner sat up a little straighter in his bed and took a sip of water before beginning his story, his thorough and chronologically-accurate accounting of not only his life at the point when he met Evelyn Maija Squire, but also of the thirty-three year lie that was the relationship with his one and only son.

"I'd gone with my father to Dove's Nest for whatever reason the day I met her. My father and your grandparents were going over some paperwork that I now know was connected to the land deals they'd been making around the country. They started with Charlotte, changing all of the wards downtown by moving out the blacks who lived there and trying to make the housing and businesses more upscale."

"Yes, my grandmother told me about that when she was giving me a history lesson on Bryant Holdings."

The senator was glad he didn't have to go into that whole story. He was getting tired quickly and that was a large chunk he could leave out. Senator Tanner closed his eyes and smiled as he remembered their first meeting. "She was so lovely, Eric. I don't know that I'd ever seen anyone so fresh and glowing before. My breath was taken away when I saw her, slowing coming down the staircase, wearing a pretty yellow sun dress with these tiny purple and red and blue flowers. Her hair was lustrous and shiny and it came to about her shoulders.

"She smiled at me and introduced herself. My father and your grandparents excused themselves which left me alone with her. I was no nervous. Now, even though they'd had this association and the bank had only been up and running for a short period of time, I was well aware of whom your mother was. We didn't run in the same circles, of course, but I'd heard through the grapevine that she was a little fast." He saw the look on Eric's face and apologized. There was no other way for him to put it. "But that didn't bother me one bit. In fact, the second I saw her in person, I put it out of my mind. I was captivated by her.

"Now you've got to remember that this was the very early seventies and Charlotte wasn't nearly as progressive as it is today. Blacks and whites may have worked together, but the concept of interracial dating and marriage was still too taboo to broach. Loving versus Virginia was still fresh on the minds of so many in the south. So your mother and I began an underground relationship. I would take every opportunity I could to see her and just be with her. But right when our relationship started flourishing, your grandmother found us out."

"She knew about you and my mother?" Eric asked, eyes wide.

"Yes," Senator Tanner said, nodding his head. "Well, at least she knew that something was going on between us that

Chief of Staff

she didn't like. She knew we were much closer than we had let on and I think it worried her."

"Why? Was it her social reputation?" Eric asked, sarcastically. "God forbid if anyone disrupt the mighty agenda of Christine Squire."

"Don't speak that way about your grandmother, Eric. I'm not defending her or her actions, but you have to understand where she was coming from. Her dislike of me seeing your mother may have been purely economic as it related to the bank, it may have been purely social as it pertained to the judgments of her friends and other family members, I don't know. But after she found out about us, I was banned from seeing Evelyn, period." Senator Tanner shuddered from the pain in his gut, took a couple of moments for it to subside and resumed his story.

"When you tell someone that they can't have something, I think it's true that they go after whatever it was even more zealously than before. Your mother and I found ways to sneak out of our houses, lying to our parents and pretending to visit our respective friends, meeting up at different out of the way places so we could see each other. It was all a game until the day she came to me and said she thought she might be pregnant."

"I'll bet that scared the crap out of you."

"It did, to say the least," the senator said through a half-smile. "We talked about what we were going to do, keep the baby or...," he said, looking down at his hand in Eric's, "have an abortion." He squeezed Eric's hand as hard as he could and said, "I know that even with everything we've put you through, we made the right choice."

Eric told the senator to keep talking, not wanting to focus on the possibility that he could have been aborted before his life even began.

"When your grandmother found out about our relationship, she went crazy. Yelling at Evelyn and saying that this could potentially put an indelible stain on their

Chief of Staff

family. How could she have fooled around with me, let alone allow herself to be compromised before marriage? Christine was no fool, though. I'm quite sure she was aware of Evelyn's old reputation. In fact, I sat her down, your mother, that is, and told her that I knew she was fast before she met me. I knew that there had been some talk about her with this boy and that boy, but that if she was going to be with me, she couldn't do that anymore. I didn't care about kissing or petting or other stuff, but I made her swear to me that she wouldn't have relations with anybody but me, and I swore the same thing. Evelyn assured me that I was the only man she'd been with – sexually - and I believed her."

"Until when?" Eric asked, wondering if this was leading up to how Cole entered his mother's life.

"I guess she had been seeing Cole at the same time, I don't know. I was crushed, of course, that she'd lied to me but something inside told me not to let go of her, to let her run this course because one day, I just knew it, we would be together again, the way we were meant to be."

"Are you sure, though, that you were the father of the baby and not Cole?" Eric asked. As soon as the words came out of his mouth, he wished he could have turned back time and shoved them back in.

"I'm sure," Senator Tanner responded. "I'm sure now, that is. You see when she came to me and told me she was pregnant, she also told me that she had met this boy at the bank, Cole, and that he was trying to court her. Things went too far one night and he forced her to have sex with him."

"He raped my mother?" Eric asked, angrily.

"Yes. By that time, she was already pregnant by me – and she said she never touched Cole again – even during their eight years of marriage. So, based on when the doctor told her she had gotten pregnant, and when Cole raped her, there was no doubt that you were my child."

"How did you find out that Cole and my mother were going to be married?"

Chief of Staff

"Ha. Christine took the liberty of spilling that information. She called me on the phone, directly, and said 'my daughter is going to be married. And she's going to have a child by her husband. I'll thank you kindly to never see or speak with her again' and then she hung up on me before I could say anything in response."

"Talk about a modern day Romeo and Juliet," Eric said.

"I don't know if it was anything at all like that, Eric," the senator said smiling. "But it was heartbreaking. The woman I loved had cheated on me. But she had been raped and there was nothing I could do about it. She was carrying my baby, she was going to marry this other guy because her mother had forced her to, and I was left out in the cold. In fact, that was the night we took that guy and beat him up."

"You're kidding me."

"No, sir. I remember it distinctly. I didn't want to go out with them that night, I was too depressed, but they wouldn't take no for an answer. While they were in Jessup's buying the beer and hassling that guy, I sat in my car listening to the radio and dreaming about what life would have been like if I'd been the one who was going to marry your mother. And that's when all hell broke loose."

"You didn't tell me that on the yacht. You just said something about being tired from working for your father all day and wanting to relax."

"Do you remember me telling you that there were two things that haunted me in life and would follow me in death?"

"Vaguely."

"That was the other thing, well a combination of things, but the most important was the fact that I was going to be a father and could never tell anyone."

"Because she was black?"

"That had something to do with it, yes. I'm so ashamed looking back on everything."

"Like you said, it was the times. People forgive things like that."

"Not me. I can't stand when other people use that excuse. 'Oh, don't mind him for being a racist asshole, he was raised in the times when that was the norm'. That's a crock of shit. If you've got half a brain in your head, you know there's a good way to treat people and then there's the coward's way out. People are people no matter what their color." The senator had gotten a little too worked up and began to cough.

"Okay, okay, back it down," Eric said, softly stroking his hand. "It's okay."

"It's not okay, Eric," Senator Tanner said, recovering from his coughing fit. "That's why I hurt that guy we took. I was hitting him and hitting him and hitting him because I was so goddam angry. I was angry at the world. I was angry at myself. I was angry at your mother. I was angry at not being able to be a true father. And I just kept hitting that man over and over again. Thank God I looked into his eyes and he did whatever it was that made me stop. I think I really could have killed him by myself. The frustration and malice I held for everybody was spewing out of me. I ran back to my car in disbelief and just waited for everybody else to come back, too."

"What stopped you?"

"From what?"

"What stopped you from continuing to beat him?" Eric asked.

"Honestly?"

"Yes, of course," Eric said, waiting for the answer.

"I think it was you." The senator put his oxygen mask back in place and took several deep breaths. "I didn't know if you were going to be a boy or a girl, naturally. But I knew you were on the way. My child was going to be borne to this world and there was a chance that he or she wouldn't have a father. Yes, you would have had Cole, but that was of little comfort. He wasn't the man you should have been raised by. It boiled me to think about you calling him daddy. I would have gone to prison if I'd hit that guy one more time. My child would have grown up without me to love them and to care for them – even from a distance. I didn't know how or what I was going to do, but I swore that I would do whatever I had to in order to get Evelyn back and raise our child together. But it didn't work out like that. I got arrested and taken in."

"How did you not go to prison? You' never told me that."

Senator Tanner couldn't look at Eric when he said what came next. "Your grandmother and my father had made some kind of deal, it would seem. In order to keep me from going to prison, which would have exposed the fact that your grandparents weren't actually the majority-owners of a black-owned bank, and to keep from losing their lucrative government contracts, and my father's business from being destroyed, they bribed a young judge to only charge me with reckless driving. They lied and said I didn't know what was going on and that I was manipulated by my friends, all of whom had bad reputations for getting into trouble, into driving them around that night."

"They paid off a judge?" Eric was astonished.

"It was easy to do then, Eric. Deals were made under the table all the time. There were only about twenty families who really controlled what went on in Charlotte, and it's the same way today. At the time, Christine had a lot of power and she was able to influence a lot of people to do a lot of things for her. The judge got some ownership in the bank and the demolition company, my charges were officially assigned as reckless driving, and everybody was happy."

"And my mother?"

Chief of Staff

"Well, she was not happy. She had this quickie marriage to Cole and had the baby. Other than her teaching job, she seemed to be depressed a lot of the time. It should honestly pain me to say this, but during her entire marriage, Eric, your mother and I carried on an affair for the ages." He didn't care to hide his smile in front of Eric and beamed. "I can't explain to you what was going on in my head, let alone your mother's, but nothing could have kept us apart. It killed me when our time together would come to an end and she would have to slink back to Dove's Nest, and then to her own home once you all had moved in there.

"I promised her one night that I would love her forever. She promised me the same and said she wished things had been different. We accepted our lot in life and moved on as best we could. I got married a couple of times, as you know, each with disastrous although lucrative endings. I never could shake Evelyn from my heart. In a way, it was the perfect relationship"

"How in the world do you get that?" Eric asked, smiling.

"It was like the difference between the kinds of relationships, or I guess just friendships, that men have and women have."

"I don't follow you."

"My second wife, Elizabeth, was one of these women who felt like she had to be in everybody's business all the time because that made her feel like she was being a good friend. If she didn't hear from her friend for a week or two, she got worried that something was wrong and she'd call to find out what was going on. It happened like that with her over and over again. Always trying to make sure that her friends knew she was still their friend."

"And guys? What about their relationships?"

"What do you do every year in May, regardless of the weather, Eric?" the senator asked, waiting for Eric to see his point.

Chief of Staff

"I go to the All-Star Challenge at Charlotte Motor Speedway. That was a silly question."

"And do you keep up with those guys, your friends you go to the race with, every week of the year?"

"Of course not. Hell, that one weekend is pretty much the only time I see those guys the whole year." And that's when the light bulb turned on. Eric understood.

"And you aren't any less friends with them are you?"

"No."

"And you pick up with each other right where you left off the year before, right?"

"I get it. That's how you and my mother were, right?"

"Right. We could go months, and once a couple of years without seeing one another, but when we got the chance, it was like old times. She'd send me letters and pictures of you every now and then to keep me up-to-date on how you were coming along. I saw the way your face changed, when you lost teeth, the way you started to resemble me in those subtle ways only strangers can see. She even photocopied your report cards and mailed them to me. I saw you grow into a young man, and then, when she got cancer and died, I decided that I wasn't doing enough."

"I had Cole, but I didn't really have a father, I guess. When he left, you kind of showed up on my doorstep."

"I made up this story for Christine, telling her that you needed to have a man in your life and that I was going to be that man to help teach you the things men ought to know and how to live life respectfully and doing whatever it took to help you find the path in your life that would let you achieve your goals, whether the hell she liked it or not."

"So that's where you came from," Eric said. "Like Superman, you swooped out of the sky to rescue me."

"Like Superman," the senator said. But he wasn't. He was just a man. He wasn't a bulletproof super hero that

Chief of Staff

swooped out the sky and stopped speeding trains and leapt tall buildings. In a sense, he was a tragic actor, deluged with emotional baggage he was too weak to lift, too scarred to carry around, deciding instead to hide in a bottle, using alcohol to drown his shortcomings and subdue his pain. No, he was nothing like Superman. The I.V. drip and the fact that death was upon him was a sobering reminder of his mortality. The warmth of his son's hand in his felt better than he could explain with words. Senator Tanner told Eric he loved him and laid down to rest.

Before he closed his eyes and drifted off to sleep, he said, "You can't live your life like I did, son."

"What do you mean?" Eric asked.

"Find a woman you love with all your heart and don't settle for anything less. Treasure her and do whatever it takes for you to be together, to live a long and loving life."

"That's easier said than done, Senator," Eric said. "I can't just blink and suddenly find the woman of my dreams. It doesn't work that way."

"Yes, it does. Trust me. You already know who she is. You just have to take that next step."

"What are you talking about?" Eric asked.

"Kathryn."

"You think Kathryn Greenich is the love of my life?"

"Grab her. Never let her go. Call her, Eric. Don't let this chance slip by. Don't let the opportunity to be happy vanish...," he said, and fell asleep.

*****

FOR the next three days, Eric sat in that hospital room with his father. He watched the rise and fall of his chest as the ventilator breathed for him and wondered what he may have been dreaming about. Senator Tanner would go in and out of consciousness, and Eric took advantage of those short moments to try and connect a little more deeply with him.

Chief of Staff

They shared quiet moments and even ate several horrible tasting hospital meals together. Senator Tanner told Eric that as his only child, he would be heir to his entire fortune; everything he owned was to be bequeathed to Eric upon the senator's death. Eric thanked him but said he didn't want to talk about it anymore. He excused himself and stood in the hallway crying.

It was unavoidable, due to the nature of his job, but he found time to work with Claudia over the phone and via email on his laptop to put the finishing touches on the hate crime bill, sending it to the floor for a vote. Eric released a simple statement regarding the senator's health to give reason for him not being present to vote on the bill that he had co-sponsored. During one of those conscious moments, he whispered to him that the bill had passed, that new laws would be enacted to protect those people who had been victims of unspeakable crimes due simply as a result of their race or sexual orientation or religion. That was the last time Eric saw Senator Tanner smile.

The pain that shrouded his body was becoming more and more debilitating. He'd lost the ability to speak and his breathing had become laborious and shallow. You could feel the hospital bed shake when a wave of pain hit him; he would groan and wince, but never was he fully aware of his surroundings. Well-wishers from every part of Senator Tanner's past sent notes and cards to him expressing their hopes that he recover and get well soon. The senator had asked that none of his friends or family know the truth about how gravely ill he was. Eric was the only person the senator wanted with him to live out his last days.

*****

AT 1:40 in the afternoon, after Eric had returned from the hospital cafeteria to get a quick lunch while the senator slept, he was greeted by a nurse outside the senator's door. Uncontrollably, Eric fell to the floor, sobbing. The nurse told him that while they were preparing to give the senator a

sponge bath and to shave his face, he stopped breathing.
He had died. He was no longer in pain.

Chief of Staff

Chapter 56

ERIC stood next to his father's body in the hospital room, slowly stroking his hair and talking to him, saying goodbye. He processed a mountain of paperwork related to the senator's wishes, settled the hospital bill and spoke to the mortuary service about what, if any, funeral plans the senator had dictated. There were so many details to take care of, only hours after the senator's death, that everything soon became too much to handle. He snapped at anyone who was trying to help him, eventually apologized, and snapped all over again at the next person. Eric was exhausted as he stood at the back door of the morgue and watched his father being rolled into a hearse. This isn't happening, he told himself. As many times as he repeated it, the reality couldn't be escaped. His father was gone.

Eight hours later, sitting in his car in the hospital parking deck, he was trying his best to console Claudia. He called her at home to let her know the senator had died and she dissolved. Claudia told him that she simply couldn't talk about it anymore and hung up. Eric hadn't told her that he was the senator's son. That was a conversation for another time.

Eric was still processing the tragic day when his cell phone rang again. It was Christine. Instantly, his blood began to boil. Every bit of this was her fault. Had she allowed his mother and father to have a life of their own, maybe the senator wouldn't have had to resort to drinking away his guilt and pain. That meant they would have been a real family. It was she who allowed Cole into his mother's life, safeguarding her social standing, but damning her daughter to a miserable life, one in which she had to lie about the man she loved more than anyone else. It was her fault that the senator was dead. And she was going to pay for it.

"We need to talk," Eric said, answering his phone.

Chief of Staff

"Yes, thank you, my trip to France was lovely. Thank you so much for asking," Christine said. The arrogance of this child had come to an end. "Your attitude is going to change where I am concerned, Eric Julian. And it's going to change now."

"Where are you?" Eric was still fuming.

"If you must know, I am about to land in Charlotte. I told you that I would call you upon my return. Why? Where are you?"

Eric started his car and shot out of his parking space, narrowly missing an oncoming car. "It's 9:45," he said checking his watch. "I'll be at Dove's Nest by the time you land. I'm looking forward to seeing you, grandmother."

"Now that's the grandson I know and love," she said, smiling broadly. "I'll make sure my driver gets me home as quickly as possible."

"Not too fast," Eric said. "I'd hate for anything to happen to you."

"Oh, thank you. I've been worried about you what with all of this nonsense concerning your father. I'm glad to hear you're in somewhat better spirits."

"When I see you, dear, everything will be just fine. Hurry home."

Eric hung up and dashed directly to Dove's Nest. A terrible accident on the highway brought traffic to a standstill and Eric sat in his car, no option of a different route, for almost an hour.

Speeding up the long driveway and screeching to a halt, Eric jumped out and stormed into Dove's Nest unannounced and on a mission. The target, of course, was Christine and he wasn't leaving until his point had gotten through to her to his complete satisfaction. The time had come for her to face the music over what she had done, how she had unapologetically twisted his reality to serve her own purpose. Congeniality be damned, the day of reckoning had

Chief of Staff

come, and all pretense of civility had been tossed out the window.

"Grandmother!" Eric yelled out. "Get down here right this instant!" After several calls, Christine still had not shown herself so Eric went looking for her.

You are going to explain yourself to me, Eric fumed over and over again in his head as he had driven to Dove's Nest from the hospital. Despicable. Self-aggrandizing. Ruthless. Sickening. There weren't any pleasantries on his mind. He sought revenge of sorts. At the very least, she would be forced to come to grips, through an extremely invasive interrogation, of how her manipulation echoed through Eric's every fiber.

"Grandmother!" he continued to scream as he searched the house. Evan ran to Eric from somewhere deep within the mansion, alerted to his presence by the incessant howling.

"Master Eric," he questioned, out of breath. "What is the trouble?"

Eric grabbed Evan by the lapels of his suit jacket and pulled him close. "Where the hell is she?" he growled.

"Of whom do you inquire?" he asked, his head leaned as far back over his shoulders as they could have moved.

"You're already on my list, Evan," Eric said, Evan's eyes growing wider. "Get in my way and I'll level you with everything my grandmother has ever taught me."

"She just returned from Marseilles. I think you'll find her in the study going over some papers related to the company," Evan said nervously and quickly shot his hand out, pointing up the stairs.

Eric flew up the steps and marched angrily down the hall. Normally, the house would be full of servants arranging flowers, making up the guest bedrooms, and doing their assorted daily chores. It was ten minutes until 11:00 now and the house was empty, all of the servants with the exception of

Chief of Staff

Evan, had gone home for the night. The double doors to the study were locked and he repeatedly jabbed at the handles while he called for Christine to, "open this door and right now!"

Still noncompliant, Eric stepped back and kicked the doors open, revealing a stunned Christine Belmont Squire huddled behind her magnificent, picture-strewn desk. "I was calling you, grandmother," Eric said, walking slowly toward her. "Perhaps you might have done the favor of providing me with a response."

"What are you doing, Eric?" Christine asked. Her voice was cracked and shaking. She was scared out of her mind at what could be making her grandson act this way. As regally as she could, she stood and planted herself in her desk chair.

"I'm looking for you, that's what I'm doing."

"I don't know what would be so important as to come into my home, destroy everything in your path and confront me so viciously. You're scaring me, Eric," she said as she started to cry.

"Save your tears, old woman."

"You will not speak to me that way. I am your grandmother. I raised you. It is hurtful and it defiles your character."

Recalling one of the best lines in movie history, Eric looked her deep in the eye and said, "I have not yet begun to defile myself, grandmother." He moved swiftly toward her, trapping her in the chair. "Why?"

"Why, what, Eric? Honestly, I have no idea at what you are so upset."

"You stole my life."

"I did no such thing," she said, still crying.

Eric spun her around to face the pictures displayed on her desk. "All of these memories have been forever tarnished.

Chief of Staff

They are not reality. They are fantasy; a fantasy cooked up, nurtured, held secret and propagated by your insufferable ego." He picked up a picture of them together and threw it across the room. It landed in the fireplace and the ornate glass frame shattered into a million little pieces. Christine started to speak and Eric instantly covered her mouth with his hand. He leaned down behind her and whispered into her ear. "It ends today."

When he spun her around, Christine kicked him in the knee and escaped her trap. She leapt out of the chair as well as she could and ran out of the study. Eric massaged his knee and hobbled after her. There was no need to run. Old women don't travel fast.

Eric threw open each of the ten doors on the second floor hallway. Each of the doors led to a guest bedroom and each guest bedroom had its own bathroom. At the tenth door, after having almost separated it from its hinges, Eric saw a maid crouched on the floor on the far side of the bed. He hadn't expected to see her and was as startled as she was. Timidly, she pointed toward the bathroom door. Eric motioned for her to get out and she streaked passed him.

"I know you're in there, grandmother," he said. "You have two seconds to open the door or I will knock it down." In hopes of preserving at least one of her doors, the latch clicked and Christine appeared. Her hair was disheveled and her eyes were smeared with mascara and eyeliner. Without waiting for her, Eric reached into the bathroom, grabbed her by the collar on her blouse and pulled her to him.

"Don't hurt me, Eric," she pleaded. "Don't hurt me. Everything I did was out of love."

Chapter 57

"THE only person you've ever loved is yourself!" he screamed.

"That's not true," Christine said. She was crying hard and her nose was running. Eric still had her by the blouse, having lifted her up off the ground just a little, only the balls of her dainty feet touched the floor. She tried to kick him again, but Eric blocked her.

"Kick me again and I'll break your leg." Fire and rage consumed Eric in a way that he didn't know was possible. "My father is dead."

When Christine heard that, the most involuntary of reactions happened: she smiled. And just as quickly wiped it away. "I'm sorry to hear about Cole, Eric. But I don't understand why you'd be so upset with me. I had to do it. There was no way I was going to give in to his demands. Cole had to die." Eric let go of her and, straightening herself out she said, "If I had to do it all over again to protect you and this family, I would. And I'm not going to apologize for it. Not to you, not to anybody."

Eric snatched her up again and dragged her back down the hall, past the staircase and back into her study. He pushed her down onto the sofa, pulled the coffee table close to her, and sat down on top of it. He was so close to her he was almost straddling her legs, not allowing her to move. "What are you doing?"

"Cole Julian was not my father." He growled so deeply his throat hurt.

"I don't follow," Christine said. "Of course he was your father. Who the hell else could your father have been? Granted, your mother had her days in the sun, frolicking around, but Cole told me, himself, that he was your father. What reason did I have to not believe him?"

"You're an idiot. Stop lying to me this instant. I now know a lot of things, grandmother, that you never wanted me to find out. I know quite a bit about you that you tried to hide from me. You're going to pay for that if it's the last thing I do."

"You know a lot about me, do you? Well, there are certain things I know about you, too, Eric. Things that you've tried keeping secret from me."

"Like what?"

"Like the summer you spent slumming with those poor, criminal negroes at FedEx." Eric's eyebrow raised. "Oh, don't think I didn't know where you were, what you were doing. I have people all over this city who will keep tabs on anyone I ask them to. My network is vast, young man. Shame on you for lying to me."

"Shame on me? I learned more about life at FedEx with those poor, criminal negroes than you ever taught me. I enjoyed going there every night just to escape you."

"And what did I do that was so bad? What have I done to warrant this kind of behavior?"

"My father was Senator Scott Tanner."

Christine's face drained of its color. She looked at Eric, head titled and inquisitive, and said, "How did you know that?" You could hear in her voice that she'd been caught. Finally.

"He told me before he died."

"He's dead?" She was honestly taken aback by that. And then she realized what she'd said about Cole, confessing to having him murdered. "And Cole? What of him?"

Eric slowly shook his head and took Christine's hand in his. "Your hit man didn't have the chance to do your dirty work."

"You've been spying on me?" She was trying to think how he could have known that.

"I had your phones tapped, sweetheart. But you trying to murder the man who knew all of your sordid history doesn't concern me. I knew you were the devil, but I didn't know you would go to the lengths you did to keep the truth about my parents hidden from me."

Christine was searching the room for some kind of weapon. She had to get away from Eric. She didn't know what he was capable of, what he was going to do to her, but she would not allow him to keep her prisoner in her own home.

"I know everything," Eric said, standing up and moving away from Christine. She was breathing hard and still trying to find anything she could use to fend him off. "I know about the truth behind Bryant Holdings and you being a slum lord."

"I am nothing of the sort!"

"I know the truth about Cole's stealing from the bank and the deal you made with him to marry my mother."

"That was a business decision, Eric."

"It wasn't a business decision!" he screamed. "That was my life! You were so scared that your friends would find out that my mother had gotten pregnant and that that information would bring you and your superfluous aura falling to the ground!"

"It was unacceptable and improper for Evelyn to have been an unwed mother, Eric. She wasn't going to ruin what I had so painstakingly created."

"So you married her off to the man who raped her?"

"What?" Christine's mind was spinning. Cole had never said anything to her about having raped her daughter, and for that matter, neither had Evelyn. "She was most certainly not raped. A tramp, yes, but when you put yourself in that position, you can hardly call what happened to her being raped."

"Don't you speak of her that way!" Eric screamed and rushed her again. He held his hand up like he was going to slap her and stood there. "You take that back! You take back everything you said about my mother."

"What kind of woman jumps into bed with men she hardly knows? Given her position in society, she had the opportunity to meet eligible young bachelors from the finest families in the country. But she chose to sleep around, to act like a common whore, defying my rule and making a mockery of me." Eric couldn't take it any longer and slapped his grandmother across the face, leaving her cheekbone reddened and bruised. Instinctively, she reached up and put her hand to her face.

"Just like her mother," Eric said. "Just like your affair with Lauren Tanner."

Christine had been looking at the floor, massaging her cheek and looked up at Eric. "Who told you about that? No one knew about that."

"Cole told me about a great many things connected to you the night I tricked him into spilling his guts. You sicken me."

Eric walked away from his grandmother and started for the door. "Wait, Eric! What are you going to do?"

"You took my mother from me. You took my real father from me. You've done everything you can to manufacture my entire life." Eric turned around to face Christine. "What would have become of me had my mother not died when I was eight and you decided that I must be worth loving? What would have become of us had you not poured yourself into using me to promote Jewel Box, working me over like a con artist, plying me with gifts and empty love? What would have happened if you'd allowed my parents the love they had for each other, the love that gave them me, their only child? What about Senator Tanner and the father you took from him? Did you honestly have to have him killed?"

Chief of Staff

Christine stood there not knowing what to say. Everything she'd crafted was crumbling in front of her. The life she had sought to protect by any means necessary was disappearing in front of her, and it was all being revealed to her by the one person she had counted on to protect her and keep her safe. Her favorite grandson had chased her down, destroyed her home, yelled at her and struck her out of the anger she had instilled in him. Now, as he stood in front of her and continued to belch out the indignities and crimes she's perpetrated that had consumed her life, she wondered where it had all gone so wrong.

Her only daughter was gone. Had she been wrong in mandating her marriage to Cole? Would Evelyn's out-of-wedlock child really have caused irreversible damage to her reputation? Had she taken the wrong path in her life? Was it too late to do anything about it? Would Eric hate her for the rest of his life? "What do we do now?" she quietly asked Eric.

"We don't do anything now, grandmother." Eric stood at the top of the steps with his back to Christine. Tears fell down his cheeks as he spoke. "I never want to see you as long as I live. You are dead to me. You are nothing to me. You're not family. You're nothing." This moment, no matter what she had done to ruin and manipulate his life, was excruciating. He was cutting his grandmother out of his life for good.

Christine rushed to Eric and reached for him, taking his elbow firmly in her hands. "Please don't say that, Eric! Please. Forgive me! Please say that you forgive me! I don't know how I would live without you!"

Eric whipped around to free his arm from her grasp. She held on tightly and as he swung around to confront her, she lost her balance and fell head-first down the grand staircase. "Grandmother!" he screamed. He watched as, in slow motion, she bounced down the steps, hitting her head several times along the way, before finally coming to rest at the bottom. Out of nowhere, Evan appeared and stared up at

Eric. Eric didn't know what to do. He stood there, frozen in place. This wasn't supposed to happen. How could he have let this happen?

Evan bent down to feel Christine's pulse just as Eric bounded down the steps. He stopped on the last step when Evan looked up at him and said, "She's gone."

"Oh my God!" Eric screamed. "Please, check again. Tell me she's not dead. Oh my God, what have I done?"

Evan felt for a pulse once more. Nothing. "I'm sorry, sir. She's dead."

Eric felt himself getting nauseous. "No. No. No, she can't be dead."

"You need to get out of here, Eric," Evan said.

"What? I can't leave! My grandmother just fell down the steps because of me. She's dead because of me! I can't fucking leave!"

With an even and evil tone, Evan said, "Old women fall down the steps all the time. This was simply an accident." He raised an eyebrow to Eric as if to say, I'll protect you.

"I can't leave, Evan."

"There isn't anyone else here." He pulled out his cell phone and began to dial 9-1-1. "It's simple: she was tired from her international trip. Making her way down the steps for a midnight snack, she must have lost her balance, fallen down the steps and broken her neck, killing her instantly."

Eric was staring at Evan and couldn't believe what he was hearing. At the same time, he thought about his mother and father, his chance at becoming a senator, and the crimes Christine was guilty of that ruined his life. He was torn and didn't know what to do.

"Leave," Evan commanded. "I'll take care of this."

"Why?" Eric wanted to know. "Why would do you this for me?"

Chief of Staff

"I knew this woman for a long time and I witnessed the brutality with which she commanded everyone in her life. You're free now. We're all free."

"I'm not leaving, Evan."

"Hello? Yes," Evan said speaking into the phone, "there's been an accident." He looked back at Eric and nodded toward the front door. Leave, he mouthed.

He didn't know how his feet were moving, but Eric was making his way to the front door. He turned to look at his grandmother lying lifeless at the bottom of her staircase and looked once more at Evan.

And then he slowly closed the door behind him.

Chief of Staff

Chapter *58*

THE funeral for Christine Belmont Squire was as tasteful and beautiful as the public perception of the woman thousands of people came to honor and memorialize. St. Luke's Episcopal was awash in Lily of the Valley, her favorite flower, each person receiving a tiny bouquet and a funeral program as they entered the sanctuary. For all of her flair and the luxuriousness of her galas, the service she had planned for herself was reserved and quaint. A single portrait of her rested atop her simple, brushed aluminum casket. The organist softly played several of her favorite hymns as the congregants found their seats and waited for the service to begin. The rain that fell outside rang like angels knocking on the copper roof of the church.

Eric gave an eloquent and moving eulogy for his grandmother. He made reference to the zeal with which she tackled not only life, but the minutiae that made life worth living. Digging back into the past, he told a couple of stories about her, the only ones he could honestly remember that had anything to do with the love she showed him, making sure to impart to the audience what a fabulous and ever-vigilant grandmother she had been to him. Where would he have been without her in his life, he asked, reciting his own answer to himself. After Clarence made his remarks and a few people expressed their love and devotion to Christine, a long procession drove Christine's body to the cemetery for the last ritual before internment in the Squire family plot.

After the service, Eric stood in the receiving line next to Clarence and his Aunt Annetta, dutifully shaking hands and saying thank you to each and every person who had come to pay their respects. The events of that night at Dove's Nest had never left his mind. He felt like a fraud, a criminal, and what's worse, he thought everyone knew the truth. People were looking at him in a way that made him uncomfortable and wary. He imagined, through his plastered on smile and mono toned 'yes, my grandmother was a wonderful woman'

Chief of Staff

response he'd rehearsed, that everyone who touched him could somehow feel the truth. He was far from innocent. Far from the kind of grandson everyone thought he was.

Following the internment, and after everyone had left, he stood in front of the marker. Funny, he thought, that his grandfather would be stuck next to her, the one person he'd tried so hard to get away from, for eternity. He bent down and wiped away some dead grass from his mother's headstone and slowly stroked the marble, tracing her name with his fingers. At what point, Eric wondered, would he be there, too, lying next to the most-influential women of his life, one good and the other evil.

Looking back at his grandmother's marker, he took a deep breath. Eric hadn't gone back to Dove's Nest following her death, and he had no plans to. The last time he saw her was when she lay on the floor, broken and lifeless. How ashamed he was to be standing in front of her right now. He imagined her calling to him, like in that scary dream, asking him to help her. This was a devastation no one should ever have to endure. But he had brought it on himself. No matter her actions, had it not been for his rampage through Dove's Nest, his being hell bent on taking from her what she took from him, none of this would be happening.

He was cold and rain-soaked, but he had to do this. He had to be here right now. It was the right thing to do. After everything, it wouldn't have been enough to say a few words about her in front of God and country. His mother was watching him now more than ever. It embarrassed him to think what she must have been thinking of her only son. Saying good-bye to Christine was even more excruciating now than he thought it would be. Standing in front of a grave had been painful and haunting for him ever since his mother passed. The dreams, the nightmares, didn't end for six months. The graveside was not the place for a child. He knew that now. But now he was a man. Staring at the marker, he squinted as raindrops pelted his face. No nearer to the headstone would he get than he stood right then. Grown men have nightmares, too.

Leaning forward, he read what had been etched into the polished granite face of the headstone:

"Man is the only animal that laughs and weeps; for he is the only animal that is struck with the difference between what things are, and what they ought to be."- William Hazlitt

Hand to mouth and shaking his head back and forth, the tears mixed with the rain, both streaming down his face as he sobbed uncontrollably. Why, he asked himself. Why did this have to happen? What had gone so terribly wrong? Had he done the right thing?

A firm hand pulled gently on his shoulder. "Senator?"

Eric turned to Claudia with tears in his eyes. She didn't say anything. She put her umbrella over them both, and hugged him for the longest time. "We should make our way back," she said, pulling away. "They're going to be starting soon."

Eric composed himself as best he could. One long, last sigh and he turned toward the waiting limousine. At the door, he stopped, turned back to the grave and quietly whispered, "I'll always love you."

*****

"GOOD morning, ladies and gentlemen," Governor Lewis said as he stood at the podium trying to quiet the audience. "This is a day in the history of North Carolina that is both sad and inspiring at the same time. On this day, I was tasked with several things, not the least of which was comforting a friend at the funeral of his dear grandmother, Christine Belmont Squire, a true friend of, and servant for, the state of North Carolina. Her accomplishments in the world of business, her tireless fundraising for breast cancer awareness, and her infectious personality will be missed more than words can artfully express.

Chief of Staff

"I have traveled to Charlotte today not only to pay my respects to Christine Squire and for all that she did to inspire North Carolinians in their everyday lives. I stand before you to announce that I have selected Eric Julian to replace our beloved and committed senator, Scott Tanner, who passed away recently from complications related to liver disease. Eric brings with him a wealth of political knowledge and cunning; he has the savvy to influence colleagues and the deftness of hand with which to support initiatives that may run opposite of the popular vote."

The members of the press in the audience took notes and listened to the governor, but their mouths watered as they waited to pose questions to Eric, himself. The governor was interesting and spoke well, but that's not why they all showed up. Eric had been selected by the governor to take Senator Tanner's seat in the senate for the remainder of his term, a little short of three years. Although it was a rare occurrence, it was well within the governor's state-given powers to select him. Eric was the best person for the job, and it didn't hurt that the governor was also fulfilling the Jewel Box promise he'd made, telling Eric he would do whatever he could to get him into office.

During his tenure as a United States Senator, Eric would have the chance to fully expose his values, his work ethic and his utter commitment to providing the best opportunities and sound opinions as they related to his state. He tasked himself with not only living the life of a senator, but doing his utmost to change the perceptions and preconceived notions many voters, not just Republicans or North Carolinians, held for politicians. An ambitious goal for a junior senator, and one Eric felt he could not only reach, but surpass. The crowd quieted even more when he took the microphone and began to speak.

"Good morning." God is good, he imagined Zeke saying. "I would like to welcome you all to Charlotte. And I would like to thank the Westin Hotel for providing such a lovely space in which to hold this press conference. I suppose

Chief of Staff

an introduction is in order. My name is Eric Julian and I am the grandson of Christine Belmont Squire, the son of Evelyn Maija Squire Julian, and the son of Senator Scott Tanner." Pens dropped and mouths fell right along with them. This was the first time he had revealed the truth to the general public. He told Claudia as they drove from the cemetery to the hotel and she couldn't believe what she was hearing, either.

"Trust me," Eric said, smiling and holding his hand up to bring some order back to the room, "that shocked me just as much a week ago as I'm sure it shocked you all just now. Yes, I am the son of Scott Tanner, the man at whose feet I grew up believing he was just a friend of the family, a confidant to me in my teenage years and my early twenties, a best friend as I graduated from college and began life as an independent young man. He is also the man that I have been picked to replace. The honorable Governor Lewis a moment ago began his remarks by saying that this is both a sad day and one that is, at the same time, inspiring. What a profound and remarkably resonant statement." Eric turned to the governor who was standing behind him and off to the right. "Thank you, Governor Lewis, for all you have done for me and my family in this, our most pressing time of need." The governor nodded politely and Eric returned to his address.

"Governor Lewis is correct, of course, in stating that this day is both one filled with sadness and well as unbelievable inspiration. I have lost two people I dearly loved and treasured; two people who were closer to me and cared for me more than you can ever know. If you do not know me or know of my family's accomplishments, I will tell you that I do not come from humble beginnings. I know that it is the standard practice, even somewhat fashionable, if you can believe it, for politicians to report how they grew up deprived of certain fundamentals of life, that they struggled and worked their way to the top, only to realize their dream of becoming a senator or congressman. My life, from the moment I was born, has been one of luxury, privilege, entitlement and riches. I say that not to be boastful, but in an effort to express

Chief of Staff

to you that I will bring honesty and integrity to my position from the outset. As a political consultant, having established my own firm before graduating from college, I understand the concept and necessity of hard work. Growing up rich afforded me a great many opportunities many Americans and many North Carolinians didn't enjoy.

"But with the guiding wisdom of my family, and taking advantage of the shoulders on which I was raised, I have been lucky enough to exist in a duality, fully aware of my position, and making every effort through public service, charitable contribution and a general understanding of the way the world works to improve the lives of others. I have worked tirelessly to promote the underdog both in my clients and their stands on certain unpopular positions – so I am very much in tune with the citizens of this state and the high ideals they expect their governing officials to hold.

"I bring with me to this office, as a former chief of staff the ability to guide change and recognize the limits of what I can do to influence that change. I learned from my grandmother what it means to hold yourself up and stay strong in the face of adversity and turmoil. I take from my mother a love of children and teaching, the guidepost of education representing the true center around which true progress is not simply obtained – but sustained. From my friend and mentor, and most importantly my father, I have learned how fabulous and fulfilling it is to dedicate your life's service to bettering our fellow citizens in all aspects of their lives.

"I will miss my father most in those times I question my ability or have doubts in my resolve when facing a turbulent and challenging task. I will remember in those moments, precious and wholly committed to memory, the words he would say, never once giving me the opportunity to let me defeat myself. 'Shut up and get over yourself.'" The crowd let out a respectful, yet uncomfortable laugh. "It's okay to laugh. Laughter, and a lot of it, is yet another pearl of wisdom he shared with me."

Chief of Staff

Eric grasped the podium and fought back tears. "I pledge to you all, each and everyone one of you in this room," he said and then looked into the television cameras, "and every citizen of North Carolina, home or abroad, that I will do my level best to represent you and the issues of this state in a manner that would make my grandmother, my mother, my father, and the registered voters proud to call me your United States Senator."

The crowd burst into applause, and everyone jumped to their feet for a standing ovation.

"Thank you. Thank you," Eric said. "Please, everyone, take your seats. That was very kind of you. Regretfully, at this point, and I know the timing could be better, I need to depart. I laid my grandmother to rest not hours ago. Now I need to keep a promise that I made to my father." The crowd groaned a little, wanting to hear more from this new political powerhouse, untested though he may have been. They understood his reason for leaving, though, and broke into applause once more.

"Before I leave, I would ask that you direct your questions to my chief of staff. With a steadfast adherence to policy, unwavering commitment to the job they currently have and the position they will be assuming, I know this person has the ability, the fortitude, and the attitude," he said, raising a cheer from the audience, "and the moral compass to make sure that as a team – no, as a family – we not only meet but exceed your expectations for many, many years to come. Already having proved herself in the work she put into reworking the text of the hate crime bill, which passed with flying colors, she's set up for a bright, bright future. Please welcome Claudia Eldridge was warmly as you have welcomed me."

Claudia had been jotting notes down on some ideas for the office that came to her while Eric spoke. She had agreed to accompany him to his grandmother's funeral, but had little interest in standing on stage during his press conference. When she heard her name announced, she was more than surprised. This wasn't what she had expected at all and didn't know what to say to Eric. She looked at him as if to say, 'Me? Really'? Eric motioned her to the podium, they hugged and Eric stepped off stage.

Not missing a beat, Claudia's entire demeanor changed on a dime. Not that she hadn't been a consummate professional five seconds ago, but now she seemed one hundred per cent authoritative, and even her diction changed. "Good morning. Since today is not about me, but about remembering two fallen patriots of North Carolina, and introducing the newest star of the senate, I will be brief. In order for you all to get the facts straight, I'll put together a bio and you'll be able to access it...," she said and stopped. "On second thought, I'll have my Executive Administrative Assistant put something together and get it out to you." She smiled and the reporters all smiled with her. "Make sure you get this right. My name is Tomilyn Claudia Eldridge, but you can probably guess why I go by Claudia," she said, instilling more laughter. "I am 35 years old and proud of it. My weight is none of your business and I am southern through and through. I will make no apologies for my accent or the liberal use of the word 'honey'." The reporters thought that was hilarious and it seemed she was off to a great start as Eric's new chief of staff. "As golfing legend Tiger Woods said when he announced that he was turning pro, 'Hello, World'."

As Eric walked off stage, he was overcome with flashbacks, instigated by Claudia's revelation of her first name. Tomilyn. TE. The other initials on Byrum's spreadsheet. I'm not the only one. Cole admitted that during his interrogation. Eric thought back to their lunch at Lola's where Claudia blew up at him. It would be easy to write a book about your family. Partial photographic memory. Everything ever published. Socialize, lift up, and benefit your own. Profit off of the backs of real black people, whether you know it or believe it. Insular, deranged and disgusting display of bigotry and self-loathing. Not enough to just be rich. You have to throw your light skin, your good hair, your fancy colleges and your exclusive clubs in everybody's face.

Chief of Staff

Bougie and privileged and sickening. Hate what you represent. And the day after she'd read 'Betrayed'. Byrum asked for my help on his first novel. Knew about my photographic memory. Hate what you represent. Hate what you represent. Hate what you represent.

Eric felt the feeling drain from his body, turning cold and stiff. He stopped in his tracks and turned back to look at Claudia, standing prominently in the limelight, exactly where she'd always intended to be. She turned when she noticed Eric hadn't left the building and smiled at him. Eric smiled back, waved good-bye and left.

Chapter *59*

WHEN Eric's helicopter touched down on Trinity, once again he thanked the pilot for not killing them and got off as quickly as he could. The captain met Eric once he was aboard. "Your father was genuinely a great man, Senator Julian."

"I've got an idea, captain," he said smiling. "How about whenever I come to spend time on Trinity, you just call me Eric."

"Agreed," the captain responded. He noticed that Eric was carrying the urn holding Senator Tanner's ashes and removed his hat. After a moment of silence, he snapped his fingers and a steward approached. He took Eric's bags and told him that there was a present from the senator waiting for him in his stateroom, explaining that the senator wanted it delivered to the yacht as a surprise the next time Eric visited.

When Eric opened the door, he found a large package lying on his bed. Unwrapping it, Eric shook his head and laughed. It was a huge, framed picture of Mark Twain. A gold square at the bottom of the frame read: 'Trust Me. It's going to be a Great Adventure.'

"What a sweet, sweet man you were," Eric said of his father. "I'm going to miss you terribly." He called the captain and asked if he had received the coordinates that were emailed to him earlier in the week. Yes, the captain said, and in fact, we've almost reached that point. Eric asked the captain to have a steward come for him as the sun was beginning to set. He sat down on the bed and got out his cell phone. Now or never.

Clearing his throat, his heart skipped a couple of beats when she answered. "Um, hello? Kathryn?"

"Yes. Who's calling?"

"It's Eric. It's Eric Julian." He felt like he was back in high school, calling the girl he liked for the very first time.

"Oh, hi!" she said, excitedly. "Hi, Eric."

"How are you?" What's with the small talk, he asked himself. Get to the point.

Before he could do what he'd intended, what the senator had also made him promise he'd do, Kathryn started talking. "Eric, I am so sorry for everything that happened to you last week. I can't imagine how you're holding up."

"Thanks, Kathryn. I appreciate that a lot."

"Is there anything I can do for you? You just name it and I'll do whatever you need to help get you through this."

It couldn't be that easy, Eric thought. "Actually, and this may sound odd right now, but I'm okay. I've tried to focus on all of the good things in my life, the things that make me happy and make me smile and remember the funny and crazy times I had with both my grandmother and my father, little did I realize it back then, you know?"

"I can only imagine," she said softly, trying not to say anything out of turn. She was very excited that he'd called her, but she didn't want to make too much out of the situation. "I'm glad you kept my card. I've been thinking about you a lot lately." There, she'd gone and said it. She kicked herself right after the words left her mouth. Here he was, going through unimaginable pain and she'd just thrown herself, rather tastelessly, at him.

"I've been thinking about you a lot, too," Eric said, matching her soft tone. "I was wondering if...well, I wanted to know if....God, Kathryn," he said, laughing. "I'm so nervous. I feel like a schoolboy and I don't know why. I'm sorry."

"Don't apologize, Eric. I think it's cute. We kind of have a history, don't we?"

"Kathryn," Eric said, looking at the Mark Twain picture and thinking back to the senator's none-too-random interruption of the interview in his office. "I've been in love with you since we were in the eighth grade."

Kathryn was silent because she was trying not to cry. Had she uttered one single word, the waterworks would have been unstoppable.

"Say something. Say anything, Kathryn. Tell me I haven't just made a complete fool out of myself. That's why I never said anything to you in all these years. I just knew that if I told you how I felt you'd think I was an idiot and that you'd never want to…"

"I love you, too, Eric."

Now it was his turn to be silent.

"Eric?"

"Uh, yeah. I mean, yes?"

"Did you hear me?"

"I did." He refocused and stood up. The steward sent to retrieve Eric at sundown had just knocked on his door. "I did, Kathryn. I'm so happy and amazed and unsure of what the hell I'm supposed to do next, I don't even know what I was going to say."

Kathryn giggled and smiled.

"Listen, I've got to do something now. In fact, I'm going to be taking a little vacation before the insanity that has now become my life begins."

"That's right. Mr. Senator. Look at you," Kathryn joked.

Eric smiled right along with her and said, "When I get back to D.C., how would you like to have dinner with me? We'll start over, like we were kids, the way I should have asked you out a long, long time ago. Would you like that?"

Chief of Staff

"That sounds like heaven. I'll be waiting for you to call."

"I'm already looking forward to it."

"Before you hang up, where are you going on your vacation?" Kathryn asked.

"I don't know," Eric said. "But I have a good idea it's going to be between somewhere and nowhere. I'll call you just as soon as I get back. I promise."

Eric hung up, took a deep breath and looked in the mirror. "You are the freakin' MAN!" he screamed and quickly settled himself for what he was about to do.

Gathering up the urn, Eric headed to the aft deck of the yacht. Stepping down onto the transom, he looked up into the sky. Only the brightest stars were visible; the others were selfishly withholding their brilliance until later that night, but Eric could easily make out several constellations. "Hello, mother."

Carefully unscrewing the cap to the urn and leaning over the transom railing, Senator Tanner's ashes delicately spilled into the water, spreading themselves quickly with the current. "I love you, Senator." Eric stopped himself because he'd never said these words before, at least not to Scott Tanner. He held them inside for a moment, and let their true meaning and feeling soak in, selfishly, before he released them to the world. Slowly and deliberately, he said, "I love you, daddy."

Eric teared again up when he asked him to take good care of his mother, and to take care of himself. "I'll always miss you and I'll always love you for how you changed my life, daddy." He turned around to see each and every employee on Trinity, dressed in their crisp red and white uniforms, standing on the top deck, saluting their friend and boss, giving him a final wave of good-bye and remembrance. Eric carefully screwed the top back on the urn, looked out into the distance, and muttered between somewhere and nowhere.

Chief of Staff

He smiled and disappeared inside Trinity to begin the rest of his life.

Chief of Staff

Chapter *60*

CNN BREAKING NEWS: *CNN is reporting that Claudia Eldridge was arrested earlier today following an anonymous tip on the FBI's Art Theft Program website. Investigators raided her Alexandria, Virginia, home this morning and charged her with several crimes including possession of stolen property, intent to distribute stolen property, and obstruction of an ongoing federal investigation.*

According to an unnamed source, the FBI has recovered several paintings and a sculpture from Ms. Eldridge's home that were stolen during the second World War from a prominent Jewish family in Poland. Two of the paintings, alone, are valued at more than five million dollars, each. Program Manager, Sherika Howell, was quoted as saying, "This is a very unexpected and certainly very important discovery. The arrest of Ms. Eldridge should serve as notice to anyone who harbors stolen artifacts, no matter their heritage, or knows someone who is. We will find you and we will bring you to justice."

Newly appointed as chief of staff for Senator Eric Julian, Claudia Eldridge is the first African-American woman to hold the position. It was partially on the strength of her work crafting pivotal hate crime legislation for the late Senator Scott Tanner that propelled Ms. Eldridge into her new role. No name was affixed to the website tip, just the following scripture: "Blessed is the man who does not walk in the counsel of the wicked."

Senator Julian is on vacation and could not be immediately reached for comment...

THEN END

Chief of Staff